In a world divided by war, falling in love is the ultimate betrayal.

Galena Shantos has never questioned her loyalty to Eden. As sister to the Myren king, she serves as a healer, one of the best in the army fighting to suppress the brutal Lomos Rebellion. She's never doubted the importance of stopping the rebels bent on enslaving humans, until she spots a warrior across enemy lines—and knows instinctively that their destinies are entwined...

Rebellion warrior Reese Theron has nothing left to lose. He's been forced to fight on the wrong side of a war he abhors in order to protect his family secret. His honor lost, as well as the trust of his own people, Reese has thrown himself into a battle he cannot possibly hope to survive. But after being rescued by a beautiful woman whose exquisite eyes seem to see him for more than the traitor he's become—he may have just found a new reason to live...

Books by Rhenna Morgan

Eden Series
Unexpected Eden
Healing Eden

Published by Kensington Publishing Corporation

Healing Eden

An Eden Novel

Rhenna Morgan

LYRICAL PRESS
Kensington Publishing Corp.
www.kensingtonbooks.com

Lyrical Press books are published by
Kensington Publishing Corp. 119 West 40th Street New York, NY 10018

All Kensington titles, imprints, and distributed lines are available at special quantity discounts for bulk purchases for sales promotion, premiums, fund-raising, and educational or institutional use.

To the extent that the image or images on the cover of this book depict a person or persons, such person or persons are merely models, and are not intended to portray any character or characters featured in the book.

Special book excerpts or customized printings can also be created to fit specific needs. For details, write or phone the office of the Kensington Special Sales Manager:
Kensington Publishing Corp.
119 West 40th Street
New York, NY 10018
Attn. Special Sales Department. Phone: 1-800-221-2647.

Kensington and the K logo Reg. U.S. Pat. & TM Off.
Lyrical Press and the L logo are trademarks of Kensington Publishing Corp.

First Electronic Edition: December 2015
eISBN-13: 978-1-61650-989-7
eISBN-10: 1-61650-989-9

First Print Edition: December 2015
ISBN-13: 978-1-61650-990-3
ISBN-10: 1-61650-990-2

Printed in the United States of America

To my husband, Victor. For never giving up, growing, and loving me just as I am. You've healed us both.

I Love You Sweetheart!

Rhenna Morgan

Acknowledgements

The discipline it takes to get from, "Once upon a time," to "The End," is pretty intense. Well, for me it is anyway, and there are lots and lots of people who keep me sane in the process. My heartfelt thanks to T.D. Hart, Lauren Smith, Dena Garson, Lorenda Christensen, and Lucy Brower for your many interventions.

I'd also never make it to print without some very important people—Penny Barber, Sarah Hegger, CJ Burright, and the amazing Kensington/Lyrical Press team. Seriously, between reading all my drafts and pulling me back from the ledge when my devastatingly handsome muse goes on strike, you guys deserve a lifetime supply of coffee and chocolate.

I've got a pretty killer support team too. People who keep the engine running at Mach speed even when I'm writing at a snail's pace—Jay Donovan, Fiona Jayde, Laird Sapir, and Kami Adkison.

And finally, endless hugs and kisses to the family for putting up with me day after day, and skillfully hiding those eye rolls when I say, "I gotta get my words in." I couldn't do this without you, nor would I want to.

Chapter 1

A lightning bolt sheared past Reese into the smoke-filled night sky and left an acrid stench in its wake. Streaks of fire and blue-white fingers of electricity flared so bright he could barely focus. He wasn't getting out of this. Not this battle, or this life, with any modicum of honor.

Darting through the air, he dodged another electrical strike.

An elite flashed into view and swung wide, his bloodied dagger aimed at Reese's gut.

Reese barrel-rolled up and over his attacker, wrapped him in a chokehold, and masked their presence from the rest of the fighters. Praise the Great One, he should be fighting beside this warrior, not against him.

The warrior flailed and tried to break free, the lack of footing giving him zero leverage. He slumped, unconscious, into Reese's ready hold seconds later.

He lowered them both to the tree line at the battle's edge, out of site from the rebels. The man couldn't be more than twenty years outside his awakening. Probably barely into his elite torc and cuffs. Beneath Reese's fingers, the man's pulse thrummed slow, but steady. At least this innocent's death wouldn't be on his conscience.

A twenty-five-foot wall of flame exploded across the open field and rattled the air and earth around them. The bright flare faded under heavy night, and more rebellion warriors thunked to the mottled field.

The sharp rustle of leaves against the forest floor sounded down the tree line, one quick shift and then silence.

Reese backed deeper into the foliage and strengthened the mask that kept him hidden. It couldn't be a rebellion man. All those were engaged against the malran's warriors. Focusing his thoughts, he sought the soulless black thread that represented the link he'd grudgingly created with Maxis Steysis, and traced his location.

No, not the rebellion leader either. His energy showed more than ten miles to the east, well away from the fight. Reese levitated off the forest floor and floated through the trees. Gnarled and leafless branches scraped his cheek and shoulders. Darkness enveloped him, broken only by the bright attacks where the forest opened to the battle beyond.

There. Not five feet from the tree line, a figure knelt facing the battle.

He drifted closer. The sweet, damp scent of soil and decomposing leaves overpowered the metallic residue of electrical strikes floating on the wind. Grunts, shouts, and the too-frequent thuds of perished men sounded in a haphazard pattern.

A flash spotlighted long, auburn hair. A woman. Bowed over a body, she cradled a fallen companion's head in her lap.

Reese angled to better see her and nearly faltered in holding his mask. His heart kicked in an awkward rhythm and reality faded to nothingness. Galena Shantos, sister to the malran. The last person he wanted to witness his disgrace.

Seventy years since he'd seen her this close. Her elegant features were still as staggering as the days when he'd trained to serve the malran, but there was more to her now. A confidence in the way she protected her charge and watched the battle. Knowledge behind her tropical blue-green eyes that spoke of experience and age.

And he fought alongside the men who battled her brother.

Galena flinched at another blast and hugged the limp body she cradled tight. As the light dimmed, she uncurled from her burden.

Another woman, her long blond hair stark against Galena's black tunic and leggings, and her sightless eyes aimed at the heavens.

No. Surely not. Reese crept closer, pressure building at his temples. The zings and thunder of battle rumbled louder, and his gut clenched.

Phybe. She'd been alive when Reese left her, tucked away in a zeolite mine where Maxis couldn't trace her link. He touched down in the thick carpet of leaves at Galena's right and dropped his mask. "I failed her."

Galena jerked and reached for something beneath one leg. "Who are you?"

Smudges marked Phybe's ashen face, her blue gown torn and satin slippers stained. Somehow Maxis had found her and finished the job he'd sent Reese to do. "He'll kill me for trying to save her."

More strikes burst through the thick residual smoke, the malran's fighters airborne and casting one attack after another. Fewer than twenty rebellion men still lived, half retreating north.

"A cause that fights without honor isn't worth fighting, is it?" he said.

Galena straightened and squared her shoulders. "I'd have a hard time counting on honor from any man who fights with Maxis."

"You're right. I gave that up the moment I agreed to his schemes." He crouched beside them.

Galena tensed and tightened her grip on whatever she hid beneath her leg.

Reese palmed Phybe's forehead, cool and lifeless. *May your journey be swift and your spirit find peace with The Great One.* The same Myren prayer he'd offered his mother when she'd drawn her last breath. He stepped back. Maybe it was time to find his own peace. On his own terms. "You don't remember me do you?"

She shook her head. A terse, barely-there jerk as she eased from beneath her dead charge, crouched on the balls of her feet and coiled for escape.

"My name is Reese Theron."

She froze, flashes of light from the battle winking off the edge of her blade. She assessed him head to toe, no spark of recognition.

Maybe if he'd been braver all those years ago, he'd have had a chance with her. Or broken his vow and killed Maxis himself when he'd had the chance. He shook the memories off. He'd taken the wrong path and now it was time to pay. "Call your guards. Make sure they know you're in danger."

A gunshot rattled the skies and a woman's blood-curdling scream sounded across the battlefield.

Galena lurched to a stand and then stopped, zigzagging her attention between the shouts along the battlefield and Phybe's body.

Now was his chance. Either he took the brave farewell, or he'd die by Maxis' hands. "Your face is a good one to remember. Go with The Great One, Galena." He shot to the sky and built a violent ball of energy in his palm, sharp tendrils darting from its center. Drawing back, he aimed the bogus attack at Galena. Surely The Great One would understand.

An elite guard spun from across the skies and drew back for counterattack.

Reese braced for impact.

A streak of auburn flashed below him. Galena, spearing through the air, her trajectory centered between the elite and Reese.

The energy in his palm fizzled. Not her. Not Galena.

Lightning fired from the elite's palm, sheered past Galena's cheek, and pierced his shoulder. He jerked and spasmed, locked in place by the force of the strike. Blue-black spots dotted his vision and his lungs seized.

A woman's scream ripped through the air.

Wind whipped around him, dead weight as he fell, and darkness took over.

* * * *

Galena twisted midair and shot toward Reese, wind blurring her eyesight.

His arms and legs flailed boneless as he hurtled to the earth.

She'd never make it before impact. Even if he survived the fall, Jagger's strike had been a killing shot, off by inches at most.

Reese crashed against the unforgiving ground, his head and limbs thunking against the trampled turf.

She landed seconds behind him. The sticky iron scent of blood, dirt, and sweat surrounded her. So many men strewn across the grass, their bodies contorted in unnatural shapes.

Less than ten feet away one of her brother's men struggled for breath, unconscious with a trail of blood at his temple. A loyal fighter who'd battled against an indecent and cruel rebellion.

But it was Reese her palms burned to touch. To feel the beat of his heart. She dropped to her knees and rolled Reese to his back, muscles surging with wells of strength she'd never felt.

His pulse fluttered beneath her fingertips, faint and irregular.

A thud sounded behind her. Her name registered, a voice she recognized.

She ignored the call. Shedding her mortal form, she dove into Reese's unconscious body and let her spirit spread and assess. Gaping, charred flesh at least two fists wide, muscle and sinew around it lifeless from the electrical shock. She followed the damage, too much impairment radiating dangerously close to his heart. She couldn't lose him. Traitor or not, her instincts didn't care. Only knew this moment would shape the rest of her life in a way she didn't dare ignore.

Shouts rang out beside her. Short, brusque words delivered with a frustrated bite. Footsteps shuffled around her and the injured moaned. Detached in spirit but still connected to her physical senses, the muffled distractions rattled as she healed.

Five inches. That was the gift of her intervention. Had she not flown in the path of Jagger's bolt, he'd have pierced Reese's heart. Blood seeped from the violent gash and his heart trembled with the aftershocks of the delivering jolt.

Swift and sure, she spread her spirit, cauterizing and mending the most critical lesions. A touch here. A brush there.

Near his heart, a fine opaque mist appeared.

Her spirit vision faltered. The odd substance settled into every nook and cranny. It shimmered and sparkled, a mix between morning dew and midnight fog. Seventy years she'd been healing men and not once had she seen anything like it.

"Damn it, Lena, we need you." The admonition rang in her ear and a firm hand clamped on her shoulder.

Galena ripped her spirit from Reese's body and spun in a levitated twist to a defensive crouch, hands lifted to protect herself. Her vision wavered.

Ramsay came into focus, the whites around his gray eyes glowing in a way that promised dire loss of control and a vicious scowl aimed squarely at her. "What in histus is wrong with you?"

Her knees nearly buckled. Maybe she'd put too much into her healing. "He's wounded."

"He's a traitor. To me and to Eryx." Glaring at her, he swept his arm behind him. "What about them?"

There were dozens of them. Good men, battered, bloody, and fatigued. Most were upright and lumbering across the battlefield, checking for rebellion survivors. Six were laid out for triage close to Maxis' estate, Eryx and Ludan seeing to their care.

Her cheeks burned and her stomach pitched. There wasn't any logic to defend her actions. She'd acted on pure emotion and instinct, and put the lives of loyal men at risk, but she still wouldn't change what she'd done. Not a second. A truth she wasn't altogether sure how to process.

"Focus on the ones worthy of your gift. Not someone—"

"Enough." She straightened and met her brother's scowl. Every muscle shook with fatigue. "I watched an innocent woman die tonight. Held her in my arms while she screamed."

"Trust me." Ramsay glowered at the unconscious man behind her. "He's not innocent."

For years she'd trusted her brothers. Loved and followed them with unwavering loyalty wherever they asked her to go. Until this moment. She inched forward on trembling legs, hands fisted at her sides. "Innocent or not, I saw goodness in him. Watched him say a prayer over Phybe's body and felt his grief. Healing is my gift to use when and how The Great One guides me. Not to be commandeered and directed by a man swept up in the heat of battle. Life is life, no matter whose heart feeds it."

Ramsay sneered. "Even Maxis Steysis?"

Nearly six hundred years their families had been at war, since their grandfather left Maxis' grandmother pregnant at the altar in favor of a commoner.

"Everyone has a shred of goodness in them." Well, maybe not Maxis. But she'd be damned if she let Ramsay question her judgment. There was a reason she was drawn to Reese. She just needed a little time to figure out why. "If you'd stop and think for a minute you'd know saving him is a smart move. If he fought with Maxis, he knows things. Things you won't be able to learn anywhere else."

Reese's chest rose and fell, slow and steady. With a push from her senses, she registered the faint but solid rhythm of his heart. More than anything she ached to kneel beside him. To finish the job she'd begun and skim her fingers through his wild hair. Perhaps link her fingers with his long, tapered ones and rest alongside him while she waited for him to wake.

Praise The Great One, what was wrong with her? This protectiveness didn't make sense.

Eryx's best friend and somo, Ludan, shouted from the furthest edge of battle. "Ramsay."

Galena knew that tone. Had heard it after too many battles. Another warrior in need of care. With a last glance at Reese to placate herself, she headed in Ludan's direction. "I've got it."

Three steps in she stopped and glared at Ramsay. "You may not care for him. May see him as the vilest of men. But do not disrespect my gift by hurting him."

She left her frowning brother behind, and prayed the promise of a traitor's information would stay Ramsay's hand until she returned.

Chapter 2

Seventy years. Seventy fucking years since Maxis had been this dumbfounded, with not one thought, word, or deed to spur him forward.

The sun beamed brighter than normal through the thick Asshur clouds. The faint winds at his back were unseasonably warm, as though nature conspired to lure him from his trance.

He wasn't interested in moving. Couldn't fathom his next step, and wasn't sure he cared to bother.

More than three-quarters of his men, gone. On the red clay valley below, what remained of his army jerked and stumbled through an embarrassing display of drills.

It wasn't possible. If he hadn't seen the scorched fields and twisted bodies surrounding his home for himself, he'd have never believed it. When he'd left with Serena the night before, the malran's men had been grossly outnumbered. There was no way they should have survived. But Eryx and his men had done it. Done it and saved the new malress and Maxis' best-trained slave in the process.

All because of his traitorous strategos.

His eye twitched and the slow ache at the back of his jaws sharpened. He'd trusted Reese Theron as he'd trusted no one since his grandmother's death. That fucking betraying, shortsighted bastard. If he'd killed Phybe as instructed, Eryx would never have found Maxis' home or been able to save Lexi.

The warriors dropped their weapons and took up bickering like a nest of hormonal bitches. Not an ounce of organization among them. Unsurprising given the limited time Reese had led them, but still, one would think some of their brawn would extend to their brains.

Maxis reached through his link for Reese. Still not so much as a flicker, the same as every other time he'd checked this morning. Reese was either dead, or captive in zeolite.

Serena's sultry voice crooned behind him. "If the look on your face is any indication, you should have stayed in my bed this morning."

Maxis winced. He knew better than to lose sight of his surroundings. With Eryx out for vengeance, daydreaming was a bad idea no matter how many of his warriors were within spitting distance. That a woman had managed to catch him unaware only validated his level of distraction.

A wisp of yellow fabric billowed beside him, no doubt another of the elegant gowns Serena preferred. Why the malran had abandoned his relationship with her years before was beyond Maxis. With vivid blue eyes and ridiculously long blond hair, she was the picture perfect model for a malress. Fortunately, her thirst for revenge as strong as Maxis'.

"No good morning for your lover?" She gripped his hips and nuzzled his neck. The brush of her soft breasts at his back pricked his temper.

"Enough." He pushed her away and crowded the ledge overlooking the training grounds. He had enough to contend with without Serena adding petulance to the mix.

Serena glided beside him and scowled at the men. "I guess if I had to take credit for that mess, I'd be bitchy too."

He spun so quickly she gasped and took a step back. He gripped her hair before she could escape and yanked her so no more than inches separated them. "Watch. Your. Mouth."

She froze, but the challenge in her exotic eyes held. Only four or five inches beneath his stature, she carried herself with a regal grace, and damned if her lemon and honey scent didn't taunt him as boldly as her stance.

"Damn it all." He shoved her away and stalked along the ridge, watching his men.

"You could talk about it." Patronization at its finest, with a bit of dare mingled in for good measure.

"Which part? The fact that I've lost a chunk of my men, or the fact that Reese is captured or dead?'

She shrugged. "Both are replaceable."

The warriors, yes, though at the expense of time. But Reese? He'd wanted to kill his strategos. To watch his eyes stretch wide with pain while Maxis shredded his brain to bits via link the same way he'd killed Phybe. So why in histus was he so agitated with the prospect of his demise?

"Recruitment's a must with the plans you've laid out, but we'd be wise to find others to handle the legwork," Serena said.

Maxis faced her. "We?"

The imperious chit lifted an eyebrow. "You got me in this mess, so yes, it's a 'we.'" She glared at the men below and her dusty pink lips curled in a vicious grin. "From the looks of things, you could use a little help."

Finally. A moment of clarity. A spark of anger he could mold. He prowled forward. "Let's be clear Serena."

She retreated one step. A wise move from her for once.

He followed. "You're nothing more than a fuck. A beautiful and convenient one to be sure, but a fuck nonetheless. Any plans for the rebellion will be guided by me. Not tempered by a bratty social butterfly who spreads her legs on a whim."

She flinched, though she covered it as well as any longstanding queen and swept her arm out over the disorganized mass of men below. "By all means then. Lord over your precious kingdom. Thank The Great One my name's not attached to it." She shot to the sky, never once looking back.

"And here I'd thought you a smart man."

Maxis spun toward the voice behind him. A grated baritone with a nasally bite. Familiar, yet foreign.

Adobe ground stretched unbroken but for random clumps of gray spindly bushes. Not a soul in sight. Nothing pinged against the bubble-like surface of his sensory gifts.

"Only an idiot would piss away a delectable and advantageous piece of tail mourning over a traitor." The voice hovered around Maxis, like a shout from the center of a cavernous room.

Maxis planted his feet at shoulder width, weight forward, ready for defense against the unidentifiable presence.

"I'm the least of your worries." The voice held more substance this time.

Maxis whirled the other direction.

A lithe, dark-haired man stood in clothes unlike any he'd seen in either the human or Myren dimensions. His black tunic shone like silk, and formed an H across his chest before it dropped to his shins. Tall and lean, the man needed a good dose of sun. As it was, his pale skin struck a harsh contrast to the black, ruler-straight hair that fell from his widow's peak to the tops of his shoulders.

The clang and shouts of men drilling below sounded in the distance. Not one blip in their efforts to indicate they saw the unexpected visitor.

"I trust no one," Maxis said. "Least of all a stranger."

A low, sinister laugh filled the space, though the man's lips barely moved. "I'm no stranger to you, Maxis. Quite the opposite."

He lifted a hand, palm forward, and his jade eyes sharpened.

The landscape dimmed, replaced with snippets of Maxis' life. His grandmother Evanora's death. His mother abandoning him when he was only nine in favor of the half-human child she carried. The human bullies who'd beat him before he'd come into his Myren gifts. The subtle resistance of Maxis' blade in his father's chest as he'd plunged it deep. Every critical moment of his life sped by with alacrity. One voice threaded each one.

Maxis' memories dissipated and the desolate landscape returned. "Who are you?"

The stranger's smile grew. "Your spiritu."

"Don't fuck with me. I asked who you are, not what you are."

"Ever the clever one." The man eased into a more casual stance. "I've always appreciated that about you. That is, when you're not sniveling over your worthless strategos."

"Your name!"

The stranger crossed his arms and waited several breaths. "The name given to me by my people is too complex for your mortal mind, but you may call me Falon."

"And your people?"

"I thought my race didn't interest you."

Maxis fisted his dagger's hilt.

Falon sneered. "You cannot force my demise. Spiritu are not susceptible to mortal death. Only The Great One rules us in such a fashion." Uncurling his arms, he stalked forward, the air snapping with electricity. "I, on the other hand, can force yours quite nicely."

He stopped a stone's throw away, lifted his hand, thumb and fingers spread as though coiled around an unseen substance.

An invisible pressure blocked Maxis' airway and crushed his windpipe. His elemental gifts wouldn't respond to his commands. No call of earth, no fire. Darkness crept along the edges of his vision and his heart thrashed.

"I'm the voice in your mind, Maxis. The one who's guided you throughout your life and lifted you when most needed."

The memory of his father, bleeding out on his vast bed seconds after Maxis plunged the knife deep, leapt to life.

"Then most of all." Falon whispered in Maxis' mind. *"It was I who guided you to that moment, and every critical juncture after."*

As quickly as it had begun, the tightness in his throat disappeared, and a fresh wave of chilled Asshur air rushed his lungs. Maxis stumbled back a step and braced his palms on his knees.

The crunch of Falon's boots on clay pebbles crackled, slow, casual steps promenading around Maxis. "My people are the guides for Myren and humans alike. The passion and inspiration that feed their souls. I am of the dark contingent, those who focus on the headier passions."

Maxis' vision spun and his knees trembled. He couldn't show fear. Everyone had a weakness, this man included. He just needed to find it.

"So you've suddenly decided to make a house call?" Maxis glared at Falon. "Don't play me for a fool. Even if I were to believe in your assertions, your change in behavior calls for suspicion."

"Your blubbering heart pushed me past the point of reason." Falon paused, gripped his hands loosely behind his back, and paced away from Maxis. He studied the barren tract of land. "Deny it all you want, but your dead strategos has done a number on your head. One I'm not willing to stand by and watch. We've worked too long and hard on your future for you to go soft now."

His future. Revenge on the Shantos line for the wrongs handed his family and the throne to go with it. The stranger was right. He needed to get his head in the game. Get his plans under—

"What did you say?" Maxis strode the handful of steps to Falon, gripped the spiritu's shoulder, and spun him around.

A devious grin crept across Falon's face. "I said dead strategos. As in not among the living."

"You know this for certain?"

"I know his presence is no longer within the plane in which my people have purview, so yes. Dead."

Maxis staggered and his gut lurched. "He could be in zeolite."

Falon's voice dripped with disgust. "Praise The Great One, what difference does it make? Look at yourself. You need to focus, reformulate your plans, and reengage. I've already given my light brethren an opening they don't need by appearing in person. The light contingent and the malran don't need any more advantages."

Important information. Words he'd need to study. Later.

Reese was dead.

Falon clamped an unforgiving grip on Maxis' shoulder and roared loud enough his voice echoed off the gorge walls. "Hear me."

Maxis fired a defensive bolt of electricity toward Falon.

It passed through Falon's chest, and his maniacal laughter filled the air.

Maxis tottered backward.

The warriors kept to their exercises. Even with Falon's raging guffaws echoing through the canyon, not one seemed to notice.

"You want an empire, Maxis? Then make one." Falon's arms swept out in dramatic fashion. "Build your own. Start with family."

Family. A poignant chord that rattled more than flesh and blood. His father had never offered a mating link to his mother. She'd escaped too easily because of it, not that his father had bothered to try and find her. He'd finished his life alone with nothing more than a broken rebellion. Evanora had been the wise one, surrounding herself with loyal family and friends. Wasn't it she who'd fueled Maxis' goals?

Falon had a point.

Shouts and grunts lifted from the training fields. "What about them?"

Falon inched closer, still on the furthest reaches of Maxis' periphery. "Reese was never your best choice for strategos. You were biased with him. Always were. If you'd paid closer attention, you'd have noticed someone much more suited to your nature."

The men had found a rhythm, groups pairing off for practical training. In the furthest section of the field, a bellow rang out. A man collapsed to the ground, a harsh line of crimson stretched across his neck and sightless eyes aimed to the sky.

His partner gripped a wicked dagger with a charcoal hilt and a blade coated in blood.

Maxis shot from his place on the high ledge across the vast valley to intercede before the man charged more of his fellow warriors. He knocked the weapon from the man's grip. "We need more fighting men, not less."

The warrior glared at Maxis, his odd green eyes unflinching. Sweat coated his bare chest. His short black hair was equally drenched and scattered. "If they're weak, they're not worth it."

Hard to argue the man's logic. "Give me your name," Maxis said.

Silence settled around them, the shuffle of feet and the whisper of wind the only sound.

"Uther Rontal."

The men around them glanced back and forth between Uther and Maxis, weight on the balls of their feet, waiting and ready.

They feared them both. With fear came control. How had he missed such a discovery among his troops?

Falon's voice rang in his head. *"Like I said, a much better match."*

Chapter 3

The slow, steady rumble of hushed, masculine voices nudged Reese toward consciousness. Every muscle hung heavy and useless, his eyelids as dead weight as the rest of him. Cold radiated from the hard surface beneath him. Stone maybe, rough and uneven. He shifted and sharp jolts webbed down his spine. Praise the Great One, what the hell had he done? The last thing he remembered—

The warrior's strike, shooting past Galena's cheek and nailing him in the shoulder. He should be dead.

Cool, damp air swished across his torso, tainted with the scent of mold, earth, and something else he couldn't quite place. He pulled in another breath, ignoring the tiny stabs poking beneath his ribs. Herbs. Nothing he knew by name, just a clean, crisp edge out of place with everything else. And flowers. Definitely flowers.

Out of nowhere, a pressure built at his wound, ratcheting from warm to blowtorch hot in seconds. A scream punched from his lungs and jammed in a vicious knot at the back of his throat. He needed to move. To thrash and strike at whatever it was attacking him, but his body couldn't move, too paralyzed by pain to break free.

The pain flashed to nothing in an instant, the heat of the assault falling away with it.

He shuddered, chilled to the bone with goose bumps covering his flesh.

A flutter brushed across his mind.

His memories. Someone was trying to read him. An invasion. He forced his eyes open, tried to push away, and froze. His voice cracked. "Galena."

Light from the torches behind her flickered off her auburn hair, and her lips curved in a tight, practiced smile. "I know that was painful, but you'll be fine now."

She'd healed him. That was the burn beneath his skin. But guilt shone in her eyes too. Had she read his memories before he shut her out?

"That's enough."

Reese flinched at the clipped reprimand. He knew that angry tone all too well. The same one Ramsay Shantos had flailed him with all those years ago. He didn't dare look up. Didn't trust himself.

"Get him up and in the cell." His former strategos, the man who'd trained and then denied Reese entry into the warrior brotherhood, dipped into Reese's line of sight and pulled Galena away.

Two guards hustled forward and hoisted Reese up by his armpits and thighs. They lugged him toward a cell, every jerk and bounce lashing fresh torment against his bruised and battered body.

An icy wave pummeled him, and his stomach lurched. Zeolite. The crystal showed no mercy, crushing his powers as soundly as a boot heel on a bug.

His guards grunted beneath the impact as well, their dagger sheaths thumping against their belts with each shuffle. They tossed him toward the corner.

He slammed into a thinly cushioned cot, and his teeth clacked together, rattling as hard as the cell door the guards slammed on their way out.

Praise the Great One, he ached. Everywhere. He pushed upright, holding his breath until the fresh wave of agony settled.

A candle burned on the weathered wooden table beside him. Eden didn't utilize electricity the way humans did, and no sane jailer would risk piping in light from above. Too much opportunity for prisoners to feed on Eden's energy through the opening and past the Zeolite to feed their powers.

On the other side of his door, Ramsay's voice roared, ripping someone a new asshole.

Reese struggled to his feet, locked his knees and slowed his breath. He knew Ramsay like few others did. It'd take his once friend another thirty seconds tops before he stomped through the cell door and unleashed his venom on the person he was really pissed at.

Reese.

He rolled his shoulders and exhaled through the pain. Damn it, if he wouldn't find his pride and meet Ramsay's attack upright. His drast was gone, leaving his chest bare. Understandable with the charred mess covering his wound, but least he still had his pants and boots.

The latch on the door kachunked and the door whooshed open.

Ramsay prowled inside and shoved the door closed. His jaw looked hard enough to snap. Thank The Great One, zeolite would keep things on an even keel where powers were concerned.

Reese glanced at the door. "Where's Galena?"

"My sister's not your concern," Ramsay said, harsh and cold as the dungeon.

Like histus she wasn't. For whatever reason, she'd saved him. "Was she hurt?"

Ramsay crossed his arms and tilted his head. "Why would you care? You tried to kill her."

Seventy years and Ramsay's glare still sliced him.

"A warrior with something to hide has no place in the brotherhood. This candidate is unworthy to serve."

The memory tore through Reese, slicing open old wounds poorly healed. "Why did you let her heal me?"

Ramsay uncurled his arms and stepped forward, nostrils flared. "Because you've got information and I want it."

The blood rushed from his head and his knees threatened to give way. Of course, that's why Galena had saved him. She'd thought of her race. Of her brothers, and saved him for what he knew. Not some spark of mercy or kindness.

The door flew open and the thick wood cracked against the stone wall. "Ramsay, let him heal."

"Not now, Galena." Ramsay kept his gaze locked on Reese.

She swayed, her face pale. Whatever she'd done to heal him, her empathic gift had taken its toll.

Ramsay stalked toward Reese. "You're well enough. I'll bet I can find a way to get what we need out of you."

"Ramsay." Galena darted forward and stumbled.

Reese dodged to the side. His legs gave out beneath him, but he broke her fall, his good shoulder snapping against the stone floor.

Galena twisted in his hold and studied his injury, her eyes flared in alarm and her mouth parted. "Reese."

Screw the pain. Every bit was worth it to have her this close. To have her lips this close and her breath on his face. To feel her soft breasts pressed against his against his chest and let her flowery scent cart his mind miles and miles away from here.

Ramsay scooped her up and out of Reese's arms.

"I'm fine." Galena shoved Ramsay and tried to wiggle free. "I'm fine. Put me down."

"You're not fine." Ramsay shifted her in his arms. "You look like hell."

Reese pushed himself from the floor on wobbly legs, his breath shallow and huffing.

"I just need some rest." She still struggled. "Now put me down."

"No." Ramsay spun for the open door, his guards hovering outside the door. He paused at the entrance and scowled at Reese. "She saved your ass. Not once, but twice. If you care so much about her, you'll thank her for her efforts in the form of answers when I get back."

The door slammed behind him and quick footsteps faded into nothingness.

Reese dropped to the cot and the wooden legs grated against the floor. What in histus was wrong with him? He was a POW, would probably hang within twenty-four hours, and all he could process was the way Galena felt next to him. He couldn't twist the scenario more if he tried.

He fisted the cot's coarse brown blanket. Galena shouldn't have wasted her energy to heal him. The zeolite negated his gifts, but it also sheltered him from Maxis. The minute he stepped free of the protective crystal Maxis would find him via link and shred his brain the same way he had Phybe's.

He laughed and banged the back of his head against the wall. What was he thinking? Ramsay and Eryx would hang him for treason whether he gave them the information they wanted or not. Even if they offered mercy in exchange for what he knew, he'd spend the rest of his life behind zeolite, which was worse than death.

Two death sentences or a lifetime in prison. He let out a harsh exhale and hung his head. No matter which way things went, he was well and truly screwed.

* * * *

Galena bolted upright in bed and gasped. Her pulse thrummed at either side of her neck and her breasts ached, tight and heavy. Cool air hit her sweat-slick skin as she blinked her eyes into focus. Emerald curtains framed a window open to dark skies. A favorite painting hung along the far wall. Her room at the castle.

Now she remembered. Ramsay hadn't let her go home. Had insisted she sleep at the castle instead of her cottage.

Plucking the damp silk against her belly, she took a slow steady breath and dropped back to the pillows. Wisps of erotic images clung to her thoughts. Her and Reese, lips and tongues, tangled and sweaty. She pressed her legs together and groaned at the lingering ache between them.

In her dream, he'd devoured her. Touched her in a way no man had in real life. Bold. Decadent.

A traitor.

She flicked the covers aside and shoved upright. She didn't have anything to be ashamed of. So what if her subconscious put Reese's face on her desires? It didn't mean she wanted him literally. Just that she wanted to be desired. To be more than someone's political advantage or empty-headed house warmer. Completely reasonable.

Pulling her hair off her neck, she plodded to the window and rested her elbows on the stone ledge. If she'd minded her manners and stayed out of Reese's head in the first place, her imagination wouldn't have had so much material to work with.

Her cheeks flared hot and a strangled cough bubbled up. She'd just wanted to gauge his intentions at the battlefield. To see if he'd meant her harm. Boy had she ended up with a surprise. Her image. Front and center in the bulk of all his last memories.

Did he really see her that way? That sexy? Voluptuous?

The wind coiled around her neck, teasing the damp stands. The barely lightening skies fell out of focus. What would it feel like to have Reese touch her there? To feel his hands in her hair? His breath at her neck?

She pushed away from the window and stomped toward her closet. Nursing those ideas wasn't healthy. Or realistic. Dawn was close, so she'd been out what? Twelve? Thirteen hours? Plenty of time for her to bounce back. The Great One knew, she had enough to catch up on.

With a tiny mental push, she set the candles in her room to light. Bold colors and soft fabrics lined her closet. Some elegant gowns, but mostly tunics and comfortable leggings. Other women stuck to the old ways of formal attire, but those outfits didn't serve well for her line of work.

She tugged on an emerald set and brushed her hair in quick, efficient strokes. What in histus was wrong with Ramsay anyway? Out of everyone in her family, Ramsay was the happy one. The playboy who wrestled panties from women with a wink and a smile. Even in battle, he'd find something to joke about. So, why was he angry? Yes, Reese had served the rebellion. Yes, Reese was hiding something. But this level of anger? It didn't add up.

She tossed her hairbrush aside. The wood clattered against the marble countertop and muffled her frustrated huff. Was she being shortsighted? Siding with the enemy? Ramsay and Eryx were the only two living relatives she could call her own. How could she betray them by even thinking about someone who served the rebellion? Let alone fantasize about them.

She shoved the thought away and grabbed her toothbrush. She needed to check on Brenna, not piddle around in her room sulking. Eryx healing the brave human who'd saved Lexi during the battle was a gutsy move. No one knew what the impact on a human would be, and the intervention put Eryx in a tenuous place. Malran or not, violating the Myren law prohibiting intercession in human destiny was a death sentence.

A few guards nodded at her on her way to the kitchen, but most kept their gaze locked straight ahead.

So many warriors. Maxis might have gotten to their family once, but Eryx clearly wasn't taking chances for a second bout. She'd bet there were guards stationed at her cottage too.

The scent of freshly baked bread and something sweet tempted her nose before she reached the kitchen. As she turned the corner, the warmth from the fire ovens wrapped her in a fierce hug.

"What on Earth are you doing up?"

Galena shrieked and spun. "Orla." Galena rubbed her palm over her agitated heart and glared at the silver-haired woman. "You scared the hell out of me."

Orla flicked her hand in Galena's direction.

A snap of electricity shot across the room and zapped Galena in the butt. She jerked her hip to one side, more in reflex than in pain.

"Manners, Galena. Human slang from your brothers is one thing. It's not nearly as appealing on a young lady." She shut the pantry door with her hip and bustled to the island countertop with a fresh box of yeast. Her long hair swished free behind her, and she grinned far too brightly for this early in the morning.

Galena rubbed the sting Orla's shock left behind. "You don't correct Lexi and she curses more than most of the men."

"Of course, I don't correct her. She's the malress. Besides, she needs to speak in a way they can relate to if she's going to keep their attention." She stepped around the counter and tapped Galena's cheek. "On you, however, it's like graffiti on a fine piece of art."

Galena let out a sigh and leaned into the island.

Orla bustled to a cabinet for a bowl.

So much for being hungry. She'd be better off snipping thorns or yanking weeds from her garden. Why everyone put her in the classic art category she'd never understand. "Graffiti has its own beauty."

Orla turned, head slanted in a questioning angle.

"Is something wrong?" She set the bowl aside and gave Galena her full attention. "You look a bit...out of sorts."

Well, that wasn't surprising. If her outsides matched her insides, she probably looked like she'd been on a five-day strasse bender.

Galena hesitated and rubbed her hands together. Orla had a warm heart and bubbly personality, but was one hundred percent old school. *"Until your brother takes a mate, you have to fill your mother's role,"* she'd said. *"Royals set the standard. You, in particular, for our next generation of women."*

She stifled a harrumph, the sound coming out like a half-hearted sneeze. No. Orla wasn't the best candidate for a heart-to-heart. She pushed from her perch and gave Orla a warm hug. "It's nothing. I'm just off my schedule. I'll be fine once the sun's up."

"Well, get some food while you're here. There's fresh bread and briash on the stove. Lexi begged me for lastas again, but I won't start those for another few hours." She glanced around the kitchen and patted the pockets on her apron. "Galena can you run and get my hair clip? I think I left it near the rear entrance when I came in this morning."

Galena nodded and snagged an end cap off the loaf of bread on her way.

Yep, right on the side table near the coat hooks at the back door. She snatched it, turned for the kitchens, and drew up short.

The dungeon entrance loomed just ahead, sealed tight with no guards or witnesses in sight. It made sense, really. Eryx was worried about intruders getting in, not getting out. The zeolite cells had never required guards before. Why now?

Temptation wrapped around her waist and gave a none-too-subtle tug. She could check on Reese. No one was there to report she'd been by. And if he wasn't there, what difference would it make?

No. Reese was none of her business. If Ramsay or Eryx needed her help, they'd call. She beelined it for the kitchen. "Got it. Right where you left it." Was that too bright? Too bubbly? She laid the clasp aside for Orla and grabbed another slice of bread. "Call me when it's time for lastas. I'm headed to check on Brenna."

Orla barely glanced up from her dough. "Of course, dear. Let me know if you need my help for anything."

Galena strode toward the guest wing and Brenna. This was where her time was best spent. She'd done what was necessary to keep Reese alive for his knowledge, but now her time with him was over.

She paused at the bottom stair. What if Reese hadn't given Ramsay the information he wanted? Ramsay had been awfully angry when he left her. She backtracked, skirting the kitchen on quiet, swift feet. Two guards stood outside the rear entrance, faced away from her. Mindful of the noisy latch, she opened the door.

A dank draft swooshed her hair off her neck. Her sandals patted down the stone steps and the scent of torch oil and pitch filled her lungs.

No guards waited in the hallway, just a long stretch of cells, each with their doors closed. One slow-burning torch smoldered outside Reese's cell.

She inched closer, fingers trembling at her sides. No sound came from the cell, at least none louder than the pound of her pulse in her head. She traced the iron latch and its chill ran clear to her shoulder. Her brothers would be livid.

She stepped back and clutched her hand at her chest. This was insane. If she did this she'd be a traitor, no different than Reese. She spun for the exit.

"Galena."

Reese's ragged, low voice rumbled and pulled her to a stop. Was his infection back? Had Ramsay tortured him to get his information? And how did he know it was her?

"Don't leave." His request barely reached her, rough and pitched with pain. "You have my vow, I won't hurt you."

Chapter 4

Reese braced himself against the cell wall, his knuckles hard against the smooth, cold crystal. It had to be Galena. Warriors wouldn't have such quiet footsteps, and they damn sure wouldn't carry the soft, flowery scent that crept beneath the cell door. He strained his ears against the silence. His eyes stung, trained on the motionless iron latch, like his constant stare might somehow will her to lift the lever.

"I only want to talk. To thank you. I never would have set the strike free." It wasn't an outright confession he'd sought to end his life, but it still stung to admit. Reese shoved away from the wall. She wouldn't open it, and he sure as histus couldn't blame her, but at least she'd heard the truth.

Metal clunked on metal, and Reese's heart lurched.

The door creaked open and Galena's scent whooshed through the still widening gap. Shadows hid her face and the torchlight cast her outline in an otherworldly, gold glow. Her long tunic and leggings hugged her body in the backlight. Perfect curves. Hips made for a man's grasp.

His throat caught on a swallow. He should say something. Thank her at least, but his jaw wouldn't cooperate. He edged to the furthest wall, giving her space.

She took two steps across the threshold and stumbled.

Reese darted forward to catch her.

Galena gasped and jerked away, hands raised in defense.

He backpedaled. "Sorry."

Smoothing the front of her tunic, she straightened and dipped her chin. A subtle tremor shook her voice. "The zeolite caught me off guard."

"If you stay in it long enough, you adjust." He motioned to the cot. "You can sit if you like. I'll keep my distance."

She gauged the space between him and the makeshift bed and frowned.

Hard to blame her hesitation. Few women would deem a POW and a cot a safe combination. He slid to the ground, the smooth crystal wall chill against his bare back. He drew his knees up and rested his forearms along the tops. "What time is it?"

Her tension loosened and she folded her hands in front of her, formal and a little uncertain. Though, a one-on-one in a dungeon had to rank pretty high on the scale of awkward situations. "It's a little before dawn." She glanced around the room. "Has Ramsay been back?"

He shook his head. "You haven't seen him?"

She peeked at the cot again. "Not since last night."

"I gave you my word. I'll stay where I am. If you'd rather, I can move the cot closer to the doorway."

Something in her demeanor shifted. A mantle of certainty settled into place just as powerful as the confidence her brothers wielded, but quieter and more graceful. She waved him toward the plain narrow bed. "I'd rather you sit on the cot and let me check your wound."

He stood, slowly so as not to frighten her, and shifted to the rickety cot. "You're very trusting."

She froze halfway to him and quirked her head to one side. "What makes you say that?"

He motioned toward the still open door with his chin. "I don't know many women who'd walk into a cell without a guard. Let alone leave the door open."

She scowled and strode to the small side table, dragging it and the lone candle closer. "You gave your word. My instincts tell me you wouldn't break your promise. If that makes me trusting, then so be it."

"Ramsay would disagree."

"I'm not Ramsay."

"I see that." He grinned. Hard not to with the quick fire he'd lit with their conversation.

"He's not himself right now. We've got a lot to contend with between Maxis and the rebellion." All business and matter of fact, she dropped to her knees and reached for his shoulder.

Reese caught her by the wrist before she could make contact. "You don't have to justify his behavior, Galena. I deserve everything he gives me and then some." Praise the Great One, she was beautiful. Earthy and sensual, but innocent too. Beneath his fingertips, her pulse tripped fast and furious. "You're also smart. And brave. None of the warriors thought to spare me for the information I hold, but you jumped in and saved me."

"You're giving me too much credit." She tugged her arm free and touched the edge of his mending wound. "I didn't think, I just acted."

Reese hissed and shuddered beneath the contact.

Galena jerked away. "Did I hurt you?"

Did sensual torture count? She may as well have stroked between his legs. "I'm fine."

She frowned and leaned back in, albeit more cautious than before. "Healer's instinct then?"

No response.

"If not for my knowledge, then why?" he asked.

Her gaze was the only thing that shifted, a quick, sideways peek, then back on the wound, but a sweet flush spread across her cheeks. She checked the pulse at his wrist and averted her face. "Why try to label my actions? Why not just be grateful you're alive?"

"Because it's a temporary reprieve at best. I'll either die in this cell, by your brother's mandate, or at Maxis' hand."

She froze.

He should tell her. Ramsay was right. She'd saved him not once, but twice, and deserved the truth. "Your willingness to heal me meant something. To me, anyway. No matter what your reasons."

With only the candle's glow her hair gleamed more chestnut than auburn. She dipped her head and the flowery scent he'd struggled to name registered with a kick. Lotus flower. A fitting match for her exotic eyes, like water off a white, Caribbean shore.

He'd never dreamed he'd get this close to her. Not even when he'd visited the castle with Ramsay all those years ago. "I used to watch you." Probably not his wisest confession. Then again, he'd be dead in who knew how many days. As repercussions went, they couldn't get much worse.

Her gaze met his and her lips parted.

"It was a long time ago," he said. "When I trained with Ramsay. Did he tell you about me?"

She ducked her head and studied his wound with extra focus. Not a yes, but not a no either.

"I didn't come to the castle often, but when I did I'd watch for you. You were barely past your awakening. I thought you were perfect." He cupped her cheek. "Still do." He traced her cheekbone. "Your skin's just like I'd imagined it. Warm. Soft."

She leaned into his touch. Not much. Probably didn't even realize she'd done it. Her eyes softened, lids dropping, and her hair slicked against his knuckles. "Reese." A whisper. Nothing more.

"You see the good in me, but your brother can't pardon what I've done. Nor should he. I'll die for my actions in days, if not hours." Was he really going to do this? Could he live with the humiliation if she refused his request?

Absolutely. He traced her lower lip and her breath skittered against his finger. "I always imaged what your lips would feel like. Will you give me that gift?"

Galena froze. "You want…"

"A kiss." He chanced another glide along her mouth and the tip of her tongue trailed the path he left behind. "Just one."

She swallowed and her eyelids fluttered shut as she pressed a kiss into his palm.

He braced, ready for her shutdown.

Her eyes opened and he jolted beneath the passion in her gaze. "One." So much emotion. Need. Urgency. Fear and shame. All rolled into one power-packed word.

He leaned forward and curled his free hand around the side of her neck. A decent man wouldn't follow through, but a far more primal part of him was in charge now, instinctive and not at all gentle. Her lips were close enough his own tingled. He held himself there, soaking in the sensation. Something to remember.

"Please," she whispered.

Tightening his fingers, he angled her face for his advance. Slow. Careful.

Her mouth gave way, soft and sweet, parted just enough to lick along the lower one. She moaned and edged closer, opening to the bold sweep of his tongue.

He growled at her taste, mint and something that reminded him of long lazy mornings and sunshine. Her breath mingled with his, hot and heavy between each slick glide of their lips. Fuck ordinary air. This. This was what he wanted to live on. In his lungs, day in and day out.

Her fingers splayed across his pecs, blowtorch hot. He wanted them lower. To feel them slide down his abs and curl around his straining cock. Splaying his hand at the small of her back, he tucked her between his thighs so her hips nestled tight against his hard length.

She flexed her hips and a sweet, needy mewl vibrated against his lips.

He nipped her lower lip and slanted deeper, sweeping the plush texture of her tongue with his. Lost. No worries and no fears, just sweet, perfect abandon.

Traitor.

He jerked away and fisted the cot's edge, fighting for control.

Her voice rasped between the rapid rise and fall of her chest and her eyelids hung heavy. "What's wrong?"

He'd give anything to flame that look. That fire. To take her where it needed to go and watch her shatter. "You offered one kiss." His grumble matched the unsatisfied hunger beating him. He gripped her shoulders and eased her away. "I won't break my word. Not to you. If I hadn't pulled away, I wouldn't have stopped."

Her eyes rounded and her kiss-swollen lips formed an O.

His resolve faltered. He fisted his hands at his sides and forced himself against the too-cold crystal wall. "Go. Get Ramsay. I'll give him everything I know." Better to serve the malran's needs with what he knew and honor her healing gift in the process than to waste away here.

Galena hesitated, her face flushed and still kneeling between his thighs. His ideal and wet dream rolled up into one.

Her expression hardened and she shoved to her feet. "I'm glad to hear it. Good I offered the incentive you needed to do the right thing." She spun away and slammed the door.

The latch clanged into place, and his heart echoed with the same finality. It was better this way. Felt like shit, but was definitely better. He'd just replay the bullshit line until it took root. Besides, once she learned his secrets, she'd be glad he'd pulled away when he did.

* * * *

Galena stormed the dungeon steps and out the rear entrance of the castle.

The guards spun at her abrupt arrival, arms up and ready for attack.

She waved them off in what she hoped was an authoritative gesture and stalked deeper into the exotic garden. "Pair up with the men from the outer walls for now. I'll call you when I'm done here."

Neither moved.

Galena stopped and crossed her arms. She peered over her shoulder only enough to portray annoyance. Playing the royal card wasn't her style, but prying eyes weren't something she wanted right now. "This space is royal sanctuary. Eryx may want us on high alert, but neither he nor Ramsay will countermand my order. Now go."

The ranking warrior fisted the hilt of his dagger, scanned the perimeter, and motioned his partner to the iron gate at the garden's edge with a jerk of his head. Their heavy footsteps clipped along the flagstone path until the roar of the ocean's surf overpowered them.

Thank The Great One. She hung her head and a shiver rippled through her. The sun was barely up. Shadows coated every corner of the tiny paradise, the air too cool against her bare arms.

But the tremors came from somewhere else.

She shook her head to clear her thoughts, and ambled to the alcove overlooking the sea below. What in histus was wrong with her? She'd kissed a traitor. Willingly.

No. It was more than a kiss. She'd surrendered to him. If Reese hadn't stopped when he did, she'd have followed any and every lead he'd taken. Maybe initiated a few of her own.

The ocean breeze stung her tear-dampened cheeks. Her heart thrummed as loud as the waves below. She still craved his touch.

An ironic, self-deprecating chortle shook her. He'd been the one who pulled away, not her. She should be furious, or at the least indignant. The Great One knew, she'd done her best to storm out with such a facade. He'd probably only asked for the kiss in some sick ploy for mercy. He fought for the rebellion, for God's sake. To do such a thing took a certain kind of perversity. And she'd proved to be the perfect sucker.

A tear slipped free and she dashed it away. She'd felt desirable. For one tiny sliver of time, a man had really touched her. Not handled her like a snowflake.

She plunked to the teak bench, planted her elbows on her knees, and rested her forehead in her hands. No matter how she tried, the way he'd reflected her in his memories kept circling in her mind. Sultry and sexy, like one of those early screen goddesses in Evad, but softer. Easy as the ocean breeze ruffling her hair. She hadn't imagined it. Memories didn't offer the insight of emotion or thoughts, only sights and sounds like a movie. But to him, she was beautiful.

So, what was she supposed to do? Follow Ramsay's distrusting lead and let things take their course? Pretend nothing ever happened? Or was Reese sincere?

Surely he wasn't so duplicitous. Her pride might have stung when he sent her away, but he'd fisted his hands at his side as well. Desire had weighted his eyes just as much as her own. And at the battle he'd seemed genuinely distraught at Phybe's death. She'd sensed his goodness. Felt it as warm as a setting summer sun. Condemning a decent man to death seemed wrong. Even if the kiss was nothing more than a ruse, everything else pointed to a man of character stuck in a difficult place.

She scrubbed away her tears with the back of her hand. Even if she wanted to intervene, she wouldn't be able to stop Ramsay in his current mood. For whatever reason, his mind was made up where Reese was concerned. No one stopped Ramsay once he'd chosen his path.

No one but Eryx.

She gasped and sat up straight. The wind buffeted her as much as the rush sprinting through her. Talking to Eryx might work. He likely didn't trust Reese any more than Ramsay did, but he seemed to be lacking Ramsay's extra wallop of hatred. Maybe he would listen to reason and consider leniency in exchange for the information Reese provided.

She stood and rubbed the goose bumps along her upper arms. It might work, but she'd have to word her request carefully. Going to bat for a man who called to her instincts was one thing. Losing her brothers to him was something else altogether.

Chapter 5

Creaks and muffled voices sounded above Reese's cell. It was probably the castle staff settling into their morning routine, but without natural light or his senses to gauge the sun's position, it was hard to tell for sure.

Where in histus was Ramsay? Surely Galena had tracked him down by now. He couldn't sit still. Couldn't pace enough to dull his anxiety. No matter how many times he replayed Galena's kiss, the ugly look of betrayal it had ended with always smacked front and center in his head. He'd hurt her. Badly.

He stretched out farther on the cot, as if lengthening his torso might somehow unhook the guilt snagged beneath his sternum. Pulling away from her ranked at the top of his most difficult list. There wasn't a single word worthy of what he felt for her. It went beyond need, or even want. More fundamental, like air, or water.

Damn it. He paced the tiny space. The sooner he unloaded his burdens, the sooner he'd be free from his past. The damned things weighed three times more now that he'd decided to talk. Of course, the sooner he talked, the sooner he died. He stopped and hung his head, huffing out a resigned breath. At least he'd have those minutes with Galena to take with him.

"Your life may yet serve a significant purpose, warrior."

Reese spun toward the voice behind him, poised to fight.

A female with an angelic face stood in the center of his cell, an ethereal glow around her. Straight black hair hung to her waist accenting pale mocha skin. Her white gown gripped her slim body and shimmered as though the cloth were embedded with bits of the moon.

His muscles uncoiled and he straightened from his stance. A weird kind of peace moved through him, the same bright sensation of a quiet afternoon in spring. "Who are you?"

Dusky pink lips stretched into a smile brighter than the noonday sun and her pale blue eyes twinkled. "My name is Clio. I am your spiritu."

What? One hundred and forty-three years old and trained for all manner of human and Myren interaction, but he'd never once heard the term. Either someone had a sick sense of humor, or he'd finally skipped one region past sanity.

Laughter filled the cell, the sound light and laced with wind chimes. "You won't find what you seek through logic, only through your memories and your heart." She glided forward. Sparkles along her brow winked in the candlelight, white, pearlescent jewels in varied shapes and sizes. Like a crown, but without a base to hold them together. "We do not make a practice of showing ourselves to our charges, but there are times when it cannot be avoided." She tilted her head. "Search your mind. Do you recognize my voice?"

Reese closed his eyes, his brain jumping to obey before his curiosity could argue. He had heard it before, a lilting sound colored with flutes and the laughter of children, but where he'd heard it he couldn't quite place.

"I've been with you since you were born."

Reese snapped from his trance.

Clio drifted closer, her feet never appearing to move, and touched his shoulder. "I've been with you even when you chose to forgo my guidance."

The cell fell away.

Warm, sunny skies surrounded him. The barest breeze touched his sweat-slick skin, and he knelt on one knee. The gold-flecked sand from the warriors' arena floor surrounded him, Ramsay's boots the only other object in his line of sight.

It was his swearing-in. A crystal-clear replay of the moments he'd lived through all those years ago. Ramsay gripped Reese's forearm. A warrior's greeting. Ramsay's spirit brushed through Reese's mind, gauging his memories.

"Trust him. Open your heart and find your dreams." Clio's voice had drifted through his mind, soft, but strong.

The dark, dank cell crashed back in place and left a fresh gash on the old, festering wound. His lungs burned to let loose a ragged shout. He'd ignored her. Locked his secret in an iron-willed vault and blocked Ramsay out.

"It's in the past, Reese." Her comfort wrapped around him, as tangible as a down blanket in the coldest winter. "You cannot undo wrong choices, but you can make new ones. Choices to change your life and the lives of those you love."

Reese shook his head. "I don't have any choices left. No one left to love." It was a lie. Maybe love was the wrong word, but if he'd ever hoped to gain the love of someone it was Galena. "I'm past saving."

"Your healer doesn't think so." A verbal punch straight to the gut, one that wrenched his insides tight. A beautiful thought, but cruel as histus.

Clio cupped his cheek, the movement so similar to something his mother would have done his stomach quaked. "You have many more choices to make. Far-reaching ones. It's why I'm here."

Reese jerked away from her touch. He couldn't afford fantasies, let alone hope. "Time and riddles aren't my friends right now. If you've got something to say, get on with it."

An impish smile graced her face. "The spiritu are your guides. The inspiration in your thoughts. We aid the human and Myren race, and represent the light and dark passions."

"But you don't show yourselves."

"No. To do so would be to sway your conscience from free will."

Free will? She wanted to talk about free will and inspiration? Now? Why in histus should he care about either when he was locked in a dungeon and headed to the gallows?

"Because the law of reciprocity has been violated."

"You can hear my thoughts?"

"And feel what you feel." She tilted her head with childlike delight. "I am connected to you in a way that transcends this plane."

Odd. The whole concept was a little disconcerting, both intimate and a violation in the same breath.

Her smile dimmed. "I stand before you because you have an important choice to make."

Blink.

Blink.

His brain refused to cough up anything. No witty retorts, no questions, just a great big fat blank space. He gestured to his cell. "Have you missed my situation? I can't do anything here."

"Quite the contrary. You were already on the path to your choice."

"You mean giving Ramsay and the malran the information they need."

She inclined her head, slow and regal. "There is a human, a man close to the new malress who Maxis has taken hostage. The knowledge you have can aid in his freedom, but there is still more you can do."

Reese thumbed through what he knew, what might be a benefit to the malran and his men. "I don't have anything else to give."

Clio stared at him, her face deadpan. "Maxis."

A ripple shot down Reese's spine.

"Whether you realize it or not, you are the one decent spark in Maxis' life. You have a chance to fan that spark. To aid the malran in freeing the captive human, but also to use your own light to guide Maxis' soul."

"You've got to be kidding me." He spun and fisted a chunk of hair at the top of his head. "Of all people, you want me to be a guiding light? For Maxis? He thinks I'm a traitor." He threw up his hands and faced Clio. "Even Ramsay thinks I'm a traitor. There's no way he'll let me out of here. Least of all evangelize to the man whose family has hurt the Shantos line for centuries."

"You assume too quickly, warrior." Her genteel demeanor disappeared. Whether a trick of shadows or actual manifestation, Clio loomed larger, angled for attack with a steel-laced voice to back it up. "You've assumed wrong before. Perhaps you should put your strategic abilities to task and favor a different path this time. One that serves the greater good and stands for what you know is right."

Her stance eased, and her tension settled as swiftly as it had come. She folded her hands in front of her. "The choice is yours to make. Search yourself and make the right one."

Her image dimmed.

Reese lurched forward to try and stop her, but met air.

She was gone. Poofed to nothing. If he'd found the cell dismal before it was worse now. His soul itched with discomfort.

He covered the cell's width in three long strides and slammed his palms against the wall. A roar knotted at the base of his throat, neck straining for release. All the pain, all his bad decisions, balled into one giant barricade.

Lead Maxis to goodness? With Ramsay and Eryx's blessing?

He rested his forehead against the cold crystal and groaned. He'd need more than strategy to bring what Clio wanted to pass. He'd need a fucking miracle.

* * * *

Maxis stuck to the shadowed side of Cush's main thoroughfare, the other sparkling with gold flecks in the morning sunshine. Serena's link pulsed a pastel yellow in his mind's eye, its mental map showing her location barely a block away, just over the next rise.

The stubborn minx. If it were anyone else he'd have avoided the sun and waited until nightfall to do his business, but delaying with Serena was a bad idea. Mending the hole he'd blown in her pride would take some impressive sucking up. Leaving her alone to stew on it longer would only up his deficit.

He shielded his degenerative eyes from the reflections and ambled up the hill. Every flicker plucked at the nerves behind his retinas and left a path of bruises on his brain. He'd trade cheery, searing sunshine for dark or cloudy skies any day. He sidestepped a well-dressed lad running down the sidewalk. It could be worse. Serena's parents could live on the poor side of town.

"Maxis. I need a word."

Maxis groaned at the mental summons. Thyrus was a pain-in-the-ass middleman and a glutton on a good day, but damned handy when it came to information. *"What do you want?"*

"Yes, well." A stammer and string of garbled noises brought to mind Thyrus' flapping jowls. *"It's Angus. Says he needs a word with you posthaste. Seems he's still a bit agitated over his last confrontation with Eryx. The old man didn't take too well to being made the fool."*

"He made himself a fool," Maxis replied. *"He wasn't supposed to use the information until we had proof. Let alone confront the malran in front of the whole damned council. If he can't hold his tongue or his temper, that's hardly my fault."*

He stopped in front of one of the cootyas. Wooden crates were stacked in chaotic yet artful patterns and filled with Eden's bold colored fruits and vegetables. Dealing with Angus was the last thing he needed today. Charming Serena alone would suck up a year's worth of charisma. *"Where is he?"*

"At my office. Was here when I arrived this morning. Very fidgety and quite loud. Not good for business."

No, probably not. Thyrus might be a finger-licking meat eater in search of his next buffet, but he had a healthy legal practice to pay for his gullet's demands. If said business handed Maxis frequent insight into the cracks and scandals of the Myren elite, then so be it. *"Keep him there."*

Thyrus huffed and dropped their connection.

This part of the capital was surprisingly quiet. A block away an ostentatious fountain shot steams of water from moss-green marble, a centerpiece for one of Cush's most exclusive neighborhoods. The light chatter of early morning business droned behind him.

Dealing with his future bride wouldn't be a straightforward affair. And while she might come up with a half dozen more ways to make him pay for his harsh statements between now and when they next met, she wouldn't go off half-cocked like Angus.

Rerouting to Thyrus' office in the business district, he took to the skies. Better to nip the ellan's frustration while he could. He'd use the delay to his advantage and offer a fresh spin to keep Eryx and Angus at each other's throats a little longer. Maybe even long enough to let Maxis bounce back from his losses.

Sunshine slanted across the ivory domed rooftops and taupe brick-laid streets. Street vendors settled their carts for a new day, canvas awnings stretched to battle what promised to be an over-warm morning. The trip took no more than five minutes by air, but was enough to stoke the slow ache behind his eyes to a nasty throb.

He stormed the stairs to Thyrus' office, his bootheels clipping against the smooth gray sandstone. The top floor opened to a long, open-air corridor with three Blackwood doors along each side. Faint, muffled voices sounded from the far end, the other spaces void of energy.

He opened the last door on his right.

Thyrus' voice hung in the air, his jaw slack on an unspoken word.

Angus scowled and spun toward the entrance. At least Maxis though it was a scowl. It could have been the old man had left his dentures at home.

"You." Angus shuffled forward with hunched shoulders. "You and your bogus information left me and my constituents in a bad place with the malran." He stopped a foot out of Maxis' reach and wagged a bony finger. "Give me one good reason I shouldn't divulge my sources and turn you in."

Constituents his ass. If Angus gave a damn about the people of his region Maxis would hang himself at the malran's request. "I'll give you three reasons." A cream-colored sofa stretched beneath a high, wide window. Maxis strolled around Angus and settled on one side. "Number one, Eryx already knows your source. To think anything else would be to discredit his intellect. While I find his family to be a generational string of pompous do-gooders, he's not stupid."

He propped his booted foot on the ornate glass and iron table in front of him. "Number two, the information you were given wasn't bogus. And, three." He stretched his arms out along the sofa back. "You can use that information to make Eryx's life hell, if not cost him his throne." He paused and tilted his head. "That is what you want, isn't it?"

Angus straightened as much as his stooped frame would allow. His fingers twitched at his sides and sent a ripple through his crisp white council robe. "How?"

The fickle bastard. Maxis ought to make him grovel after the attitude he'd thrown around. Probably, not the best time to posture though if he wanted to keep Angus as an ally.

Thyrus waddled around his oversized black desk.

"My sources tell me you challenged how Eryx knew Lexi was Myren before he brought her here," Maxis said. "Are they correct?"

Angus nodded.

"And what was his response?"

The councilman harrumphed and waved a dismissive hand. He tottered toward the high maroon wingback at Maxi's right. "A bunch of evasive nonsense about not being able to disclose such matters until certain security aspects were researched." He eased into the chair, stiff, like he had more than a proverbial stick up his ass. "Considering my recent episode with the malran, I wasn't about to crawl any farther up his bad side in a public forum."

Ah, yes. The episode. He'd heard about Angus convening criminal trials in Eryx's absence. Damned if Eryx hadn't judged him guilty of treason for daring to act on his behalf.

Maxis scratched at his jaw. "So, the malran stripped your rank. You're still a valued ellan, sworn to act in the best interest of the Myren people and to champion the malran's vision. Correct?"

Angus narrowed his eyes. "What of it?"

"So, you play the concerned, agreeable councilman." Maxis stood and straightened his overcoat. "I understand the malress has professed a desire to find more lost Myrens, such as herself. The best way for you to support our newest leader is to support her causes. To jump on the bandwagon, so to speak."

He paced to Thyrus' desk and plucked a pink hard candy from a delicate ivory dish at the edge. "Of course, to find our lost, we'll need to know how Eryx identified our malress. That type of information can't be withheld from the council. It should be public knowledge so we can better seek and protect our people."

"A good angle." Thyrus nodded. "We have a moral obligation. Can't have any of our lost folk traipsing about in Evad all alone."

Maxis couldn't help but smile. Such support, and without the mention of food. "A nice touch, old friend." He squared his attention on Angus. "You're a gifted politician with a host of solid connections. What do you think? Can you make it work? Or did the...episode...affect more than your placement on the council?"

Angus straightened in his chair, torso angled forward and shaking. "I can make it work."

"Good. I look forward to watching Eryx squirm from the sidelines." Maxis headed toward the door. That hadn't gone bad at all. If anything he had more bounce in his step. Who'd have thought it possible? "Now, if you two will excuse me, I'll return to my errand. But do keep me updated on your progress."

Angus' voice cracked across the room. "Maxis."

Maxis paused at the threshold and lifted one eyebrow.

"A word to the wise. Rumor has it the malran's men are searching for the rebellion leader." Angus anchored his elbows on his armrests and steepled his fingers beneath his chin. His grin looked about as innocent as a dagger. "I'd hate to lose a valued colleague."

Chapter 6

...with all council agenda items completed and new business assigned, the formal session between our esteemed malran and the region representatives of Eden were concluded at fifteen spans past sunrise in the year of our race, three-thousand, six-hundred and thirty-eight.

Eryx snapped the old journal shut and leaned back in his desk chair. He anchored his elbow on the armrest and rubbed his chin. Pale sunlight speared through the library's arched windows, distant and annoyingly chipper voices slipping through the open panes.

His muscles twitched and a restless simmer crept beneath his skin. His mate was only just now recovering from being kidnapped, her human best friend was still held captive by his worst enemy somewhere in Eden, and a whole mess of politicians were breathing down his neck.

And he was drudging through old transcripts.

He'd kill for a dagger and decent fight. Histus, he'd even take a quick spar with Ludan. At least his somo wouldn't pull any punches.

"Here. Take a look at this one." Lexi shoved a new tome beside the one he'd finished. The damned things would've made tolerable bricks in the castle walls. Eighteen by eleven and an average of four inches thick, they ate up a whole wall, their leather covers weighting the room with the scent of age and dust.

Lexi hustled to the other side of the desk. She'd spurned the closet full of gowns and tunic sets he'd given her in favor of Levi's and a soft purple tank. The way the denim hugged her ass, he had half a mind to commandeer the whole damned Strauss empire.

She opened a new book and ducked her head. The sun shot across her long, soft-black hair to call out hints of blue.

His bainenann. His malress.

And he'd nearly lost her.

The restlessness jumped from a simmer to boil, and pressure knotted at the base of his throat. "What makes you think this one's any better than the last one?"

"Dirt." She winked, flipped the page, and reclined into the chair she'd dragged from her matching desk across the room. "I figure the more layers, the older and juicier the information."

Not exactly how he'd hoped to spend the second week of mated life. Then again, it beat how he'd spent the first. Considering she'd been nearly killed by Maxis and his rebellion fanatics, he'd halfway expected her to cut bait and head back to Evad. But no, she was here, sharing his desk, helping him dig for a historic precedent to bail his ass out of hot water with the ellan.

Helluva woman.

"If I did the math right, mine starts around 1760." Lexi smoothed her hand down the parchment. "It would be nice if you guys counted years the same as us."

"Them."

She looked up, a silent question on her face.

"Humans," he said. "They're a them. You're Myren."

She waved him off. "Semantics. I was a them a long time and always will be. How far back is yours?"

Eryx glanced at the spine. "1520 to 1580."

She squinted, gaze distant for a few seconds before it sharpened. "That's like...your great-grandfather's reign?"

He rubbed his eyes, the burn from hours scanning faded ink on yellow parchment going nowhere fast. "No. Grandfather."

"Pfft." She frowned and turned another page. "Generations were hard enough to track with an average life span of eighty. An average of five hundred years is gonna take a while to wrap my head around."

"You'll get there." No doubt faster than most. For a woman who'd spent her whole life with few friends, no family, and scraping to make ends meet, she'd done pretty damned good taking on his hodgepodge clan, a sizable estate, and a royal title.

A soft knock sounded at the door.

Lexi peeked over the back of her chair. "Hey, Galena."

Galena shut the door and glided across the rug emblazoned with the Shantos family mark, a black horse reared back with wings spread wide on a backdrop of deep maroon. "Am I interrupting? Orla said you're trying to find something."

"Political ammo." Lexi marked her place on the page with one finger. "Eryx needs arguments to warrant his bringing me here and healing Brenna."

Or else he'd lose his throne. No one ever said it out loud, but his brain sure offered it up often enough. Intervention in human destiny or disclosing their race to humans were the two sacred tenants that had ruled his race from the very beginning, handed down from The Great One, himself.

And he'd broken them both for Lexi.

If it meant keeping her in his life he'd do it again. Repeatedly. Still, if he wanted to protect the throne, he'd have to find a convincing argument for his ellan.

Galena rubbed her hands together and checked the doors behind her.

A brush of intuition fanned along his shoulders. "Something up?"

She hesitated and glanced at Lexi, buried in her book. "I know it's not a good time, but…" She bit her lower lip and gripped her hands tight enough her knuckles turned white. "…Reese is ready to talk."

Lexi straightened and shut her book.

Eryx leaned his elbows on his desk and tried to rein in a surge of adrenaline. If Reese knew even half as much as they hoped about Maxis, they had a decent chance of tracking Lexi's still-missing friend, Ian.

"Wait." He shoved from the desk and the beads holding his braids in place clicked around his shoulders. "Why are you the one telling me this? Ramsay said Reese was healed, but not willing to talk. He wanted to let him stew a while in zeolite and see if it changed his attitude."

Galena's lips snapped together tight, and she lifted her chin. "I went to check on him this morning. He indicated he was ready to share what he knows."

"And where was Ramsay?"

"I have no idea."

He crossed his arms and firmed his stance. If he couldn't intimidate her, at least he'd be far enough away he couldn't choke her. "So you went there alone."

The corner of her mouth quirked and she mirrored his stance, stubborn as the day she'd been born one hundred and twenty-one years ago.

"Um, hello." Lexi waved as though trying to stop two idiots from stepping in a heaping pile of shit. "Does it matter? She's here. She's fine. Reese wants to talk. I say we go hear what he has to say."

She had a point. Still, undercutting Ramsay's authority didn't sit well. And while he might be the most powerful of his race, he couldn't make the library search itself. "Ramsay's running the search for Maxis and Ian. We've got more than enough to handle on this end." He poked a stern finger in his sister's direction. "You. Stay the hell out of Reese's cell."

He sat back down and tugged the over-sized tome closer.

Galena planted her hands on his desk and leaned in, more determined than he seen since she'd demanded he sentence a bully at school for picking on someone half their size. "I think you should talk to Reese. Ramsay's temper is all over the place. He'd just as soon beat Reese than listen to what he has to say."

"Reese fought for a group of people who think human slaves are a good idea. What do you care what Ramsay does to him?"

"Are you out of your mind?" Lexi got side-by-side with Galena and glared at Eryx. "She's healed the guy twice. And thank God for that if he's willing to talk. I'd say she's got a right to care. You think she wants to do it a third time?"

Well, now. This was interesting. Eryx reclined into the high, cushioned chair and laced his hands behind his head. The leather groaned as he stretched his booted feet out in front of him, crossed at the ankles. The two made quite the unexpected tag team. Sure they'd come a long way at developing a bond in a short period of time, but enough to have Lexi jump to her defense? Over a man she knew nothing about?

Lexi's gift. That had to be it. As an emotional empath, she'd pick up on the slightest tweak to Galena's feelings. And, Lexi being Lexi, she'd jump to Galena's defense in a heartbeat. Lucky for him, he carried the sum of all Myren gifts. Maybe not as fine-tuned as Lexi's, but enough to sneak a peek for himself.

"Stop." Galena pushed away from the desk and took two shaky steps back. Her cheeks flushed bright red. "Don't think you can brush around on my emotions without me noticing. I'm your sister, not some stranger off the street. I've felt your nosy prodding since I was twelve. When I want you to know what I'm feeling, I'll tell you."

She pushed back her shoulders and lifted her chin, the tail end of her tirade hanging in the air. "Now, are you coming with me or not?"

* * * *

Maxis landed near the center of a residential square in the most exclusive part of Cush and let out a delighted chuckle. Such finery. Elaborate mansions loomed on every side of him, as though they jostled to make the most impressive statement.

He'd never visited this area. Never wanted to. For the last seventy-plus years, he'd been far too busy in Asshur and Brasia, building the infrastructure for his grand plans, and expanding the meager gifts The Great One had failed to grant him at birth.

Pride radiated warm beneath his sternum. Everyone thought the malran and his brother were the only ones capable of stripping another's gifts, but they were wrong. He'd found a way. Granted, the contributing Myrens didn't come out breathing on the other end with his method, but that wasn't his problem. His secrets had burned alongside the dead men's bodies.

A fine mist dusted across the side of his face. The high marble fountain at his right gurgled and whooshed in a roar too potent to be peaceful, a monolith of wealth that screamed for attention.

The same taupe and gold-flecked stone paved the roads here as along the main thoroughfare, but the walkways leading to the grand homes were closer to ivory. Eight manors formed the square, two on every side. Intimidating for the average man.

He wasn't an average man.

Serena's bold yellow link pulsed in his mind's eye, luring him toward the two residences on the left. One was crafted in the standard Myren architecture, rounded rooftops and arched windows with walls of mocha stucco. The other held a more ornate feel, somewhere between Baroque and Renaissance with its dark roof, pointed spires, and intricate details.

He closed his eyes and fine-tuned her location. His laughter spilled out into the early afternoon air, a brash intrusion against the quiet lawns. He should have known her family's home would be the ornate one. Something about its outspokenness matched her personality, a trait he imagined ran rampant in her clan.

He strode across the square and up the walk, a low-line iron fence guarding the plush green grass on either side. The rhythm of his heart mirrored each step, and his muscles hummed with an anticipation he hadn't felt since the day he'd found Reese.

On reflex, he reached for his strategos' link and slammed against the mental equivalent of a marble wall. He stopped at the massive Blackwood entry with its opaque glass insets, and tucked his chin tight to his chest. Now wasn't the time to look back. As surreal as Falon's visit might have been, his message was likely accurate. Reese was dead. Better to focus on his future, the key to which lay on the other side of these doors.

He lifted his hand to knock, then hesitated. Angus might be a short-tempered politician, but his warning had merit. He might be unrecognizable to most after so many years out of the public eye, but servants were a gossiping lot and no one else would answer the door.

He reached out through his link to Serena. *"You have a lovely home. Are you going to continue the cold shoulder? Or come open your door and welcome me inside?"*

No answer. If anything a chill pushed down the link to sting the back of his head, but her presence hustled within the house.

He tucked his hands into the pockets of his black overcoat and waited. Not one soul wandered the courtyard, the pretty details locked in place like some landscape on a wall.

The door jerked opened and the knocker at its center clattered against the wood.

"Are you crazy?" Serena grasped him by the forearm and glanced over her shoulder. She tugged him past the entry and through a black and white marble foyer to a receiving room off to one side. "Warriors are all over the place looking for you and they've got a damned good rendering to go with it."

She strode to an end table situated between two wingback chairs covered in a pale plum fabric and flicked her hand toward the door, shutting it with a mental push. With quick fingers, she sorted a stack of papers and thrust one in his direction. "Whoever drew it is surprisingly good. See for yourself."

The paper wavered from the tremor in her hand.

"You're worried about me?" He strolled forward. It was a comfortable room, easy and warm with its creams and purple accents. Serena fit right in with her loose, flowing pants and tunic. The dusky rose color matched the slight flush on her cheeks.

She thrust the parchment toward him again. "Worried about my connection *to* you is more like it. If I'm nothing more than a fuck, I'd prefer to keep my distance."

He took the drawing. The hair was certainly right. Past his shoulders and sporting the waves he hated. They'd nailed the angles of his face and the color of his eyes, but they'd gone a bit overboard with the maniacal expression.

No, his identity was no longer a secret. Not with this floating around. And he'd definitely dug a hole for himself with Serena. She pulsed with a nearly tangible energy, the lines of her neck so taut it looked painful. If he wanted to lure her across party lines and solidify her beside him and the rebellion, he'd have to do something big. Something he'd never done before.

He sat the flyer atop a haphazard stack of papers. He stepped closer, not enough to touch, but enough to enter her space. "I was wrong." He held her stare, the taste of his words foreign and uncomfortable on his tongue.

Quiet settled, broken only by muffled movements and voices in the rooms beyond. The scent of citrus and crisp linens hung in the air, more noticeable in the stillness. The nerves along his spine bristled and the urge to pace beat at his feet.

He waited.

And waited.

She met him eye to eye without a quaver. An iron will behind a deceptively beautiful woman. Few men could hold themselves with such dignity. The only woman he'd known to match her strength was his grandmother. Maybe he'd been wrong in his assessment of Serena.

Sharp footsteps sounded on the tiles beyond.

Serena's head snapped toward the door and her gaze sharpened. "Stay to the far corner of the room and mask yourself."

Maxis heeded her directive and spread his senses along the home's perimeter. The patterns were the same. The courtyard was bare, the same number of bodies moving at a steady pace around the house.

Serena situated herself in one of the chairs and picked up the drawing, making an overblown act of studying Maxis' image.

The door opened.

"Put those down." The terse command came from a tall, slender man with shoulder-length salt and pepper hair tied back in a formal queue. He strode to the table and plucked the drawing from her fingers. "You know better than to meddle in my affairs."

Serena looked up, eyes wide with sickening innocence.

Maxis stifled a cough.

"I'm sorry, father." Not the least bit of hesitation, not even a flinch. "I only stopped to study the image. Who is it?"

"No one you need to know about." Her father tucked the stack of papers into a leather satchel, one worn enough to indicate a life of actual work. If his trousers, boots and overcoat were any indicator, he worked as a merchant, and a pretty successful one at that.

"Is he dangerous? I've never seen the malran post such a warning."

"It's nothing to concern yourself with. Just a political matter you wouldn't understand." He turned for the door. "Tell your mother to arrange for dinner at the customary time. Your brother and I will be bringing home a few contacts from work."

The door clacked shut behind him, rattling the frame.

Selena held her place, back straight and frowning.

Maxis dropped his mask. "You handled that well."

His voice seemed to shake whatever haze held her. She shrugged and pushed from her seat. "He's a busy man."

"He's a fool." Maxis prowled across the thick gray carpets, the glimpse into Serena's life brewing an urge he couldn't quite wrap his head around. As if he needed to shield her, or at least snap something, or someone, in two. "He has no clue of the intellect behind your pretty face, does he?"

For the first time since he'd met her, the cool facade faltered. "No." Her expression hardened and she pierced him with her startling blue stare. "And neither, apparently, do you. Now go."

Maxis shook his head, stepped in close, and cupped the back of her neck. "I told you I was wrong." He teased the hair at the top of her spine. "I came to make amends. To offer you something you'll never find within these walls."

Goosebumps lifted along her exposed shoulders and her breath shallowed. "What could you possibly give me I don't already have?"

She couldn't have handed him a more perfect invitation, a prime opening to lure his future mate. His heart surged and his muscles tightened. "Power."

Chapter 7

Reese sat on the edge of his cot, elbows planted on his knees, and hung his head. The space between his temples throbbed, slow and heavy. Too much thinking, too little sleep, and a fat zero on what he should do next.

"Use your own light to guide Maxis' soul."

Right. Like his "light" cast a big enough glow to work with. Kind of hard for anything bright to get through all the hate he felt for Maxis.

He massaged the tight muscles around his healing wound and circled his arm to loosen the stiff joint. What was he missing? How could the spiritu possibly think he had any influence where the malran was concerned?

A rumble sounded beyond the door, and heavy, confident footsteps clipped against the stone.

Reese stood. He pumped his fists, open and shut, over and over. His heart worked double rhythm, but his gut was steady, braced for whatever lay ahead. This was it. Ready or not, he'd face Ramsay and give him the truth. His old friend deserved that much.

The latch echoed and the cell door opened. Ramsay's shadowed form filled the entry.

The back of Reese's neck tightened to the point of pain, but he snapped to attention. "Ramsay."

"Wrong brother." Eryx stepped from the darkness, the cell's candlelight glinting off the royal torc at his neck and the metal beads holding his braids in place.

Maybe they didn't need his information any more. If Eryx was here to give his sentence, then there was nothing left but—

Galena walked out from behind her brother, and Reese's lungs emptied on a whoosh. She clasped her hands loosely in front of her, a formal pose best suited for strangers. Or detachment. "Eryx has agreed to hear what you have to say."

Eryx crossed his arms and dipped his chin, a non-verbal warning of the deadliest variety. He might be Ramsay's twin, but the warrior garb of silver drast and black leather pants sent his intimidation factor off the charts. "Galena says you're ready to talk. That true?"

Reese jerked a nod, his throat too clamped to speak.

The soft flutter of the torch's flame beyond his cell and a muffled creak from the castle above filled the silence.

Eryx motioned toward someone in the hall to enter.

Two warriors bustled in carrying simple ladder-back chairs.

Galena perched on the edge of hers, her posture so rigid his hand twitched to rub the back of her neck.

Eryx spun his around, straddled the back, and pointed at the cot. "Sit."

Reese edged back until his knees met the cot, Galena's steady, patient gaze so heavy he could barely take a breath. He didn't want her here. Not for this.

"Got a lot on my plate, Reese. For whatever reason, Galena thinks I need to be the one to hear what you've got to say. I'm doing her a favor, but I'm not in the mood to screw around. We clear?"

She went for Eryx on purpose? Why?

"We clear?" Eryx snapped.

Reese forced himself to look at Eryx. "Clear."

All he had to do was start simple. The basics. The location of the training grounds, Maxis' underground hideout deep in the mountains of Asshur, the coordinates Eryx's men would need. The words rolled off his tongue, one secret after another, Galena steady and unmoving in his periphery.

"Any prisoners at those locations?" Eryx said.

Reese blinked, mentally stumbling from his trance-like fog. Right. The spiritu had mentioned a captive, one special to the new malress. "I don't know of any prisoners. Maxis kept everyone on a need to screw basis, but if he's got one, the hideout in Asshur would be the best bet. Hard to scan with the rock density and even more difficult to locate on sight. Only those closest to him know where to find it."

Not so much as a twitch from Eryx. No hint of his thoughts or emotions. "And you'll corroborate this information with your memories?"

Reese's mouth dried up and his heart kicked. He tried to swallow, but his tongue seemed stuck to the roof of his mouth. "I will, but I need to share something else."

He glanced at Galena. She'd never view him the same. How could she? How could anyone? He coughed around the catch his throat. "My mother fled the rebellion ranks when she learned she was pregnant with me. She wasn't mated, but was afraid the man she lived with would kill her if he learned she was pregnant with another man's son."

Galena perked up, her voice soft and curious. "Why would he kill her?"

Adrenaline rushed so thick his body felt twice its normal weight, and a sharp steady pain pressed behind his sternum. "He was abusive, the type of man who viewed women as little more than cattle. They'd already had a son together. From his perspective, her job was to satisfy his physical needs and see to their child. That was it. For her to come up pregnant with another man's child would have been one thing, but to come up pregnant by a human slave? That was something else. So she ran."

Reese focused on Eryx. Now that he'd started, he couldn't stop. Didn't want to. The onslaught of information burned from the inside out. "My mother never believed in the rebellion. She was trapped because of her first-born child. She risked her life to save me and raised me to do the right thing. She wanted me to fight against the rebellion, not for it."

Eryx frowned and curled his fingers around the top rail of the chair. "Your mom ended up in a bad place, but you being half human's not exactly earth-shattering news. I'm not seeing how her background with the rebellion has any tie to the information I need."

A steady hum started in the back of Reese's head and the air around him thickened, weighting his shoulders. "It's important because of who my mother was."

Praise the Great One, he hoped he did this right. He took a deep breath. "Maxis Steysis is my brother."

Eryx and Galena gaped.

Reese propped his elbows on his knees and let his head fall forward. It didn't matter now. It was out. Done. And strangely, the truth hadn't stung as bad as he'd thought, a good chunk of the emotional dead weight in his soul gone. How the information would serve the spiritu's purpose he couldn't fathom. The only thing good he and Maxis held in common was their mother. He'd have killed Maxis himself if she hadn't made him promise to protect him.

Wait. Maybe that was it. His mother had loved Maxis. Reese had wished him dead over and over since the day he'd fully understood what the relationship meant, but their mother loved him. Had hurt and prayed for him every day after she'd escaped. Had Maxis ever known love? Would it make a difference?

"Half brother."

Galena's voice pulled him from his thoughts. "What?"

"He's your half brother," she repeated, glaring at Eryx. "It's not a crime, it's genetics."

Eryx kept his expression blank, the only tell a slight tilt to his head. "That's what you wouldn't share with Ramsay. You were afraid of what we'd think."

A full, pent up breath huffed out, and the fear and doubt he'd held captive burst free with it. He slumped against the crystal wall, exhausted. "You. Ramsay. The other warriors. If I'd shared it, no one would have trusted me. How could anyone believe Maxis' brother would have their back in battle? Or believe I wasn't there to feed information to the rebellion? If I wanted to serve, I didn't have a choice."

"We always have a choice." No sympathy from Eryx, just conviction. "Some are more difficult to carry than others. It sounds like your mother understood that."

Reese straightened. That was it. The different path the spiritu had told him to find. "I need to ask you for something."

Eryx huffed an incredulous laugh. "You think you're in a position to barter?"

"No." He needed to watch what he said. It was one thing to drop his history for the malran, but another thing entirely to expect him to buy a mission from some unknown being. "My choices were wrong. I knew it the day I blocked Ramsay. I knew it watching rebellion men die for a cause I wanted nothing to do with. I'll pay the price. Willingly. All I want is a chance to make things right before I do."

Eryx sat up taller in his chair, eyes narrowed and wary. "How so?"

"Let me lead you through the tunnels to Maxis, maybe act as a distraction while you look for the prisoner you're after."

"You realize that sounds more like a trap for me and my men veiled as a shot at redemption." Eryx smirked. "I might not be ready to rip your head off like Ramsay is, but that doesn't make me an idiot."

"That's not what this is about," he said.

Galena studied him, a wary uncertainty coloring her expression. If he wasn't reaching her, then he'd never win Eryx's approval.

Fuck. What the hell could he say that wouldn't sound insane?

"The truth." A swift answer, wind chimes and laughter behind it.

Clio.

Okay. The truth. He focused on Eryx. "It killed my mom that she left Maxis behind. She saw what Evanora's hatred was doing to him. There was no way to get Maxis out without the whole lot of them following, but she could keep at least one child safe. I want the chance to let Maxis know our mother regretted leaving him. To see if it might make him let go of, or at least revisit, his need for vengeance."

Eryx's laugh ricocheted through the cell. "You know that's got a snowball's chance in histus of happening, right?"

"I do. But if it takes him off his current path, then it's worth trying. If Maxis balks, I'll kill him myself. If not for my race, then for what he did to Phybe."

The two stared at him, Eryx tight-lipped and Galena openly stunned.

"I wanted to serve you and Ramsay because I wanted to balance the scales for my mother," he said. "For her to die knowing at least one of her sons stayed to the good. I screwed up with my choices. Let me try to make it right."

"Eryx—"

Eryx glowered at Galena.

She clamped her lips tight and ducked her head.

The silence scratched and grated.

The musty dankness filled Reese's lungs until he thought he'd choke. "He killed Phybe on purpose."

"As a distraction," Eryx said.

"No, as a message. To me. Maxis blackmailed me into forming a link with him, threatening to share our relationship with others if I didn't. When he found Phybe at his house with you and the rest of your men, he realized I'd helped her, which brought you straight to his door. Killing her was his way of saying I'm next."

"Then you can't leave zeolite," Galena said. "He'll kill you the minute he sees you."

Something inside him warmed. Even in the darkened cell, her light and goodness shone on his soul. A benediction he didn't deserve. "Galena, I'm dead either way. Life in here will be a slow, torturous death. My only other options are death at your brother's order for treason, or to die trying to save the soul of my mother's other son. Which would you choose?"

Her shoulders dropped and her hands tightened in her lap.

Reese stood and motioned to the hallway beyond. "Take me out long enough to offer my memories and my link. As a Shantos male, you're as capable of killing me via link as Maxis is. If at any time you sense treachery on my part, you can strike."

"Anything else?" Eryx said.

"I'd ask one last night in my mother's homestead to say good-bye."

Eryx studied him another moment, stood and motioned Galena toward the door. He parked the chair against the wall and followed her out. "We'll see."

* * * *

"Stop squirming, Serena." Maxis tightened his arms around Serena's torso, her body soft and giving against his as they flew through the Eden skies. The wind bit his cheeks, and the setting sun took what was left of the day's warmth with it.

Serena nestled closer. "I can't believe I let you talk me into this. I can't trust you with my eyes open, let alone blindfolded."

He'd been surprised too, a small win in his grander plan. With a little luck, he'd cinch the war before the sun rose. "I gave you my word, you're perfectly safe. Now relax and let me make my amends."

A line of clouds spanned the horizon, soft gray outlined in shimmering pinks against blue velvet. Nature's demarcation between two opposite regions, Cush's bright heat to Asshur's stormy existence.

Maxis steered left toward Brasia's multi-hued mountains.

Veins of violet, red and yellow covered the foothills, blending where they overlapped for a rainbow effect. Evanora's Peak stood the tallest. A behemoth of color, its temperature set in perma-freeze. No matter how much snow nature dumped on the mountain, those same varied colors pushed through the white, pulsing and hypnotic.

Gold sparked in the distance, brilliant flecks off castle spires that marked their destination. Each flash stabbed his retinas, but the tightness in his chest unfurled. They were almost home.

He landed in a frigid crosswind so fierce the unforgiving gust penetrated his thick overcoat.

Serena shivered and lifted a hand to the blindfold. "Praise the Great One, where are we?"

"Not so fast." He captured both her wrists, pinned them behind her back with one hand, and splayed the other across her abdomen. Her rose silk tunic slicked against the firm flesh beneath.

He dragged his lips along the shell of her ear. Caramel and vanilla scents teased his nose—there a moment, then pushed away on the wind, a promise of hearth and home unlike anything in his stiff and cold childhood. "If you rush, you'll ruin the surprise."

She stilled, but her brow furrowed above the blindfold.

He loosened the fabric and stepped to the side.

She blinked and squinted against the twilight before her face softened, mouth parted in a soft O. "Where are we?"

Warmth and a sated lethargy radiated through him, a lion stretched beneath the sun after gorging on its fatted prey. "My family home, situated where Asshur, Cush, and Brasia meet. Evanora commissioned it not long after my father was born."

White limestone walls sat on an elevated acreage and stretched to the sky, topped by forest green tiles and gold-tipped spires. Wrought-iron accents lined each oversized window and exotic hedges wound in intricate patterns around the perimeter. The staggering structure spanned two hundred feet to either side and reached three stories high.

The wind tossed Serena's moonlight-colored hair around her neck and shoulders, and greedy rapture twinkled in her bold blue eyes. "It's magnificent."

Ah, yes. He'd definitely chosen the right lure for his mate-to-be. "Evanora had a thing for daring statements. This one was aimed at the man foolish enough to forgo choosing her as his mate." He held out his hand. "I won't be as dimwitted."

Serena studied his outstretched hand, his face, and the manse stretched out before them. She licked her lower lip and laid her palm in his. "Get me out of this cold."

He ducked his head to hide his triumphant smile and ushered her toward the main entrance. Two guards dressed in black stood at either side with others stationed in regular intervals around the perimeter.

Uther strode out the front door as they approached and bowed. "Maxis."

"Serena, this is Uther Rontal, our new strategos."

She offered her hand with a benevolent air, not the slightest hint she'd caught the "our" in his statement. "Serena Doroz."

Uther accepted and kissed the top. "Maxis has good taste in women."

Electricity arced, unbidden, between Maxis' fingers and thumbs, palms tingling with the need to strike. He clenched his fists and the energy fizzled. Stupid of him. What in histus did he care if Uther found her pleasing to the eye? "How are the plans moving along?"

Uther released her, albeit far too leisurely for Maxis' taste, and motioned them forward. "As you requested. We'll have everything ready for you in the morning. For now the men are on high alert and ready for action."

"Excellent." He steered Serena through the soaring entry by the small of her back, the urge to distance her from his strategos a buzzing, nearly palpable force. "Rest tonight. Tomorrow we start fresh."

"What happens tomorrow?" Serena's muscles tightened beneath his hand.

Maxis' boots clipped against marble, reverberating off the gold and ivory walls. He tucked her in the circle of his arm. "Your father keeps everything from you doesn't he?"

"Mmmm." She appraised the rounded columns interspersed down the long hallway, her glower making clear just how sensitive she was to the topic without saying a single word.

He stroked the curve of her hip and gave a slight squeeze. "I vow you'll know my plans. No secrets. But not tonight. Tonight is for something else. Agreed?"

She pursed her lips. "I'll play along. For tonight."

The tour of the main floor was quick, the library, an overlarge kitchen, a stately golden dining room, and servant's quarters. Serena soaked in the surroundings, her expression contemplative and focused throughout. He'd bet half his inheritance Serena's father hadn't a clue of his daughter's attention to detail.

A platinum throne sat at the back of Evanora's receiving chamber, paintings of the many Steysis generations hung along each side in gilded frames.

Serena drifted through the cavernous room, subtly angled toward the embellished chair.

"My grandmother knew what she wanted," Maxis said. "When the malran turned her away, she built her own kingdom and an alternate route to the seat she believed would be hers."

Serena's hand slid across one armrest and a lock of hair spilled across her angelic face.

"You have that vision," he said. "You merely lack the partner and leverage to make it happen."

She paused behind the high back, tracing the filigree and smirked. "You've been dancing around your topic all day. I think it's time you get to the point."

Ah, so the lady suspected his intent. She probably also thought she held the upper hand. Perhaps, in a way, she did. He'd give her due respect and a slice of power, but there would be only one ruler between them.

He stopped in the center of the room. "You want to know what I offer? What opportunities I provide for you and your future?"

Quiet pressed on every side of him. The room's shadows deepened, building in height and depth. "Come to me and find out."

"No." She finished her circuit and stepped down from the wide dais. "I offered myself, but you rebuked me. Only a foolish woman returns for a second bout."

"I admitted my error, an offering no other being on this earth has ever received." And it still burned on his tongue. "What I offer isn't about supplication or amends. It's about something deeper. Something necessary for what you seek."

"Such as?"

"Step forward and find out."

Her fingers twitched at her sides. Curious little cat.

"It's not weakness, Serena. A man needs to know where a woman's trust lies. A malran needs to know the loyalty of his malress. Where is yours?"

Anticipation hummed in his veins. Each moment ticked and tocked in slow, torturous lifetimes, and the air crackled and hummed with palpable tension.

She stepped forward, and Maxis' heart kicked. With each slow stride, her hips swayed, a feminine testament to power even as she acquiesced. The sweet scent of vanilla coiled around him as she stopped, close enough to touch, but not enough to kiss.

He could live with that. She'd made her offering, now it was time for his. He lifted her hand and brushed his lips across each knuckle. "Be my mate. Stand beside me and lead those who follow us in our mission. Help me take the throne and raise our race's power across the realms."

She smiled, slow and devious. "You're not following protocol. Males always approach the father of their intended first."

His cock lengthened, a heavy, eager weight ready for its perfect sheath. He brushed his lips along the pulse at her wrist. "Do you really want your father's blessing?"

Her tremor vibrated through his touch and her voice dropped to a husky purr. "No. No I don't."

Chapter 8

Galena shut the door to Brenna's room, and leaned into it with an exhausted huff. The last few days had been a physical strain, but the morning's emotional turmoil was enough to make a woman want to hide for a solid week. Lexi's kidnapping, Ramsay's odd behavior, and now the weight of what she'd found in Brenna's memories. It was too much.

And that was with her own turbulent feelings for Reese locked in a mental strong box.

She closed her eyes, and the memory of his kiss rushed to greet her. Never had she felt so desirable. So possessed. From the bold sweeps of his tongue to his palm's hot press at the small of her back, he'd touched a part of her she'd never imagined existed.

A shiver rustled down her torso and her thighs tightened. Five heartbeats and she'd leapt from fatigue to painful awareness. Her conscience might insist anything between them was wrong, but the slick heat between her legs said the rest of her was very on board.

For a dead man.

She shoved from the door and stomped down the hall. Her senses clocked the sun at early evening and Eryx somewhere near the royal chambers.

Unlike his usual decisiveness, Eryx had put any decisions for Reese on hold until he talked with Ramsay, Ludan, and Lexi, leaving Galena's thoughts with way too much open range. She'd killed time with a thorough once over of the still-unconscious Brenna. Four hours later she was exhausted, but certain it was the girl's subconscious holding her in a dreamlike state more than any physical ailment.

Rounding the upper landing in the castle's guest wing, Galena hurried toward Eryx's private study off the royal chambers and tapped out a quiet knock. The double doors opened without aid of a hand and the scent of wood smoke whispered past her nose.

"That's twice today you've knocked." Eryx sat at his desk, head down. The room was dark but for the firelight beside him, the golden-tipped shadows slanting across one side of his face.

It was an imposing image. One she'd have walked away from if his greeting hadn't intimated old-fashioned brotherly ribbing. "You're mated now. The way you and Lexi go at it, I'm never sure what I'll walk in on." She waved her hand and lit two candles stationed at the corner of his desk with a mental nudge. "You'll ruin your eyes in that light."

Eryx grumbled and pushed from the desk. "There's too much to look at and not enough time. I've got two days, three tops, before Angus starts pushing for answers. Stalling with rebellion concerns can only last so long."

"So where's Lexi?" She settled in one of two crimson wingbacks in front of his desk, and feigned a lightness she didn't feel. "I thought she was looking too."

"She's teamed with Graylin in the library. I'm hitting dad's personal stuff here." He lifted his chin toward the still open doors. "How's Brenna?"

Her stomach roiled. "Still out."

"Did I miss something?"

Galena shook her head. She'd combed every inch of Brenna's body and knew full well Eryx had nearly matched her own healing abilities in caring for the girl, which was saying something. "I think her mind's locked down."

"Trauma from the injury?"

"Trauma from before." She'd witnessed the atrocities in full color with crystal clear audio in the girl's memory. Speaking the details aloud seemed a travesty. "Maxis raped her Eryx. Not once, but over and over. I can't tell from her memories how old she was when it started, but her life's been histus. If I were her, I wouldn't want to wake up either."

A prominent tic kicked at the back of Eryx's jaw and his hands fisted on top of his desk. He shook his head and huffed out a sarcastic laugh. "And Reese thinks he can save him. Maxis is a sadistic bastard. He deserves anything but decency."

There wasn't much she could add to that. From all she'd seen, Maxis was a vile creature, void of conscience. But he was Reese's brother, too. A man whose mother had loved him and suffered for leaving him behind to save her other son. Was Reese right? Could the truth change Maxis? Did the worst creatures deserve such a chance after a lifetime of wrongs?

"Have you talked to Ramsay?" She'd been hesitant to broach the subject, too afraid of Eryx's answer. Not that there seemed to be a decent outcome for Reese.

Eryx strode to a built-in cabinet spanning the rear wall. The candles and firelight gave the mahogany wood more depth than in daylight. "He and Ludan had leads to follow. They're on their way now." He poured a hefty dram of strasse, and tossed back more than half in one gulp.

She didn't know how the men tolerated the stuff. It sported enough kick the fermented Myren berries and wood cask scent carried from fifteen feet away. "So, what are you going to do?"

He stared into the burgundy liquid and his thumb dragged along the tumbler's crystal edges. "What would you do?"

She blinked, then did it another ten or so times. Eryx might ask her opinion on remedies or healing, but Ramsay was the go-to guy on strategy. Her instincts quavered. It could be an honest question. It could also be well-hidden bait. "I think it's a good shot at finding Ian."

Eryx's thumb stopped moving.

She should leave it at that. Not say another word. "But I don't want to see him die."

Eryx tilted his chin in a way that accented his frown. "Why? He's a traitor. You saw what Maxis did to Brenna, and Reese was his right hand."

"And you heard the situation. Would you have done anything different in his circumstance? Can you say without a doubt you'd have owned such a relationship? It doesn't seem right to judge Reese over something he had no control over." Just like she had no control over how she felt about Reese. She'd have staggered a step or two at the realization had she not already been seated.

"No one's judging him for his birth." Eryx took his seat and the leather let out a muffled groan. "They're judging him for his lies and the choices he made."

"Choices who made?"

Galena surged upright at the sound of Ramsay's voice, and found Ludan striding through the door beside him. The two packed a visual punch. Standard-issue silver drast stretched over powerful warrior bodies, black leather pants and boots, and hair long enough to graze the tops of their shoulders.

"Choices Reese made," Eryx said from behind her.

Ramsay had looked irritated when he'd walked in, but when Eryx answered his expression flipped to lethal.

He halted next to Galena's chair and volleyed his focus between her and Eryx, ending on her. "What the hell did you do?"

Instinct urged her to shrink away, or apologize, but sibling defiance bubbled up instead. "I checked on my patient. It's within—"

"You did what? Without guards?"

"I didn't need guards. He gave me his vow."

"His vow? And you believed him?"

"Enough." Eryx's command cut through the brewing argument.

Ludan's chuckle rasped right behind it as he ambled to the sofa situated along the side wall. He grinned and sunk into the deep, blood red cushions, spreading his arms along the back, knees wide. "Family."

"You find this funny?" Ramsay glared at Ludan. "Reese could've killed her."

Ludan craned to see around Ramsay and a chunk of wavy ink-black hair fell across his forehead to accent his ice-blue eyes. He shrugged. "She's breathin'." He straightened and the smirk grew. "And hell, yeah, it's funny. Haven't seen you and Eryx this worked up since Galena's first date."

Oh. Shit.

Neither brother said a word, but both lasered their attention square on her.

Ludan's mood shifted right behind theirs, his stare just as heavy. He might not have meant the comment the way Eryx and Ramsay had taken it, but all three of them were mentally tiptoeing way too close to the truth.

"Can we focus?" She had enough years of sidestepping her overprotective brothers to know the best offense was a quick redirect. "You've got an offer on the table and a chance to find Ian. So are you going to take it?"

Ramsay faced Eryx. "What offer? He either talks or he doesn't."

Ha. Worked every time.

Eryx downed his strasse. "Actually, he's got more." He sat the tumbler on his desk and reclined into his chair. "He's willing to tell us all he knows, even lead us there and offer himself as a diversion, in exchange for two things. A chance to share some info he thinks might make Maxis repent, and a night at his mom's place before he dies. Says he'll share every memory in his head to confirm his info and give his link so we can kill him if he turns on us."

"Ballsy son of a bitch." Ludan pushed from the sofa and headed for the bar.

Eryx held his empty tumbler up for seconds as his somo passed. "No shit."

Ramsay's eyebrows shot high. "And you're actually considering it?"

"Why wouldn't he?" Crystal tinked as Ludan poured a glass full. "Save us a lot of manpower and gets us a bead on Ian. Once we've got him, it's open season on Maxis no matter which side Reese is on."

"But Maxis will kill him." All three men regarded her as though she'd appeared out of nowhere. "He killed Phybe with his link and he'll do the same to Reese."

Ludan capped the decanter and handed Eryx his glass. "And he'll die for treason on this end. Gotta spin your angles where you can."

That son of a bitch. "Spin it?"

The men went on alert. Call it instinct or male preservation, but every one of them knew they'd struck a nerve. She could see it in their eyes.

"We're talking about a man who's admitted to his faults," she said. "Who's offering to share what he knows, and is willing to lay his life on the line to make the wrongs in his life right before he dies, and you want to spin it? What the hell happened to decency in this family? Or maybe a little compassion?"

"Compassion?" Ramsay got up in her face. The whites surrounding his soft gray eyes burned a harsh white, a sure sign his formidable powers teetered close to loss of control. "He gave up the right to compassion the day he threw my trust in my face."

Galena wobbled back a step, and the hairs along her forearms stood straight, no doubt from the violent energy sparks snapping around Ramsay. She glanced at Ludan, then at Eryx. "What's he talking about?"

Ramsay held his tight stance a second longer, huffed, and then backed away. He dropped into the wingback beside hers.

"Tell me," she said.

Ramsay sucked in an audible breath and his jaw tensed.

"If you want her to understand, you're gonna have to tell her," Eryx said to Ramsay. "Otherwise, you just look like a dick."

Ramsay fisted his hands atop the armrests and fixated on the far wall. He was the spitting image of Eryx, minus the ridiculously long hair and covenant braids. One wouldn't think a man so hard and formidable on the outside could be hurt, but in that moment she sensed a vulnerability he wasn't altogether comfortable with.

The grit in Ramsay's voice raked her. "Reese was my friend. I love my brother. Hell, I'd die for him in a second, but he was always with Ludan. Reese…" He dragged a hand through his already mussed hair and sat forward, a grimace on his face. "He seemed genuine. Not a suck-up. Not a dick. Just a good guy. Or that's what I thought."

She knew what Ramsay meant. She'd felt Reese's warmth. The genuineness of his presence. Under normal circumstances she'd have been sensitive. Maybe tried to lure whatever bothered Ramsay out with soft words or a gentle tone, but the very tangible hatred for Reese kept her question tight. "What happened?"

The corner of his mouth curled in an ironic smile. "I trusted him, Lena. I was so damned happy for him at his swearing in. I knew how much it meant to him, or how much he'd said it meant to him. Then, to have him not share his memories? His bullshit friendship was nothing more than a bridge to get through the swearing in. It was a farce. For all we know, he was scamming to get on the inside for Maxis."

Galena crossed her arms. Stupid, emotionally negligent men. "Or maybe he was afraid his secret was so bad you wouldn't be able to see past it."

He cocked his head and scrutinized her. "What in histus is so bad you can't share it with your best friend? With a man you're prepared to fight beside and die for?"

No point in pulling her punch. "Maxis is his half brother."

Ramsay's jaw dropped.

Ludan let loose something between a hiss and rumble, then poured a fresh drink.

Part of her wanted to stop there. To quietly leave the room as she normally would and hope her point hit home, but if she was going to make a difference for Reese, now was the time to drive it home. "Do you have any idea how hard it is to expose your deepest secrets for fear you'll be judged for it? Put yourself in his place and tell me if you'd have done any differently."

"Hey, babe. Guess what...we...found..." Lexi's voice trailed and she looked from person to person. "Who died?"

Galena nearly bit her tongue in half.

"No one." Eryx rounded the desk and headed for his mate. "You got something?"

"A precedent." Despite being wrapped in Eryx's welcoming embrace, Lexi stared at Galena, a concentrated stare that made Galena want to twitch. Her voice went flat, bordering on curious. "We haven't combed out the details, but it's enough to cover what you need with the ellan."

"Then you're set." Ludan sprawled into his place on the couch, a reloaded glass of strasse in one hand. "Let Reese do his thing, blast Maxis, and short-circuit the council."

Ramsay shook his head. "Reese teamed with Maxis is a risk you don't need."

"I'm done playing it safe." Eryx faced the rest of them, Lexi tucked tight to his side. "I was too short-sighted with the rebellion before. If I let Reese have his chance at Maxis it gives me more stroke with the ellan. Proof I gave the traitor a chance before I took him out. I've got enough political problems without adding more headaches and this circumvents a hell of a lot."

"And what if it works?" Everyone turned Galena's way, a mix of incredulity and confusion painted on their faces. All except for Lexi who still watched her with way too much insight. She focused on Eryx. "What if Maxis surrenders? Then what?"

"Reese is a traitor." Venom coated Ramsay's voice. "Traitors die."

Slow, near-to-bursting rage shook her. "So you'll use him. Give no quarter for his efforts. Is that it? And here I'd thought my brothers played fair."

They glared back at her, the hurt and surprise in their expressions so potent it torched her from the inside out.

She stormed for the door. To histus with them and any answers they coughed up. She'd heard enough in the last thirty minutes to shake a lifetime of perceptions. Using her mind, she slammed the doors behind her. She needed air. Air and enough distance she couldn't use her Myren gifts to lob the heaviest object she could find toward their heads.

She abhorred the rebellion as much as anyone. Hated what they stood for and the atrocities they'd committed against humans and the throne, but in this her brothers and Ludan were wrong. The past was the only thing driving their actions, not any sense of decency. Not factoring Reese's circumstances into the equation was just stupid.

She threw the gate to the private castle garden wide, and a gust of ocean air slapped her head to toe. Reese was going to die. Either by her brothers' hands or Maxis'. And there wasn't a thing should could do to stop it.

She doubled over on a quiet sob and slid to a crouch, her arms wrapped tight around her stomach.

Lexi's voice cut through her thoughts. "There's more to this than you're letting on."

Galena surged to her feet. The wind cut a cold path along the tears trailing her cheek. "Why? Because I'm championing a traitor?"

"No, because my scary emotional mojo latched onto some serious worry this morning." Lexi strolled forward, her saucy jaunt not the least bit dimmed by the simple blue gown she wore. "Couple that with your comment about exposing your deepest desire for fear of being judged? The guys might be too stupid to see what's going on, but I'm not."

Damn, but her shalla's new gift was scary. Galena cleared her throat and shuffled to the rock ledge lining the garden.

"You know," Lexi's voice grew closer. "The first time I was around your family as a whole, I was floored. You're so fiercely loyal to each other. I'd never seen anything like it. Never felt anything like it." She took a spot beside Galena and mirrored her study of the churning waves below. "I guess I can see why a woman would be afraid to upset that dynamic."

Galena spun to face her. "What's that supposed to mean?"

Lexi shrugged, gaze still locked on the horizon. "I mean upsetting the family balance to take care of your own needs would be a little frightening." She laid her hand on Galena's and faced her. "But there comes a time when a woman needs to stop looking at what everyone around her needs and start taking care of herself."

Chapter 9

Eryx strode through the dungeon, Ludan and Ramsay's booted footsteps rumbling alongside his to fill the cavernous space.

Ludan glanced at Eryx. "You call the council session yet?"

"After the raid," Eryx answered via link just outside Reese's cell. After a long night and significant back and forth with Lexi, he'd decided Reese was likely telling the truth, but that didn't mean he was willing to toss info around so Reese could hear it. *"We've got nothing to prove Angus is hooked into Maxis, but with the information he knew about Lexi, I find it hard to believe anything else. I'm not up for tipping him or anyone else off to our plans before Ian's safe and we've got a bead on Maxis."*

He buried all thoughts but the task ahead of him and checked Ramsay on his left. He dropped his mental connection to Ludan and isolated his link to Ramsay. *"You sure you're up for this?"*

If his brother could do the Superman laser vision bit, there'd be man-sized hole in the cell door already. *"He's a traitor. Nothing to feel."*

"That's bullshit and you know it." Man, but Reese had done a number on Ramsay. While Eryx sympathized with Reese and the awkward position having Maxis for a brother caused him, he still wanted to choke the bastard for the blow he'd dealt his brother. Ramsay kept most people at bay with his laid-back persona, but he'd let Reese in. Taken him under his wing, trained him, and treated him like a brother. *"You want to stuff your shit, that's your business, but keep it tight while this goes down. We've got enough irons in the fire without you blowing up the whole damned forge."*

Ramsay scowled back at him, but thankfully held his tongue.

Eryx mentally triggered the latch, braced for the slam of zeolite, and stepped across the threshold.

The crystal's power-stealing impact sluiced from head to toe, ripping and clawing every organ and muscle along its path. Myren powers were more than bonus options for their race. They were inherent to each person's being, no different or less important than a spleen or a kidney.

Reese stood, the whites of his eyes shot with red and fatigue weighting his stature. Confession might have been good for his soul, but it didn't appear to have done much where sleep was concerned.

"Malran." Reese shifted his gaze to Eryx's left and his voice lowered. "Ramsay."

Fuck if this whole scenario wasn't a brawl waiting to happen. "I've got an answer on your offer," Eryx said before shit could get out of hand.

Reese's Adam's apple bobbed.

"You'll take point in the raid on Maxis' hideout," Eryx said. "You'll draw your brother out for whatever it is you feel you need to say to him. If he surrenders, we'll take him into custody and bring you both to zeolite. If he doesn't, we attack." Sufficient details for now. Highlighting Reese's low odds for returning alive seemed about as heartless as Galena had accused him of being the night before.

Reese jerked his head in agreement. "Done."

"Not quite." No way was Eryx letting him off that easy. "I'm not foolish enough to buy your claims without confirmation. You give your memories, all of them, from birth to now. You hold anything back, we take you to trial tomorrow, and we know how that ends. Clear?"

"Clear."

"And you give your link."

"Agreed." Reese's gaze stay locked to Eryx. His body language remained loose and open, but there was still no a guarantee he wasn't a lying son of a bitch with an gift for acting.

Ramsay prowled forward and offered his hand, grim enough to scare the diabhal.

Eryx stopped him with a palm at his chest. "No. This one's mine."

"Like hell it is." Ludan stepped between them and glared at Eryx, the idea of a traitor having a link with his malran clearly not high on his list of bright ideas. Links made it easy for bad guys to track and kill. Not exactly an ideal situation when your primary job in life was to keep the malran breathing.

Eryx spun for the door. "Not your call, Ludan. Reese, outside. Now." His powers roared to life as he stepped into the barely lit corridor. He turned in time to see Reese sway beneath the same onslaught. After nearly three days behind the crystal, the rush had to pack a wallop. "You good?"

Reese focused on the wall behind Eryx and shook his head as though to clear it. His eyes were still glassed over, but the torchlight and the rush of power made the rest of him look better. "Yeah."

Eryx crowded close and offered his hand. "Time to show your cards."

Reese clasped it, his grip solid, albeit weak. Not at all the tentative or shaking grasp he'd expect if things weren't on the up and up.

"Hold him," Eryx said.

Ludan and Ramsay snapped forward and seized Reese by his upper arms.

Eryx speared into Reese's mind, and Reese's knees buckled, his body sagging into Ludan and Ramsay's firm grip.

Snippets of Reese's youth plowed by. Not the whispered, painless sweep Ludan's unique gift provided, but a slow, detailed study that left a burning trail of discomfort in its wake. Intelligence gained, and a warning given all at the same time.

He slowed through Reese's training years. So much time with Ramsay, Ludan and Eryx absent for most of it. Galena was prevalent then too, picture after picture, though most were captured from a distance.

He lumbered through more recent years. A solemn stretch spent alone, Maxis finding and blackmailing him, all of it confirming Reese had spoken the truth. He slowed at Reese's memories of the battle, scrutinizing every moment. What the—

Galena hadn't just healed Reese on the battlefield, she'd talked with him. And the way Reese registered her appearance wasn't anywhere near the way Eryx saw her. This woman was exotic. Sensual and enticing.

He fast-forwarded and growled at the site that greeted him. Galena, on her knees between Reese's thighs and locked tight to his chest. He shook his head to clear the vision and refocused on Reese in real-time. His gut roiled, energy pounding for release. He should make the link and get out. Take advantage of the traitor while he could. But damn it if he didn't want this man's head.

He stabbed his link through Reese's palm, and spasms wracked Reese head to toe. The thread pulsed neon red in Eryx's mind, loaded with enough energy to jump Reese's tremors to outright shakes.

Lexi's warning from the night before shuttled past his thoughts. *"He means something to her. Right or wrong, the emotion is there. You, of all people, should remember what it's like to have to choose."*

Reese's emerald green link inched toward Eryx's. It coiled around Eryx's angry red strand, slow, but determined.

The link snapped tight and the colors merged to solid black.

Reese's eyes rolled back in the back of his head and he sagged deeper into Ludan and Ramsay's hold.

Eryx dropped Reese's hand and stepped away before he could snap Reese's neck.

Reese staggered and tried to push upright.

The image he'd witness flashed back in full color. The flush on her cheeks when she'd knelt so close to Reese. The need in her eyes. Eryx knew that rush firsthand. Felt it every time he looked at Lexi. Histus, every time he thought of her. Galena would suffer enough at Reese's death. Better for Maxis to bring his downfall than her brothers.

He sucked in a lungful of air. "Your mother's homestead's in Runa?"

Reese rubbed his forearm and stared almost defiantly at Eryx. "Close to Cush's border, halfway through Big Valley on the east side."

Good. Far enough to keep him away from Galena until tomorrow.

Eryx motioned to Ludan and Ramsay to step back, but kept his focus on Reese. "You've got twenty-four hours. We meet on the ridge across from Maxis' rat hole at ten AM. You're so much as a minute late, I'll make the burn you just experienced feel nice in comparison." He spun for the door. "It'll last a good, long time before I kill you."

* * * *

Reese touched down in front of his mother's homestead. Crosswinds whipped his bare torso and cheeks, easing the noonday sun's heat. Compared to the rest of Eden, Runa paled in terms of beauty and its sweeping winds were hellacious on a tame day, but no other region beat its fertile soil.

The stretch of land in front of him was no exception. Waist-high wheat stretched twenty acres wide and five deep, the color more a rose gold than what grew in Evad. The puffy topped stalks bobbed a happy greeting and their familiar honey-cinnamon scent grounded him in a way no other place could.

Praise The Great One, he'd missed this place. More than he'd realized. Life had been simple, he and his mother farming a tiny section of their acreage and renting the rest to farmers just starting out. She'd joked about how Maxis' father would hemorrhage if he ever learned the jewels she'd smuggled in her escape went to finance something as sensible as agriculture.

Their modest cypress cabin stood more weathered than when he'd seen it last. The windows were clean, the porch tidy, and pretty little ferns he'd probably kill in three days sat perched on the porch rail. The nearby couple he'd hired to tend the place after his mother's passing had done their job well. Still, the years had taken their toll. The ivory-hued wood now glowed a deep honey gold, the cherry slate roof more carnelian.

His footsteps rang hollow on the porch planks. No activity bristled against his senses for at least a good hundred feet out, nor had he scouted movement from the skies on his way in, but he couldn't afford to be complacent. Not with Maxis on the run and undoubtedly eager to slit Reese's throat.

Reese buried the thought and triggered the door's hidden lock with his mind. He'd have more than enough time to ponder all things related to Maxis after he'd eaten and found some decent clothes.

The above-ground level was a simple, wide-open space split into quarters with the kitchen and living area up front, and a bed and bathroom at the back. More a bachelor's dwelling than a hideout for a woman with a small child on her own, which was exactly what his mother had intended.

She'd always feared Maxis' father would find them, and had built in as many warning and escape features as her jewels had allowed. The single inhabitant guise was one, the escape tunnels below ground another. Probably smart to make sure the latter were still operational. After food.

The pantry sat mostly empty, long lasting staples lined neatly on the middle shelf and lined with dust. Pretty depressing as last meals went, but enough to keep him alive until morning.

He snatched a spoon and a jar of drishen preserves, and ambled toward the poor excuse for a bedroom at the back of the cabin. Second best to food was a shower. A long, scalding shower to drown his time in zeolite, and maybe a set of clothes clean enough they couldn't stand on their own. Then he'd think. And pray.

With a flick of his mind, the oversized bookcase slid open to show the hidden staircase, and candles flickered to life. How many times had he raced these steps to find his mother as a child, or handle chores as he'd grown older?

Long-forgotten memories poured over him, steady and cleansing as the shower waters, heavy as the musty scent permeating every room. It felt right to swim in them. To ground himself in the past before he faced his end.

He finished his shower in a haze, and rummaged through what clothes he'd left behind. Jeans he'd tucked away from an old trip to Evad and a well-worn green T-shirt sat folded at the back of a drawer. Not the best pick for tomorrow's outing, but they'd do fine tonight.

Histus, who was he kidding? They'd be fine for tomorrow too. Not like there would be much of a fight. He'd either pull off a miracle with Maxis, or end up dead, neither of which required a warrior's getup.

He checked the escape tunnels off his room and the main corridor. Caked in dust and thick with heady earth scents, the two were still fully functional.

One more to check.

He hesitated in the hallway and stared at the closed door to his mother's room, palms damp and breath shallow. It was a door, nothing more. Decent logic, but his emotions didn't give a shit. All they sensed was the looming judgment crouched on the opposite side.

The knob twisted without a sound.

He nudged the door open, and the breath he'd been holding rushed free.

Sunshine bathed every surface, piped from the ground above to highlight the vibrant styles and colors his mother had favored. Blackwood furniture, bold impressionist paintings, and purple and cobalt fabrics.

"Not purple, periwinkle," his mother would have said. Such a damned girly word, but his mother had loved it.

Draped across the large bed was the coverlet she'd fashioned in the rich hue, her family symbol embroidered at the center. She'd toiled for months on the image. Artemis perched at the tip of a crescent moon, her bow stretched taught and aimed at the heavens.

He strolled through the room, pausing here, touching there, every item a testament to her personality, alive and in tune with Mother Earth.

Much like Galena.

His stomach clenched. Galena was the last thing he needed to think about right now. Especially after the glower Eryx had pierced him with after scanning his memories. No doubt about it. Eryx had seen the kiss. How Reese had made it out of the dungeon alive was a mystery he'd never solve.

He stopped at his mother's bookcase and traced the leather jewel-toned spines. Classics from Evad and Eden, fiction from little-known authors she'd met in Cush, and her journals. He pulled the first in the series free and opened it, the spine crackling in protest. All the emotion he'd felt reading them after her death rushed forward. The fear as she'd escaped, the pride at watching Reese grow, the agonizing guilt for leaving one son behind. It was all here. One entry a day until the day before her death.

Maybe the spiritu was right. Maybe there was some value for what he was about to attempt. Maybe he could atone for the wrong steps he'd made.

Wood groaned from the ground level, roughly in line with the front porch.

Reese froze and fanned his senses wide. He snapped the journal shut. Whoever was at his front door had come alone.

His reflexes pushed to check for Maxis' location via link, but he reined the urge in at the last minute. Even a tiny mental brush could alert Maxis. That left the escape tunnels, or facing his unexpected guest head on.

He slid the book back in place, hesitated a moment, then strode toward the door. He'd had enough hiding. His lifespan might only stretch to tomorrow, but he'd damn sure live what was left head on.

Chapter 10

Galena stole across the cottage's raised porch toward Reese's front door, her heartbeat droning loud enough to overpower the constant whirr of Runa's unforgiving wind. Farmland stretched out behind her, not a soul in sight to witness her arrival.

She tossed her head and squared her shoulders. No, she wasn't doing anything wrong. She had absolutely nothing to feel guilty about.

Except slinking off behind her brothers' backs to visit a traitor.

She still couldn't believe she'd gotten away with spying on her brothers with Reese. The strength of the Shantos line might run through her veins, but her masking and detection skills were nowhere near her brother's and Ludan's.

Then again, Eryx had seemed pretty pissed off. Whatever was under his skin must have made him too preoccupied to check and allowed her to catch Reese's directions to his homestead.

One thing was certain. If she wanted to see Reese, she'd need to take action and knock on the damned door, not waste what was left of his time waffling on the front porch. It wasn't like he could read her mind to answer the door, assuming he was even here.

Only one way to find out. She huffed out a breath and lifted her hand to knock.

The door swung wide before her knuckles made contact.

Galena gasped and jerked her hand to her throat. "Reese." She cringed a bit at the startled quaver in her voice. Who had she expected to find behind the weathered door?

Reese stared at her, locked in place. His emerald eyes shone with an intensity that made her want to fidget, and the matching color of his T-shirt only made their impact more pronounced.

The cotton stretched enticingly across his warrior body and her palms tingled with a need for touch. She pressed a hand to her belly instead, and remembered her own attire. Compared to his casual appearance, her simple gown seemed foolishly out of place. "I know it's rude to stop in unannounced, but—

"How did you find me?" Brusque. Bordering on rude.

What should she say? Confess she'd eavesdropped? She licked her lip and tried again. "I—

"Did Ramsay send you? Or Eryx?"

Well, histus. It would seem that way from his angle. "No." She cleared her throat and lifted her chin. "I came on my own. I masked myself when Eryx came for you and overheard where you lived."

He relaxed a little, but kept his wary focus.

Damn, but this was difficult. Challenging situations weren't exactly a stretch for her, and she'd tangled with some crazy personalities, but this? Awkward.

The wind swept around her, whipping escaped tendrils from her single braid. She was tempted to swat at the wisps, or at least try to smooth them into place, but didn't want to come off any more foolish than she probably already did.

Praise the Great One, she could never match the woman in his thoughts. She'd primped and worn her favorite dress, a deep evergreen with inlaid black velvet swirls, and she still didn't measure up.

So far, the encounter wasn't playing out anywhere near how she'd hoped. "I'm sorry I bothered you. I'll go."

She turned to leave.

Reese caught her by the wrist. "I never thought I'd see you at my door." His words might have been simple, but the humility in them rocked her to the core. He gently urged her to face him. "Please stay."

Stay. Yes, she could do that. Assuming she could find a way to put herself in motion. Or at least manage a nod of acknowledgment. With her blood rushing as furious as the wind behind her, she stepped forward.

He adjusted his grip and held her hand, the warmth of his palm scattering most of her reasonable thoughts. The memory of his touch at the small of her back blazed bright. What would it feel like lower, pulling her tight against him?

"I'd offer you something, but the cabin's not very well stocked."

Praise the Great One, she needed to get ahold of herself. He was offering something to drink while her daydreams hosted sexually decadent ideas. She'd come here to spend time with him, not use him to scratch an itch.

"I'm fine. I just." Just what? Wanted to spend time with you? Maybe see if I was imagining things between us? "I wasn't sure if you'd be alone and thought you might like some company."

"Do your brothers know where you are?"

The hairs along her nape and arms lifted and the blood in her head felt as though it plummeted to her toes. She'd put him in a dangerous position coming here. The least she could do is share the truth. She ambled toward the empty fireplace and the comfortable mango colored chairs cozied around it. "No. I don't often disagree with my brothers, but when I do it's difficult."

"Why did you come?"

She stroked the back of one chair, the softly woven fabric tickling her palm and fingertips. "I told you, I thought you might like——"

"Galena." He prowled toward her. Not a predator about to pounce so much as one unsure of the creature before him. "You came to a confessed traitor's house without your brothers' knowledge. You expect me to believe you risked making them angry for a social call? I've got roughly twenty hours left before my existence gets shaky. Whatever brought you here, whatever it is you want or need, you need to say it."

She clenched the cushion, and her heart high-jumped into her throat.

Reese stopped just out of reach, but his heat filled the distance. It lulled her. Tugged and crooned for surrender.

"Talk to me, Galena." His smooth voice moved over her, warm as the press of his palm had felt. "Whatever it is stays between us. Tell me what you need."

She swallowed and licked her lips. She'd told herself the visit was for Reese, that she wanted time to talk with him and would walk away and return to the castle after a few hours. Now, hearing his honest request, not admitting the truth seemed an insult.

She met his steady stare and sucked in a shaky breath. "I need you."

* * * *

Reese's heart stumbled then took off at a pounding gallop. Of all the reasons he might have rationalized to explain Galena's visit, a personal request hadn't been one of them.

She needed him. Not wanted, but needed. His cock stirred, and a rush of something dark and primitive swamped his reason. He shifted to ease the hard press behind his jeans, caution the only thing that kept him locked in place. Surely he'd misinterpreted things. Yesterday's kiss had just been a gift, a sendoff from a generous woman before he met his death. Hadn't it?

"Say something." Galena whispered, the rasped request so vulnerable it raked inside his chest.

Maybe he hadn't misunderstood.

She ducked her head, gripped the chair at her side for a beat, and turned away. "I should go." Chin high, she strode toward the door.

"No." He burst across the room with Myren speed and slammed his palm against the door to block her escape.

He caged her against the wall, her back to his front. Her ear nearly brushed his lips, her neck exposed by the long, thick braid down her back. He dragged his finger down the center of the plait. Myrens rarely bound their hair in any fashion outside of a relationship as it signaled commitment. The idea she'd come here bound to someone else rankled. "Why did you bind it?"

"The wind." Energy bristled off her, and her stance made her seem torn between flight and surrender.

"There's no one else?"

She peeked over one shoulder and shook her head, eyes trained on the floor.

The breath he'd been holding released and stirred the fine hairs at her nape. He toyed with the platinum bead keeping the braid in place at the tip. "Will you let me free it?"

An innocent question for a human, but for a Myren it was intimate. A gift restricted to deeply tied lovers and mates.

She lifted her gaze, bringing her full lips close enough her breath fluttered against his face. "Please."

His heart jolted, just the illusion of intimacy with this woman driving adrenaline through his bloodstream like a mainlined drug. He kissed her barely parted lips and groaned, imagining her soft, plump mouth stretch around his cock.

"Turn around," he breathed against her mouth.

She shivered and turned, but kept her gaze locked to his until the last moment.

Using his mind, he warmed and loosened the platinum bead, and slipped it free. He sifted through the soft strands one section at a time until the fiery mass spilled down her back, unleashing more of her unique scent. He nuzzled the spot behind her ear. How easy it would be to lose himself with this woman. In her scent and her warmth. He let out a rough exhale. "This is wrong."

She stiffened, but he tightened his grip on her hips and kept her locked in place.

"The secrets." He pressed a lingering kiss where her neck and shoulders met. "They'll hurt you and your brothers."

"They're only secrets if you're not willing to own them." She met his stare and a shiver rattled through her. Covering his hands with hers, she urged them up her torso. "I'm willing to own this."

The predator in him wrenched free, her confidence and sweet curves heady enough to drown his reason. He cupped her breasts, full and free of the undergarments so common in Evad, the only barrier her gown's slick fabric. He wanted to see her. To stroke and suckle the hard tips raking against his palms. To find every spot that made her arch and moan. To whisper salacious thoughts in her ear and watch her come.

He tweaked the tiny buds through the material.

Her eyes fluttered shut and she sighed, dropping her head back on his shoulder. "Yes."

Fuck, that word sounded sweet on her lips, a desperate plea that shot straight to his dick and drew his nuts up tight. He shouldn't do this. It was unfair and a gross abuse of trust, but damn it, he'd be dead tomorrow, and she'd been the one to come to him. What was the harm in pleasuring them both?

He swept her into his arms and forged toward the stairs, pulling the hidden door open with a hasty thought.

"Where are we going?"

The bookcase thunked closed behind them, and the quiet snick of the lock ricocheted down the shadowed hallway.

Galena tensed. "Reese?"

"Shhh." He cradled her close and strode through the darkness, brushing a kiss across her temple. "You're safe."

She loosened her grip, but craned her head to take in her surroundings, eyes widening as he carried her into his room. "The upstairs is a ruse," she said with undisguised awe.

"The rebellion taught my mother caution if nothing else." He lowered her to her feet, and she padded deeper into the room, examining every detail. To him it was barren and nondescript. Minimalist Blackwood furniture, pewter curtains and bed covering, and not a single accent or personal object to add personality. But watching her, the way her mouth parted with a tiny smile, made him wonder how she saw it.

She paused at the foot of the bed, her gaze locked on its center and the stark white sheets turned back at an angle. "This is your room?"

He should give her distance. Wait and gauge her intent.

To histus with that. Galena was in his room, an arm's length from silk sheets and sparking with sexual tension. He stalked forward. "There's nowhere else I'd take you." He caressed her upper arms, her back to his front, and brushed his lips along her neck. "You don't know how many nights I lay there, hard and ready, thinking of you."

The grumble in his voice couldn't be helped, his throat too tight to offer better. Admitting such a thing was probably too much. Too bold and too fast, but he was mighty close to not caring.

"What did you think about?" She turned in his arms. Just looking at her made his body tighten and crave things he never should. "Tell me what you imagined."

Their naked bodies tangled together. Breathy moans. Slick, heated skin.

No. She couldn't want him. It had to be a trick, all of it. "Thinking of giving a dying man his last wish?"

Galena shrugged him off and took the tiny step left between her and bed. She lifted her chin. "You seem to always assume people have the worst of intentions." Her lips pressed tight and her eyes flickered with what looked like guilt. "I asked for me."

Trapped with the bed behind her, he crowded close and gripped her face with both hands. Not harsh, but enough she couldn't escape his study. "Why?"

Her aqua eyes deepened, more like deep ocean than shallow beach waters. "Because I scanned your memories."

Fuck.

He swallowed past the emotional vise gripping his neck. Granted, he'd already confessed, but what else had she seen?

"It was just a glimpse." She gripped his biceps, a nervous, urgent squeeze. "It was rude and unforgivable, but I wanted to see if you'd meant to hurt me. Nothing more." She fanned her fingers across his pecs, the cotton of his T-shirt heightening the touch. "But the way you view me." She shook her head and tried to free herself from his grip.

He held fast. "What of it?"

Raw need flashed before her eyelids fluttered closed. "I want to be that woman. Just once."

Every muscle unwound, his mind gobsmacked. She wanted to be what? Sexy as hell? Earthy and sensual down to her toenails? Surely she knew her effect on men.

She squeezed her eyes tighter.

Histus, she didn't. "Look at me."

She shook her head.

"Galena, look at me."

She opened her eyes, slow and hesitant. Vulnerability shone bright in her glassy gaze, honest and open, rearranging every priority down to the very reason for his existence.

He released her and stepped back, limbs shaking. The exact opposite of what he craved, but the right action to give her what she needed.

Her breath shallowed and her lips parted. She pushed her shoulders back, a proud defiant stance that raised the swell of her breasts above her neckline. "I'm sorry I threw that on you. It was wrong. Completely unacceptable."

"Undress."

Galena gasped. Silence rumbled in behind the breathy sound and a tiny blush stole across her cheeks.

"Only a fool would turn you away, Galena. You asked what I imagined. Lose the gown and I'll show you."

She licked her lip.

Oh, sweet mother of all that was holy. Her whole demeanor transformed, a spark he'd never seen before flaring soft, but beautiful. Her lips curved, slow and sultry, and she trailed her fingers up between her breasts to toy with one strap of her gown.

"Like this?" Her smooth voice wound between them as she pushed one strip of evergreen fabric over her shoulder. In hung, teasing around her bicep, prevented from traveling farther by the gathered waist of her gown, but displaying the upper swell of one breast.

She traced a path across her collarbone to the other strap, toyed with the slick fabric long enough to make him wet his lips, and tugged the material so it hung lose and matched its mate. The bodice barely covered her nipples, and the smile on her face taunted him to step in and finish the job. A test of wills and a greedy game of anticipation all rolled up into one. Definitely a game worth playing.

With a grin, he pulled his T-shirt free and loosened the top two buttons of his jeans. Not nearly enough to ease his aching cock, but enough to tease her with what lay beneath. "Show me, Galena." He palmed his dick through the denim, and her eyes darkened to near black, locked on the motion of his hand. "I've had enough of fantasies. Show me the real thing."

Her gaze lifted slowly along his torso, and his muscles flexed as though she'd physically touched him.

She nibbled her lip and hesitated, the barest tremble where her hands hovered at the top of her gown. She sucked in a shaky breath and pushed the fabric free.

The gown pooled at her feet, and all the air in Reese's lungs followed suit, his feet anchored only by the lust paralyzing his mind. "Perfect."

Had he said that out loud? It was all he heard in his head. He'd dreamed, but reality was so much better. Luscious curves, rosy nipples, and full breasts. This was happening. Really happening. Tomorrow didn't matter, because he'd already found nirana.

Her flush deepened and crept down her neck to the top of her chest.

He prowled closer, the air between them fairly snapping with energy. "My imagination didn't do you justice." He traced a path along her jaw, down her neck, and between her breasts, the perfect mounds so ripe and ready for touch, it was all he could do not to give in and fill his palms with their delicious weight. At her navel he drew slow, teasing circles. "Will you let me show you more?"

Galena whimpered. "Please."

Eager to oblige, his cock twitched behind the painful confines of his jeans. Hell, he'd give her everything. With a mental push, he swirled cool air around her legs and up her torso, stirring the hair at her shoulders. He streamed a thin gust between her thighs.

Galena whimpered and her eyes fluttered shut. Her nipples jutted hard and ready for his mouth.

Praise the Great One, he wanted to touch her. To explore and sample every inch of her until he found the spots that made her moan and beg for more. He fisted his hands at his sides and tried to bank his escalating lust. He couldn't give in yet, not until he'd proven his point. "Lie on the bed."

She moaned and reached for him, her fingertips grazing his abs.

He captured her wrist, her pulse frantic beneath his thumb. "That's not what I said. I want you in my bed and stretched across my sheets."

She tugged until he freed her, a conflicted scowl on her face.

"Your call, Galena. I'd never force you into something you don't want, but I won't shortchange you either."

Seconds ticked by, every damned one of them prodding the pacing beast inside him.

Slowly, she turned and crawled to the center, her perfect, heart-shaped ass swaying with each movement. Auburn hair spilled nearly to her hips, fire against golden, Myren skin.

He'd take her that way. Not now, but soon. Drape himself against her back and plunge deep.

She rolled to her back and rested her head on his pillow, knees crooked to one side.

Dear God, her hips were meant for a man's hands. His hands. He sucked in a breath and reached deep for control. Tonight was for her. To show her the image she'd seen wasn't just his perception, but reality. The same reality for any sane man with a beating heart.

Popping the remaining buttons on his jeans, he pushed them past his hips. His cock sprang free, his pulse a steady, pounding presence along the shaft. "Draw your knees up and wide. Bare yourself me."

She tensed, and splayed her fingers at either side of her hips against the sheets.

"Look at me." He couldn't give in. Wouldn't let her give in until he'd shown her the truth. He fisted his staff, the touch not nearly enough to sooth the raging throb just looking at her created. He teased her thighs with another swirl of wind, an invisible but subtle pressure at the insides of her knees. "You can do this."

Her eyes went wide, so trusting and vulnerable. She sucked in a shaky inhalation and shifted, centering her knees. Her thighs parted and she arched her back, head thrown back and eyes closed in surrender. She stroked between her folds and a ragged moan filled the room. "Reese."

Enough. More than enough to prove his point and light years past the amount of temptation he could bear. He kneeled between her legs and covered her hand with this own, their fingers sliding together through her wetness.

Her eyes popped open and locked onto his.

"You see?" He overpowered her movements, guiding her slender fingers and gathering her juices to slick around her clit. "You can't be the woman in my mind *just once*." He circled the swollen nub and teased one nipple with his tongue. "You are that woman. Always." He pressed one finger deep and sucked the tip in his mouth.

Galena cried out, her hands fisting in his hair, holding him to her breast while her hips undulated in a slow, sexy cadence.

He nipped the tight peak and laved the sting away with the flat of his tongue, reveling in her ragged moans and the thickening scent of her arousal. Bracing himself on one arm to see her face, he added another finger. Her walls clamped around them with each thrust, so wet and tight his cock flexed against his belly. "That's it, sweetheart. Let it happen." He licked her lower lip, no more than a tease. "Ride my fingers. Let me watch you come undone."

Her eyes flared and a tiny whimper huffed past her lips.

He circled her clit with his thumb once, twice.

Her hips quivered.

Angling his wrist, he stroked her front wall and pressed his thumb against the swollen nub.

"Reese." Her grated wail filled the room, husky and so damned enticing his nuts tightened to the point of pain.

Ah, but the clench and release of her pussy was heaven. He worked her sex and kissed his way down her torso, milking every drop of her climax while he feasted on her sweat dampened skin. "So slick and sweet."

"Reese." Galena clawed his shoulders, her efforts useless against his determined path. "Let me touch you, please."

He sat back on his heels and palmed her hip with one hand, her legs still wide, but now boneless from release. Her release coated his fingers, still leisurely pumping in and out of her pretty pink pussy. He pressed her knees wide and his mouth watered. "Later. Right now I want you on my tongue."

Galena wriggled beneath him, pressing up to her elbows. "But you—"

"I'm the happiest fucking man alive." He tugged her hips up to his ravenous mouth and devoured. In every dream, every fantasy, this was how he'd wanted her. Spread wide and open to every touch, every lap of his tongue and scrape of his teeth. God she tasted good, a decadent feast he'd never get enough of.

Galena collapsed to the bed and widened her legs farther.

He licked and sucked her labia, gathering up every trace of her pleasure, driving her for more.

She clenched the sheets at her sides, and her whimpers stroked like velvet along his staff. "It's not enough." She fisted his hair, pushing him closer one second and tugging him away in the next. She clenched her fists harder and the bite of pain shot straight to his nuts. "I need more."

Hell, yes, more. And then some.

Pressing one of her legs high and wide, he dragged his cockhead through her folds. The site of his flared head against her deep pink core nearly yanked his climax free. A growl rumbled from his chest. No more waiting. "Say it again."

She met his gaze, her breaths short and ragged. "I need you. Please."

Thank The Great One.

He surged forward and their rough shouts mingled, her nails scoring his back. Damn, but she was tight. Tight and so damned perfect he could barely breathe.

He pulled back slow, nearly to the tip, and powered deep, angling his hips to rub her just right. Over and over he pounded, punctuated thrusts and the gentle smack of his sac against her flesh spurring a wild rhythm.

She tossed her head, her auburn hair tousled against his sheets. Squeezing his hips, she dug her heels into his flanks and met each spear of his cock. With every lunge, her breasts bounced. The most delicious torment on the planet topped by nipples hard and berry-ripe.

His climax built, balls drawn tight and full. Lifting her legs to rest on his shoulders, he drove deep. "You're coming with me, sweetheart. Show me how it feels to have you come on my cock."

He fired energy at her every pleasure point, relentless, rasping pulses to match his unforgiving rhythm.

"Yes." Galena's relief rang out and her pussy fisted his length.

His climax fired and his hips rammed home, his shaft flexing in time with his frantic heart. He kissed and licked her sweat-dampened shoulder, lungs burning for air as he rode the ebbing storm with slow, leisurely rolls of his hips.

Damn, but she'd turned him inside out. Dragged him miles past bliss and rocketed him to rapture wrapped in slick heat. He'd never get enough, never be able to settle for anything less than what burned between them in this moment. And didn't that just figure. The fates had finally given him a taste of perfection the night before he was sure to die.

Chapter 11

Maxis cracked one fifty-pound eyelid open, his blood sluggish and muscles unresponsive. Sunshine framed the closed black velvet curtains across the room, and dull red embers glowed in the large hearth on his left. He tugged the thick gold coverlet to his chest and settled into the warmth along his side.

Warmth. He snapped awake, his hazed focus sharpening in one blink.

Serena lay stretched out on her belly with her pillow tucked lengthwise against her. Her near-white hair spilled in a well-fucked mess down her back, her breaths deep and even.

He'd actually done it. Claimed a mate.

He propped himself on one elbow and rubbed his chest. The flesh stung where welts rose in a starburst over his heart. A growl rumbled in his throat and an odd approval stirred. Serena had met him pound for pound in the course of their joining, insatiable, demanding, and downright dirty.

A flash of black caught his eye and he stretched out his arm. Her mark.

He'd forgotten that little aspect of his new turn in life. Hard to think about anything else the night before with Serena's slick heat gripping his cock.

He sat up for a better view.

Oh, she'd marked him, all right, and with flowers, no less. Five-pointed blossoms, the long wavering petals crushed beneath a warrior's fist. The blooms spilled down his forearm toward his wrist, deceptively beautiful. One, lone petal stretched and rounded at the end and formed a drop of blood.

The ivory silk sheets rustled beside him and Serena inhaled slow and sleepy. She pushed to her side, a sliver of white hair pointing toward one uncovered breast. Her screams and moans from the night before sounded in her roughened voice. "They're oleander."

"I know what they are." Maxis pressed her to her back and gripped the hair at her nape. Damn, but the skin along her neck was decadent. Creamy perfection. "They're deadly." A message he'd be wise to heed, as well as appreciate.

Serena wrapped her arms and legs around him, lips tilted in a sultry smile and a sated glow on her cheeks.

"Eager to play again, my baineann?" He cupped one breast, the mound filling his palm, but not overflowing. "I would have thought you had your fill last night."

"You could always fill me again." She flexed her hips and chuckled, a delightfully wicked sound.

Maxis played her stiff nipple with his thumb, a languid back and forth that made her arch into his touch. Oh, yes, he'd be wise to exercise caution where she was concerned, else he'd wake up one day and find his balls canned and stored in the kitchen pantry. "Don't think to lead me around by my cock, Serena."

Her cool blue eyes fired hot. She bucked against him and fisted her hands at either side of her head. "Get off me."

"Mmm. Perhaps I grazed too close to the truth." Maxis rolled to his side of the bed, tossed a fresh log into the hearth with his mind, and strode toward the closet. "I offered you a partnership. More than I've offered anyone else. It's best you remember that and mind your place."

He summoned Uther with a thought and dressed in leather pants and black drast to match the warriors they'd soon meet.

Feminine grumbles sounded from the bedroom, and muted heel strikes beat against the carpet.

Serena rounded the closet door and planted her fists on her hips. A flush spread across her collarbone and cheeks. "Mind my place? Or you'll what?"

He'd give her credit for her fire and fearlessness. Still, better to solidify her place before things got out of hand. He tugged on his last boot, straightened, and prowled close until he towered over her. "You'll keep to your role as my mate and confidant. You will not rule me, Serena." He paused long enough to ensure he had her attention. "I slit my own father's throat. Don't think for a minute I'd hesitate to choke yours."

A knock sounded at the bedroom door.

Maxis pulled his robe from its hanger and tossed it her direction as he strode past. "Cover yourself."

At his command, candles throughout the bedroom and his adjoining office flared to life. He rounded his desk. "Enter."

The whitewashed doors swung open and the fire's glow caught in the gold filigree. Uther filled the entrance, outlined by vicious sunshine.

Leaning back in his brocade chair, Maxis propped one foot on the corner of the French antique desk and laced his fingers behind his head. "Give me an update."

Uther sauntered forward. Either he'd pulled off several feats in the two days Maxis had given him to work, or he didn't give a shit how well or poorly his efforts were received. "Men are relocated. Slave pens are ready. Drills start after you meet with them this afternoon."

Impressive indeed. Maybe he'd earned that cocky stride. "We'll meet within the hour at the main training hall. I need an hour—"

"Did I hear someone at the door?" Serena, glided into his office, all sugar-sweet and fabricated innocence with his black robe precariously cinched at her waist. Nothing so flagrant as walking naked in front of his new strategos, but enough to make it clear she wore not a stitch underneath.

Uther spun and stepped back.

"Oh." She halted mid-stride, a hand at her mouth. "I thought I'd imagined the voices."

Troublesome wench. "I'm not buying it," Maxis said. "Neither is he."

She shrugged with an unrepentant smirk and aimed a come-hither look at Uther. She lifted the black sleeve, not enough to show the entire mating mark, but enough to register her new status. "We had a busy night."

Uther took her hand, a roguish glint in his eyes. "So I see." He glanced at Maxis. "It appears congratulations are in order. May I?"

Damn it all, the two made an impertinent and troublesome pair. If he denied Uther, he'd give Serena too much power. If he approved, The Great One only knew what message he'd send to Uther. He nodded.

Keeping her hand in his, Uther pushed the sleeve to her elbow with his free hand.

A Deathstalker scorpion covered her forearm, its pinchers reaching toward her elbow and its tail wrapped around her wrist. Two swords crossed the center of its back. It should have been obscene on her delicate frame, but Serena made it elegant.

"A powerful mark." Uther laid a chaste kiss to her knuckles.

"Enough." Maxis shoved to his feet and stomped toward the bedroom. This was why he chose to work alone. Less drama and infinitely less bullshit. "Get a man to Serena's home and move her things here. Serena it's time for your tour."

"No."

Maxis halted, clenching his torso muscles to keep from backhanding and marring his mate's beautiful face. He pivoted. "You think to be my mate and live under another man's roof?"

"I think I've waited years to see the look on my father's face when I slide out from under his thumb. No one, not even you, will steal that from me."

She pulled her robe tighter. Only a sliver of creamy skin showed beneath the dark silk. Her chin lifted, mouth as stiff as her spine, and wary.

"Fair enough." A small win he'd allow. "Dress in the gown you wore last night. You'll not meet our men like some common slut. We'll retrieve your things together later." He motioned for Uther to follow with a jerk of his head and resumed his trek to the bedroom. "We'll wait for you in the tunnels."

"What tunnels?" Serena scurried behind them.

Maxis unlatched the hidden mechanism deep within the gilded ivory walls. "Dress and find out."

A section of wall framed in gold trim cracked open, and the hinges groaned from limited use. Another office, a mirror of the one he'd left behind, sat shadowed beyond.

A frigid draft pushed the hair off his neck, a mere taste of the bitter cold that waited.

Serena drifted to his side.

"You're wasting time, mate." Maxis ambled to the hidden room and set the hearth's kindling ablaze.

Serena hustled away and disappeared into the closet. Leave it to curiosity to set his baineann in motion.

Uther strode toward the main tunnel entrance on the opposite side. "I'll ready the men."

"Not yet. There's something we need to discuss." More like catch his strategos unaware. He'd have to be damned quick to glean Uther's memories before he shut him out. He motioned for Uther to shut the door between his hidden room and the bedroom.

As soon as the latch snicked into place, Maxis struck, snatching Uther's hand and darting for his memories. His energy slammed into an unforgiving barrier, and painful reverberations ricocheted down Maxis' arms and legs. He staggered and dropped Uther's hand.

An arrogant smirk spread across Uther's face, his arms loose and unaffected at his sides. "If you want my memories, you'll have to ask."

Interesting little gift his strategos had. Not exactly a welcome development on the quality control scale, but interesting nonetheless. "I'm not inclined to ask for anything when it concerns my baineann."

"Mighty protective for a woman you've only just met."

"She wears my mark. You'll keep your distance."

"I have no interest in Serena, or any woman like her. Too high maintenance and standoffish for my taste." Uther offered his hand. "Though you're welcome to see for yourself if you'd like."

Solid, steady. Not so much as a tremor.

Maxis motioned his offering away. "Keep your distance from Serena. Managing her is challenge enough without you fanning her ideas."

Uther grinned. "Duly noted."

"Now explain that handy gift I barreled into."

Uther studied him. His chin shifted back and forth as though he rolled the taste of possibilities on his tongue. "It's exactly what it felt like. A natural shield. No one gets in I don't want in, either mentally or physically. That's the only explanation you'll get. For now."

Arrogant bastard. He'd have to find something to bring his strategos down a notch, or at least some leverage to keep him in line.

"Maxis?" Serena's muted query issued through the walls.

"Go." He waved Uther toward the door and the tunnels beyond. "See that the men are ready."

Uther ambled off, and Maxis triggered the latch holding the hidden door in place.

Serena stood, hands on hips. "I couldn't reach you via link or sense you."

"Of course you couldn't." Maxis ran his hand along the bared gap between the walls. "It's lined with zeolite. Not enough to hinder our gifts on either side, but enough to block detection on line of sight." He held out his hand.

She stepped forward, her fingers chilled against his palm. The simple cut of her blue gown left her arms bare, not at all appropriate for their pending tour.

"Stay here." Returning to his closet, he pulled a fur coat from a section deep in the back, a white, ankle-length affair Evanora had favored. Back beside her, he thrust it at her. "Put this on. The blue does nothing for your skin when you're cold and where we're going it will only get worse."

She studied the coat. Then him. One corner of her mouth lifted and her eyes sparked as she reached for the opulent fur. "Careful, Maxis. One might think you care." Slipping the heavy coat in place, she freed her hair from the neck.

"Of course I care." He plucked his own black fur from a peg beside the door and halted beyond the tunnel threshold. "First appearances are everything. I'll not have my mate looking like a popsicle." He lifted his eyebrows. "Coming?"

"Of course." She pulled the lapels closer together so the soft edges framed her smug smile, and glided forward.

Black rock walls surrounded them, the tunnel two men tall and five men wide. The surface was crude, hewn solely by determination and his natural Earth gifts. Despite the obvious curiosity on Serena's face, she held her tongue. "For a woman eager to learn my secrets, you're awfully quiet."

"You said you'd show me. I trust you." Nothing else. Just sweet acquiescence.

He stopped.

She stopped as well. "That is what you asked me to do, isn't it?" The sneaky bitch batted her eyes.

Praise The Great One, the woman was a manipulative landmine waiting to happen. He continued his trek. On the bright side he wouldn't be bored.

"Have the tunnels always been here?"

Finally. A face-value topic. "No. Evanora built the training grounds and slave farm you'll soon see, but she didn't live long enough to put her plans in place. I've spent the last seventy years mining the tunnels and updating the infrastructure my father let fall in disrepair."

"Why the tunnels?"

"Trackers."

Serena surveyed the dark walls. "Trackers?"

"If we traveled the distance between the estate and the warrior camp above ground we'd be too easy to find. Trackers can't scan us below ground, not with this much rock between us. That, and I like knowing I have an escape few others know about."

He stopped at a dead end. "You and I both know our efforts may turn ugly before they turn in our favor."

She gripped her lapels more tightly and burrowed into the coat's warmth, wary, but thoughtful.

"Second thoughts?"

She tilted her head. "Merely studying the angles. As you point out, it pays to be prepared."

Maxis harrumphed. Whether or not she was telling the truth was hard to tell with his new baineann. She could just as easily be plotting his demise. He pushed the rock slab aside to show another hallway.

"This is the main corridor." He waited until she cleared the opening and pushed the rock back in place. "The warriors can enter from four locations, each spread a good mile from the main camp. They're being trained to mask their presence prior to approaching, all efforts geared toward protecting our location as long as possible."

Voices rumbled and the scent of freshly cut wood filled the tunnel. The steady draft was a good twenty degrees colder here than the one they'd left behind.

Serena burrowed deeper into the coat's high neckline.

"We're in Brasia now." Maxis steered her down one offshoot tunnel. "The temperatures range from ten to thirty below outside, another deterrent to keep Shantos and his men away. Not exactly a hospitable environment, unless you know what Evanora uncovered."

They rounded the last bend.

Serena gasped and halted.

It was a rather magnificent surprise. He'd been honing it for decades and it still jumpstarted his pride.

"It's not possible."

"It's entirely possible." Maxis drew her forward and leaned into the stone railing, a balcony of sorts jutting over a cavernous opening, skylight tubes shining muted gold above. "There's a mountain range that marks Brasia's border."

"The one beyond the estate," she whispered, eyes wide with wonder.

"Exactly." Below him, men hustled back and forth between large stone and wood buildings. The warriors looked even more impressive with their thick coats adding to their physical bulk. "We're in the belly of the biggest, Evanora's Peak. Measuring it has proved difficult, but my best estimations are somewhere in the space of a square mile."

He pointed at the balconied decks jutting out along either side. "The senior warriors and their families will be appointed living space in the top tier. Seasoned men have apartments situated at the corner quadrants, and new recruits stay to the barracks along the back."

Serena faced him. "No one man could do this."

"No." Maxis shrugged. "But a man can take advantage of what nature and his grandmother's vision started."

He slipped an arm around her waist and took to the air, sweeping them both toward a squat structure centered along the furthest stretch.

"Evanora's husband found it. His gifts aligned with the Earth as do mine. My grandmother made the most of it, though she started late in life. I merely finished it."

They landed outside the main entrance, and Maxis urged her through the wide double doors. "And this is where we'll store our resources."

Lanterns hung in regular intervals down the long hallways, the partitioned cell doors open in preparation for use.

"When you said slave farm I'd thought it an elaboration." Serena peered inside one cell, the ten by ten space barren but for a bucket, and a cot. "How many will it hold?"

"Two hundred. Though we're nowhere near ready to handle so many at present."

"You'll never get that many. Not without gaining notice from the human realm."

"Humans go missing all the time." He strolled beside her, her dumbfounded expression firing a pleasant buzz beneath his skin. "They'll just continue to do so."

"How do you plan to take them? Won't it take time?"

Maxis grinned and led her out into the hive of activity. "That's what our men are for, Serena. They capture, they guard, they fight. Simple as that."

She frowned, and stared into the distance. "What if you use humans to do it?"

"Pardon?"

Head tilted in a detached study of the senior quarters above, she worried her lower lip. "Wouldn't it make more sense to have human middlemen to do the job? We wouldn't be exposed, and even if Eryx does get suspicious, his investigations and the disappearances wouldn't point back at us." She grinned, her attention now solely on him. "At least not until we're ready."

She was out of her mind. Humans wouldn't traffic—

Well, histus. They did traffic their own kind. At least some of them did. But finding that particular resource might prove problematic. Although, there was the malress' friend. A retired officer, still safe and sound in his Asshur hideaway. No one knew better where to locate mercenary types than their jailers.

In the center of the square, men lined up, Uther moving with long arrogant strides to ensure their placement.

Serena watched. The lick of greed and excitement he'd sensed in her from day one burned bright across her cheeks.

"It seems my choice of mate has been most fortuitous." He tucked her hand in the crook of his arm and guided her toward their waiting troops. "What say we introduce you to the men so we can get on with our plans?"

Chapter 12

Reese shifted against the crisp, cool sheets. Too cool. Empty.

He opened his eyes to dawn's soft gray kiss and swept his hand along the space beside him. Galena's floral scent billowed from the pillowcase.

So, he hadn't dreamt it.

He rolled to his back, shoved his wild hair from his face, and fisted it at the top of his head. He couldn't blame her for leaving. She'd risked a lot in coming here with zero to gain in the long run. He was a dead man and everyone knew it.

Memories of the things they'd done through the night flashed bold and vivid in his mind, and the husky way she'd groaned when he'd pushed inside her the first time rang in his ears. Even the taste of her lingered on his tongue.

Fuck. He gripped his hardening shaft and gritted his teeth. So, she'd left, but she'd also left him with the most profound experience of his life. He had no right to complain, not after what they'd shared.

He tossed the sheets aside and snatched his jeans on the way to the bathroom. Now wasn't the time for memories. If he wanted to make it through the next few hours, he'd need to pull his head out of his ass and focus. Not whine about Galena skipping out on a morning cuddle. She'd shown her courage last night. Now it was time for him to suck it up and show his own.

With a mental push, the shower sprang to life. He tugged a towel from the cabinet and tossed it near the open ledge. Praise the Great One, he was crazy entertaining thoughts he might live through this. Not impossible. Improbable, but not impossible. If he did, would he even have a chance with Galena?

Now there was the impossibility. Ramsay would cut his nuts off if he knew the things he'd done with Galena last night. Worse if Reese instigated something more tangible.

Damned if she wasn't worth it, though. If nothing else, he'd grip that notion tight when he faced Maxis and pray he made it to the other side. He'd move a whole damned mountain range if it meant so much as another second with Galena.

Water raced down his body, an erotic touch, so much like Galena's. He braced against the shower wall and hung his head, muscles loose, but eager in a way he hadn't felt in years, if ever.

All he had to do was lead Eryx's men to Maxis, tell his brother he hadn't really been abandoned, and try to sway his plans for vengeance.

He lifted his head and caught his reflection in the mirror. Who in histus was he kidding? He was a dead man.

* * * *

Stubborn, good-for-nothing humans. Maxis stormed the length of crude rock cell and gripped his kneeling prisoner by the neck. "Names. All I need are names and this is all over. No more pain."

Ian Smith grunted and spit near Maxis' boots. Only one slow burning torch smoldered near the door, but it was more than enough to spotlight the bruises and angry welts that covered his legs and torso. The flesh around his neck was charred and blistered, a byproduct of his bullheaded silence. No wonder he and the malress had been such fast friends. The two were entirely too much alike.

He tightened his hold and unleashed another torrent of electricity.

Ian jerked and spasmed, blue sparks zinging all around him. His choked gurgles filled the tiny space as his face reddened and swelled with pressure.

Maxis released him, and Ian slumped to the rock floor, unconscious.

"Fuck." Maxis crouched beside him. The whites of his eyes were streaked with red and his pupils dilated, his pulse thready and barely detectable. Fuck, fuck, fuck.

Maxis surged upright and paced the tiny cell. His heart hammered and his torso was slick with sweat. Damn it all, Ian knew all kinds of potential middlemen. The images were there, but Maxis needed details. Learning and logic didn't transfer with the audio and video play-by-play, and he'd never get what he needed from a borderline corpse. Maybe he should get a healer. Human or not, Ian was leverage. The one thing preventing Eryx from killing Maxis on sight. If Maxis died, Ian's location went with him.

"That's not your only problem."

Maxis spun toward the voice behind him.

Falon. The spiritu blended with the shadows. There, but not there.

"What do you want?" He didn't have time for games. Not if he wanted to keep his prisoner breathing.

A growl emanated through the cell, though Falon's face didn't move. "Reese is alive."

Seconds stomped past, each heartbeat ricocheting in his head. The room spun and adrenaline rushed his bloodstream. "Care to repeat that?"

"You heard what I said. Your damned brother is alive and well."

"I thought you said—"

"I know what I said." Falon crept forward, shadows falling away to make him a solid substance. "The Light hid him from me. A camouflage I wasn't aware they could manage. They did it when he was injured in the battle at your estate. Fortunately for us, he indulged in a little fun between the sheets last night. A lot, actually. Burned a big enough hole in their cover I was able to find him."

Ian's breath hitched, followed by a wet cough.

Reese was alive. He had a mate and a brother. Family.

"Don't kid yourself." Falon prowled closer, and a dark, cloying scent seeped in with him. "Your mother abandoned you. Filled Reese's head with lies about you and your grandmother. The only reason he linked with you was because you threatened to share his lineage with anyone who'd listen."

No. Not true. He'd seen a flicker of himself in Reese. A promise of what they could accomplish together. "He needed a cause to fight for. In time he'd have willingly participated."

Falon leaned in, inches from Maxis' face. "He betrayed you. Saved a simpering female and screwed your plans in the process. Three days ago you were ready to kill him for his treachery. Now is no different."

It was different. The need for vengeance no longer existed. Maybe taking a mate made Reese unnecessary. Or Uther's eager participation replaced Reese's hesitant presence. "I've got bigger issues to contend with. Plans to put in action. I'll not be swayed from my course."

Falon straightened and ambled a half-circuit around the wheezing prisoner. He nudged Ian's leg. "Your plans will fail without me. My plans will fail without you. Deal with Reese or both our schemes are doomed."

"What's that supposed to mean?"

"The dark passions." He tilted his head, eyes squinted. "Do you really think the Myren race will actively adopt the implementation of slavery without freedom from their conscience? Their darker desires will never run free if my men fail, and my men need your dark deeds to feed the way. So, I'm telling you to do it. Make your brother pay for his treachery."

"It's a needless killing. You want someone dead, give me someone deserving."

"You suddenly find your brother to be worth redemption? Reach out, Maxis." A wicked smile crept across Falon's face and he crossed his arms. "I doubt you'd grant your precious brother a pass if you checked his location at this very moment."

The hairs along his nape lifted and his belly cramped. He reached for his link to Reese and his brother's presence pinged against his internal map. On the ridge, just beyond this cave, no more than two hundred feet as the crow flies.

"He's not alone," Falon said. "He's brought some company. People who've been most interested in tracking you and your human captive."

Maxis fanned his senses along the perimeter. Twenty, maybe thirty men placed at every quadrant. Perfectly placed. Positioning Eryx and his men could only manage if they knew the details of his hideout.

Traitor.

Falon's chuckle rumbled through the room. "Yes, your dear brother, leading your enemy to your doorstep for the second time." He uncurled his arms, glided closer, and rasped in Maxis' ear. "Now what are you going to do about it?"

* * * *

Another thick and ominous cloud drifted in front of the sun and lifted a fresh wave of goose bumps along Galena's arms. She hated Asshur. The whole region reeked of desolation with its crackling clay terrain and sparse, gangly vegetation. Tucked into a twenty by twenty indention along a desolate canyon wall, at least she and the rest of her group were isolated from the cool winds.

A chill racked her from the inside out. For the last ten minutes, she'd barely ripped her gaze from the barren horizon, waiting for Reese. One minute she couldn't wait for him to show, and the next she prayed he wouldn't.

Jagger and Ludan muttered behind her. Every now and then Lexi chimed in, a light and sassy sound against their deep, rumbling voices. Hard to believe she'd only been a part of their lives for less than a few weeks.

Ramsay stood beside Eryx and glowered at the skies. "You think he'll show?"

Unlike his brother, Eryx's attention was locked on her, a nearly constant weight she hadn't been able to shake. "He's on his way. The link shows him two or three minutes out."

The link.

Praise the Great One, she was an idiot. He'd scanned Reese's memories before he'd made the connection, and then turned scary angry. He must've seen the kiss.

And then she'd spent the night with him. If he checked both their links last night—

A muted thud sounded behind her.

"My Malran." Reese's voice rumbled behind her, followed by an awkward pause. "Ramsay."

Male greetings rang out from the other men, polite, but insincere, and Eryx jumped in behind them with quick, staccato orders.

Galena swallowed past the lump in her throat and turned toward Reese.

Praise the Great One. Wrong choices or not, Reese had brought his pride today. He stood before Eryx, shoulders back, hair unbound and wild. Instead of a drast, he wore a loose ivory shirt with black leather pants and boots. Rather a new age pirate with a rugged edge.

He lifted his chin in answer to whatever had been said, a resolute hardness to his mouth.

What she wouldn't give for contact. Even just one glance. She couldn't tell him how much last night had meant, how sorry she'd been to leave before the sun rose, but her eyes would say enough.

"You get one shot." Eryx cut into her thoughts, his words aimed at Reese. "Two minutes to share whatever it is you want to say. If Maxis so much as twitches, all bets are off."

Galena edged closer.

"Fair enough." Reese jerked his head toward the canyon wall opposite them. "The main entrance is about a hundred yards north. A flat ledge juts out with a natural rock slab sheltering the opening." He faced Ramsay and his gaze swept right past her. "You'll want to cover the secondary openings at the coordinates I gave you yesterday. Not a lot of guards since he doesn't tell many about the place. Only a handful at each entrance."

Why wouldn't he look at her? Her heart cramped and her lungs burned with a need to shout. To rant and rail.

A hand cupped her shoulder. "You okay?"

Lexi stepped into sight, her slate-blue eyes filled with concern and pity.

"I'm fine." Or she would be eventually.

"I'm not buying it." She pursed her lips and sidled closer, eyes pinched with too much intuition. Damn, Lexi and her emotional radar. "He's doing what he feels is right. No one's forcing him to take this route."

The same way she'd followed her instincts the night before. It might have meant nothing to him, but for her it was everything, a feminine liberation and an exploration of a part of herself she hadn't even known existed.

And now the man who'd given it to her was marching into death.

"Men are in place," Ramsay said from somewhere behind her.

Eryx strode to the center of the group. "Ludan, you're with me. Jagger, you're with Lexi until we have the cave secured." He peered over one shoulder at Reese. "You're up."

Reese nodded, hands fisted at his sides, and stared at the rocky ledge beyond. A muscle ticked at the back of his jaw. "I'll incapacitate the guards up front, but I won't take them out. You want them dead, it's up to you."

Wind gusted past the ledge and he shot to the sky, never once looking back.

Galena's heart lurched and she stepped forward.

Lexi clamped onto Galena's wrist. "This isn't your battle. Let it—"

A grated scream rent the air and Reese freefell toward the Earth.

Galena darted after him, the wind a sharp whistle in her ears.

Reese crashed to the ground and curled inward, clawing his head the same as Phybe had only days before.

"Eryx, it's Maxis!" Galena landed beside Reese and shoved him to his back. Straddling his waist, she gripped either side of his neck and froze. She hadn't been able to save Phybe. Maxis' mental destruction had been too quick and vast to risk the healing. What in histus made her think she'd live through the same with Reese?

She could do this. She would do this. No one's healing surpassed hers. Not even Eryx's.

Shouts rang out behind her and someone tugged her arm.

She tightened her knees at Reese's sides and speared her spirit into his.

"Galena," Eryx barked. "You can't save him. Get out."

She mashed her eyelids tight and visualized her path, up through the carotid.

"Eryx, let her go." Lexi, thank The Great One.

Someone gripped her shoulders and footsteps shuffled on the sandy rock.

Her spirit turned at the cerebral artery. Damaged brain tissue spread in all directions, what should have been a healthy pinkish-gray a charred and blood-streaked mess. She healed as she ghosted along her path, scanning for the source.

"Galena, tell us what you need." Lexi's voice lilted through her mind, an echo behind each word that said she shared her words with others.

Galena's fingers trembled and her arms ached with fatigue. She'd never healed this much damage this quickly. No way would she stop whatever Maxis was doing alone. Pulling in a lungful of air, she shoved a summer green blast of healing energy across Reese's cortex. *"The damage is everywhere, but I can't keep up."*

A muffled curse grumbled nearby and large hands covered hers, rough calluses abrading her knuckles. "Ramsay, we're going in with her," Eryx said.

"You sure about this, Eryx?" Ramsay whispered beside her.

A tear slipped down her cheek, the wind cold in its path. They'd always question Reese's motives. No matter what he did right. And if anything happened to her, they'd lay the blame at his feet.

Eryx's hands tightened against hers. "I can't stop her, and if she's determined to fight, then we fight with her." His energy surged to meet hers, his powerful white aura bathing everything around her and lightening the weight of Reese's pain on her spirit.

Another wave rushed in behind it, this one tinged with silver. Ramsay. *"Now what?"* Ramsay asked.

"Find the link." Eryx's spirit pushed in front of hers, Ramsay right behind it. *"Ludan stop worrying about me and feed Galena. Her energy's too low."*

A giant hand pressed between her shoulder blades, and power jolted through her veins and sinew, feeding her starved cells.

"I don't see anything," Ramsay said, his mental voice distracted.

Of course they wouldn't see the connection. The link was between Reese and Maxis. To find Maxis they'd need a connection to Reese.

"Eryx, that's it." Galena's arms shook, palms slick against Reese's neck. *"Your link with Reese. Use it."*

"How?"

"Stream through your link to Reese." Galena kept healing, a fresh jolt of adrenaline and hope pushing her faster. *"See if you find Maxis that way."*

"Shit, that's genius." Ramsay's spirit swirled around hers. *"You look, I'll cover Galena."*

Eryx's light wavered and disappeared.

Ramsay weaved his energy with hers, amplifying her healing with his warrior strength.

Cracked squeaks ripped passed Reese's throat.

"*Son of a bitch,*" Eryx said. She'd never heard him so stupefied.

Ramsay's energy formed a barricade around hers, protective. "*What?*" Hope fluttered in Galena's stomach. "*You found him?*"

"*Yeah, I found him.*" Eryx's deadly tone sent a chill across Galena's heart. "*Ramsay, funnel through my link. We'll attack the thread on two fronts. Pull the link tight and do not let him connect. Ludan, need you ready to hit the center.*"

"*Got it.*"

"*Galena, whatever you do, stay back,*" Eryx said. "*Do not engage. We clear?*"

"*Just do it.*"

Ramsay's spirit faded. Left without his strength, Reese's injuries slammed heavy against her.

She pulled in a steady breath and narrowed her focus. If they could fight, she could heal.

Reese bowed beneath her and Galena opened her eyes. His face was a mottled red, his neck strained.

"*Ludan, now.*" Eryx commanded.

The steady stream of Ludan's energy dropped to nothing and her spirit staggered, slamming back into her body in a dizzying recoil.

Reese convulsed, his entire body shaking as though an entire lightning bolt coursed through him.

Darkness hovered at the edge of her vision, her energy almost depleted, but she leaned forward and pinned Reese by his shoulders.

Lexi jumped in to help a second before Reese slumped, his jaw slack and muscles limp.

"Reese?" Galena's vision blurred behind tears and she cupped his face. "Reese."

"Galena, it's okay." Lexi's arms wrapped around her, and a fresh wave of energy surged behind it. "He's fine, but he needs you to heal him. The men need their strength, but you can have mine." She covered Galena's hand with her own and laid it over Reese's heart. "Feel his heartbeat."

A weak thump registered beneath her palm, and her shoulders sagged. His vitals were haggard, but steady, no more violent reverberations like she'd felt during Maxis' attack. "What happened? Where's Maxis link?"

"Snapped that bitch in half," Ludan boasted behind her.

Ramsay rose beside her. "Yeah, but what about Maxis?"

"Hard to tell. He can't feel good though." Eryx shoved to his feet. "And if he's stunned, that means he's vulnerable." With a quick, reassuring squeeze to Lexi's shoulder, he spun toward Maxis' cave. "Ramsay, prep the men, we're goin' in."

Chapter 13

Eryx flew a second pass along the cavern wall, Ludan off to one side. Their masks were in place, but speeding this fast anyone with baseline detection skills would sense them a mile off. *"You see anything?"*

"A two-mile stretch of ugly." Count on Ludan to make urgency sound boring. *"You catch anything in Reese's memories?"*

He had, but everything looked the same up close. Stopping, he replayed what he'd gleaned of Reese's time at the hideout. The most prevalent exterior memories had shown a flat rock jutting from the canyon wall with a shelter hiding an opening. Spindly bushes with straggling sage green leaves marked either side. *"You see any bushes?"*

Air gusted across Eryx's face, and Ludan's energy zinged across Eryx's mental radar. *"Back this way. Thought I saw something closer to the top."*

Eryx followed and tried to wrestle his escalating impatience into submission. Every damned nook and cranny looked the same.

"Here." Ludan's energy stopped.

Sure enough, there it was. Maxis might be an underhanded blight on their race, but he had to give him credit for originality when it came to subterfuge. *"Ramsay, we've got the entrance. You found yours?"*

"Just found it." Ramsay's voice resonated with an extra bite. *"Two rebellion guards tipped us off. Not the best training. They're out."*

"Out for a nap, or for good?"

"Out for good."

Well, that explained the extra bite. *"Might want to save the rest for questions, brother."* Eryx drifted forward. *"Slow and easy going in. We've stirred enough to wake anyone with half a pulse. I don't want to give anyone else inside reason to run."*

Ever the mother hen, Ludan flew in front of Eryx's path. *"Ever consider you're killin' our job benefits?"*

Eryx let his somo have the lead for the moment, but if they found Ian or Maxis, a mountain wouldn't be able to block his path. *"Find me Ian and you can have free rein at the training grounds Reese told us about."*

"A bonus. Nice." Ludan touched down on the landing, Eryx a second behind him.

Ten or fifteen feet into the tunnel, a torch glowed bold orange, near red. Behind the puddle of light, was nothing but black void.

A steady draft slithered down the corridor and energy pinged against Eryx's senses. *"Up and on the right. Whoever it is is strong. Too strong to be human."*

"Rebellion lackeys." Ludan shimmered into view. *"I'm done with the cloak and dagger bit."*

Eryx dropped his mask as well and grabbed Ludan's shoulder. *"They fight, they're out. They surrender, they get a hearing. We clear?"*

Ludan's jaw shifted side to side.

"Reese made bad choices for the wrong reasons," Eryx said. *"There could be more like him. They roll, they get a chance to come clean."*

Ludan nodded and strode forward, his clipped steps a calling card for whoever waited.

Two warriors stepped into the tunnel, eyes wide with fear, hands fisted and ready to engage.

One swung a punch at Ludan.

Ludan dodged and gripped the fist as it flew past his check. Torquing the man's arm behind his back, Ludan leveled a dagger at his throat. "Knees. Now."

The warrior hit his knees.

Ludan glared at the other man, still shell-shocked. "That means you too." He wrenched his hold on the man in front of him enough to elicit a whimper. "Unless you want to take me on."

Shell-shocked dropped and put his hands behind his head.

Ludan grunted and stowed his dagger, but kept his captive's arm locked at a painful angle. "Maxis didn't dig deep for you boys, did he?"

"You two are lucky he's in a good mood." Eryx stepped between the kneeling men. "You get two choices. Get us to the heart of this beehive or take your chances with my moody somo. What's your pick?"

The men wide-eyed it with each other.

"I'll take you," Shell-shocked said.

The other one flinched and glared at his partner. "Maxis will kill you."

Ludan wrenched his arm again and crouched close. "I won't. But I'll make you wish I had."

The two kept the silent eyeballing up for another second or two before Ludan's captive relented and ducked his head.

With his dagger hand, Ludan motioned Shell-shocked to his feet. "You lead."

The four of them headed down the tunnel. Not-so-tough guy shuffled behind Eryx as best he could with Ludan twisting his arm between his shoulder blades.

Eryx nudged Shell-shocked in front of him. "How many more of you?"

The warrior cast a guilty glance over one shoulder, but trudged forward. "There are three entrances, two men at each entrance and one near the pens."

Ludan chuffed. "Shit for security."

"We had more," Shell-shocked said. "Uther's pulled most out on some big—"

"Neil." Not-so-tough lurched from Ludan's grip and aimed for his fellow warrior.

Ludan intercepted and a sick crack rattled down the dark corridor.

Not-so-tough slumped to the rock in a lifeless heap, his head at an all-wrong angle.

With a careless step over the body, Ludan rolled his shoulders and got up close to Neil/Shell-shocked. "You were saying?"

"Later," Eryx said before Neil could answer. He jerked his chin toward the blackness. "I want this over with." He switched to tell-coms. *"You're up, Ramsay. Got another entrance we need to cover, two men at each one. I want prisoners."* He stepped alongside Ludan and raised an eyebrow. *"Not dead men."*

Ludan shrugged, though it was shallow enough to admit he might have been trigger-happy. *"He was about to shut our source up."*

Ramsay's chuckle wound through their open link. *"Guess I'm not the only bloodthirsty bastard. I'm heading up the ramp. Wesley's hunting for the other exit."*

Eryx followed Ludan and Neil around a wide corner and the tunnel opened to a thirty-by-thirty circular room. A lifeless fire pit sat at its center, squat oak chairs arched around one side, and a tall-backed, onyx wanna-be throne at the other. Otherwise the place was a big zero.

"Not feeling all that impressed." Eryx strode toward the black tunnel on the other side of the room. "Where's that go?"

Neil swallowed and the color drained from his face. "The pens."

"I'm thinking not the animal variety." Ludan stepped up tight behind Neil. "Am I right?"

Neil nodded, but the action looked damned pained.

Eryx motioned with his head. "Move it."

Hustling around the far side of the fire pit, Neil took up point.

"Report," Eryx said to Ramsay.

His brother sounded a whole lot more pissed off than he had a few minutes ago. *"Wes found the second entrance. Men are contained. Got a talkative one who said Maxis took off five, maybe ten minutes before we got here and didn't look so good."*

Fuck. Not fast enough. The lights in this tunnel were fewer, the dullish red glow barely enough to cast a shadow. Eryx stepped up the pace. *"Anyone with him?"*

"Not a soul."

Well, that was a plus, he hoped. "How much farther?"

Neil ducked around a sharp curve, then V'd to the left. "Fifteen yards, on the right."

Eryx opened his emotional senses and damned near tripped. "He's here."

"Who's here?" Neil drew up short and his eyes widened.

"Not your fearless leader, that's for sure." Ludan shoved Neil forward. "Move."

Eryx shot forward and Ludan cursed behind him. *"Follow my link,"* he said to Ramsay. *"Target the emotions if it helps. The damned place is a pain powder keg."*

He rounded the last turn and stopped. "Shit."

Ten scarred wooden doors lined a crude hallway, five on each side. Agony pulsed from each one, the impact enough to churn his stomach.

"Almost there," Ramsay said.

Ludan pushed Neil toward the center. "I'll take the right."

Eryx nodded, eyes to Neil. "You really think this kind of shit's right?"

Neil shook his head.

"Then make yourself useful. Get 'em open."

Neil turned for the far end on the left side, notably as far as he could get from Ludan.

Eryx took the first door on his right.

Metal latches clanged up and down the rock walls as they unlocked the doors, and quiet sobs and gasps sounded in their wake.

No light shone inside the first one. Eryx stepped in and nearly buckled at the stench. He coughed, covering his nose with the back of one hand, and lit the room with a steady flame from the palm of the other.

A woman lay huddled on her side, naked. Long, matted black hair covered her face and shoulders, her skin a sickly color. He crouched beside her and touched her arm. Dead. "That son of a bitch."

Ramsay barreled in behind him. "You find—" He stared at the lifeless woman, his jaw slack.

"Yeah." Eryx stood. "Hopin' they're not all this way."

They checked more cells and found seven other women, all with a pulse. Barely. None had clothes, and all were curled into tight, defensive balls. Ludan stroked a shorthaired redhead's back, her tremors so violent Eryx thought she might be mid-seizure. Neil cradled another weeping woman's head on his lap.

Two more doors to go.

"I'll get one, you get the other." Ramsay headed to the next to the last door, leaving Eryx the corner cell.

Eryx pulled the latch, bile and doubt churning in his gut. At this rate, he wouldn't eat for a week. If Ian wasn't here—

Nope. Not going there right now. He fired a thin flame from his palm.

Another woman cowered as far from the door as possible, her knees pulled up tight to her chest. Her voice cracked, thin and desperate. "Please."

Ramsay shouted from the cell beside his. "Eryx."

The woman flinched and ducked her head.

"It's all right." He scooped her up and hurried out to the others .

Ludan met him at the door and took his burden. "I got her. Go."

Two steps into Ramsay's cell, Eryx froze. It was Ian all right, but he'd seen roadkill in Evad look better.

Ramsay crouched beside him, two fingers at his carotid. Third degree burns circled his neck and his belly was bruised and bloated, a marquee for internal bleeding. "He's got a pulse, but it's thready."

Eryx kneeled beside him. "Go help Ludan. Get the girls out and get them home."

"I'll help—"

"Get 'em out and get 'em home." He met Ramsay's stare. "Take care of Lena and Reese, and get the prisoners in zeolite. I want this place cleaned out and Maxis unable to track anyone. Got me?"

"What about Ian?"

"I'll handle Ian." He'd already broken the laws. He'd be damned if he fucked up Ramsay's future too. "Now go."

* * * *

Maxis cracked one eye open and the harsh orange and red-rimmed Myren sun blasted across his sensitive retinas. He squeezed them shut and a tear slipped down his temple. Cool air dusted one cheek, dry, gritty soil beneath the other.

He tried to push upright. Pain stabbed his lower neck and shot across his shoulders and arms to tingle in his fingertips. Sweat broke out along his forehead. Where the fuck was he? The last thing he remembered he'd been in the air and headed for home, burning through Reese's cortex via link.

The presence. Somewhere along the way, another energy source had intervened. Maybe more than one. The next second, he'd been trapped, pulled taut between two anchors before a mix of fire and ice cleaved him down the middle. He'd been a good thousand feet in the air, his muscles unresponsive to any command, pain stabbing through his limbs and brain.

Voices sounded in the distance. Serena, maybe, and someone else.

Uther.

Fire burned up his neck and face, legs desperate to push upright. He couldn't be caught this way. Serena was one thing, but not Uther.

Nothing. Not so much as a twitch from his thighs or feet.

"Maxis?" Serena's urgent voice rang out and her slippered feet padded against the hard dirt. "Uther, hurry."

Maxis tried to speak, but all that came out was a chortled cough.

"Don't move him," Uther said.

A shadow fell across him, and the sun's glow behind his eyelids went dark. Uther's voice rumbled close to Maxis' ear. "Brace yourself."

Pain, fierce and unforgiving, darted up and down Maxis' spine, and then blessed, forgiving black.

Chapter 14

Reese shifted in his bed and a cool spring breeze brushed his naked torso. Galena's flowery scent wrapped around him, her softness pressed against him.

Perfect.

Whoa, wait. Galena? He opened his eyes.

Galena lay nestled in the crook of his arm, her hair trailing over his skin and onto crisp, white sheets. Morning sun shone through a large, arched window with panes thrown wide to let in fresh air. The room was huge with stone walls that soared a good ten to twelve feet high and quality accents that spoke of limitless wealth. Definitely not the homestead.

He rolled his head on the pillow and a sharp, stabbing pain pierced the back of his neck. Maybe moving wasn't such a great idea. What the hell had he done?

The meet point. Galena had been there, so much pain on her face he'd nearly dropped his plans and his pride to hold her. He'd taken flight instead and been lashed with something every bit as powerful as a thunderbolt.

"You're a blessed man."

Reese tensed and Clio shimmered into view at the foot of his bed. How in histus he'd kept from jumping out of bed on instinct was beyond him.

"Because you know my voice," she answered as though he'd spoken aloud. "Your mind recognizes me as one of its own."

"Is there anything in my head that's a secret to you?"

No answer, but her smirk said plenty.

Shit. Reese tightened his hold around Galena and tried to shift more protectively around her. Aches radiated from every joint.

"She'll not come to any harm by my hand, nor can she hear my voice." Clio touched the blanket just above his waist, and an instant peace settled over him. "Be at ease. I'd say you've earned your time with her."

Reese kept his grip anyway, her soft curves against his length an opportunity he wasn't passing up no matter who walked in. "What happened?"

For all the glow and glitter that surrounded the spiritu, her aura wavered. "One of the dark spiritu found you. A rogue by the name of Falon. We'd protected you, veiled your spirit to hide you from the rogues, but your relations with Galena made you vulnerable." She grinned, lightness twinkling in her eyes once more. "We probably should have accommodated for that contingency. Free will has a tendency to throw wrenches in the best laid plans."

So she saw that too. Kind of brought a disconcerting spectator aspect to any kind of intimacy. "I don't remember anything. Just a blinding jolt, nothing but piercing white behind my eyes."

"He attacked you."

"Falon?"

Clio paused, her mouth pursed. "Your brother."

The news shouldn't have fazed him, but somewhere along the way he'd begun to hope he might actually make a difference. "So I failed you."

"No. You haven't failed."

"But I didn't talk to him. I didn't even see him."

She smiled, soft like the first bit of sun over the morning horizon. "There are always new opportunities. The Great One willing, a new intersection will present itself. At least that is what we're hoping for. Such a chance may be the only way to stop what the dark rogues are working toward."

"What's a rogue? I thought there were only dark and light."

Clio lowered her head and trailed her fingertips along the foot of the bed as she floated toward the open window. "The law of reciprocity allowed me to tell you only so much." She folded her hands at her waist and studied the green landscape before facing him. "With the steps Falon has taken, I now have more leeway. Not that I wish you or any of your race to be caught up in his schemes."

"Whose schemes? Maxis'? Falon's?" The second his question was out, he regretted it. He'd lived through an undertaking he barely hoped to survive and Galena was stretched out beside him. The idea of additional risk didn't much appeal.

She shook her head. "Both, though Maxis is more of a pawn."

"Maxis? A pawn?" Reese slowly combed his fingers through Galena's hair, and the scent of flowers strengthened around him. "Maxis makes pawns, not the other way around."

"He's too blind to see the situation clearly. Falon is a powerful spiritu. Of the dark contingent, he's one of the most advanced." Clio drifted toward the side of the bed. "Your brother is the tipping point in bringing the light and dark passions out of balance. If left unstopped, his plans for slavery will snowball throughout the human and Myren races. Panic will rule the human realm, and greed the Myren realm. Once tipped, the scales will be near impossible to rebalance."

"Then why have me talk to Maxis? If he's the linchpin, why not just kill him like I wanted in the first place?"

Clio settled beside them and smoothed Galena's hair from her face. "You're so quick to draw your dagger." She folded her hands in her lap and fixed her attention on him. "Think about what you're advocating. Murder, however necessary, feeds the dark. And, while its act is simplistic, its weight is significant. The only way to counterbalance the weight of murder is to sway your brother via his conscience, to appeal to the goodness inside him. To win through persuasion carries more weight than if you kill him, weight that falls to the side of the light."

"You're saying the pen is mightier than the sword?"

She lifted one eyebrow, a look reminiscent of his mother the first time Reese had dared lie to her face. "Every courageous act has a different weight, just as every darker act has its own. The balance between the two is cumulative."

"Sounds like you'd be smarter to work this angle through Eryx." Anyone but him. Courageous acts weren't exactly his strong suit.

"Eryx has his own path to walk. My responsibility is to you and your future. You have many decisions ahead of you, none of them easy." Clio's gaze shifted to Galena. "All of them worth it."

The iron latch clunked, and the wide mahogany door opened.

Eryx strode through the opening, Ramsay and Ludan shoulder to shoulder behind him.

Wait. Clio was—

Gone.

The three warriors stared down at him from the foot of the bed, their scowls ranging from pissed off to outright murder.

Eryx crossed his arms and chin-lifted in Galena's direction. "You wanna explain this?"

Shit. Reese dropped the strand of hair he'd had between his fingers and rolled to his back. He'd be damned if he unwound his arm from around her torso, though. "I woke up this way." Galena stirred, and Reese lowered his voice. "I couldn't remember much past Maxis frying my brain cells, but I figured she had a lot to do with why I'm still breathing, so I let her sleep."

Galena pushed up with a hand at his chest. The deep auburn in her hair shimmered with the sun behind it, and the strands hung haphazard and sexy close to her cheeks. Her sleepy voice matched her languid eyelids, the lack of tension at her temples giving her an innocent quality he'd kill to protect. "You're awake."

"And alive," he said. "I have a feeling I have you to thank for that."

A sweet flush crept up her neck and across her cheeks. She ducked her head and beamed at the three still frowning men at the end of the bed. "Not just me. They had something to do with it to. Most of it, really." She sat up, putting her back to Ludan and her brothers. "They broke your link."

Silence.

Reese rewound through what she said, but it still didn't make sense. "Come again?"

"They broke your link with Maxis. He can't attack you anymore."

He looked to the trio. "How?"

Eryx's gaze shifted to Galena and a wash of pride eased his harsh expression. "Galena figured it out. I traced Maxis' presence with my link to you, Ramsay and I anchored the link on either side——"

"And I sliced it," Ludan finished.

So, he was free. A tiny detail with huge implications Clio hadn't mentioned. He had a feeling it had an angle in the other news she'd shared.

Galena stroked his forehead and a lock of her hair fell forward. "How do you feel?"

He lifted his hand, ready to smooth the long fiery piece between his fingers, but checked the action and rubbed his chest instead. "Like a night after too much strasse and a nosedive from a mountain. Other than that, tolerable."

"Well enough for a trip to council?" Eryx glared at the hand Reese had narrowly diverted.

"No." Galena cut in before he could answer. "He needs time to heal. You saw the damage in his——"

"Wasn't asking you, Galena." Eryx stared at Reese, a perfect poker face. "You up for a trip to council?"

His throat tightened and a cautionary buzz hummed at the base of his skull. "If that's what you need."

Ramsay looked away, a muscle on the side of his neck twitching.

Ludan stayed stone-faced, no doubt ready to dish out cold merciless judgment.

Eryx's face was a blank slate, impossible to read. "Maxis got away."

Not good news.

"We did get my baineann's friend," Eryx said. "That makes my mate happy, which makes me feel a whole lot more generous where you're concerned."

Better news.

"It doesn't, however, absolve you of your actions with the Rebellion."

Shit. And then Eryx had walked in to find his sister cozied up next to a traitor on top of everything else. He still wouldn't have moved away.

"Here's what I'm offering." Eryx uncurled his arms and planted his fists on the footboard. At that angle, his appearance went from warrior to fuckin' scary. "Your testimony of Maxis' plans and actions in the time you've conspired with him, complete with the names of those involved, in exchange for a pardon."

Galena sucked in a sharp breath and her hand fisted on the bed.

Ramsay glared at Reese.

Ludan stayed rock still.

Reese should have been sucking in huge gulps of air and offering a hand to shake on, but all he could focus on was the gaping hole spinning bigger and bigger in his soul. What had he expected would happen? That all would be forgiven? That he'd somehow end up serving the malran?

He pictured himself in front of the council, admitting his involvement with the rebellion. He imagined the disappointment on his mother's face, and the sadness that had always shadowed her whenever she spoke of Evanora and her schemes now aimed at him. Clio hadn't been lying. He had loads of decisions to make and not a damned one of them easy.

Ramsay's feelings weren't too much of a stretch to untangle, his scowl practically dared Reese to take the offer. Galena, on the other hand, kept her elbows tucked to her sides and her lips mashed up tight.

If Reese did what Eryx asked, he'd be a free man, able to start over. And maybe, just maybe, get to a place where Galena might consider him for more than one, secret night.

He met Eryx's stare. "I accept."

* * * *

Galena trudged toward the castle's vast guest wing, her muscles better from the few hours she'd napped beside Reese, but still sorely in need of a solid night's sleep. Men. Overbearing Neanderthals deep down, every damned one of them. Maybe it was a good thing they'd asked her to leave while they plotted their strategy with the counsel. Anger alone had fueled her trek to check on Ian in Eryx's old room in the royal wing, and it was probably the only thing keeping her up and moving to see Brenna now.

Voices rumbled from the vast dining hall below, staff gathered for the noonday meal, beef brisket by the smell of it. The bite of bay leaf and rosemary were unmistakable even from this distance, and Orla almost always paired the two for her brisket buffets.

Galena's belly grumbled a not-so-subtle request. Probably smart to stop for a bite or two after she checked on Brenna. If she snuck into the kitchen from the back rooms, she'd have a better shot of missing Orla and having to explain why she still had on yesterday's wrinkled tunic and leggings. She'd get in, get out, and then nothing had better come between her and her bed for at least eight to ten hours.

Gripping the handrail for an extra tug, she forced her way up the gray stone steps, her sandals quiet in the shadows. Eryx needed to find a way to get Lexi to rest. Galena hadn't asked how long Lexi had held her bedside vigil, but the dark circles under her eyes said plenty. Eryx had done a great job healing Ian, but whether or not he'd wake up was another worry altogether. And even if he did, how was Lexi going to explain where he was, her role in her new realm, and everything she was now capable of? Not an easy task no matter how one sliced it.

Yeah. Like figuring out how to deal with a rebellion warrior who'd turned over a new leaf as a love interest would be any simpler.

"Humph." Galena strode down the long guest hall, the thick maroon rug muffling each step. For the life of her, she couldn't decide what to do. First Reese had ignored her at the meet point. Then he'd covered for her falling asleep beside him. She'd never figure out the look he'd given her before accepting Eryx's offer. Was it interest? Or was he trying to tell her to keep her mouth shut about their night together?

Well, yeah. She couldn't blame him being cautious on that score. Eryx might have been decent, but the two of them weren't going to be best friends anytime soon. Ludan had seemed sort of human in his detached killer kind of way. But Ramsay? Total jerk. Nowhere near the forgive and forget stage.

Galena rounded the corner, knocked on Brenna's door, and pushed it wide. Lexi was right. Her brothers' opinions shouldn't factor into her decisions. It wasn't like Reese had done anything——

She pulled up short, one hand shooting out to the rough stone wall for support. Spring sunshine poured through the open window, every detail in its proper place. Except for one.

Brenna was gone.

Chapter 15

Eryx stormed the council hall steps two at a time, Ludan and Ramsay at his side. He motioned Reese up from behind them and paused inside the vestibule.

Reese stopped in front of him, clad in the same leather pants and cotton shirt combo he'd worn the day before, though the getup looked a whole lot better now thanks to Orla. Under normal circumstances the outfit would've stood out, but with Eryx, Ludan, and Ramsay in warrior gear it wasn't as bad. No better way to make it clear warfare lay ahead than a visual.

"When we get to the front, fall out beside Ludan and hang close to the East wall," Eryx said to Reese. "They'll assume you're here in a military capacity and I'd rather not tip my hand before I'm ready." He paused long enough to let his instructions settle. "You good?"

Reese nodded. "I am." Not exactly a convincing response. More like a man resigned to a visit with a guillotine. Though in a way, he was. By the end of the day he'd have so much nasty social stigma glommed onto him he'd probably wish for death.

Outside, the council bells gonged, and a crush of ellan streamed toward the main hall, their voices punctuated with animated gestures.

Ludan glared at them over one shoulder, arms crossed. "You sure got their panties in a wad."

"Two unexpected summons in less than two weeks?" Ramsay smiled despite Reese being so close. "Hell, yeah, they're in a tail spin. Word in the ranks is they're worried the prophecy is somehow gonna upend their jobs."

Eryx kept his silence. The light-hearted banter was well and good, but he couldn't afford to lose focus. Delivery was key in what he planned. One misstep and he'd dig up more political pitfalls.

When only a few straggling council members remained, he stepped from the shadows and angled toward the main hall entrance. "Remember what I said. The message needs to be clear. No holds barred as it relates to Maxis."

Ludan sounded almost cheerful. "That mean I get to have a little fun?"

Twisted humor for sure, but Eryx could use a little levity about now. "If you can scare 'em with a look, have at it. Everything else stays on lockdown."

They stepped into the cavernous room.

Ludan shrugged. *"Better than what I normally get."*

"Sick bastard," Ramsay said.

Ludan grinned. *"Hell, yeah."*

Their boot heels struck the concrete in heavy, rhythmic strides. By the time they reached the steps to the dais, the crowd's rumbled conversation silenced.

As ordered, Reese made for the side wall.

Ludan and Ramsay faced the council, feet shoulder width and arms at their sides, their tension evident. Two predators prepped to pounce.

Eryx climbed the steps to his platinum throne, Lexi's empty one beside it. Sunlight highlighted both from the domed windowed above. Fuck he wished she was here. If nothing more than to balance him. But her place was with Ian. With the injuries he'd sustained, he'd need all the support he could get, assuming he ever woke up.

To histus with sitting. He faced his council and nursed his anger toward Maxis. So damned many atrocities visited on undeserving people. Two dead women, and seven others too skittish to talk or do more than huddle in whatever corner they found, Ian, Brenna, Reese. His mate.

The weight of every gaze pressed heavy on him. Vendors from the street outside shouted and children laughed, all of it muffled by tall glass windows. "There have been rumors of increased actions with the Lomos Rebellion. I'm here today to confirm the Rebellion has indeed resurfaced."

Whispers rippled down the cavernous room, council members leaning into each other, mouths covered. Nirana forbid they actually hold their snarky comments until a more appropriate time.

"Up until last night, certain security matters required I keep my silence. Now that I've secured those in danger and procured my evidence, it's time you learn the details." He paused, waiting for everyone's attention. "All of them."

From his height on the dais, Eryx zeroed in on Angus in the back row, his wild gray hair making his presence easy to single out. "You each know our malress was one of our lost. What I have kept from you is her Myren heritage was not assured before I brought her to Eden."

Grumbles and whispers filled the room.

"Silence." An eerie stillness settled in the wake of his outburst. "I'd planned to research her history first. In fact, I'd scanned her memories without her consent for clues, and intended to have my sister scan for any Myren markers to confirm her ancestry. Before I could, we were attacked by Maxis Steysis."

The grumbling ignited once more, and this time he gave them free reign.

Angus bellowed from the back of the room. "So you broke the tenets."

"You called that one right." Ramsay's telepathic thought brushed through Eryx's mind.

"Bitterness is pretty predictable." With a little luck, the rest of his dominos would fall in the right order as well.

"I did what was necessary to protect a woman I suspected was Myren," Eryx said. "Maxis Steysis attacked us without provocation and in plain sight of humans. Through *his* actions, our race was exposed. My duty, my right, as malran, is to see to the safety of all within our race, even those I have not yet confirmed as one of our own."

Those who'd twisted to witness Angus' accusations slowly faced the front.

"Alexis was taken to a secluded section of our realm and, at her agreement, participated freely in the awakening ritual, confirming my suspicions as to her race. Had I brought this matter before you, I risked alerting Maxis of my search and giving him means to flee." Eryx paused long enough to make eye contact with those most influential. "Shortly after my mating, Maxis solidified his treasonous actions and kidnapped a human male, an honored friend of our malress. We've now retrieved the male and found eight human women he captured from Evad as well, all in abhorrent health."

A younger male ellan situated midway in the assembly stood, his face flushed. "I move we charge Maxis Steysis with treason against our most sacred mandates, both in revealing our race, and in interfering with human destiny."

"Then our malran is guilty too." Angus stood as quickly as his aged body would allow. "If you charge Maxis, you must charge Eryx as well."

"His charge is to protect us," the man answered. "I see no wrong in his actions."

"You might want to hear the rest." All attention snapped to Eryx, his words silencing the murmuring crowd. "I, too, have interfered in human destiny, though I believe my actions were warranted."

He prowled down from the dais. "The human male and one of the females were in dire condition when they were found, wounds inflicted by Maxis and his lackeys. On the basis of historic precedence, I healed both humans."

"What basis?" Angus spat his words with enough venom to sear the air. "You expect all to be held accountable to the tenets, but you're to be spared the consequences? You think—"

Angus flew through the air and slammed against the rear wall, his torso snapping against the stone a mere second before his head did the same.

Eryx stood, calm with his hands behind his back. "I can hold you there for days and not break a sweat, Angus. I hold this throne, as my family has since the beginning of our race, for two reasons. Power, and the honor with which I yield it."

Angus' shaky breaths reverberated through the cavernous room.

Every ellan ignored the old man, eyes riveted to Eryx. "In my grandfather's reign, a rebellion fighter fled to Evad and slit a human's throat in an attempt to divert his pursuers. My grandfather ordered his healing, stating the intercession corrected a wrong inflected by one of our own. The council reviewed the action and approved it. This case is no different."

He loosened his mental hold on Angus, and the old man collapsed to the floor in an ungraceful heap.

"Now you know the facts," Eryx said. "All of them. I stand by my decisions and the integrity with which they were made. Had it not been for Maxis and the rebellion's actions none of them would have been necessary."

"What became of the human healed by your grandfather's men?" This from a woman in the front row, her question more sincere than argumentative.

"The human never knew how he came to be healed as it occurred when he was unconscious."

"And the impact of the healing?"

Eryx tried to make eye contact with whoever asked the question, but couldn't find them in the crowd. "There are no records of the human beyond the healing, though I intend to research it."

The same ellan who'd motioned for the charge against Maxis stood. "The captured humans are still in Eden, my Malran?"

Eryx nodded.

"How do you propose they be dealt with? If their treatment was as you say, modifying their memories is no longer an option."

And that was the kicker. The wrinkle he'd been unable to iron out no matter how he'd angled the situation, save one. "I propose these humans be given the choice to remain and live in Eden for the rest of their days, abiding by Myren law. If they agree, they can remain here, safe and alive."

Angus' voice shook. "And if they don't?"

"Then the council will have to decide if they live or die. If they choose death, then I will be the one to carry out the sentence."

* * * *

From his place along the side wall, Reese shifted his weight. Not enough to call attention to himself, but enough to shake the tension gripping his spine. Man, the malran had balls. No doubt about it. Playing chicken with your own skin was one thing, but stepping up and saying you'd take an innocent's life if someone else said it had to happen?

Yeah, kind of made his tiny, upcoming confession look like a cozy, fireside fantasy. If the spiritu was right and courageous acts held more influence, then Eryx had just put a few extra weights on the light side of the scale. Reese wasn't entirely sure how anything he could say would make that kind of difference.

Eryx eased onto his throne, arms relaxed against the gleaming platinum armrests. "The humans' fate is in the council's hands. As to sanctions against me for my actions, you'll have to do what you think is right. However, as malran, I have the right to take my own measures." He motioned the council page from his place on the front row. "Dunstan, make note. Maxis Steysis is hereby formally charged with treason against the throne and the Myren race."

Dunstan scribbled in his overlarge tome, his long ruby-colored tunic wavering with each broad pen stroke.

"Ramsay."

Ramsay snapped to attention at Eryx's command.

"Effective immediately Maxis Steysis is wanted by me and this council. Should he resist arrest, any and all force, including death, is acceptable in bringing him to justice. Further, any individual suspected of affiliation with the Lomos Rebellion will be apprehended and brought forward for trial with this council."

Ramsay jerked a nod and resumed his original stance facing the assembly.

Another ellan stood, his hands gripped nervously at his belly. "So you believe there to be a greater threat beyond Maxis? That the rebellion is truly active?"

"It's beyond belief," Eryx said. "I have proof Maxis is intent on not only promoting Lomos Rebellion ideals, but plans further transgressions against the human race."

"My Malran." An elder ellan situated in a box along the rear wall stood at her ivory balcony. "Perhaps it would be wise to share your evidence with the council. While your judgment and information may not be in question, as your advisors and representatives of the people, we have a right to know what challenges our race faces."

Gaze locked on the ellan, Eryx nodded. *"You're up."*

Eryx's summons right-hooked through Reese's head. He'd expected and braced for it, but hearing it rattled everything from head to toe.

Council members ducked close to each other and their whispers rippled across the room.

Reese's knees shook, thighs tensed and prepped to run. Sweat broke out along his spine and pressure circled his throat. He'd been in this same situation before, felt the same cloying response at his swearing in, and look what he'd done.

No one looked his way. Not Eryx. Not Ludan or Ramsay, not another word spoken aloud or via link.

Because the choice was his. His heart kicked at the realization and adrenaline buzzed beneath his skin. Clio believed in him, and Galena claimed to as well. Surely he could follow his mother's example and live with honor.

He stepped forward and the room spun. "The evidence is mine."

The chatter among the council settled. Dunstan's quill scratched the journal parchment.

Odd, the only person he could bear to watch as his gruff and grated admission slipped free was Ramsay. "I've shared Maxis' plans with the malran and confirmed them with access to my memories. I offer those to the council as well."

"And who, exactly, are you?" The question came from the old man Eryx had slammed against the wall.

"My name is Reese Theron." He chanced a glance at the crowd, faces blurry beneath his hazy vision. He could do this, get it out and be done with it. Be free and live a good life. A right life.

The image of Galena, lying beside him, peaceful in sleep, blasted to the forefront of his mind, and a root of resolution wrapped around his heart. "I know Maxis' plans because he's my brother."

Gasps and shouts filled the hall.

An ellan stood and spoke.

Another right behind him.

Then Eryx.

The voices ricocheted without context. The white noise in his head and the thrum of his pulse buzzed too loud to make sense of their meaning. Someone gripped his shoulder, and Reese shook himself into focus.

Eryx stood beside him, Ludan and Ramsay at his left. The ellan filtered out of the room, half of them already gone, the rest in line to exit.

"You did good," Eryx said.

"What happened?" Praise the Great One, he sounded vulnerable. Kinda wimpy, really, spotlighting how he'd strolled off to la-la land at the absolute worst time.

Eryx glanced at Ramsay and Ludan, and jerked his head toward the grand entrance. "Give me a few. And put a tail on Angus. That son of a bitch is on my last nerve, and I've got a good idea he's hand-holding Maxis."

Ramsay nodded, but his stare was on Reese. For once, the contact didn't seem based in anger, but whatever his once-friend was thinking, Reese couldn't discern it.

"What you did took courage," Eryx said after they'd walked away. "I know the last thing you wanted was to make that info public knowledge, but you probably saved a lot of lives."

Reese swallowed, bile sloshing in his gut. If Eryx knew what had finally gotten his lips moving, he wouldn't be so quick to offer praise.

"The pardon is yours, but one wrong move negates your clean slate. We clear?"

Reese cleared his throat, even a simple answer difficult to formulate. "Yeah. We're clear."

"Good. Then let's clear something else. This fresh start? I think step one is you clearing out of the castle."

If he'd felt upside down and disconnected before, it was nuked now. "I'm sorry?"

"You. The castle. Fresh start. I think space is a good thing for everyone involved. Too much history and hot tempers with you and Ramsay in fighting distance. Frankly, I don't need that shit right now."

And it got him a long damned way from Galena. Yeah, if he were in Eryx's shoes, he'd be shuffling the traitor out the back door too.

"I'm assuming you'll stay at your homestead?" Eryx said.

Reese stared out the two-story arched window on his left. The gold flecks from the brick-laid thoroughfare winked in early afternoon sunlight, and the rainbow-laced sky stretched without a single cloud to the horizon. "To start."

"Got anything you need sent there?"

Translation: *No, you're not gonna say good-bye to her either.*

"Nothing I need." At least not that he'd admit. He faced Eryx and straightened to attention. He could whine like a damned dog when he made it home, but for now he needed to keep his back up. "If I think of something, I'll go through you."

A nod, a handshake, and that was it. Eryx, Ludan, and Ramsay were gone, and he was as free as the day he was born. No commitments, and no threats or hidden shame hanging over his head. So, why in histus did he feel like the world had just gone to shit?

Chapter 16

Galena took the stairs down the main foyer as fast as she dared, her footsteps as frantic as her heart's rhythm. Brenna wasn't anywhere. She'd searched every guest room, scoured the living areas, and even checked the royal wing. Not one worker had seen any unfamiliar women up and about.

"Praise the Great One, Lena. Are those yesterday's clothes?" Orla stood beside a castle maid, a checklist in her hand and a frown on her face. "You've got more wrinkles on you than I have on my forehead."

"Now's a bad time, Orla." Galena strode to the soaring window overlooking the entry gardens. Empty, not a single soul wandering the well-tended paths, at least not from what she could see at this angle. "Have either of you seen Brenna?"

"Is she awake?" Orla joined her at the window.

"I hope so." Galena glanced over her shoulder. No sounds filtered from the dining room or receiving room, and no guards roamed the halls. "If not, we've got problems because she's gone."

Orla's eyebrows rose. She held out her tablet to the castle maid. "Wait for me in the kitchens. Not a word to anyone until I tell you otherwise."

The woman scurried off, her long skirts swishing with each step.

Orla lowered her voice. "What do you mean she's gone?"

"I mean I went to check on her and her bed was empty."

"Maybe she's just looking—"

"I've looked everywhere. The guest wing, the rooms down here, the royal wing. If she's inside the castle, she's huddled tight." From the foyer all she could see were the garden's white sand paths up front. She'd have to walk the garden if she wanted to be sure Brenna wasn't there.

"You think someone's taken her?"

Galena swallowed. "I don't know what to think. Maxis took Lexi. What if he wanted his property back?" She shook her head. "The things he did to her were horrid."

"We need to alert the guards, Jagger at least."

"No." Galena gripped Orla's shoulder. "The last thing Brenna needs to see is a man bearing down on her, let alone one of our warriors."

Orla scowled, the tiny age lines around her mouth making the movement even more pronounced. "I don't like it, Lena. If the castle's been breached——"

"Thirty minutes. Thirty more minutes and I'll find Jagger and tell him myself. If you help me and we split up we can cover more ground."

Hands planted at her hips, Orla let out a huff. "All right, thirty minutes. I'll get Jilly to help too, but we meet back here and stay in constant contact, agreed?"

Galena opened the front doors with her mind, and the warm afternoon air rushed against her face. "You two search the house. I'm checking the gardens."

"Galena."

Orla's voice stopped her mid-stride.

"Constant contact every five minutes or I'm contacting Eryx myself. I don't like the way this feels. Not one bit." Orla white-knuckled the stair rail. "You may not be my blood, but you're still my baby girl."

Galena's heart and breath hitched. For all the high expectations Orla may have had for her through the years, she'd also nurtured and held her when no one else would. "I'll be fine. Just help me find her." She turned away before Orla could say anything else, the fear in her former nanny's demeanor more than she could process right now. It couldn't be Maxis. The guards posted at the castle since Lexi's kidnapping were elite, loyal to the core. Even those she'd known since childhood underwent regular screenings now, their memories constantly scrutinized for signs of treason.

Opening her senses, she hurried through the labyrinth paths, carefully combing the sections with tall grass and hip-height flowers. She might not be as skilled as her brothers in detection, but she could at least reach a good twenty to thirty foot perimeter. Even if her senses didn't lead her to Brenna, a little early warning system wouldn't hurt if Maxis had more people on the grounds.

The paths ended on the east side of the house. Nothing but workers and warriors wandered near the castle. Vibrant green grass with silver sparks stretched in a slow downward slope to her left, and the evergreen and indigo forest beyond it looked more like puffs of bold color than actual foliage. Surely Brenna hadn't made it that far. She might have been fully healed physically, but with no more than forced broth and water for nourishment, she had to be weak. Too weak to make the forest on foot.

To Galena's right, the iron gate and stone wall surrounding the private Shantos oasis stretched twelve feet tall, impossible to breach for a feeble human.

She let out a frustrated breath and closed her eyes. Wind gusted against her face and briny ocean air filled her lungs. The tiny hairs at her nape tickled her skin. If she was Brenna and she woke up alone in a strange place after years as a prisoner, where would she go?

Galena opened her eyes. She'd run, as far and as fast as her legs could take her.

Ahead, the bluff stretched in a crescent shape. A three-foot sandstone wall sat ten feet back from the ledge, more to prevent unintended falls than any type of access deterrent. The sea tossed below and slammed its waves against the white beaches and black lava-like cove walls.

An ugly weight built inside Galena, mushrooming out to plunk heavy in her stomach. Not the bluff. Praise the Great One, not the bluff.

She hurried forward, then ran.

Orla's voice sounded in her head, fear resonating loud and clear. *"Galena?"*

Galena didn't stop, taking to the air to cover more ground. *"I'm fine, but haven't found her. Anything on your end?"*

"Nothing yet."

Galena dropped the connection without another thought, her focus too honed on the ground below. She finished one half of the cove's arc and circled back for the other. Maybe it was time to call the men. If Brenna made the forest, waiting would only make the search more difficult.

A flutter of white flashed, a tiny flicker along the rock wall near the gate.

Galena landed, keeping her distance so as not to startle. Her pulse hammered at her neck. The ocean's push and pull turned deafening, and the wind frayed her nerves. She edged forward and the breath in her lungs left in a rush.

Brenna sat wedged in a small offset between the fence and the gatepost, knees tucked in tight with her forehead resting on top.

"Brenna."

The girl's head whipped up and she squeaked.

"It's okay." Galena knelt beside her and the ocean-damp grass seeped through her cotton leggings. "You're safe. My name's Galena. I'm a friend of Lexi. Do you remember her?"

Such soulful eyes, so dark they bordered on black, a perfect match to the twin braids on either side of her head. Tears streaked her face, and her nose and cheeks bloomed a splotchy red. Her voice eked out, scratchy and broken. "The woman from Master's home?"

"Maxis, you mean?"

Brenna shivered, pulled her knees in tighter, and bobbed her head.

"Yes, that's Lexi. She'd very much like to see you. Would you come with me so we can let her know you're all right?"

"She's okay?"

"She's perfectly fine. Do you remember what happened?"

Brenna stared at the ocean, her gaze distant. "The man with the gun. He aimed it at her."

"He did, but Lexi's fine." Galena hesitated. "You saved her, Brenna. The bullet hit you instead."

Looking down, Brenna felt her shoulder, her work-hardened fingertips snagging on the soft cotton sheath they'd dressed her in. Her nails were short and jagged. "I don't feel anything."

"That's because Eryx healed you."

She rubbed the exact spot the bullet hit, the heel of her hand pressing deep. Her lower lip trembled. "Why would he do that?"

A slow, steady ache blossomed. She was so damned young, twenty-two or twenty-three at most given her body's composition, yet her voice wavered with the weight of an elder. "Because you're worth saving."

Tears welled in Brenna's eyes, but she dropped her forehead back to her knees before they could fall.

Galena eased closer. Laying a hand on one shoulder, she sent her calming energy through the girl. "You're safe now, Brenna. Nothing can hurt you here. All you need to do is rest and heal."

"I want to go home." Brenna sniffled and lifted her head. "I want to see my family."

Avoidance wasn't Galena's strong suit, at least not outside her personal life. Her feelings for Reese she could avoid all day long, but in this situation, a diversion seemed almost necessary. "Let's go back to the castle. You need to eat and we can get you some dry clothes."

Brenna shook her head and swiped one cheek with her shoulder. "I like it here."

"By the ocean?"

Brenna nodded.

"Did you live near the water where you grew up?"

"We lived in Texas, but my parents took me to a place like this." Her voice cracked at the end and her lips locked up tight. "It wasn't as pretty as this, but it was nice. The next day we went to Disney World. That's where Maxis snatched me."

Galena kept her silence and rubbed Brenna's back, pushing calming energy into her quivering muscles.

Brenna's gaze sharpened and her voice firmed. "I want to go home."

A placating lie rose to Galena's lips, but she swallowed it. Too many wrongs had been thrust on this sweet girl for her to add any more. She took a deep breath. "I'm sorry, Brenna. We can't take you home."

* * * *

A noise echoed over and over in Maxis' head, short on the upswing, long and winded on the way down. With every repetition his chest burned and tiny zaps scampered along his rib cage.

No, it wasn't a noise, it was him breathing, each push and pull far too labored and shallow.

Serena's voice echoed as though it came from a tunnel. "Maxis?" Her peppermint breath fluttered against his face, and smooth cool skin skated against the back of his hand at this side. "Open your eyes."

He pried open his eyes and tried to turn his head. Fiery jolts shot through every nerve from his neck to his fingers and toes, and his lungs seized on a strangled moan.

"Uther." Serena disappeared from his line of sight, her near-white hair flying out behind her. "Uther he's awake."

Whitewashed walls stretched twenty or so feet, a wide window at its center with thick navy curtains pulled tight.

Bootheels struck wood-planked floors, heavy, but not hurried.

Uther rounded the bed. Had it not been for the dark circles under the man's eyes, Maxis would have almost bought his careless facade.

His throat was too dry for more than a croak. "Where."

Uther raised a negligent hand and a utilitarian tan club chair slid into view. He settled himself, resting one ankle over his knee. "You're at my homestead in the Underlands."

Serena cupped the back of Maxis' neck, lifted him, and pressed a glass against his lower lip. "Drink."

Cool water rushed across his parched tongue. He swallowed and nearly choked, sputtering as he fought the liquid's sweet sting.

"Smaller sips first." She backed the glass away and gave him a chance to settle. "You've been out almost twenty-four hours. You need fluids."

Maxis tried again, more successful the second time, though painful darts shot down his spine. "No one lives in the Underlands." His ragged-old-man-ish voice sent him back for another drink.

Uther shrugged. "I do. At the border of Asshur, anyway. Far enough out to avoid guests." He assessed Maxis' prone position. "All things considered, I didn't think you'd want witnesses. I sure as hell wouldn't."

Serena eased his head to the pillow and the pain dulled to a steady throb.

"What happened?" Maxis aimed the question at Serena.

Uther answered. "We were hopin' you'd tell us."

An impotent rage billowed through him, his useless body preventing even the tiniest outlet for his emotion. "Reese." He coughed and a fresh shockwave rattled his torso. "He's still alive. I found him and others around the cave and attacked."

"Attacked how?" Serena settled on the bed beside him, her head slanted at a wary angle.

Fuck. The pain was making him sloppy. "A gift. A protective measure I hold with those I share a link with."

Uther leaned forward and rested his elbows on his knees. "Looks like Reese fought back."

No, not just Reese, but Maxis wasn't going to share that with these two. Reese and whoever was with him might have found a way to fight it, but he wasn't stupid enough to pass such info around. He needed what links he had to keep the people around him in line.

"I was midair when he struck." Maxis closed his eyes and let out a ragged exhale. "How bad's the damage?"

The cushions from Uther's chair groaned. His heavy footsteps sounded around his bed, and up on his right. "Bad. I stabilized you, but I'm no healer. Neither is Serena."

"Then get one." He'd meant it as a roar, but all he got was a garbled croak and fresh torture.

"Not thinking that's wise," Uther said. "Any healer who gets their hands on you gets a long, clear look at your memories. You sure you want that?"

Maxis opened his eyes. Freshly whitewashed boards stared back at him. If Uther had healed him, he'd had the same uninhibited access as a healer.

The son of a bitch towered in Maxis' periphery. "Didn't think so."

Maxis let out a slow breath and experimented with moving his feet. "What have you heard? Any news?"

"Not yet," Uther said. "Men are on lockdown at the camp. Wanted to wait until you were stable before I headed out."

Serena fidgeted at his side. "I could go." She straightened the blanket stretched across his bare chest, his family mark on her arm sinister in the room's dim light. "You heard the kind of man my father is. He'll know the latest." She glanced between him and Uther and shrugged, though something about the move seemed off. "I'll go, grab a few things, and pretend I'm headed somewhere else."

"That wasn't the plan." A fierceness he couldn't quite identify spread through him. "Your father's an ass. When you go, you'll go with me."

Scowling, she pushed to her feet. "I've handled my father fine this long, and it's not as if you're in any shape to stop me." She strode toward the bedroom door.

"Serena," Maxis said.

She kept going.

Uther intercepted and grabbed her by the arm.

It took everything he had to twist his head to see her. The scorpion he'd marked her with stretched along her forearm, as fierce as the woman who bore it. "Take Uther with you and cover your mark."

Chapter 17

Reese flew toward the morning horizon, eyes stinging from the wind's bite and lack of sleep. The grass below shimmered from rains the night before. The moist air left a damp sheen on his bare arms and his cotton tank clung to his chest.

He landed just outside a ring of Lyrita trees. Their smooth chocolate trunks reached toward the morning's bright pink skyline topped by exotic pearl blooms the size of his fist. All night he'd thought about his actions, what steps should be the first in his new lease on life. Most had steered toward Galena, a drive he wasn't sure he could define or explain shoving him toward actions that scared the hell out of him. But the one he was about to take took terror to a whole new level.

The Lyritas lined a quarter-mile arch and protected a quiet clearing in the valley's center. He'd lost count of the times he'd been here, every one of them with Ramsay, his old friend's go-to place for natxu. Now, here he was again, ready to atone for the wrongs he'd dealt his friend in the name of pride, even it was a fool's errand.

He trudged through the trees, and the morning breeze brushed his bared arms and neck. The contact on his arms was one thing, but the sensation on the back of his neck was something altogether intimate. He'd never bound his hair before. Not that he had a justifiable reason to bind it today. In truth, the timing was rotten because Ramsay certainly wouldn't miss such a detail. No Myren man would. But he was done with half-truths and deception. It might take months, even years to earn Galena's attention, but he'd make his intentions clear from the start.

A blue larken swooped from its perch with a happy chirp, its wings tipped with lavender.

Reese's soft steps echoed through the forest, a delicate *schlip* where his boots met wet turf.

The rising sun filtered through the trees ahead. Another thirty or so steps and he'd know if his trip was a wasted one. Adrenaline pricked beneath his skin. He was stupid to get himself worked up, melodramatic and highly assumptive. For all he knew, Ramsay didn't even use this place for training anymore.

Twenty feet away from the clearing, he levitated two hand spans from the ground and drifted forward, more out of respect than secrecy. He'd timed his arrival to catch Ramsay at the end of natxu, not interrupt mid-drill. No point in starting off on the wrong foot.

A fat shaft of sunlight crested the treetops on the far side of the glade as Reese stepped into the clearing.

Shit.

Ramsay faced away from him, a towel around his neck and head rolling side to side as if to loosen up for a fight. "A rhino would've stomped through there quieter."

So much for not starting off on the wrong foot. "Stealth wasn't the point."

Ramsay turned, scooped his drast off the ground, and strode toward Reese. "You got balls coming here." He stopped at punching distance, hands loose at his sides. Only an idiot missed such a clue. Ramsay's stance wasn't about attitude, it was about a man pissed off and ready to throw a jab at the first provocation. "Someone better be dead or planning an attack." He paused long enough to scrutinize Reese's bound hair. "Better sure as hell not be about anything else."

"I'm here because I owe you something."

Ramsay scoffed and walked the opposite direction. "You don't owe me shit."

Reese lurched forward and pulled him to a stop.

Ramsay acquiesced, but glared at Reese over one shoulder. "You wanna drop that hand and you wanna do it quick."

Reese released his hold. "Five minutes. Your brother gave me a chance. Give me five minutes to make it worth his gift."

Leaves rustled in the treetops and random birdsong lilted from the skies, but everything else lay quiet.

Ramsay stared at the opposite end of the field, the muscle at the back of his jaw working overtime. "Talk."

Fuck. He'd thought about what he'd say for a good chunk of the night, but damned if any of it came to mind now. "Your family was perfect," he said. "Not the royalty, but the family. A mom and a dad, a brother, a sweet little sister, friends. Everything I wanted." He cleared his throat, everything he wanted to say jumbled with years of embarrassment and shame. Laughable really, enough so he probably needed to fork over his man card.

To hell with holding it all in. He'd come this far, so he might as well get it out. "Your friendship meant a lot, and I didn't want you to see how ugly my situation was. It wasn't about using you and it wasn't a trap. I just didn't want to lose your friendship."

Ramsay glared back at Reese, chin aimed low and body angled to jet. "So you lied. Makes a helluva lot of sense." He stormed away.

"I was wrong."

Ramsay stopped.

"I knew it then," Reese said before Ramsay could take another step. "It was fear. Praise the Great One, put yourself in my shoes. Would you be so quick to claim Maxis as a brother?"

Ramsay glowered back at him. "So you've finally owned it. You think that makes it better? That my friend didn't think to trust me?"

"For you? Probably not. Trust isn't something you can refill. Once it's gone, it's gone. I get that. But I can try to take what your brother's given me and fix it going forward."

Silence.

Ramsay tensed and fisted his hands. He spun without another word and stomped toward the forest.

"That's it?" Reese followed. "Fuck, if you need to throw a punch, then do it."

Ramsay paused and shook his head. "Right now, walking away is the only option." And then he was gone, shooting to the sky as his mask settled into place.

* * * *

Galena strode down the guest corridor toward Brenna's room, her full skirt giving way to her long strides. The gown's cut was overkill for this early in the day, a crimson underdress with a long-sleeved, corseted overlay in black velvet, but for once she didn't mind dressing up.

Reese was free. He'd given his testimony and, with a little luck, she might run into him. No point in kidding herself, though. At best they might be able to start fresh. At worst, what they'd shared was a one-night-only deal. Either way, today she intended to find out.

Praise the Great One, she practically bounced with each step. Of course, ten hours of sleep, a hot shower, and clean clothes helped. A trifecta really, and easier on the eyes and nose. She knocked twice on Brenna's door and pushed it open a crack. "Brenna? You up?"

Rustling bedcovers sounded behind the thick wood. "I'm up."

Galena stepped into the room and stopped. "Brenna, you don't have to do that."

Brenna tugged the sheet and turned the down blanket over it. She smoothed the edges. "I'm used to it."

How sad was that? Making the bed itself wouldn't have been so bad if it hadn't been coupled with such a grim face.

Galena shuffled close and stilled Brenna's hands. "It's okay to let us take care of you for a bit."

Brenna trembled and backed away. "I always…It's what I know."

"So now you're going to learn something new." Galena turned her with a hand at her shoulder. "How to receive instead of give, at least for a while. All right?"

Brenna nodded and focused on the floor.

"Good. Did you see the dresses Jilly brought you?" Galena marched to the closet and glanced back.

Warily, Brenna followed her.

"I'm pretty sure you two wear the same size and her closet is packed thanks to Eryx and Ramsay. She loves them, and they love to hear her squeal." Pulling the doors open, Galena flipped through gowns. "If none of these work, we'll send the boys shopping."

Brenna ran her work-hardened fingers over a gown's royal blue sleeve, the velvet some of the softest made in Eden. Her eyes watered, filled with awe and longing.

Galena swallowed around the gargantuan knot in her throat and pulled the dress Brenna had touched off the rod. "You want to start with that one? The color would look great on you. Your eyes are amazing. The way they match your hair is very exotic." She smoothed one of Brenna's braids. "Is there a reason you keep it braided?"

Brenna answered without hesitation even though her focus was still locked on the dress. "Maxis."

"Well, then I vote we do something different. A new look for a new day." Galena bent her knees enough to make eye contact. "What do you say?"

With another quick peek at the dress, Brenna tugged one of the clasps holding her braid in place. "Okay."

Thirty minutes, a new gown, and pair of sandals later, they were headed down the stairway toward the main receiving room. Brenna had protested meeting Eryx at first, but when Galena promised Lexi, Orla and Jillian would be there too, she relented. No matter how things played out over the next few days, she'd have to be sure Eryx kept the men at a distance.

"Remember what I said." Galena wrapped an arm around Brenna's shoulders. "This is informal. Eryx just wants to get to know you and thank you for saving Lexi. No one here will hurt you." She mentally opened the double doors and voices rolled out to greet them. She leaned in close. "If you get nervous, come to me or one of the other women. Okay?"

Gaze darting in all directions, Brenna gripped her hands at her waist. "Okay."

Two steps in, Jillian stepped to Brenna's free side like a long lost friend. "You're going to love Uncle Eryx and Uncle Ramsay. Uncle Ludan acts like a brute, but he's really a teddy bear."

Well, histus. Galena had expected Eryx, but Ludan and Ramsay put the testosterone level through the roof. She steered Brenna toward the trio situated around Eryx's corner desk. "Eryx, I want you to meet Brenna Haven."

Brenna studied the empty thrones centered at the rear of the room.

"Brenna?" Galena waited, giving the woman time to wrap her head around whatever it was chewing on.

Blinking a few times, Brenna shook her head as though to clear it.

"This is my brother Eryx." Galena motioned at the far side of Eryx's desk. "The other two lugs are my other brother, Ramsay, and my might-as-well-be-brother, Ludan."

She measured each man, back and forth between Eryx and Ramsay, as she put the twin connection together. Her gaze shifted to Ludan and then shot to the floor, one shaking hand smoothing her unbound hair. "It's nice to meet you."

God, Brenna's voice, awkward and trembling, but still firm. She and Jillian couldn't be more than four or five years apart, but Brenna had years of life under her belt, years she hoped Jilly never got a chance to see.

Eryx shifted to the edge of his seat, but thankfully didn't stand. "You don't have to be so formal here, Brenna." He offered his hand, palm up. "Though I would like to thank you for what you did for Lexi."

Brenna stared at Eryx's outstretched hand.

To Eryx's credit, he didn't waver in his offering. Didn't speak or try to hurry her along. Just waited, patient as always.

"Will you take me home?" she asked, still staring at his palm as if the answer might show itself there.

"I can't answer that question yet. What I can promise is I'll do all I can to make up for the wrongs you've been dealt. Will you trust me?"

She studied his face for long, tense seconds, and placed her hand in his. "I can try."

He dipped his head. "Fair enough." Easing to his feet, he squeezed Jillian's shoulder. "Why don't you take Brenna on a tour? Keep to the main hall and meet me in the foyer in about thirty minutes." His gaze slid to Brenna. "Lexi wanted to be here, but her friend, the one she was looking for at Maxis' house, woke up this morning."

"He what?" Galena said.

Eryx shook his head, glancing away from Brenna only long enough to make sure Galena got the point. "I thought I'd take you up to see her. Would you like that?"

Brenna bobbed her head.

Jillian stepped in quick. "Do you like books?" She gripped Brenna's elbow and tugged with teenage enthusiasm. "The library is huge. Ramsay brings lots of books back from Evad too. That's what we call where you're from. And I can show you where my room is, too."

By the time they rounded the corner, Jillian's conspiring dwindled to nothing more than a girlish mumble.

Galena spun to Eryx. "What do you mean he woke up?"

"To wake. To be conscious." Eryx settled in his chair, knees falling open in a far more casual pose than he'd used in front of Brenna. "What else would I mean?"

"I mean why didn't you call me?"

"We did, Lena." Ramsay's sprawl matched Eryx's, though he had one foot propped on the edge of the desk. Despite the languid posture, he seemed a little off this morning. Tense in a fashion that seemed to be reserved for going head-to-head with Reese. "You didn't answer. When I went to check on you, you were out cold."

Shit. She must've been more tired than she'd thought. She raised both eyebrows at Eryx. "And?"

Eryx mocked her with a subtle headshake and his own set of raised eyebrows. He stopped teasing and grinned. "And he's fine, Galena. Tired, sore, and ready for a little unsupervised time with Maxis in zeolite. Other than that, I can't find a thing wrong with him."

"So you're not worried? No ramifications?"

Eryx shrugged and kicked a leg up to match his twin's. "None that I can see."

"Don't stare that gift horse down too hard." Ludan's gruffness seemed harsh compared to Eryx and Ramsay's light tone. Come to think of it, his mouth was nearly white he pressed his lips together so tight. She'd never seen him so fidgety.

"You okay?" Galena shifted for a better angle. "You don't look so good."

Ramsay guffawed loud enough to echo through the room. "He always looks like a beast."

"I'm fine. Drop it." He lifted his chin at Eryx. "You need me, or you stayin' close to the castle? Got somethin' I need to do."

Eryx held his surprise pretty well, but Ramsay's jaw dropped. Ludan never had "something else to do." The man took shadowing Eryx beyond serious.

"I think I've got it covered, Mom," Eryx answered.

"Fuck you." Ludan shoved to his feet. The words might've been terse, but didn't carry any venom. Just the same boyish back and forth she'd heard as long as she remembered. He was out the door in about half the strides it would have taken Galena.

"Wonder what that's about?" Ramsay ambled to the side bar and poured two fingers of the Balvenie Fifty Eryx kept stocked from Evad.

"Don't know and don't care." Eryx motioned for Ramsay to make him one too. "This is the first damned day I've had of peace and quiet without a shitload of worry. He'll tell me if there's a problem. Otherwise, I'm enjoying the silence."

"It's barely ten-thirty in the morning." Galena inclined her head to the amber liquid Ramsay poured. "A little early, don't you think?"

"Depends on the time zone." Ramsay crammed the stopper into the decanter and grumbled something else she couldn't make out.

Fine. If it meant getting him in a better mood, Ramsay could drink all day. She focused on Eryx. "How's Lexi? When I saw her yesterday she was worried about how she'd tell Ian everything when he woke up."

Eryx took the glass Ramsay offered and grinned. "Ian thought she was playing a joke until she pulled a few parlor tricks. He still didn't believe it until I threw in a few she hasn't learned yet." He shook his head. "Priceless."

Galena settled in Ludan's chair. "Does he know about Jillian?"

Ramsay leaned into the sidebar and crossed one foot over the other.

Eryx took a long drink of his Scotch. "Not yet. Lexi wanted to tackle the unbelievable stuff first and end on a positive note. I was just about to head up when you got here." He motioned toward the door with a jerk of his head. "How's Brenna doing? The real version?"

"Fine," Galena answered. "Just like Ian. Healthy from everything I can tell. She was weak yesterday, but anyone would have been after so much time in bed. Today she seems great."

Eryx got quiet and stroked his armrest, pensive. "This bit about going home...I've gotta cover that with Ian too. I'm thinking if we do it together it'll go better for both. You think she's up for it?"

Praise the Great One. Galena thought about the things she'd seen in Brenna's mind, all the suffering and degradation. The fact that she couldn't go home to the people she knew inherently she could trust seemed brutally unfair. Still, she'd made it through this much. She might be quiet, but the woman had a pretty stout backbone. "With Lexi there? Yeah, I think she'll be fine."

"Aren't you coming?"

"I'd actually hoped to talk to Reese. Do you know where he is?"

Twin glares lasered in on her.

"He's gone." Eryx picked up his drink and took another gulp.

Gone on an errand? Gone to visit someone? Damn, she hated when her brothers went vague on her. "What do you mean, 'Gone'?"

"I mean gone." He plunked his drink on the desk, nearly sloshing what was left of the amber liquid over the rim. "To the homestead I guess."

"What did you say to him?"

"I said, 'Thank you.'" He shrugged, like the piecemeal info was enough.

Stupid, pain in the ass men. "What. Did. You. Say?"

"Why do you care is a better question?" Ramsay stood and scowled. "It's no concern of yours, right?"

Her lungs seized hard enough she nearly wheezed. Why would it be her concern? She certainly hadn't done anything to show her brothers or anyone else it should be, not even Reese. She kept her silence, her brother's glares bearing down on her as sharp as a sword. Did she want Reese to be her concern?

She stood and shook out her skirts, avoiding their stares. She had enough to think about without either one of them forcing their opinions on her psyche. "Good luck with Ian and Brenna. I'm sure you'll handle it fine." She ducked her head and made for the door.

"Where are you off to?" Eryx asked, more suspicion in his voice than she cared to analyze.

"I've got something I need to fix."

Chapter 18

Eryx drained the last of his Balvenie and debated his next play with Galena. She was a woman now, more than capable of making her own choices, but something in her stride as she'd left screamed trouble.

"Got a funny feeling about whatever it is she's out to fix." Ramsay turned to the sideboard and his crystal tumbler clinked on the granite top.

"You mean Reese." Not so much a clarification on Eryx's part as voicing his fears out loud.

"Of course I mean Reese. She's always supports the underdog. She needs to stay the hell away from him."

"I'm not so sure about that." Lexi sure didn't think so. She'd let him know it for the better part of two hours last night. *"It's a wonder that girl can even breathe with you and Ramsay around, let alone want something that doesn't tie in perfect with the family modus operandi."*

Eryx traced the cut edges of his crystal glass. "Do you think we pressure her?"

"Galena?" Ramsay huffed out an exasperated breath. "In the long run she always gets what she wants. You know that."

With causes and niceties, sure. But now that Lexi had him thinking about it, he couldn't remember a time he'd seen her excited about a man. Not like what he'd seen this morning, and she'd been pretty decked out too.

He shook himself from his thoughts. "I gotta meet up with Jilly and Brenna." He gestured at Ramsay's empty glass. "You headed to the training center, or are you exorcising whatever demon's crawled up your ass with Scotch."

"Fuck you." Ramsay turned for the side bar and fisted the decanter.

Eryx shook his head and strode for the door. "You need me, I'm here."

Twins or not, they had their differences, but they matched each other neck and neck on the stubborn gene. When the time was right, Ramsay would talk.

Praise the Great One, it was good to have quiet. For at least a minute. He rounded the corner to the foyer and stopped.

Jillian and Brenna sat side by side on the long settee, Brenna with a soft smile. Granted he'd known her all of a few days, the majority of which she'd been unconscious, but the smile changed her appearance, lifting away Maxis' grime to reveal a light and innocently pretty woman. And without the braided pigtails, she looked a whole lot more her age.

"Uncle Eryx." Jillian stood and urged Brenna up alongside her. "After we meet Lexi's friend, I want to show Brenna the stairs to the cove."

He hadn't used those since he was seventeen. Once a teenage boy learned to fly, hoofing it up or down stairs didn't hold much appeal. "Sounds great."

Wait, had she said, "After *we* meet?" One look at Jillian is all it would take for Ian to know she was related to him, and no more than twenty seconds after that to figure out she was the perfect age to be his daughter. Probably a little too hardcore a way to break the news his daughter was not only alive and well, but a Myren too.

Eryx rubbed his chin. "Jillian, would you mind if I introduce Brenna to Lexi's friend alone today?"

Jillian's bright smile fell.

He squeezed Jilly's arm. "I promise you'll meet him, Squeak, but right now we've got things to talk about. Things they need to hear alone." He jerked his thumb toward the kitchen. "Now, go find Orla and tell her to be ready for my call. I'll ask her to come get Brenna and bring her to you when we're done."

Jillian shrugged in half-hearted surrender and glanced at Brenna. "Come find me when you're done and we'll go to the cove."

Brenna's tiny smile crept back in place.

"She'll make you do that," Eryx said, drawing Brenna's attention.

"Do what?"

"Smile."

Brenna flushed and ducked her chin. On the bright side, whether she realized it or not, she was alone with a relative unknown man and hadn't yet run for the hills. With the briefest touch on her arm he steered her toward the stairs. "Come on. Let's go see Lexi and her friend."

"Why did you call her that?" Brenna followed behind him, lifting her gown to clear the steps.

"Call her—oh, Squeak." He chuckled and motioned down the hallway when they reached the landing. "Ramsay gave her the nickname. When she was little, he'd throw her in the air and she'd let out a funny squeak. The name stuck."

A wistful look of longing washed across Brenna's face, too much understanding of everything she'd missed for someone her age. Damn it if he didn't hate the choice he was about to lay at her feet. He opened the door to Ian's room with his mind.

"Brenna." Lexi bounded from the far side of Ian's bed and wrapped Brenna in a quick hug. "You look fantastic. That color's great on you. And I'm so glad those braids are gone. How do you feel?"

"Probably better if you'd let her get all the way in the door." Ian lay propped on the bed on top of the covers, more like a guy kicked back on a couch than an invalid. He'd dressed since Eryx left this morning, the same button-down and jeans combo Ian had worn the first night they'd met, though this shirt was tan instead of blue.

"I see someone made a clothes run while I was gone." Eryx shut the door behind him. "Button-downs aren't in high demand here."

Lexi tugged Brenna beside her on the bed. "Ramsay sent one of his men. None of your stuff fit and I don't think I could get Ian to wear leather at gun point."

"That's for damned sure." Ian shifted on the bed and winced. "Who's your friend?"

"Oh." Lexi leaned back enough so as not to block Ian from Brenna's line of sight. "Ian, this is Brenna, the woman who saved me. Brenna, meet Ian. Usually he's a pain in my ass, but still my best friend."

Brenna dipped her head and laughed. A tiny laugh, but happy all the same. "It's nice to meet you."

Ian rolled his shoulders up and back as though trying to give his ribs more room move. Not surprising since five of them had been broken. "You gonna tell us what's got your back so straight, Eryx? Or would you rather stick to uncomfortable small talk first?" The man was amazingly shrewd, though as a retired cop he probably caught more than the average Joe.

Eryx winked at Lexi and mentally slid the gold wingback nestled in the corner closer to the bed. "Can't have uncomfortable small talk. We've got too many big topics to work through."

"More than unknown races, superpowers, and rebellions out to start a war?" Ian smirked at Lexi. "Helluva rabbit hole you fell in, sweetheart."

"And took you with me." Lexi frowned and traced the damask patterns on the ivory comforter.

Ian tilted his head. "Something I'm supposed to be hearing in that message?"

Lexi's head lifted, a silent apology in her eyes.

Eryx let out a frustrated breath. "Myrens have laws like any other race, most of them similar to yours. There are two that supersede all others. No sharing the existence of our race to humans, and no interference in human destiny."

"Kinda screwed the pooch on both of those with us." Ian stared at Lexi. "So you're in hot water?"

Lexi shook her head. "Not me, Eryx."

"I've already approached the ellan, our form of government." Eryx said. "If they choose to bring charges, that's on me. Though if they think to take my throne without a fight, they're in for a surprise."

Brenna piped up, a heavy dread weighting her voice. "That still leaves us."

Eryx nodded. "It does." He leaned in, resting his elbows on his knees, hands clasped. "My recommendation to the council is the two of you be given the option to live out the rest of your days here so long as you abide by Myren laws. You'd be held by the same tenets as us."

"Or?" Ian's eyes narrowed.

Eryx met his stare. "Death."

"Serious stuff." Ian dropped his head back on the propped up pillow.

Brenna gazed out the open arched window, her hands gripped tight in her lap, thumbs rubbing back and forth. "You should have let me die."

Lexi covered Brenna's hands with one of her own and glared at Eryx. "Nice delivery."

"She deserves the truth." He left his chair and crouched beside Brenna at the foot of the bed. "I'll make this right for you. After all you've done... all you've gone through, you deserve that much. Can you trust me long enough to see what I can do?"

Shiny, unshed tears welled in her eyes. "Do I have a choice?"

"We always have a choice, Brenna. Try for me. For Lexi. Find what joy you can here and trust me to do what I can to make accommodations."

A tear slipped down Brenna's cheek.

Lexi wrapped her in a hug and half-whispered, "We'll have fun while we wait. Explore, and meet new people. We'll do it together. Okay?"

Eryx sent a mental summons to Orla and sat back in his chair. Lexi could help the girl more with her innate compassion than he ever could. Ian, on the other hand, he could relate to. "Where's your head in this?"

Ian studied the ceiling. "Think Brenna hit it pretty square." He paused a second. "Hate the idea of no electricity, especially since I'm not naturally plugged in like you two. No football, no Internet."

Lexi frowned at him, her arms still locked around Brenna. "Since when are you techno-savvy?"

Ian grinned and a few beats later, he lifted his head and aimed the smile at Lexi. "Truth of the matter is, everything I care about's here anyway."

Lexi shifted, gifting Ian with her megawatt, no-holds barred smile over Brenna's head.

A sharp knock sounded and Orla popped her head around the door, her waist-length hair loose and trailing over one shoulder. She zeroed in on Brenna huddled close to Lexi. "Goodness, she's only been awake a day and you've already got her in tears."

Funny how she zoned in on Eryx as the culprit. "That's why I called. I thought you and Jillian might take her mind off things while we finish with Ian."

Before he'd even finished his sentence, Orla urged Brenna off the bed and tucked her under one arm. "Whatever the problem is, it can't be that bad. Jillian and I are elbow deep in dough. We'll talk it out and pound out your frustrations at the same time."

Brenna sniffled and laid her head on Orla's shoulder. They shuffled out together, muttered words Eryx couldn't make out sounding just before the door snapped shut.

"If you're hustling off crying girls, I gotta think there's more. Probably worse." Ian lifted both eyebrows. "Am I right?"

Eryx looked to Lexi. "He always like this?"

"Yep," she said with a smile that made him want to move mountains.

Eryx pooled his thoughts. "Some time ago, my men were called to investigate a cottage. The neighbors were suspicious, and said they hadn't seen the woman and her daughter for some time. We checked the place and found the mother dead, and a barely one-year-old child starving. We brought her here and she's lived with us ever since."

"And?" Ian's attention zigzagged between Eryx and Lexi.

Lexi squirmed on her bedside perch and fiddled with her crimson tunic. "She's nearly nineteen."

Laughter rippled up from the garden below, and a breeze whistled through the window.

"The story sounds nice, but I'm thinking if you pull the Band-Aid off quick this would work better."

Lexi peeked at Eryx, uncertain.

"It's your call, Lexi. I can tell him if you want."

She shook her head, pulled in a tight breath, and gave Ian a shaky smile. "Her name is Jillian, and we think she's your daughter."

Chapter 19

Reese thwacked another log in half and buried the axe's blade in the sawed-off tree stump. The wind whipped his bare, sweat-slicked torso and his shoulders burned, but damn it if the outlet wasn't sweet.

He grabbed a halved log and centered it over the deep scars at the center of the stump. He needed a plan, not just where Galena was concerned, but for his whole fucking life. Land wasn't his thing. The homestead's peace and quiet was his mom's dream. He needed a cause, something to protect and defend.

Hefting the axe high, he slammed the blade home. The wood snapped in two and tumbled to the ground, the strike still reverberating across the open field. Maybe he should bide his time with Galena for now, build his future first and start fresh with her. Unless she'd been the one who asked Eryx to kick him out.

He shook the thought off and set up another log. He'd doubted himself and too many other people in his life and he wasn't about to add Galena to the list. The pleasure on her face when she'd come for him, so open and honest, hadn't been a fluke. He'd find a way to win her, one way or another.

He lifted the axe, muscles tensed for the downswing, and tingles flared across his nape and shoulders. Adjusting his grip, he spun and froze mid-swing, nearly fumbling the tool. "Galena."

She stumbled back and pressed her hand above her gown's square neckline, fingers trembling against the soft swells of her breasts. "Sorry. I shouldn't have sneaked up on you." With a tremulous smile, she dipped her head toward the axe and laughed. "Especially with that thing."

"My mind was somewhere else." Like back in bed with her, pretending the real world didn't exist. He buried the axe's tip in the stump. "I should have been more focused. If you'd have been Maxis, I'd be dead right now."

"He knows where you live?"

Reese's lips twitched but he managed to hold back his grin. "Hard to blackmail a guy without knowing where to find him."

"Then you're not safe here. You'd be better off at the castle."

"I'm fine here." Though her eagerness to welcome him back into her family home went a long way toward negating her involvement in kicking him out in the first place.

"Hardly. What if he catches you unaware?"

"A run-in with Maxis wouldn't be altogether unpleasant, particularly since you and your brothers evened the playing field." If anything, that tidbit had been the one saving grace of Eryx's polite request to vacate. Out here in the middle of nowhere, Maxis might opt to finish what he'd started and give Reese another shot at furthering the spiritu's mission, or at least offer up a fair fight if talking didn't pan out.

Still, Galena wasn't safe here, not out in the open. Blue skies stretched above them and nothing pinged against his senses, but with her black and crimson gown she'd draw more than a passing glance for someone skilled at masking. "Probably not the best idea to wave your presence for anyone interested in a fly-by." He cupped her elbow and guided her to the greenhouse behind him. "Come on. I'll grab my shirt and show you another route into the main house. I'm surprised your brothers let you visit with Maxis still free."

The light in her eyes dimmed and she tensed. "I didn't ask for a hall pass. Contrary to what they and anyone else might think, I make my own decisions."

He pulled her to a stop.

She averted her face, lips tight.

"Galena?"

Her jaw hardened and her chest rose and fell in quick, shallow moves.

"Galena." Keeping his grip on her arm, he lifted her chin. No tears marked her face, but she was well and truly pissed, her aqua blue eyes sparking. "I asked for your safety. Nothing more." He traced her lower lip and the tension there ebbed, the berry-red fullness soft against his thumb. "I'm not blind to the tug-of-war you're in. I won't add to it, at least not intentionally. If you choose me, it'll be because you want me, not because you gave way."

Her lips parted, more than a little surprise coloring her expression.

Instinct pulled him, urged him to erase the confusion on her face with his kiss and with slow teasing touches.

Histus, he'd just promised her he wouldn't push her and now he was fantasizing just that. He opened the door to the shed and squeezed her elbow. "Go inside. I think you'll like what you find."

She blinked, studied him a second, and stepped across the threshold. Her gasp fluttered back to him, carried on the scent of rich, damp soil and herbs. Plants of all kinds lined either side of five rows and along the back wall. "These are yours?"

"Me?" He followed her inside, snatched the towel he'd tossed down with his shirt, and wiped his brow. "Praise the Great One, no. I'm surprised my mother even let me in here. I can kill them with a single look."

Her lightness was back in full force, her strides quick to roam the aisles of all his mother's favorite plants.

He settled in to enjoy her response. "I hired a nearby couple to keep the farm up. The wife loves plants as much as mom did."

Galena dipped to sniff a tiny pink flower with sharply pointed petals and traced the leaf beside it. She stopped at the drishen bush nestled at the far corner and lightly flipped one berry so it wiggled on its tendril. "My brothers used to eat these until they made themselves sick. These are a lighter color than what we grow at the castle though, more white instead of pink."

He looped the towel around the back of his neck and held tight to both ends. If he was smart, he'd keep his distance and stay out of trouble. He took two steps forward anyway, then two more, close enough to tempt himself, but not quite enough to touch. "Try one."

She reached for a cluster higher on the bush and traced the rib of a fat leaf. The sun streamed in from the skylights and accented the sweep of auburn hair down her nape. Stretched in that position, her breasts strained the top of her gown. It would take two, maybe three seconds for him to get the bodice unlaced.

"What am I to you?" Galena murmured.

His brain clambered up from its single-track strategy on how to get her naked. Drishen. They'd been talking about drishen.

"Earlier," she added still studying the fruit. "You said, 'if you choose me.' How can I choose if I don't know what I am to you?" She lowered her hand and turned, her raw vulnerability cranking his protective inclinations to full bore. "Am I a fling? A passing interest? A curiosity? A—"

"Everything."

Shit. So much for no pressure. His knuckles protested his grip on the towel and his forearms ached from the morning's hard use. Did he keep going? Or try to keep things light?

Fuck waiting. She was here of her own free will. If he'd learned anything the last few months it was to face the challenges life threw him head on. "I keep thinking about how to make my life right. Everything I've missed and everything I want. For me, it all comes back to you." He stepped closer, only inches and her sweet scent between them. The rough towel grated beneath his fists. "But I won't hide. Not anymore. So the question is, what do you want from me?"

She studied him, his face, his bound hair, down his neck to his chest, and his belly. She traced the top ridge of his abdominals and her voice cracked. "I'm scared." Slick from the sweat still on his skin, her fingers slid up, slow until her palm covered his heart. "But I'm not torn. Not in this."

The touch rippled through him, contractions spearing to the base of his cock. Everything he wanted was right here, his if he'd dare to reach for it. But he couldn't pressure her. She had enough of that already. It had to be her choice. Her desire. He covered her hand with his, the beat of his heart reverberating through the touch. "You're sure?"

She leaned close and the turquoise in her eyes glittered bright. Her heated exhalations danced across his skin. "I've come for you. Twice."

She meant visited. Surely that's what she meant.

With a tentative, yet innocently wicked lick, she sampled the skin along his sternum. "I'd say that shows certainty." She dipped her head as though to make another pass.

"No." He pulled away, not enough to break contact, but enough to let him catch his breath. Without conscious direction, he buried his hand in the hair at her nape, fisting the thickness in a loose grip. "Come inside where it's safer. I'll shower and we'll—"

"I don't want safer." She held his stare, regaining the distance he'd created. "Don't cosset me. Let me feel." She kissed his chest, lips parted and tongue trailing a wanton path. "Let me fly."

He tightened his hold, every scrap of his attention lasered on her plump, perfect mouth and the press of her soft breasts. Her white teeth peeked out for no more than a heartbeat, and he imagined them digging deep for a sweet, torturous pain. She wanted to fly? Fuck, he'd make her soar. "You didn't try one."

Lips still pressed to his skin she lifted her gaze, eyelids heavy, yet questioning.

He turned her and wrapped one arm across her collarbone to grip her shoulder, tucking her back against his front. Drishen berries dangled high overhead. With a quick snap, he pulled one pearl fruit free and brought it to her lips. "Open."

Her heart fluttered beneath his arm. Dropping her head to rest on his shoulder, she opened her mouth, gaze locked to his.

He pressed the fruit against her mouth. "Bite."

Damn, if the color of her eyes didn't deepen. Her perfect little teeth rent the delicate flesh in half and her eyes closed on a quiet moan. "Sweet." She licked her lip. "Like lemonade without the bite."

A marauding, almost feral need to claim and possess clawed past the last scrap of his reason. She was his to taste and touch, to consume. He ran the halved fruit along her lip and tossed the fruit aside. "My turn."

Her pupils dilated and her warm breath fluttered against his face.

He lowered his head and licked, her full, soft lips slightly parted and coated in the sweet, delicious juice. Her wet heat and fruit drenched taste sucked him in, overriding everything but the need to claim and dominate.

She moaned into his mouth and stretched back, cupping the back of his head and arching so her soft ass ground against his cock.

He nipped her jaw and cupped her breasts, her beaded nipples teasing his palms through the fabric. He tweaked the taut points. "I want you naked." He grazed her neck with his teeth. "Right here, right now."

Her husky groan wrapped around him, and her hands covered his and squeezed in encouragement.

"Tell me, Galena." He ground his hips against her, prodding her with the pulsing hardness she'd created. "Tell me you'll take what I give you."

She urged his mouth back to hers and whispered against his lips. "Everything."

* * * *

Galena's fingers tangled in Reese's bound hair, his chest against her back, her neck craned to meet each slick lash of his tongue against hers. The position was awkward and limited the depth of how she answered his kiss, but no way was she shifting from the firm clasp of his hands on her breasts.

He pinched the tight peaks and she gasped.

His voice rasped against her lips. "Here all this time and you haven't asked." He nipped then sucked the sting he'd left behind. "You noticed my hair. Why not ask me why it's bound?"

She'd more than noticed, had actually volleyed back and forth between thrill at the thought he'd done it for her, and utter rage he'd bound it for someone else. In the end, she'd been afraid to mention it.

"Ask." His thumbs flicked her nipples.

"Why?"

His lips skated the shell of her ear, and flutters danced down her neck.

"You." He growled, a delicious vibration. "I can't think beyond you. Can't want beyond you." He spun her, throwing her off center so she fell against him, his heartbeat against her palm furious. "Free it." Not a request, but a command thick with need.

Quivers rippled through her belly and her thighs tensed. She wasn't sure what provoked her more, the intimate act or the dark demand. "You're too tall."

He traced the exposed curves at the top of her bodice, drawing slow, tantalizing patterns and leaving gooseflesh in their wake. The corner of his mouth lifted, a smile of sorts, but wicked as he eased to his knees and trailed a hand down her leg. "You'd better hurry, Lena. My mouth's that much closer to heaven." Slipping his hand under the hem of her gown and coiling it around her ankle, he slid one sandal free. "Once my tongue's between your thighs, I might not stop."

His words jolted through her, and a steady ache centered at her core. She fumbled with the knot holding his hair in place. Already he'd removed her other sandal and she'd barely managed to breathe, let alone release the tight strands.

He tugged the ties of her over-bodice, unwinding the laces while his other hand skated up, up, up the back of her leg beneath her skirt. "Focus, Sweetheart." He teased her thigh, ghosting his fingers to the inside, then out along the seam between her leg and ass. "Free me so I can make you burn and beg."

She jerked at the band holding the mess in place and it snapped against her fingers. It should have hurt, should have brought a curse to her lips, but every neuron focused on his touch.

He pulled the bodice loose, leaving only the crimson underslip. "I think you want to burn." He rose, towering over her like a wild god, the tawny mass of his hair no more tame than a lion's. "Do you want to beg? To scream?"

God, yes, she wanted that. No propriety, and no formality, just raw, uninhibited passion.

Not waiting for an answer, he turned her and worked the buttons along her back. Open to her waist, warm greenhouse air brushed her bared skin as his knuckles circled the small of her back. "I love your skin." He nudged her hair to expose her neck and nuzzled behind one ear. "The color and the way it tastes." Torturously slow, he eased the fabric past the curve of her shoulders. The slip swooshed to the stone floor and left her bare. "Perfect."

Every nerve ending pricked to attention, craving his next touch. The leather from his pants whispered along her thighs. "What do you want Galena. What do you crave next?"

"Your voice." The answer ripped free before she could overthink it, and her skin tingled in anticipation. "The things you say and how you say them." She leaned back, gaining what ease she could from the hard press of him. "I feel them everywhere, like a touch from the inside out."

Reese inhaled slow and deep, a sound so sensual it ricocheted along her flesh. He gripped her hips, one hand sliding in to span her abdomen. "You feel it here."

She whimpered, his touch so blatantly possessive she nearly wept.

"And between your legs." His fingers dipped, stopping at the top of her cleft. "Is your pussy wet, Galena? Will you be slick for me? My tongue?"

Her legs shook, close to giving way.

"You do like the words." He kept teasing her, so close, and yet forever away from the building thrum at her clit. He ground his cock against her ass, thick and hard as stone. "I like them too. Give them to me. Tell me where you want my fingers."

If only she could. The words sat on the tip of her tongue, erotic images fueling her unspoken vocabulary, all of them wrong and horribly improper.

His tempting whisper tickled her ear. "Tell me. You're safe with me." One hand pinned her hips in place, the other teased her thighs. "Nothing you can say...nothing you can want or do is wrong. Not with me."

God he was close. A breath away from where she needed his touch.

"It's only us." His voice stroked her everywhere, low and sultry like velvet sin. "Let go."

She squeezed her eyes shut and gripped his forearms. "Please." Every part of her shook, desperate and demanding she obey. "Touch me."

"More."

Her lungs burned and her breasts ached. "Your fingers, I want to feel them slide between my legs."

"Where?"

Oh, God. He wanted that word. So damned wrong, but exactly what she wanted. She didn't want safe. Isn't that what she'd told him? Her hips flexed forward, seeking the contact he withheld. All she had to do was say it. "My pussy." Heat rushed to her cheeks, but a spear of pleasure rippled through her core. "I want your fingers on my pussy. Inside me."

Reese growled, the slow-rolling animalistic call of a predator who'd sighted its prey. He dipped his fingers and stroked exactly as she'd asked. "You're drenched." He teased her entrance, dragging the moisture up to circle her clit. The steady rhythm reverberated along her arms and legs. "What else? Lift your breasts, show me how you want them touched and tell me what you need."

It was too much. She opened her eyes and the environment crashed in on her. They were in the open, exposed where anyone could walk in.

"Look at me." Reese cupped her chin, urging her to face him with one hand while the other kept its enticing pattern. His emerald green eyes were nearly black with passion. "You're safe."

He'd die to protect her. Where the thought came from, or how the certainty landed at such a moment she didn't know and didn't care, but he'd give her anything and everything she asked, even what she craved and feared the most.

"Let it out." He swiped his tongue along her lower lip. "No judgment." He sealed his lips against hers, and undulated his hips against her ass in a rhythm to match his fingers.

Something savage built inside her, a powerful and ruthless force that sent fissures through all the weighted rules that had governed her life. This was her chance to fly, free from everything but the sensations crackling between them. She cupped her heavy, aching breasts and widened her stance to give him better access.

The pad of his finger circled her entrance and his thumb brushed her swollen clit.

Head thrown back on Reese's shoulder, she cried out, and her eyes flashed opened to the midday sun pouring through the greenhouse panes above.

"There she is." Reese thrust his finger deep. "So fucking sweet." He added a second finger, and her sex clamped around him.

Ah, God, sweet wasn't right. This was pure rawness, everything carnal and wicked she'd ever wanted. "Reese." She slanted forward and sent three tiny plants flying from the workbench. He'd said he'd make her beg and he was right. She'd do anything. Hips lifted, she pushed against him. "Please."

With a ragged groan, he shifted, fingers slipping from her entrance. "Finger yourself."

She was already on it, her damp and swollen labia scalding as her pulse pounded beneath her skin.

Cool air gusted along the back of her thighs and leather rustled.

His rich, husky voice wrapped around her, a dirty and primal sound that made her belly flutter. "Look at that." His fingers brushed hers and his velvet hardness teased the curve of her ass. "You need more, sweetheart? Ready to spread those wings?"

A garbled groan clawed free, every muscle from her toes to the top of her head stretched taut. "Now, Reese." She writhed against his length, mindless of anything but the edge of bliss dangling before her.

His cock nudged her entrance.

"Now, what?" The tip of his glans pressed her opening, a merciless tease that left her pussy quivering. "Say it, sweetheart. Look at me and tell me what I want to hear."

She tried to push back, to take what she needed.

He tightened his hold on her hips.

"Reese." She angled her ass higher, instinctively aiming for what he offered. The flared head slipped inside, but it wasn't enough. She whipped her head around and glared over her shoulder. His eyes burned as wild as the fire blasting through her. "Fuck me." It rolled off her tongue, the most sensual tone to ever pass her lips. She let her head fall back, her hair an erotic stroke around her ribs. "Fuck me like I need it, hard and wild."

He impaled her in one thrust, scattering her words and thoughts with the slick, delicious stretch of his perfect shaft. His calloused hands stroked her smooth flesh, and damp air kissed her sweat-slick back. Skin slapped against skin, each strike of his balls against her swollen folds spurring a maelstrom of sensation.

She was so close, a gut-wrenching finish bearing down so hard she wasn't sure she'd withstand it, let alone comprehend.

"Lena." Barely a whisper, Reese's voice curled around her, his touch decadently descending down her spine. "Hang on, baby. Let's see how high you fly."

His hand kept moving, her own gripping the workbench in front of her for dear life. His thumb grazed the cleft at the top of her ass then slid down, slow and torturous.

Oh, God. He wouldn't.

He circled her anus, a simple brush, followed by a subtle push that shoved her past the edge.

Her cries filled the greenhouse and her sex clamped his length in fierce, pulsing grasps.

"Fuck." Reese's hips rammed home, and his cock jerked inside her core's tight fist.

She arched and curled one arm back to bury her fingers in his hair, the other digging nails deep into his flank. Her hips writhed against his, milking every pulse of his shaft. She'd never felt anything so perfect, such a heady connection with a euphoric haze.

His arms coiled around her torso, one slanted across her breasts to collar her throat, the other angled across her hips, strong and protective. "Talk to me." He nuzzled the space behind one ear, his breath still hot and fast. "Tell me you're all right."

All right? The word was too shortsighted. Woefully inept for the feminine power coursing through her veins. He'd cracked her shell before, but today he'd freed her, rearranged her perspective to the point she'd never fit inside the cast she'd worn before.

She let her head lull against him and a languid peace billowed along her muscles. She was safe with him. If she fell, he'd catch her, a fact her body had registered long before her mind.

Forcing her heavy eyelids open, she cupped his cheek. "I'm better than all right." She tried for a smile to match the lightness in her heart and her cheeks trembled from the strain. "I'm alive."

Chapter 20

Galena stared at herself in the mirror, naked. Soft morning light spilled from tubes overhead, the muted pinks a compliment to the blush across her neck and chest.

She traced her collarbone. When was the last time she'd really looked at herself, not a stitch of clothes on and openly studying her curves? Yesterday the act would've made her blush. Today it was her memories. Even separated by an entire floor, the mere thought of Reese and all they'd done through the afternoon and night left her heated and short of breath. The shower they'd taken this morning was nothing short of nirana.

His room was quiet now. Level with the curve of her hip in the mirror's reflection lay the tangled white sheets on Reese's bed. She wanted back in those sheets, the crisp fabric rasping her bare skin with Reese's heat nestled close.

"You don't have to go." Reese stood in the doorway with a plate full of fruits and cheeses.

Her stomach grumbled. Something more substantial than water, sex, and exhausted sleep was probably a good idea. Her breasts tingled and tightened at the sight of everything else.

Tanned skin stretched across Reese's defined muscles, marked indentions she'd outlined with her mouth and fingers through the long, delicious night. He'd thrown on leather pants, the fastenings left partially undone. He might as well have drawn an arrow and added the caption, *Lick here.*

His hip muscles flexed and released as he sauntered her direction. She'd grown fascinated with the way they moved, particularly when pistoning against her core.

The plate clicked against the dresser's surface and his warm fingers curled around her hips.

"You could stay." A hint of forest and spice tickled her nose as he nuzzled close behind her. She wanted it back on her skin, as it had been when she'd woken. A sensual reminder of all they'd done and all he'd given her. "Let me indulge in your wicked fantasies a while longer."

Her hips rolled and a sigh slipped past her lips. Praise the Great One, he was addictive. Already her entrance was slick and ready to take him. The woman staring back at her in the mirror was a stranger, so erotic, open and free. "I can't let you have all my fantasies at once. We have to save something for tomorrow."

"I could have a million tomorrows and it wouldn't be enough. Stay. Let me pleasure you a little longer."

Her gown lay across the oversized chair in the corner of the room. Stay here, or head back home to all of her responsibilities? Back to the pieces of her life that didn't make for a nice, tidy fit. A shiver wracked her. "How do we do this? Us?"

"How do you want to handle it?" His emerald green eyes stayed locked on hers in the reflection, no pressure of any kind.

"I have no idea." She settled her hands on top of his. "I meant what I said. I'm not looking to keep things a secret. I just—"

"Don't know the best approach?" He released her hips and combed her nearly dried hair with his fingers. "You do what works for you. Until you're ready, I'll be here."

He worked the strands in small sections, each pass given patient, devoted attention. He'd offered her so much and still asked nothing in return. If the roles were reversed, could she be so forbearing? So willing to wait in the shadows until he found the strength to own what burned between them?

"Bind it." Her voice shook and a tremor snaked its way down her spine.

Reese hesitated, attention shuttling between the lock of hair resting between his knuckles and her reflection. "That's a pretty strong statement. Your brothers—"

"I'm not asking for my brothers. I'm asking for me. For us." Something she hadn't realized until the words slipped free. "If my actions lay the ground work for a conversation between me and my family, then so be it."

He pulled the strand the rest of the way through, a cautious, pensive expression on his face. He brushed it toward the center of her back, eyes locked on hers.

Stepping to the dresser, he opened the top drawer. He shifted a few items and drew out a mahogany box carved with an emblem on top she couldn't quite make out. Inside were a handful of beads the size of her knuckle, each a pale gold so smooth they glowed nearly white. He rolled one between his fingers, thoughtful, before he turned. "Hold out your hand."

He placed the sphere in her palm and cupped either side of her neck. The rasp of his indrawn breath sent flutters through her belly.

He gathered one side of her hair, then the other, reverent. The tugs along her scalp as he sectioned the mass into thirds rippled to her toes.

"Your commitment means everything." Back and forth the tension shifted as he worked her hair into one long braid. "No matter what happens, no matter what actions you might need to take in the future, I'll do all I can to be worthy of your gift."

What actions she might need to take? Did he think she'd take it back?

"Give me the bead."

She held out her palm and met his gaze over one shoulder. The respect and warm appreciation in his eyes shook her soul.

He lifted the tip of the braid so she could see and slipped the bead in place. His fingers shifted as he warmed and altered the metal with his mind, tightening it to hold the braid in place. "Until fate or your heart chooses otherwise, you're mine."

Something in her stirred. Something foreign, but comfortable and profound. The possessive tenor of his words should have struck a nerve, or made her push for distance. Instead she nearly purred, the need for intimacy coming from some place so deep she doubted it could ever be defined.

She licked her lips, imaging the slide of his tongue instead of hers.

His gaze locked onto the movement. His eyebrows dipped low at the center and his focus grew distant. He cocked his head. "Get dressed and wait here." He was out the door without another word, leaving her alone with her thrumming heart.

Maxis.

Reese had said Maxis knew where he lived. He'd even gone so far as to say he hoped his brother would show for a chance at evening the score.

Like histus she'd wait here. She drew on her crimson slip, mentally fastening the buttons along the back even as she slid one arm into the corseted outer piece. Maybe she should call for Eryx or Ramsay. Or Ludan. Ludan would come just for the chance to snap Maxis' neck and wouldn't say a word to either of her brothers out of gratitude alone.

She hustled down the hall, stopping to slide on her sandals between steps. The bookcase hiding the stairwell was nearly shut, letting only the barest stream of light shine down the stone steps. Floorboards creaked above her and a muted clang sounded from farther away.

Silence settled for a moment, followed by muted male voices. Reese's voice was easy to catch, but the other she couldn't quite gauge from her vantage point. She held her breath and pressed close to the nearly closed door-a-la-bookcase. It wasn't Maxis'. This one was too low to fit Maxis' grating tenor, too familiar.

She reached out through her links. Eryx was at home, but Ramsay—

Praise the Great One. Why would Ramsay be here? She hurried forward, shoving the door open on silent hinges.

Reese was tall enough only the tip of Ramsay's chocolate and sun-streaked hair showed. The way Reese gripped the barely opened door and jam made it clear he wasn't about to let Ramsay one step farther, no doubt an attempt to save her any pain or embarrassment.

She started forward and faltered. Maybe Reese was right. Throwing her presence on her brother wasn't the smoothest way to deliver the news. Maybe she should wait until things were calmer. Find some place with more common ground to share the direction she'd chosen.

Shaking her head, she reengaged. Reese had faced his worst fears. Had laid his heart out to her in so many ways it still made her shudder. If she couldn't face her own brothers with her feelings she didn't deserve him. She touched his shoulder and the muscles beneath her palm went rigid. "You can let him in."

Ramsay's voice faltered.

"It's okay, Reese. Let him in."

Reese stared straight ahead, no doubt meeting her brother's death stare. His stern jaw looked like it might snap at the slightest increase in pressure.

She hedged back and waited.

Reese swallowed and his grip on the door tightened until his knuckles ran white. He stepped aside.

Ramsay's scowl locked onto her then shot to Reese. "And here I thought your apology meant something." He focused on Galena. "Stupid me. You just wanted to lay a little ground work with my sister."

"You went to him?" Normally her brother's nastiness would have kept her locked in place, but surprise wedged her feet free. "When?"

"Yesterday." Reese sighed and let go of the door, letting it swing open. "A few hours before you showed up. I owed him that much."

She swiveled her head, anger bubbling beneath her skin as her brother's accusations registered. "And you think he made his apologies to lay a little groundwork?" She prowled forward.

Ramsay straightened, a cautionary light dawning in his silver eyes.

Good. He needed to be wary. "Are you saying he needed to get in your good graces so he could fuck me?"

The crude statement worked Ramsay as sure as a slap across the face, his head snapping back.

Reese stepped forward. "Galena—"

"No." She waved him off, keeping her focus on Ramsay. "First, what makes you think you hold any sway over what I do or don't do? You think he'd need to get permission from you to touch me? You think I don't make those decisions for myself?" She straightened and shook her head. "Oh, wait. Maybe the old me did, but let me assure you, the new me doesn't.

"Second." She glanced at Reese, shock doing more to loosen the tension in his jaw than any amount of soothing probably would have. "Where do you get off being so judgmental? I always believed you were reasonable and decent-hearted. Do you think it was easy for Reese to be in his position? To lie to a man he considered his friend? To man up and apologize for it years later after making such serious mistakes?"

She paused, lungs burning from her fury. "Frankly, big brother, I'm beginning to wonder if you'd man up enough to match what he's done." She huffed out a breath and what was left of her ire evened out.

Ramsay stared at her, wide-eyed.

Damned if she didn't feel about thirty pounds lighter. Not the classiest way to go about throwing out what she had to say, but she'd bet Lexi would've scored it a ten.

She smoothed out the front of her dress, cringing at the wrinkles marking the delicate crimson silk, and strolled with as much dignity as she could to Reese. She went on her tiptoes and urged him down for a kiss. "I'm proud of you."

He kissed her back, a cautious touch that seemed obviously mindful of Ramsay's shaken but steady stare. His gratitude—or was it awe—moved something in her soul. When was the last time someone had stood up for this man? Really, believed in him?

She pressed another chaste, but lingering kiss against his lips and smiled. "Very proud." With that, she pulled away and let out a satisfied sigh. "I should be finished checking in with my patients around dinner time. Why don't you pick me up at the castle and we'll spend tonight at my place?" She strolled out the door without waiting for an answer, leaving two open-mouthed men staring after her.

Liberation felt good.

* * * *

Eryx paused in the castle foyer and pulled Jillian to a halt beside him. Through the tall arched windows, Lexi and Ian sat laughing in the flower-shaded arbor, lavender and cream bell-shaped blooms dangling in the wind above them. "We don't have to do this yet. No one's pushing for you to meet Ian today. Lexi knows him better than me, but he seems like a patient guy. If you say you need time, he won't push."

Jillian hung back, only inching forward enough to peek at the stranger she'd learned last night was probably her father. "What's he like?"

Eryx sampled her emotions. The action was rude and a complete cheat, but when it came to protecting Jilly he didn't give a damn.

Curiosity tapped against his senses, a sweet, sparkling sensation not unlike champagne. Fear seemed mixed in there somewhere too, but more apprehension than terror, the difference between forged steel and the coppery scent of blood.

"He's strong," Eryx said. "Protective of those he loves."

Lexi's laughter filtered through the open front doors, her bold gestures matching her wide smile.

Ian wasn't as animated, but his face glowed with evident love for Lexi.

"Lexi said he never quit searching for you or his wife," Eryx said. "You should know that."

Jilly nodded, a shy, distracted movement he wasn't sure how to interpret. "Lexi said he loved my mother. That he kept following leads even after they chose to set the case aside."

"It takes a lot of fortitude for a man to keep going when his wife and unborn child vanish into thin air. That alone should tell you about his character."

She dragged her gaze from the window and up to Eryx. "I want to meet him. I like Lexi and Ian likes her, so he must be a good man."

Thank the Great One. If she'd said no, he'd have supported her, but he wasn't looking forward to crushing Ian's hopes. If the shoe were on the other foot, he'd be devastated at waiting so much as a minute to meet the daughter he'd thought lost.

He tucked her hand into the crook of his elbow and covered it with his free hand. "Then let's go make his day, Squeak."

They ambled along the white sand paths, the noonday sun warm, yet not hot enough to chase away what remained of the crisp morning. Jilly's fingers tightened and her body angled close to his, but she kept her head up, gaze locked on the man not twenty-five feet ahead.

"Until you tell me otherwise." he said beneath his breath, "I'm right there with you." He squeezed her hand in reassurance as they rounded the last bend.

Ian's deep voice trailed off and his jaw slackened, whatever he was saying lost behind the lock he had on Jillian. He stood, the remnants of his injuries making the move jerky and slower than his pride probably cared to admit. His Adam's apple bobbed on a nervous swallow. "Jillian?"

Lexi rose behind him and laid a hand on his shoulder. Eryx couldn't blame her for needing contact. The wealth of emotion in Ian's one word could've gutted the diabhal.

Ian inched forward.

"Call me Jilly." She held out her hand with the same cultured politeness Galena and Orla were renowned for. "No one calls me Jillian. Not unless I'm in trouble."

Ian took the hand she offered, reverently cupping it in both of his. "All right then, Jilly it is."

"*Beautiful. Just like your mother.*"

Eryx jolted at Ian's voice in his head and glanced at Lexi.

She'd moved in closer to Ian and Jillian, her light banter filling the awkward introductions between the two of them. If she'd heard Ian telepathically, she sure wasn't showing it.

It had to be his imagination. He'd probably just got caught up in the emotional moment and lost his focus.

He hoped.

"...If that's okay with you?"

Ian's voice pulled Eryx's head out of his ass. "Sorry, I was somewhere else. What's the question?"

Lexi scowled. "Jilly offered to sit with Ian for a bit while we took care of that errand we need to run." She switched to telepathy. "*Work with me here.*"

Well, he sure wasn't imagining the irritation in his baineann's tone. "As long as you two are comfortable, I'm good." He stepped aside and motioned Lexi ahead of him. "We shouldn't be long. Give Orla a shout if you need help while we're gone all right, Squeak?"

She nodded and a pretty flush dotted her cheeks, the kind he hoped Ian's presence caused a whole lot more of.

"I thought that went well." Lexi nearly bounced toward the castle, her soft-black hair swishing around her shoulders.

Histus, but he liked seeing her this happy. A far cry from where she'd been only a week ago.

Her steps slowed and her smile melted. "But that doesn't look so good."

Eryx followed her gaze and felt his levity fizzle right along side hers.

Making her way from the far end of the garden was Galena, her strides calm but purposeful. Ramsay stomped behind her, brusque, yet animated gestures flying as he shouted.

"You think we should run for it, or get a whistle?" Lexi pinched her chin. It was hard to tell if she was serious or if she'd jumped off into one of her playful spells.

Personally he'd had enough drama and wanted a little more alone time with his mate. "I'll vote for running."

Lexi shook her head and screwed her mouth up on one side. "Nope. We're too late." She tugged him closer and winked. "I think you'd better brace."

Not two seconds later, Galena strode around the last corner.

"Come on, Lena. What the hell was I supposed to think?" Ramsay ground to a halt beside her and cast a desperate look at Eryx. "You're not gonna believe—"

Galena held up a hand to cut him off. "Could you, just for a minute, keep your mouth shut? I wasn't ignoring you, I was looking for Eryx because I only want to say this once."

She took a deep breath and glared at the two of them, not sparing so much as a glance at Lexi. She ended the back and forth on Eryx. "You should know I'm involved with Reese."

Shit.

Ramsay scoffed and turned away with both hands on his hips.

Lexi smiled and snuggled tighter to Eryx. *"Oh, this is going to be good."*

"Can it, hellcat." His mate got entirely too much pleasure out of matchmaking. "Involved how, exactly?"

Lexi craned her head up at him.

Both women glared with one raised eyebrow. Did they learn that expression in the cradle?

"She means, involved," Lexi said. "As in to—"

"He knows what you mean." Ramsay crossed his arms. "And so will everyone else when they see your hair bound. Really, Galena? You think you can publicly claim a guy like that after everything he's done and it not fall back on you?"

Fuck, he'd missed the hair. Where in histus was his head today? Maybe he had imagined that bit with Ian.

Galena swung her arm between them to cut him off. "And that's what we need to talk about."

"I think you should have talked to us—"

"No." Galena sparked with a fierceness he hadn't seen since she'd caught a teenage boy hurting a helpless animal. "Here's the deal. You two are my brothers. Not my keepers. I love you and I'll support you in whatever you need, but you will not control my life. My decisions are my own. The sooner you both get that, the better off we'll be."

She paused, her gaze resting for a minute on Lexi. In that second, Eryx could have sworn some sort of feminine mojo swept between them. A silent ra-ra reserved for women alone.

"I get you don't have reason to trust Reese, and I appreciate the position you're in." She eyed each of them. "But I feel something with him I haven't ever felt before and I'm not going to pass up on the chance to embrace it." She honed in on Eryx. "You of all people should get that. You risked your throne for your mate. The last thing I want to do is risk my relationships with my brothers, but what I feel for Reese is worth the risk."

Lexi's grip tightened on Eryx's arm, a silent message he wasn't sure how to interpret. She'd hinted at something between Reese and Galena. Histus, he'd seen them kiss in Reese's memory, but had hoped it was an empty, one-time act. "What do you want from us?"

Lexi stroked the back of his arm with her thumb, a silent encouragement.

Galena pulled in a long breath and squared her shoulders. "I don't expect for you to understand my reasoning or decisions, but I'd like to have your acceptance and your support." She paused, the tension in her frame eking out enough to let her vulnerability shine through. "If I screw up, it's mine to own, but I'd like to know I have your love no matter what."

Ramsay held her stare for a heartbeat. "Always." He turned away and stomped toward the house. "But I'll kill him if he hurts you."

Galena exhaled and glared at Eryx. "And you?"

Damn. That she'd even be forced to ask the question shamed him to the core. Eryx pulled her into a bear hug, her thick braid digging into the inside of his forearm. "You shouldn't even need to ask, Lena." He let her go and tucked Lexi against his side. "But Ramsay's right. Reese will pay dearly if he hurts you."

She rolled her eyes and walked away, shaking of her head. "Neanderthals. Every damned one of them."

"Well, would you look at that?" Lexi crossed her arms, saucy and clearly pleased with herself. A satisfied smirk played on her lips. "I do believe my work here is done."

Chapter 21

The sun warmed the back of Galena's neck, nothing but her garden and her thoughts for company. The rich soil's damp musk surrounded her, a protective cocoon more effective than the high stone walls at the back of her cottage. A slow ache had settled in her back over an hour ago, but her connection to the Earth was too peaceful, too soothing to set her planting aside. Too necessary in combating her tangled thoughts and emotions.

She walked her knees two paces to the left and plunged her spade deep. The muscles in her arms shook with fatigue. Reaching with her mind, she slid the seedling tray beside her. Transplanting the tiny shoots this early was a bad idea, but she'd used up all her patience with her brothers. With a little luck and a nudge from her energy through the soil they'd find purchase anyway.

Maybe she should call Orla. The woman had a canny gift with all things green. One touch and a whispered encouragement could pull a straggling brown plant from the brink of kindling.

"I'd suggest sunscreen, but I guess sunburns and skin cancer don't last long around you." Lexi's sandaled feet stepped into sight a second before she crouched beside her. "Which brother are you digging the hole for? 'Cause if it's my husband I gotta ask you to hold off a little longer before you plant him. Technically, it's still my honeymoon and I wouldn't mind basking in the afterglow for a few more days."

Galena eased a seedling from its container, settled it in the center of the dark soil, and scooped the loose dirt around it. "I didn't hear you come in."

"I can be stealthy when I want." Lexi fingered one leaf. "Frankly, you were so focused a herd of elephants could have stomped in here and you wouldn't have known it." She dusted off one of the paver stones on the garden path and settled on her butt. "Wanna talk about it?"

Galena chuckled. "I'm a little talked out."

"Yeah, that was some speech. Pretty impressive if you ask me."

Galena sat back on her heels. "Ah, but will they listen?"

"Who the hell knows? Men are goofs. Sometimes they need repetition." She pushed to her feet and grunted on par with a man tasked with a honey-do list. "Seriously, let's save the good chats for a decent barstool and a good-looking bartender next time." She held out her hand and wiggled her fingers. "Come on."

"Come on, where?"

"Eryx needs you."

Oh, heck no. Galena edged over to the next open spot, her thick braid swinging to one side of her face. "I've had more than enough of their lectures and opinions. Unless something's wrong with Ian or Brenna, I'm taking a little time to myself. Otherwise, I might slip a little something in their food I'll regret later."

"You can do that?"

Galena leered at her new shalla.

Lexi smiled. "Of course you can. Good to know. We might need to use that someday. Right now, we gotta go." She wiggled her fingers more urgently.

"Is someone hurt?"

"No. Although, Eryx did tell me he thought he heard Ian speak to him telepathically." She shook her head as though to get herself back on track. "But that's beside the point. Eryx says it's important."

"He heard what?"

"Focus." Lexi stooped, tugged Galena upright, and gathered her tools. "I'll get these and you put your little baby plants wherever they need to go."

Galena stilled Lexi with a grip at her shoulder. "After everything you've said to me, and all the encouragement to stand up for myself, you expect me to go hightailing it over there on a whim?"

Lexi's mouth twitched and she brushed a dirt clump off the spade's tip. "I'm pretty sure it's not a whim."

"What's that supposed to mean?"

She looked away and scowled. "I don't think I'm supposed to say."

"If you're not—"

Lexi held up her hands. "Girl, don't make this harder on me than it is. Remember that honeymoon thing? If you keep digging, my allotted marital bliss period will get the kibosh. Grill me later if you want, but for right now, let's get this show on the road."

Damn but she wished she had Lexi's emotional radar detector. She dusted off her hands and grabbed the fragile seedlings. "Fine. I'll get these put up and we'll go."

She stashed the tray in the mini greenhouse off to one side of the garden, and swept the tools from Lexi and into their rightful places with her mind. She brushed the dirt from her knees as she tottered for the door. "I'll finish with these when I get back."

Lexi didn't budge.

"Aren't you coming?"

Frowning, Lexi scrutinized Galena's appearance. "Don't you want to change first? I mean, the leggings look comfy and the black's a good choice for dirt, but maybe something a little more…" She made a shooing gesture and wrinkled her nose. "I dunno. Clean and pretty?"

Galena stomped inside. The cottage's shade wrapped her sun-warmed shoulders in a cool kiss. "If Eryx wants me he can deal with me as is."

Lexi hurried past her, angling for the front door before Galena could get there. "Nope." She leaned against the door, arms crossed. "I'm pretty sure we need a wardrobe change. Gotta trust me on this one."

"Lexi, what's going on?"

"Honestly?" Lexi screwed her mouth up in a quirky pucker. "I'm not a hundred percent sure. Let's just say I have a hunch and you'll thank me later."

Galena let out a weary exhale. Praise the Great One, she needed a break. Three hours in the sun and soil wasn't nearly enough to ground her, not with all the current weirdness in her life. "Fine." She spun for her bedroom. "But if I end up changing for another lecture, you'll be the first one with a laxative in their soup."

She showered and changed quickly, Lexi jumping in and insisting on a sapphire velvet gown tucked near the back of her closet. The sleeves were long with ends that billowed out in a dramatic flair, and a broad platinum belt accented her hips before dipping in a sultry line at the center. "Kind of a bit much, don't you think?"

Lexi smirked and jaunted out the bedroom door. "I think it's perfect. Now, let's get a move on."

Jagger fell in behind them the minute they took to the air, Lexi's somo a far more discreet shadow than Ludan's brooding presence when it came to Eryx.

They landed at the main castle door and the guards on either side pulled the front doors wide.

"Lexi." Galena hurried to catch up with her shalla's long strides. "Lexi, wait. You can't expect me to walk in there without telling me what's going on."

Lexi paused outside the closed receiving room. She checked Galena's appearance, smoothing her hands along Galena's fitted sleeves. "You look great. Just take long, slow breaths and you'll be fine." She opened the doors and strode toward the thrones at the far end of the room where Eryx waited, abandoning Galena at the entrance.

So much for answers.

Everyone remotely close to her or her family was there. Graylin, Orla, and Ludan on one side of the hall, Ramsay and Jillian on the other, and Eryx and Lexi on their thrones front and center. Jagger sauntered in behind her and stood beside Ramsay.

"What is this? Some kind of intervention?" She glared at Lexi, betrayal simmering under her skin.

Lexi smacked Eryx on the arm and frowned up at him. "Now would be a good time to talk. She's one of the few female friends I have and she can slip me laxatives when I'm not looking."

Eryx grinned and waved her forward. "Relax, Galena. A formal request has been made, one that required your presence. Old-school rules demand I honor the appeal for attendance." He covered Lexi's hand where it rested on the armrest. "What it's about, I don't yet know." He nodded at Ludan who promptly ambled toward the entrance.

"You sure you don't want to clue me in?" If Galena's soft mental message startled Lexi, she didn't show it.

"If I knew for sure, I'd be tempted." She rolled her lips inward and snuck a peek at Eryx. *"As it is, I'm afraid I might be reading it wrong."*

Footsteps sounded behind her, more than one tread.

Galena turned and her heart stuttered. She pressed the heel of her hand against her chest and rubbed. Like that might somehow force it back into its normal rhythm. "Reese."

God, he looked good. She'd left him this morning in well-worn leather pants and little else, but now he was decked out in full court regalia. The leather pants were similar, yet of the finest quality and fitted to hug his thighs and grip-worthy butt. The drast wasn't like the one Eryx's warriors wore, but tinted to a pale yellow gold that accented the tawny streaks in his hair.

Loose. His hair was loose and everyone in her family was present. Puzzle pieces shifted and clicked into place, while panic shoved to the forefront of her mind. Surely he wasn't here for her.

"You've got our attention, Reese."

Galena spun to face Eryx just as he motioned Reese forward. "My sister doesn't lose her temper often, but when she does it gets nasty." One side of his mouth curled in a smile that said he remembered the lash of her earlier outburst all too well. "I suggest you share what's on your mind before she passes go."

* * * *

Reese fought for breath, air barely skimming past his tight throat. If he'd been nervous before, he was scared shitless now. Bad enough the room was big enough to fit the whole damned council. The cathedral ceiling reached at least three stories and was made of onyx planks that echoed Eryx's deep voice around the room like an omniscient being.

Lots of people stood waiting. Some he knew, some he didn't. Every one of them stared him down, Galena in particular. Even from twenty feet away he felt her pull. Her fiery hair was still braided and her sultry curves were hugged in bold blue velvet. Potential disaster or not, she was worth the risk he was about to take.

One breath at a time, step by step, he'd make it through this. He strode forward and pushed his shoulders back. The crimson rugs absorbed his footfalls, leaving only the blood roaring in his ears. If he could face the council and bare his deepest secrets, he could stand before Galena's brothers and ask for what he wanted.

Ramsay shifted from one foot to the other at the bottom of the dais, either impatient or pissed off.

Galena followed his progress, smoothing the fabric along her hips.

Maybe this was too much. Too soon.

He kept walking.

Eryx stared him down, hard and impassive. The council garb of loose silk tank and pants would have made most men look soft, almost feminine. On him it was intimidating, and the crown only made it worse.

Surely this was right. After watching Galena this morning, and the way she owned what burned between them, it had to be.

Fan-fucking-tastic words. Too bad they didn't do something to slow the jackrabbit action behind his breastbone.

Reese kneeled at the four steps leading to the dais and lowered his head. "You honor me with your audience."

A whisper drifted at his left. The rustle of the fabric issued from somewhere behind him.

"My father was the last to receive a request for private audience." Eryx paused, still not giving Reese leave to stand. "Do you accept the price?"

Indebted service without question for the rest of his life might be too large a sum for some men, but for a chance to be with Galena, the cost was paltry. He opened his mouth.

"What price?" Galena moved at his right.

Reese started to lift his head, but caught himself before he could break protocol.

"The question wasn't for you, Galena." Eryx's voice was all malran, harsh and commanding. "Answer the question, Reese."

"Gladly," Reese said.

Quiet settled on the room, the lack of sound having a unique amplification all its own.

"Rise."

Reese lifted his head.

Eryx glared from his perch, his torso angled forward and ready to pounce. The malress sat calm beside him, her hand atop her mate's on the armrest, and a gleam in her eye.

Eryx eased back in his chair and let out a slow, resigned breath. "Talk."

Every word, every thought he'd rehearsed through the day, vanished.

From the corner of his eye, the malress tilted her head, considering. Or was it encouraging?

"I've found my mate," he said before he could overanalyze any further.

Galena gasped behind him.

Someone outside his line of sight muttered. Probably Ramsay.

The malress beamed a powerful smile.

Eryx's demeanor didn't budge. "Indeed." He glanced at Galena and scooped the malress' hand into his, running his thumb along her knuckles in an absent back and forth swipe. "And?"

Reese swallowed, desperate to unhinge his tongue from the roof of his mouth. Of course the malran wouldn't make this easy. If the roles were reversed and it was his sister waiting in the wings he wouldn't either.

Every scrap of emotion he'd waded through the past many days surfaced as he spoke, leaving his voice grated. "Galena deserves the formality of this rite. I know you and your brother have no cause to trust me. I can only vow I've learned from my mistakes and demonstrate it's true through my actions going forward. But I ask you to support whatever decision she makes and know, if she chooses a life with me, I will honor her life and her trust until The Great One takes me."

Eryx stared him down. Even the affectionate stroke for his mate ceased. No one whispered. No one moved. If his mind hadn't felt so paralyzed, his senses so tuned and ready for fight or flight, he'd have prayed. Even begged if that's what it took to break the silence.

"You've got balls to come here." Eryx's voice rumbled through the quiet. Some of the tension in his frame eased. "Whether or not I like or agree with Galena's decisions, my love and support is unconditional." Eryx looked at Ramsay. "I think I'm safe in saying that goes for every person gathered in this room." He squeezed the malress' hand and nodded at Reese. "Make your request."

* * * *

Galena tried to swallow. Praise the Great One, what she wouldn't give for a time out. Just a handful of minutes she could freeze-frame long enough to catch her breath and untangle her thoughts. She'd been ready to face her family with her decision, and step into her feelings with Reese, but this?

Reese strode toward her, slow, but confident. He lowered his voice. "I told you I wouldn't push. I know this flies in the face of that promise, and if you need more time, I'll wait. But denying what I want from you is a falsehood I want no part in. I want it known, to you and to your family, my intent. My resolve."

"You might want to take a nice long breath, girlfriend." Lexi's voice in Galena's head might have had a playful irony, but her outward expression stayed locked in regal impassiveness. *"You look like you're ready to beat feet out the doors. I thought you wanted this."*

"I wanted to feel alive," Galena answered, her throat closing in as sure as a hand curled around it. *"To feel beautiful and cherished, even sexual. This is—"*

"Huge. Mind- and life-altering." If anyone knew what it was like to walk that emotional gauntlet, it would be Lexi.

Reese offered his hand.

Memories of the way Reese had touched her rushed to greet her, the rasp of his warm fingers against her skin and the scrape of his calloused palms as he swept them down her hips. The burned as fierce and vibrant as the moment they'd happened.

"Let me show you my heart," he said. "Take my hand and come with me to face our futures as one."

Galena's mind zigzagged in all directions. Seconds trudged past like hours. If anyone would understand, maybe help her find a way to sidestep this issue and save Reese's pride in the process it would be Lexi. *"I'm not like you. I can't jump in headfirst like you did with Eryx. I need time.*

Practice." That last little bit trailed off, a lack of conviction even she couldn't miss.

"Is that what you need? Or is that what you're used to?" Compassion and challenge shone on Lexi's face, not at all the sisters-in-arms Galena had hoped for. *"Seems to me you've got a man who's strong enough to let you set the pace, but willing to take you further than you yourself even know you can go."* Her gaze slid to Reese. *"But then if being cherished and appreciated for who you are at your core for the rest of your life doesn't appeal..."*

Reese waited, hand outstretched. Tension radiated from him and his emerald eyes darkened with doubt. Slowly, his fingers curled inward to form a loose fist and he lowered his hand. "I understand." His voice cracked and he coughed around it. "When you're ready, I'll come for you again."

With two quick steps back, he faced Eryx and Lexi, and dropped to one knee, lowering his head. "My debt is yours, my Malran." He rose without leave from Eryx and turned for the door, his head lifted strong and proud.

Ramsay took a hesitant step forward.

Orla and Graylin leveled worried stares at her from across the room.

He was leaving. A handful of steps away from the door, taking the air from her lungs with him. All because she couldn't muster a tenth of the courage he'd shown in coming here. Let alone promising The Great One only knew what to her brother.

"Stop!" She threw the doors closed with a shove from her mind, scantly missing Reese in the process. Her shout's echo hung above them.

Reese fisted his hands, still facing the door.

"Please, stop." Her feet moved her forward, not a conscious action so much as an impulsive need. She took his hand, smoothing the tight grip between her own. "Ask me again."

"It doesn't work that way, Galena." Eryx's voice grumbled from his throne.

"Why the hell not?" Lexi said.

God, Galena loved her new shalla. "I don't care how it's supposed to work," Galena said to Reese. There might be secret protocols and rituals, but this was between them. Between her and the man who'd faced so much in her honor. "I'm afraid, but not of you. Not of what's between us. The emotions are just—"

"Staggering," he answered.

She pressed a kiss to his palm. She closed her eyes and focused on the brush of his fingers against her cheek. "Ask me again."

He pulled his hand free and let it fall to his side, his face pensive. When he stepped away, her heart lurched. "If my malran would allow—"

"He absolutely will allow." Lexi leveled a killer smile at Eryx, one that promised all manner of indulgence if she got her way. She curled one hand around his arm and stroked his bicep with the other. "We're total suckers for romance, right dear?"

Eryx ducked his head so only Lexi could see his face, and a flush spread across Lexi's cheeks. Lifting his head, Eryx pegged Reese with a haggard look. "Ask."

Reese offered his hand, a possessive glint in his eyes that kindled a slow burn across her own cheeks. "Two hearts with one future. Will you come with me?"

A future and a family. With Reese. Flutters rippled through her and her throat clogged so thick she could hardly breathe. She placed her hand in his. "Anywhere."

Chapter 22

Reese tucked Galena tighter in the circle of his arms, the damp night cool around them as they flew. Stars and fat energy streams streaked overhead. Flowers and the crisp, clean bite of foliage scented the air. He'd been braced for disappointment. Had suffered an emotional anvil to the heart when Galena had failed to take his hand. But now, here he was, in a perfect moment surrounded by the quiet darkness of a newly fallen night.

He toyed with the metal bead holding Galena's braid in place. Customarily she'd have worn it down had she expected him, but his choosing the most ancient of rituals, stating his desire and laying his request before her in front of her family, hadn't allowed for her knowing. Not without risking Eryx's denial of Reese's petition.

"You're quiet." He brushed her ear with his lips. The lotus flower scent she favored clung to her hair and escaped wisps from her braid tickled his nose. "Regrets?"

"More confused than anything." She glanced over her shoulder, startled. "With Eryx, not us."

He couldn't blame her. The malran left him just as confused, booting him from the castle one day, only to give his blessing a few days later. Though something told him the malress had served as his advocate. If ever he proved such was the case, he'd gladly offer his new queen whatever she asked. Galena was worth any effort. "Want to talk about it?"

Beneath his arms, her chest rose and fell in slow, thoughtful breaths. "It's what he said before we left, or maybe what he didn't say." She grew silent, her thumb shuttling back and forth against his forearm in an absent swipe. "You forget, women are sheltered from the ritual. Cryptic words and pointed looks without a basis for interpretation don't do much to prepare a woman."

He hadn't forgotten. Histus, if anything he'd thought about nothing else since he'd woken from Maxis' attack with her beside him. "What did he tell you?"

"That I should be attuned to your actions. To base my decisions on the care and thoughtfulness behind each act as it should represent how you mean to go forward."

"He's right."

An exasperated sigh huffed out and she dropped her head against his shoulder. "Still cryptic."

Reese rolled, his back to the miles passing beneath them, holding Galena tight above him. "It's necessary, sweetheart. Tomorrow it'll make sense."

He might also be dead. No way would he give up until she accepted his bond. He tightened his arms and kissed the top of her head. "Relax into me. Let me fly us both while you enjoy the stars." For an independent woman like Galena who'd been flying on her own for years, surrendering flight to someone else hundreds of feet above the ground didn't come easy, but it was a decent warmup for what would be asked of her as the night progressed.

She wiggled against his grip and rolled so she peered down at him, still perpetuating her own flight. She stroked his pectorals through his drast and studied him. Inch by inch, she relaxed, her head turning so her ear lay above his heart. "You have me." Her forward movement stopped.

Reese adjusted, dropping them both a good ten feet in the process to keep her settled against him. Praise the Great One, he'd nearly failed her.

Her delighted chuckle rumbled against his ribs and she petted the rough-slick fabric of his drast. "You did say to relax."

"A test from my mate-to-be." He cupped the back of her head and reveled in his heart's rapid thump. "I'd say you took your brother's meaning quite well."

They fell into a comfortable silence, the night's steady hum and air around them a soothing song. Water trickled in the distance, growing as they covered the miles.

Galena lifted her head, her brow furrowed in concentration, undoubtedly triangulating their location. "Where are we going? We're nowhere near the homestead."

"No." And the fact that she'd followed him without question, not bothering to check their direction until now, pushed his shoulders back with pride. "I want to get your opinion on something."

Her face lit up, full of innocence and free of concerns or worry. "I'd thought we'd—"

"Maybe it's best you lose your assumptions tonight." He cradled her and angled to land. "Just let what needs to happen, happen."

Her eyes widened, focused on something behind him. "Oh..."

The cottage looked different at night than it had when he'd seen it this morning, more mystical and a bit exotic. Built into the side of a rocky mountain peak, the front half looked every inch an English village, but with a charcoal slate roof instead of thatch. The roofline was asymmetrical, one side at a standard pitch, the other with a slow, concave curve that jutted out over a cozy porch. From there it stretched back a good thirty feet before blending into the hillside.

"I've never seen anything like it." Galena studied the structure, head tilted in curiosity.

Ah, the flowers, planted in varied pots and boxes at the porch's edge. Of course she'd be drawn to those first.

Reese led her toward the front door, her awe spurring his own enthusiasm. He couldn't remember the last time he felt this light and free of taint. "Come look inside."

The tour wouldn't take long. Empty of everything but its rough, stone walls and ancient Blackwood floors, there wasn't much to show—a comfortable kitchen situated at the center, three living areas, and three well-sized, but otherwise unremarkable guest bedrooms. The master, however, packed a pretty inspiring punch he couldn't wait to share.

They moved from room to room, candles he'd left behind late this afternoon flaring to life at his command. The master suite lay ahead, all that remained of their tour. The long, dark hallway echoed their steps and drew them deeper, far away from the rest of the cottage.

Galena glanced over her shoulder. "Are we beneath the hillside?"

"For now." Pale moonlight sparkled at the end of the corridor. "A little farther and you'll find the best surprise."

She hustled faster, her full skirt flaring. Two steps from the threshold she slowed.

As he closed the distance behind her, he shifted to one side. The pearlescent light from the wide balcony window spotlighted the wonder on her face, one hand resting at the hollow of her throat.

"Reese this is..." She glided forward, slow and reverent. "I've never seen anything like it."

He hadn't either. The room wasn't obscenely large, but enough to handle over-sized furniture and still appear roomy. The entry's nine-foot ceiling vaulted to nearly fifteen feet at the center, the hillside rock exposed as it eventually opened to a balcony. The entire wall to the outside was glass, domestication wedged within an otherworldly aerie.

Galena pushed open the sliding door and the soft rumble of the waterfall they'd heard flying in filled the shadowed room. She rushed to the carved railing and leaned over, her gasp mingling with the water's rush. "It's beautiful."

Reese crowded behind her and cupped her shoulders. "You missed the bathroom, but I'll agree this was probably the more exotic choice." It also brought her one step closer to where they'd end their night, but she'd learn that soon enough. "Do you like it?"

"Who wouldn't like it? It's amazing." She scanned the deep green fauna around the tall, intimately rounded cove at the waterfall's core. "These plants...they're some of the most difficult to grow. The soil here must be incredible."

"Beth tells me there's a certain rainforest effect here, a blend where Havilah and Runa meet."

She shuffled to the edge of the balcony. A wood bridge spanned from there to a stone path beyond and down a winding trek to the cove's sandy base. She stooped to touch the charcoal soil.

"Beth?" She rubbed the granules between her fingers and thumb and peered at Reese. "I don't remember you mentioning a Beth. Is this her place?"

"Beth and Ben care for my homestead. She's the woman who kept my mother's greenhouse." Reese edged forward and urged her upright. "As for who this land belongs to, it depends on you."

She tilted her head in silent question.

"If you like it, it's yours. My mating gift to you. A home that fits your gifts and your exotic nature, free from all my past."

"Your past makes you who you are." She edged close, her breasts soft against his chest. Her fingers pushed and pulled against his drast and she swallowed, pupils dilating. "And I happen to love you. I have no desire to lose what makes you unique."

He'd thought the night was perfect before, but he'd been wrong. This was perfect. The two of them, surrounded by tropical indulgence, the water's vibration, and the pulsing, damp air. He'd never thought to hear those words from any woman.

"I love you, too." He traced her jawline. Tonight was real, not a dream or a figment of his imagination. "Enough to keep you safe and far from anyplace known to Maxis. Enough to surround you with beauty and what feeds your soul."

He lowered his head, the lure of her lips and the potent pull that crackled between them too much to ignore. "Enough to claim you if you'll have me." He hovered, close enough to feel her warm exhalations, to scent her honeyed breath, but not enough to touch. "Say yes."

She gripped the back of his head and crushed her mouth to his. Her answer tasted of impatience and her tremors echoed the need stomping through his own.

The path. He had to make it down the path, tamper his need, and see to hers. This was her time, a definition of how he meant to treat her. How he'd cherish her in the days and nights to come.

He swept her up and cradled her against his chest. Each step rung through the grotto, sharp against the bridge's wood slats, and then on to the thick stone. The air grew thicker, damper against their skin as he navigated the slow, meandering path.

Rounding the trail, he angled for the natural grotto near the waterfall's base. A push from his thoughts fired the waiting pit. The flames leapt in a powerful burst and settled beneath the air's damp kiss.

Galena pulled away on a startled gasp and fisted his shoulder. "Praise the Great One."

He lowered her to her feet, the amazement on her face worth the temporary loss of contact.

She crept forward, gaze roving across the candles wedged in clumps along the rocky ledges. She stopped at the natural raised shelf near the fire and ran her fingertips atop the forest green pallet. Understanding settled in her expression, her focus squared on the thick padding. "Here." The single word seemed more for her ears than his, a thought spoken aloud.

"It's your choice, Galena." He might go ten different kinds of insane in waiting, but he'd be damned if he pushed her in this, or gave her any reason to second-guess her decisions. "Always your choice."

She lifted her head. "You misunderstood." Never dropping her gaze from his, she toed off her sandals and unhooked the draped platinum belt at her waist. Every move held a sensual grace, an elegant stroke that called him closer. She pushed the wide neck of her gown past one shoulder, and his stomach wrenched tight. "I wasn't questioning my decision." She freed the other side and the velvet fell to the ground in a decadent heap. "I was asking you to make it happen."

Firelight flickered over Galena's tanned curves, her hair a perfect match for the flames. Every untamed, carnal thought he'd kept caged fought for release. His cock, a ready player from the moment she'd stepped onto the balcony, hardened to the point of ache. He tugged his boots free and tossed them aside. "You're going off script."

"I don't know the script, remember?" She cupped her breasts, lifting them and worrying the tight tips between her fingers and thumbs, a seductress unleashed from her confines. She prowled closer, hips swaying seductively. "Can't we make our own?

He rubbed his shaft, desperate to make room behind the too tight leather. Christ, he'd had a plan. What in histus was it?

"You're supposed to show me how you mean to go forward, right?" She slipped her fingers under his drast and pushed the fabric up, splaying her hands across his pecs. She laid a kiss above his heart. "You give me pleasure when you make love to me, so give me that."

Fuck, the woman was muddling his mind and enslaving his body with little more than a words and simple touch. He yanked his drast over his head.

Before the shirt could even clear his head, Galena unfastened his pants and kneeled before him. She peeled the leather past his hips and his cock sprang free, heavy and ready.

Her mouth parted and her delicate tongue swept across her lips, so close her breath fanned out against his skin.

His dick jerked and his balls tightened. "Galena."

She leaned in, lips at the base of his shaft. With a reverent kiss, she looked up from beneath weighted eyelids. "I want us. This. However it comes."

"So bold." Fisting himself, he grazed the tip along her lower lip. "Show me what you want."

Her eyelids dropped on a heated moan and her mouth enveloped him, sinking to the root in one insistent plunge.

Hot. Scalding and so damned intense the pleasure nearly knocked him off his feet. Galena worked his length as though starved for his taste, the sensation too much and not enough all in one breath. He had to get a grip, to keep control and see to her needs.

"Mine." He gripped the back of her head and freed the bead binding her hair as her tongue lashed his hard flesh. He worked the sections free, fingers tangling in the smooth strands. His legs shook, the need to indulge warring with the need to protect. "Mine to take." A short thrust, and then another. "Mine to pleasure."

He pulled himself from her mouth's searing heat and dragged her to her feet, slanting his mouth against her swollen lips. He pinned her hands behind her back.

She fought his hold and let loose a frustrated mewl. "Let me touch you."

He tightened his grip, and cupped her nape with his free hand. "No." He nipped her chin, kissing his way up her jawline. "Tonight you feel." He savored the skin along her neck, and rubbed his cock against her mound. "You enjoy." He tumbled them to the pallet, adjusting her hands overhead and pinning them there with his mind. He splayed her knees wide and his mouth watered, eager for her taste. "You relent."

Her bold, earthy taste exploded on his tongue, and the sharp musk of her arousal filled his lungs. Her cries echoed through the tiny inlet, and she shuddered beneath him with each lap of his tongue. This was what he'd waited and suffered for, a feast for all his senses and a succulent reward.

He pushed a torrent of energy around her breasts, plucking the tips with intense sparks she'd feel like the scrape of teeth.

"Reese." She arched into the invisible caress, straining for more of the dark touch.

"Fuck, yes." He splayed one hand on her belly, fingers stretched wide to hold her in place. With the other he teased her entrance, slipping through her wetness, and coaxing it up and around her swollen clit. "I love it when you let go." He pressed two fingers deep and her tight channel clamped around them. "Love the way your pussy grips me." Another press, crooking to nudge her front wall. "Tight and greedy for more."

She fought, legs trembling with need as she tried to wiggle her hips. "Reese, please. It's not enough." She opened her eyes, such need reflected in them he felt it like a grip at his nape. She undulated against him, writhing through a long moan. "I need your cock."

Sweet Great One on High, he loved her voice like this. Grated and husky, dirty and blatant. He shifted, anchoring one hand by her head and guiding his staff with the other. No one would ever have her this way again. No one but him. "Mine."

He surged forward.

Galena's cry fired through the grotto and her hips rocked against his in a frantic dance, two mindless souls in perfect sync, barbaric and beautiful.

Christ, he needed control. Needed to bind her and claim her before they both shot straight to climax. He shifted and put his weight on his heels. Anchoring his hand above her heart, he deepened the stream of energy at her nipples and slowed his thrusts.

"I vow to the Great One," he rasped, "to love and provide for you until I leave this life." He captured her right hand and anchored it over his own heart. "I will see to your needs and the needs of those you hold dear. Protect you at all costs, even to the point of death."

Her heart pounded against his palm, a powerful match to his own.

His lungs burned and pleasure pooled at the base of his cock. "No other will be placed before you." He hesitated and the muscles behind his shoulder blades tensed, braced for the pain. He'd bear it. He'd bear anything to earn her trust, or die trying. "You have my heart until I breathe no more."

Instinct took over, some fundamental fragment from his soul spearing past flesh and sinew to surround her heart.

Pain speared as fat as a broadsword into his chest, and heat scorched and fired out in every direction, hot enough to shrivel every vein. He couldn't breathe. Couldn't see. Wasn't even sure his heart still beat.

The trial. This was it, and it was pure, scorching torture. No way would he give in and rescind his bond. She'd either accept him or he'd die trying.

A shout filled the grotto, an agonized wail too deep to be Galena's. Darkness crowded his vision and torturous shards pierced from somewhere in the center of his brain to the souls of his feet.

If you let go, it will all be over. Peace and comfort will all be yours.

The thought lured him, dangling like a wind chime on a sunny, spring day.

He pressed harder against Galena's chest, desperate, feeling for the reassurance of her heart's beat against his palm. He wouldn't give in, never again. He'd die before he let her go.

A powerful force slammed into Reese and latched around his heart, the sting of anchor-like pegs digging deep into the vital muscle. His torso jerked on the snap of an invisible tether and his breath caught.

Galena. She'd accepted him. Pleasure lanced through him, licking every vestige of pain he'd endured in an exotic stroke. Quaking muscles roared with renewed strength and his balls drew up tight, his release not far behind.

"Reese." Galena's nails bit into his shoulders, her sweet plea smooth against his ears. Her legs draped wide over his straining thighs. Her breasts bounced with each thrust, the contrast of the creamy, soft swells to his dark hand pressed to her sternum blatant and erotic. Her kiss-swollen lips curled in a satisfied, open-mouthed smile and she splayed her legs wider. "Mine."

The husky claim spurred his beast. Hell, yes, she'd accepted him. This was his woman. To protect, to love, and to pleasure. With his mind, he unleashed a rampage of energy, swirling unmercifully at every pleasure point and simulating the sensation of both fingers and mouth. He gripped her luscious hips and pistoned deep.

She took all of him, tip to root. Decadent sensations warred for surrender, the slap of his tight sack on her flesh, the musk of her arousal, and the slippery sounds of his cock pounding through her wet channel.

A violent release burned low in his shaft, each ragged mewl from her lips lending unbearable pressure. "Come for me, Galena." Sliding a hand between their bodies, he ran his thumb through the wetness where they joined and circled her swollen clit. "Surrender."

He struck without leniency, pressing the nub beneath his thumb, and latching onto one turgid nipple with urgent lips.

Velvet heat clamped down on his shaft and Galena's haggard wail rent through the room. He came with her, long, jerking spasms he felt to his toes. In that moment, they were one. Two halves joined, male and female bound by heart and soul. His existence without her meant nothing.

The rhythmic press of their bodies eased. The kiss of water-cooled air fanned their slick flesh, raising gooseflesh in its wake. He cupped her beautiful face and grazed each perfect angle with his lips. Resting on his elbows, he pushed a stray lock of hair from her brow. "I love you."

Shocking blue eyes opened to meet his, so filled with passion his heart buckled. "My fireann, my love."

He had a mate, a baineann of his own who loved him without any secrets between them. He cradled her tight and rolled them to their sides. Their clamoring pulses warred beneath sweat-slick skin. For the first time in his life he felt centered. Complete in a way he never knew existed. For her he'd endure any pain, or kill any being that came between them.

Chapter 23

Faint light flickered against Maxis' closed eyelids, plucking him from a deep and peaceful sleep. He stretched, luxuriating in the rasp of cool, well-worn sheets on his bare skin as he blinked his eyes into focus. Two candles burned on the nightstand, barely illuminating Uther's lackluster décor and scenting the bedroom with tallow.

Throwing off the covers, he sat up and hobbled to the window, his muscles stiff from lack of use, but blessedly pain free. How long had he been out? Hours? Days? He pushed the heavy drapes aside.

The Underlands' black and barren soil stretched as far as the nearly darkened skies allowed him to see, with only a tiny hint of blue staining the horizon. Feeling for the sun's position with his mind, he let the curtain fall back in place. Barely past sunset, though it still didn't answer how many days had passed.

His clothes sat folded on a trunk at the foot of the bed. He snatched his loose cotton shirt from the top and tugged it over his head. A clean, generic scent he didn't recognize lingered on the fabric. He must've been out a long time if Uther had stooped to acting as laundress.

He pulled on his wool pants and reached for his boots. The room spun and he caught himself with a heavy hand against the trunk just before his kneecap smacked the wood floors.

Sitting on the trunk, he waited for his vision to still, fighting to calm his panting breaths. Maybe he'd had fewer days on the mend than he thought. He shoved on his boots and stood, locking his knees. From the looks of things, the only way he'd get answers was if he got up and took them for himself.

The door groaned opened and the scent of wood smoke filtered past the threshold. Gold and orange firelight danced against whitewashed walls, and the crack and roar of flames filled the silence.

Footsteps sounded from beyond the front door. A light tread.

The knob turned and Serena shuffled through the opening, her head ducked in a distracted pose. He'd never seen her in the casual tunics and leggings the newer generation favored, but the colorful blue fabric certainly fit her curves. The dirt and wrinkles down her front were another matter.

Something angry and downright proprietary punched him in the gut. "Where have you been?"

Serena's head shot up and her hand pressed against her heart. She sputtered and shut the door, scrutinizing him head to toe. "Handling details. How do you feel?"

"Like Uther must have graduated past shitty field medic."

The door re-opened as his words trailed off.

Uther strode past Serena and wiped his hands on an already filthy rag, not so much as a hint of surprise at seeing Maxis on his feet. He tossed the rag on the counter that separated the living area from the kitchen and fell into a worn, oversized tan chair. "Love to claim the promotion, but your mate's the one responsible."

The level of filth on Uther's attire topped Serena's my several degrees, his ivory shirt coated in four or five layers of dirt and his face coated in sweat.

Maxis stared at Serena. "Explain."

Serena's lips pursed and twitched on one side. "I went home for news, got it, and was about to leave when I decided to bring a little help with me."

Maxis studied Uther. No help there, not so much as a flicker of attention. He pegged Serena with a raised eyebrow.

"My nanny," she said. "Nanny turned housekeeper, I should say. She healed all but the worst of our ailments growing up, so I decided to bring her here."

"You exposed her to me? To us?"

"Would you rather I let you die?" Serena glided to the fireplace and sat on the side ledge. "Besides, we handled it." She clenched the rock ledge hard enough her knuckles turned white. Whatever she meant by handling it, it didn't seem to sit well.

"You handled it." Maxis shuttled his attention between the two of them, but neither met his gaze. "How exactly?"

Uther lifted his head, fatigue marking the edges of his eyes. "Dead healers make for fewer confessions." Uther glared at Serena. "They also result in tedious labor."

"She deserved a pyre," Serena said, shaking with passion. "Servant or not, she cared for me better than my own mother. Burying her would have been an insult to her gifts."

"You cared for her." Maxis crept forward, slow, so as not to miss the play of emotion on her face.

Serena studied the fire, her gaze distant.

"You sacrificed her to heal your mate." Maxis halted before her and steered her chin to face him. No one had ever put him first, no one since his grandmother all those years ago. "Worried I wouldn't make it?"

Serena jerked her chin from his grip and sidled out from between him and the ledge. She paced toward the kitchen and crossed her arms. "I couldn't exactly let you die. My fate is tied to you. If you die, I'm left holding the bag."

She gripped the raised countertop, the dirty rag Uther had tossed aside wadded in a disgusting heap in the middle of the sand colored stone slab. "You've been officially charged with treason. Anyone found aiding and abetting you will be charged as well."

He wasn't buying it. She could have let him die and been free of all but his faded mark. Why go to the trouble if she didn't care? Though he could understand her trepidation in admitting it after the way her father had treated her. She'd be a fool to trust Maxis blindly, but he could bring her around. Eventually. "What else did you learn?"

Uther shifted in his chair and the cushions groaned. "Eryx came clean with the ellan. Spilled every violation of the tenets he's performed and either cited precedence for the action to explain it, or pointed the cause back at you. In a nutshell, he's clear unless the council balks, which they won't."

That wily son of a bitch. Never in a million years did he think Eryx would confess, though he probably should have. The man had too much conscience for his own good.

Maxis gripped his hands behind his back and circled his thumbs. "Then we've got two choices. Either we find a way to discredit what he's done with the council, or stir bigger problems and distract from the rebellion by divulging our race to the humans."

Uther's deadpan response came lightning fast. "Going public's a shit storm. Panicked humans can do a lot to hurt a handful of powerful men. We're not ready for that, not in manpower or skills. Not yet."

"Discrediting Eryx would take years." Serena leaned one hip on a barstool. "The older ellan might want to upend his influence, but the newer generation adore him, not to mention we'd need some nasty secrets we don't have. I'm beginning to wonder if he's even capable of secrets."

Maxis smiled to himself. How alike he and Serena were, both in action and in thought, whether she realized it or not.

"There is another option." Uther stood and the wood floors groaned. His boot heels thumped against the planks as he headed toward the kitchen.

The fire warmed Maxis' clasped hands at his back. "I'm listening."

Uther leaned over the sink and splashed his face with water, running a hand along the back of his neck not the least bit hurried. He dried his face with a nearby towel before he faced them. "Maxis needs to die."

Maxis' laugh rattled the rafters. "You'll forgive me if I'm not on board with your plan."

Serena stared open mouthed at Uther.

"I said *Maxis* needs to die. I didn't say you had to die." Uther set the towel aside and leaned against the counter, crossing his arms. "If Maxis Steysis dies, he can't be tried for treason and the rebellion falls off the radar. We lay low for a bit, use the time to make our connections as planned in Evad, and keep building the army."

Arguments queued on Maxis' tongue, but he held them back, replaying Uther's words in his head. "You expect the public to accept word of my demise on good faith?"

"No, I expect you to die quite publicly."

Maxis looked to Serena. She seemed as lost as he was.

Uther straightened and lowered his arms. "Throw a strike at me." Whatever idea his strategos had must have been a solid one, because he didn't seem the least bit concerned Maxis might actually fire as requested.

Intriguing. Maxis whipped his hand forward and cast a slim volt at Uther.

Uther stood steady, unaffected without so much as a flinch. His shirt was charred and a black circular pattern marred his shoulder, but he stood upright. Burnt cloth and the sharp tang of electricity overpowered the wood smoke.

"Impressive." Maxis ambled forward. "No wonder you weren't worried your fellow warriors would strike back."

"It's only handy if I'm paying attention, and I can't keep it up indefinitely," Uther answered, a little cocky, but wise enough to hold it in check.

"A nice trick for you. Not especially convenient for my demise."

"Unless I project the shield onto you."

No wonder Uther had protected his secrets so well. "You can do that?" Maxis said.

Uther nodded.

Falon had been right. Uther was proving not only to be a better match, but offering up prime opportunity to unseat the malran at the same time.

Were those his thoughts? Or Falon's? All his life he'd thought the voice in his head was his own. Now he wondered if it hadn't all been the dark spiritu. Falon might have screwed Maxis royally with the altercation with Reese, but this opportunity was hard to pass up. "We'll go with the idea, but we'll up the ante in the process and see if we can't discredit our esteemed malran along the way."

Serena stood and raised her chin, defiant. "Your death doesn't exactly cover absolving me of our association."

Maxis prowled closer, lifted her hand, and pressed a kiss to her palm. "Not to fear, my dear. I plan to ensure my beloved baineann is well and truly cared for."

Chapter 24

Eryx sat on his throne and watched the ellan filter toward their assigned seats. Considering the vote they were about to render, they seemed a tad too jovial. Too detached from the futures they were charged with determining.

Seated in the more demure version of his chair beside him, Lexi leaned in at a conspiratorial angle. *"You need to bring Ludan down a notch. He's wound pretty damned tight."*

"He's always wound tight." He checked anyway, trusting Lexi's instincts as he would few others.

Positioned to the right of Eryx's throne, Ludan stood as he always did, arms crossed and glaring belligerently.

"Looks pretty status quo to me," he said, reclining into his chair.

Lexi didn't hide her perusal this time. *"That's because you're not looking like I am."*

"You're feeling, not looking." Eryx covered her fist on the armrest with his own. *"And technically, that's bad manners. Let him deal with his business and save yourself the heartache. Shut the filters down."*

Lexi glared at him. *"You toss the bad manners rule when it suits you. I'm not wrong on these feelings and you know it."* Her expression smoothed and a superior grin slid into place as she faced the settling ellan. *"Sure nailed it with Reese and Galena, didn't I?"*

He squeezed her hand and thrust his shoulders back a notch. Praise the Great One, he'd been blessed with Lexi. Fire, confidence, and street smarts all rolled into one. *"You're going to rub that in for a while, I take it?"*

Her grin grew, even if she didn't deign to give him the full force of it. *"You got that right."*

"Sorry I'm late." Galena hustled up beside Lexi, and Jagger stepped aside to make room.

Lexi craned her head up toward Galena. "What the hell are you doing here?"

Eryx angled to better see Galena's mating mark, the goddess Artemis perched at the tip of a crescent moon with her gown billowing out behind her. She held her bow taut, arrow notched and ready to fire toward the heavens, shrewd eyes narrowed in concentration.

Facing the crowd, Eryx relaxed into his chair. His new briyo might worry the hell out of him, but Reese had laid a damned fine claim on his sister. "Couldn't have too hot of a mating night if you're up and out of bed at noon."

Galena held her arm out to better show Lexi what he'd already studied. "I seem to remember a man who left his new mate warm in her bed at daybreak only a few weeks ago." Her saucy comment came out breathless, not at all the proper voice he'd grown accustomed to hearing.

Eryx was torn between slapping Reese on the back and congratulating him, and wringing his neck. "Point taken."

"You should be home." Lexi squeezed Galena's hand. "At least one of us should get a honeymoon."

Galena shook her head and patted Lexi's shoulder. "I wouldn't miss standing beside Brenna for this, and Reese insisted he wanted to seal the deal on our new home." She scanned the crowd. "Where are Brenna and Ian anyway?"

"New home?" Lexi perked up.

The council page, Dunstan, strode to the foot of the dais. "All are in place, my malran."

"Shit." Lexi shifted her thoughts to both Eryx and Galena, the smooth transition more fitting of a two hundred-year-old Myren than one barely two weeks past her awakening. *"Orla and Graylin are with Brenna and Ian in the antechamber. What's with the new home?"*

"Lexi." Eryx loved her vibrant nature, but right now he couldn't afford to misstep with the council. *"Remember what I said about sampling emotions being impolite?"*

Lexi tilted her head in silent question.

"For now, I don't care about polite," he answered. *"I'm scanning as well, but if you sense anything that feels off, tell me."*

A wicked smile curled her lips. She pulled her hand out from under his and trailed her index finger along his forearm. *"Going rogue, huh? That's kinda sexy."*

His belly tightened and his cock stirred with more interest than he could handle given the current circumstance. *"Focus, hellcat, and I'll give you all the rogue you want when we get home."*

A determined air lengthened her spine.

Eryx nodded at Dunstan. "Call the session to order."

Dunstan spun toward the ellan and his voice echoed down the cavernous hall, thick with the formality Eryx hated. When the pomp and circumstance subsided, Eryx stood and Lexi rose beside him. The air seemed cooler than normal, only Lexi's warmth keeping the sensation at bay.

"As promised," he said, "two of the humans kidnapped by Maxis Steysis have been brought to council today to share their memories and confirm the claims made by myself and Reese Theron. In exchange for the interference in their destiny, their testimony against the traitor, and their vow to uphold and abide by all Myren laws, I have offered asylum in Eden for the rest of their lives pending approval of the council."

He paused long enough to scan the many rows and let his attention rest on some of the more difficult members. "Heed this. The injuries endured by these humans are such I will not abide any belligerent acts or unkind words. Both have suffered enough at the hands of one of our own." For the last he focused on Angus. "I'll kill any woman or man who causes them further grief."

Heads dipped for quiet whispers and rumbles filtered through the room.

Eryx reached out to Graylin. *"We're ready. Keep Orla at Brenna's side."*

Footsteps sounded from the foyer and Ian, Graylin, Orla, and Brenna stepped into view.

Galena and Lexi moved as one down the dais steps, Lexi positioning herself between Brenna and Ian, Galena at Brenna's free side.

Eryx lifted his chin, pride for his family's unspoken support of those wronged a heady rush. They'd not just made their point, but added a few exclamation points and waved a red cape in the process.

Eryx stalked toward them, singling out Ian first. "You understand your sanctuary in Eden is contingent on abiding by Myren law in all things?"

Ian jerked a rough nod and shifted to more firmly plant his feet, keeping his eyes off the crowd. "I do."

"And you offer your memories freely?"

Another curt nod.

Eryx waved the waiting ellan forward, a man he'd personally chosen for his bipartisan and freethinking politics.

With a perfunctory approach, the ellan offered his hand, eyes passively aimed at Ian's chest.

Ian stared at the hand, and clasped it with a firm grip.

Ten seconds passed. Twenty. Thirty.

The ellan jerked, then jerked again. He released Ian and stepped away. "The accusations are confirmed. Maxis Steysis was the one responsible for bringing this person to Eden and inflicting...gruesome wounds in an attempt to harm more humans." He paused, swallowing in what looked to be a painful act. "It is my recommendation to the council this human be offered refuge in Eden as requested by the malran." With that he shuffled out of the hall, his flushed face shiny with sweat.

Praise the Great One, if Ian's torture had this much impact, he couldn't imagine how the female he'd selected would hold up with Brenna.

He waved the female ellan forward and stepped close to Brenna, keeping his voice low. "You understand what's being asked and give your memories freely?"

Lexi and Galena inched closer to Brenna.

"I do," Brenna said.

Eryx smiled in what he hoped resembled reassurance. "Give her your hand. You won't feel anything."

The female ellan held out her hand palm up.

Brenna looked to Lexi then Galena. Straightening, she laid her hand in the ellan's.

Long, quiet seconds stretched on and on.

The female ellan lowered her head, but kept her hand grasped around Brenna's. Two tears splattered to the stone floor at the ellan's feet.

Ludan lurched forward to intercede, but Eryx held him back. Barely.

The ellan clasped Brenna's hand with both of hers and lifted her head. Tears streaked her face. "I am..." She coughed and shook her head. "I am so very sorry."

She released her grip and faced the council. "The accusations are confirmed." She opened her mouth to speak again, closed it and swallowed before continuing. "This woman deserves our refuge and our justice." She didn't flee the room as the male had, but her steps were shaky as she found her place among the crowd.

Eryx motioned Graylin toward the exit with a nod. Not one of the ellan lifted their heads as the group exited, the room more hushed than he'd ever heard it.

The antechamber door thudded shut.

"You've heard my recommendation and those of your peers. Those who object, speak now."

Only blessed silence answered.

He opened his mouth, eager to adjourn.

"My malran." The female ellan stood, her cheeks red and eyes bright with fury. "On behalf of the sufferings endured by the humans and your supporting council, I'd like to know what justice you plan for Maxis Steysis."

A slow burn spread through Eryx's torso, the chill he'd felt before long gone. "The only justice befitting of his crimes." He fisted his hands and let the image of Maxis' throat beneath them fill his mind. "Death."

* * * *

Reese sat a weathered wooden crate on the edge of his mother's bed and double-checked for anything he might have left behind. He'd already committed to letting go of the past. Histus, a part of him had already left it behind, somewhere between Galena coming apart in his arms in the greenhouse, and the moment she'd stood up to Ramsay the next morning. The trick was figuring out what to carry forward. Intangibles were easier. Only the best of memories and those that shaped you. Tangibles? Yeah, that one was tougher.

He opened the doors to his mother's armoire and rifled through her jewelry. Most of them were inexpensive baubles, pieces she'd bought from vendors in Cush to support local artists. Certainly nothing she'd want her new oanan to have.

He stepped back and started to close the door.

A padded jade box was tucked to one side, so deep in shadows he'd almost missed it.

He pulled the box forward and opened it, the tight hinges squeaking. A cuff sat nestled in black velvet made of matte platinum, a metal forbidden for those not of the royal family.

Praise the Great One she'd been happy the day she found it. They seldom went to Cush, but when they did, they always hit the art vendors. That day they'd browsed the aisles until Reese's feet throbbed. The image etched on the cuff had too closely resembled his family mark for his mother to pass it up, and she'd bartered with the craftsman until he'd relented, making her swear on her son's life she'd never tell where she'd bought the piece.

Reese fingered the deep carvings, the onyx background giving the piece a mix of masculine strength and feminine charm.

Galena could wear it.

The thought whacked him hard, curiosity at the coincidence running right behind it. Not once had his mother worn the cuff, insisting it had called to her for reasons she couldn't explain. Had his mother had her own spiritu? Guiding her in ways as small as this?

He snapped the box shut and sat it in the crate. He'd drive his mind in circles if he went off down that road. He'd missed out on his chance with Maxis. Now his focus needed to be on Galena and giving her the life she deserved.

Shifting to the bookcase, he checked the sun's position with his mind. Ben and Beth couldn't be too far out with the paperwork to purchase their new home. Trading his homestead for the cottage was a steal. He'd have given four homesteads to see Galena's face light up again, and he'd never seen a home more suited to her skills and personality.

His mother's paperback books from Evad lined the bookcase, everything from classics to romance. Probably not much worth taking there unless Galena had a thing for fiction. He paused at the row of leather-bound journals and traced a sapphire blue spine. All her pain was there. Every second-guess for the actions she'd taken. Every hope and prayer she'd said for Maxis.

He turned for the closet and stopped, looking back. Pulling the stack of journals free, he arranged them in the crate. Paperbacks were one thing, but his mother's heart and soul were in those words. If he chose to let them go, he'd find a special way to do it. Something more personal than handing them off to unknown strangers.

The closet made for fast work, his mind too detached with thoughts of providing for his royal mate than considering each and every outfit. They'd have a cleaner, safer start letting go of the homestead, but his immediate income would drop to nil. He had more than enough tucked away for a while, but what did a warrior without an army do for a living?

Maybe something in the human realm would work. A shitload of Myrens made their living doing business in Evad, most capitalizing on their special gifts in ways humans would never perceive. Not that his gifts allowed for much in the way of commerce. Masking yourself to nearly undetectable levels didn't exactly draw in sales.

Came in damned handy when you had to sneak into a place though. Maybe something in security or protection would work.

The wood floors above ground creaked.

Reese stepped from the walk-in closet and spread his senses around the house. Only one presence pinged back at him. Odd, he'd expected Ben to bring Beth along since she'd insisted on hearing about the mating and how Galena liked the cottage.

He pushed the bookcase door wide and chastised himself. The absent-mindedness wouldn't do if he wanted in any kind of security firm.

He smiled, ready to greet his neighbors, and stopped cold.

Serena.

Her pale blue gown gave her skin a morbid glow and her eyelashes were wet and red-rimmed. Even her gown looked off, too matronly with its long sleeves.

"Don't hurt me." She wrung her hands, and her arms shook so badly he felt a need to reach out and steady her, a foolish notion for a woman like Serena. People like her could always fake an Oscar-worthy performance if they thought they'd get something out of it.

"I don't make a habit of hurting women." He shot a pointed look at the open door. "Then again, I don't recall inviting you in so you may need to give me a decent reason."

"I didn't know where else to go."

Reese strode toward the door and shut it. A quick check of the surroundings ensured him Ben wasn't yet nearby. "What makes you think this was the right place to start?"

"Because I need help." She hiccupped and swiped her nose. "I'm in trouble with Maxis and didn't know what else to do."

Reese lifted an eyebrow. "You're just now figuring out he's trouble?"

"You don't understand. If you knew…" She turned away and pressed a hand over her chest. The action was a little over the top, which only nudged Reese another step toward disbelief. "His plans are awful. If I'd known what he wanted for the rebellion I'd have never gotten involved."

"Then get un-involved. Tell Eryx about Maxis' plans and ask for mercy."

She bit her lip, gaze locked on the floor. "It's not that simple."

"Funny, I thought the same thing." He tilted his head. Clio had mentioned a new intersection. What if this was it? Could he discount her story out of hand? "You should talk to Eryx."

She shook her head and let out a whimper. "No, I really messed up." She lifted her sleeve.

Shock pushed Reese back a step. Of everything he'd expected, Serena hooking up with Maxis wasn't one of them.

"He thinks I'm headed to Cush to learn more from my family on what's happening at council. I learned where you live from his memories.

If I stay too much longer, he'll find me." She let out another whimper and a fresh round of tears kicked in.

"Then tell me where he is and I'll pass the information to Eryx on your behalf. We'll raid and take him before he can do anything."

"No." Her eyes went dinner plate wide. Was it fear or panic? "He'll know it was me and kill me before you can contain him." She inched forward. "You know what he can do."

Ah, so she knew. He'd have never suspected Maxis capable of sharing anything with anyone, let alone such valuable knowledge as his ability to kill via link.

"What are the plans?" he said. Anything she handed over would probably be complete crap, but it was worth a shot.

"If I tell you, will you ask Eryx to pardon me? He pardoned you. Surely he'd pardon me?"

So, she knew that too. For a woman who'd been tucked away with the rebellion, she was an informed little lady. "Eryx is nothing but fair, even for those who don't always deserve it."

She flinched and pressed her lips into a tight line. "Maxis is planning something in Evad. He said he needs to gather slaves and thought to start with teenagers."

"When?"

She hesitated, her high drama blending with a subtle tremor. "In two days."

Chapter 25

Galena landed next to the high marble fountain at the center of the prestigious Cush neighborhood and glared at Serena's home. She'd willingly left Reese this morning to support Ian and Brenna, but being kept from him for a mandated social call rankled.

Lexi touched down beside her, Jagger a tight presence at her side. "Whoa." She craned her head to take in the architecture. "I always liked those pointy things on rooftops, but I think Serena's family took it a bit far. What do you call that look?"

"Baroque." Galena trudged forward, determined to get this task over with. She'd never realized how heavy her social persona sat on her shoulders until Reese helped lift the burden. "The period's known for its drama and its tension in all things artistic." She smirked at Lexi. "Fitting for our girl Serena, don't you think?"

Lexi quickened her steps until they were side-to-side. "I was expecting all black with flames."

Galena shook her head.

"What?" Lexi tried for innocent, but it fell far short. "She's a demon bitch from hell."

A snort sounded behind them.

Galena glanced back in time to see Jagger duck his head.

"I'm sorry Eryx wrangled you into this." Lexi said, lowering her voice. "I told him I could handle it on my own."

A heavy sigh slipped out before Galena could check it. Between Lexi's earthy influence and Reese battering her long-practiced facades, she'd be swearing and pole dancing before the month was out. "It's the right thing to do. Serena's probably with Maxis and we could use some clues from her family. And trust me, you'll need a little back up for this one. More than you know." She opened the wrought iron gate and held it open for Lexi.

"Pretty uptight, huh?"

Nearing the front door, Galena angled closer to her shalla. "You ever read any historical books? Maybe a romance or two growing up?"

Lexi wrinkled her nose. "Chaperones and corsets and all that?"

"No, I mean the etiquette." Galena pounded the knocker on the Blackwood entry and stepped back. "They've got a time and place for everything. When to be seen and when to call one someone."

Lexi gaped.

"Like that, but up a few levels." Galena motioned toward Lexi's attire. The silk platinum gown she'd worn straight from council practically screamed her station, even without the crown. "The malress coming for a visit will bump that up to sheer ridiculousness."

The door glided opened and a butler in fitted black wool pants and matching black overcoat stepped forward. Talk about scary, the skin below his eyes and along his jowls sagged and what hair he had left was dull brown with peppered gray. "May I help you?"

Galena lifted an eyebrow, a regal glare straight out of Eryx's playbook. "Your malress and your malran's sister visit your household and you greet us with cold words?" She tsked and forced her lips to a considering purse. "I doubt the Doroz patriarch would be pleased."

Realization zapped the lower half of the man's face to an animated grimace. He stepped back, chin dropped formally as he held the door open wide. "My apologies, Your Highnesses. Please come in and I'll alert the master of your presence."

No sooner had they crossed the threshold than the butler strode off, his quick steps ringing on the black and white tiles.

"I'm gonna call him Renfield." Lexi managed to keep her expression in check even though her voice rang ornery in Galena's head. *"Admit it. He's one creepy-lookin' dude."*

"Dude?"

"What? It's a good word. You should try it." She paused in the middle of the soaring foyer, the overdone crystal chandelier poised perfectly above her, and frowned. *"Seriously. Try it."*

Galena smiled and pushed every ounce of beach bum she could manage into the effort. *"Dude."* She shook her head and let out a little chuckle. *"You and Reese are going to turn me into a rebel."*

Lexi's smile stretched from ear to ear. *"Excellent."*

A booming voice sounded from above and quick footsteps pounded down the winding steps. "Your Highnesses." A tall, slender man with shoulder-length salt-and-pepper hair tied in a queue hustled into view.

Judging by the bright red across his cheeks and the lack of his formal overcoat, they'd caught Serena's daddy completely unaware.

"My name is Reginald Doroz." He dropped to one knee and the door beside Lexi opened. "Please, let me show you to the drawing room where we can talk."

Lexi shifted for the door.

Reginald rose and reached for Lexi's arm.

Jagger shot forward and cut him off.

"Apologies." Reginald yanked his hand away and lowered his head. "I meant only to escort you in, my malress."

"No offense taken." At the far end of the room, Lexi settled into a high-backed plum wingback, her demeanor the epitome of sweet and innocent. "We didn't intend to upset your household. Galena's just told me so much about Serena that I couldn't wait anymore to meet her."

"You're flirting with him?" For the last two weeks, Lexi had slung four letter words with the best of their warriors. To see her batting her eyelashes at the old coot and slinging a coy drawl seemed incongruous. *"Maybe you don't need my help."*

"Oklahoma accent. Works 'em over every time if you do it right." She snuck a wink in as Serena's daddy sat ramrod straight in the chair beside her. "Is Serena here?"

"Yes, well." Reginald coughed and fiddled with his shirt collar. "I'm afraid Serena's not in residence at the moment. She's a bit of a traveler and prefers to spend much of her time at her friends' homes."

His lips twitched, like his mind wanted to form a smile but the nerves kept shorting out in the process. "The flighty creature's as reliable as an earthquake. Still, her taking off the same week as Inez has proven a particular challenge. Her mother is beside herself. So many social obligations and not nearly enough support."

"Inez?" Galena knew most of the society families, but she couldn't come up with one Inez on the list.

"Serena's nanny," Reginald said. "Or housekeeper now. My wife relies on her heavily when Serena's not home to help. Appearances must be kept." He bowed his head in Lexi's direction. "I'm sure Your Highness understands."

"Mr. Doroz, I'm beginning to think you run a rather lax estate." Galena never would have thrown such a pompous statement at a decent being, but this guy was an ass. If he was heartless enough to call his daughter flighty in front of strangers she couldn't really blame Serena for spending time away from home. "Your staff doesn't recognize their sovereigns on sight, and deign to report for duty only when it suits them?"

"Oh, you misunderstand." Reginald surged to his feet and lifted his hands in a placating gesture. "Inez is a devoted staff member, always here on time, and seldom a sick day. Not that one stays ill long in her presence. She's a tolerable healer, a gift that's blessed our family since we first hired her. Her disappearance is most unusual."

"How long has she been gone?" This from Lexi, gripping her hands in her lap and angling her torso forward with what looked like genuine concern. "Is there anything we can do to help?"

"You're kind to offer, my malress, but I'm sure Inez is fine." He scowled toward the door. "I'm sure we'll have refreshments for you soon. If you'll give me a moment, I'll check on them and let my baineann know you're here. She'll be devastated if she learns she missed you."

He hurried toward the door.

Galena edged closer to Lexi's side. *"You thinking what I'm thinking?"*

"That our boys did some serious damage to Maxis in their mental showdown and needed someone to do a little pick-me-up?" Lexi shot a grin at Galena, one that made Galena glad they were on the same team. *"Hell, yeah."*

Lexi stood and absently smoothed the silk along her hips as she glided toward the door. *"Let's ditch this place and get you home for some lovin'. Who knows, maybe I'll get lucky too."*

Reginald intercepted as they hit the foyer. "Are you leaving?"

"I'm afraid so," Galena said. "As you can imagine, Lexi has a busy schedule."

"We'll leave you to whatever business you were about," Lexi added. "When you see Serena, let her know we came by. I'm really looking forward to seeing her."

Reginald blustered a farewell behind them, Jagger wedge protectively in-between them.

"You're looking forward to seeing her?" It was all Galena could do not to nudge Lexi in the ribs. *"Laying it on a little thick, don't you think?"*

"No, I really do want to see her. And then I want to pop her eyes out with a spork."

"A spork?"

"Oh, geez." Lexi slung an arm around Galena's shoulders. *"We need to get you out of Eden more."*

* * * *

Eryx landed outside the castle entrance and threw the front doors wide.

"She's got Jagger and Galena with her." Ludan touched down a step behind him, his gruff reminder filled with confidence Eryx couldn't muster.

"You get a mate and send her into the nest of a woman who helped kidnap her and we'll talk. Until then, shut it." Eryx angled for the library.

"It was the right move." Ludan came up on Eryx's right. "They'd clam up if you went. Serena's parents will yak all day with Lexi."

Eryx strode to his study and the bar situated to one side of his desk. "You're awfully damned chatty." He tilted the first bottle and checked the label. Strasse, not what he wanted. Vodka, didn't want that either. Schnapps, oh, hell no.

Balvenie Fifty.

Perfect.

Eryx finished pouring, but kept the lid off. Ludan was right. Lexi wasn't in danger, not with Jagger with her, but he'd need at least two rounds good old-fashioned whiskey to take the edge off waiting. Maybe three.

The Scotch burned slow and warm down his throat. "Thought you were gonna do murder in front of the whole council before they finished with Brenna. How about you get loose-lipped about that?"

Footsteps sounded behind him, muted by the thick carpet, but Ludan kept his silence.

Eryx turned.

Ludan glared out the back window, the afternoon sun a hard slash on his tense face.

He could cheat and sample Ludan's emotions, but that was a shit move. "You got something I need to know?"

"No." Talkative had never been Ludan's thing and brooding was expected, but this level of agitation? Something was up. Eryx motioned with his glass and turned for the bottle. "You want one?" He poured without waiting for an answer.

"Yeah," Ludan answered.

Eryx capped the bottle and handed off the drink.

Reese's voice rang in Eryx's head, the ping of his presence registering just out side the castle. *"My malran."*

"My sister's not here, but I'm guessing you know that," Eryx said.

"I know she's with Lexi looking for details on Serena and Maxis, but I've already found Serena, and information you need to know."

Eryx sat behind his desk and opened the study doors with a thought. *"Follow my link to the library, first floor beneath the staircase."* He twisted toward Ludan. "Think you'd better get situated. We've got company."

Ludan hesitated with the tumbler halfway to his mouth. "Who?"

"My new briyo." He reclined in his chair. "Says he's found Serena and some information for me."

"You send him on a run?"

Distant footsteps rang against the foyer stone.

Eryx shook his head, thankful he could stop worrying about Lexi and Galena at least. "No, though I'd rather have that viper coiled up in his vicinity than Lexi or Galena's."

"Not sure I trust him."

And wasn't that a nut cruncher, because Eryx still wasn't sure he did either.

Reese rounded the corner, steps purposeful, but unhurried. With his work pants, tall boots, and loose shirt, he looked better fitted for tending his homestead than running down traitors. He'd knotted his hair up good and tight though. Stupid that such an innocent gesture eased his worries for his sister, but it did.

Halting ten feet out from the desk, Reese dropped to one knee. "My malran."

Fuck this was awkward. The guy had the Shantos emblem plastered on his forearm, an impressive showing from Galena if he was truthful, and here he was kneeling like someone off the street. Damn it, he hoped Galena knew what she was doing. "Pretty sure that mark on your arm means you can toss the formalities."

Reese stood slowly, the tension in his shoulders telegraphing uncertainty. "I had a visitor at the homestead today."

Eryx glanced at Ludan and sipped his Scotch. "From?"

"Serena."

Ludan plopped on the couch behind Reese. "He's in a touchy mood. Better get it all out quick."

Like Ludan was in a place to call anyone moody. "He's right," Eryx said. "Spill it."

"I was packing, waiting on the couple I planned to sell the land to, when Serena showed up. The high points? She and Maxis have mated, she's learned Maxis plans to swipe a busload of humans, and wants to wash her hands of the whole thing. But after learning what he almost did to me via link, she's afraid she can't get free of him. She's hoping you'll grant her a pardon and keep her safe in zeolite until you kill him if she turns over the info."

Ludan put a leg on the table in front of him and lifted his glass. "Nice."

"Maxis mated Serena?" Eryx had a hard time getting past Serena trusting anyone long enough to get through the ritual.

Reese nodded.

"And she came to you because I pardoned you?"

"Pretty much."

Interesting, but he wasn't buying it. The mere fact she'd submitted to the mating link said how deep Serena was in with Maxis. The question was whether Reese was in on it too.

Eryx opened his senses. Manners only mattered in polite situations, not those that could end you with a knife or elemental strike in your back. "You think she's telling the truth?"

Reese tilted his head. Not much, just enough Eryx knew he'd caught the shift in energy. If he knew what Eryx was about, he didn't show it. "No. She put on a great show, but I've seen the two of them together and there's no way she's regretting being tied with Maxis."

A bite of anxiousness and a prickle of fear registered against Eryx's gifts, but no deceit. If anything there was a smooth undercurrent of hope. "So what's your spin on their plan?"

"It's bait," he said. "They think you'll rush in to protect the humans and plan some kind of ambush in the process."

"Too simple." Ludan clunked his empty tumbler on the table and leaned both elbows on his knees. "They know you're not that stupid."

Eryx steepled his fingers and rested his chin on top. "You think Maxis would bait a trap and not be there to spring it?"

"Maxis has a hard time letting go of anything outside of grunt work," Reese answered. "He wants you, or something you being there will accomplish. He'll want to see it play out."

Ludan stood and headed for the bar with his glass dangling from his fingertips. "You better figure out what your trap is first."

"We'll figure it out," Eryx said. "If we've got a chance at catching Maxis and Serena in one place, we can permanently take him out of play."

"Yeah, about that." Reese stepped forward, some of the wariness Eryx had sensed earlier creeping back in. "I think it's time I share some news that may make you rethink your end game."

Chapter 26

Reese fought the need to shift his feet, no small task with the intensity flying off Eryx just five feet away. Maybe he should cut bait and leave while he could.

Eryx sat foreword in his chair. "Why do I have the feeling I'm not going to like this news?"

Oh, he wouldn't like it. He'd probably tag him as a nut job too, but at least he'd lay it out there this time. He sucked in a breath and his stomach muscles clamped tight. "There's a bigger deal going on than Maxis and the rebellion. Something bigger than Myrens and humans."

Eryx stared him down. "That's a hell of a segue. Think you'd better start at the beginning."

He did, starting with the first visit from Clio and the spiritu. How she'd encouraged him to appeal to Maxis on the basis of brotherhood, and how she'd shown after his link to Maxis had been severed and explained Maxis was a linchpin in some bigger deal that could screw all their races.

"So let me get this right," Eryx said. "A whole other race of beings exist who are responsible for keeping things in balance. If Maxis gets his way and starts enslaving humans, things get out of whack. Does that sum it up?"

"It sounds crazy, I know, but she was real. And she knew things. Showed me things only someone who'd known me since birth could know."

Ludan let out a tired exhale behind him.

Eryx studied him. "What else did she say?"

"If I understood it right, you get more points if you do things the hard way. Killing Maxis only puts a few points in your ledger. Getting him to surrender scores you a motherlode. If you run in and annihilate him, you're not doing much for the balance toward the good and may end up bringing Myrens, humans and spiritus up short in the long-run."

Eryx closed an overlarge leather tome on his desk and tapped the top with his thumb.

Quiet settled so thick it pressed Reese on every side. "I didn't want to tell you. I wasn't even sure I was supposed to because Clio never told me one way or the other. But when Serena showed up, I knew how you'd respond."

"That I'd want Maxis dead?"

"Exactly. It's the same thing I wanted, what I'd originally planned to ask you for before Clio came to me." He paused and tried to swallow around the lump in his throat. He nearly choked on his dry tongue. "If you think about it, it makes sense. The more difficult path is always the one to give the most payback. If I'd shared the truth with Ramsay at my swearing in, I'd have faced a bigger hurdle, but the rest of my life would've been different. Honest and free of the shame I carried around for all the years after. Why wouldn't this be the same?"

Eryx kept his eyes locked on his desk, distant.

"I took the chance in coming here, knowing what you'd think. If there's even a shred of truth to what Clio told me, I figured you thinking the worst about me was better than risking throwing things out of balance. What you choose to do with the information is up to you."

Eryx still didn't respond.

He waited a handful of heartbeats longer and turned for the door. Eryx and Ludan's stares weighted his shoulders, but neither stopped him. It didn't matter what they thought. He'd done the right thing, no matter what the repercussions. He'd learned that much and he had Galena as a mate to show for it.

Well, he'd had her. No telling what would happen when she learned the curve ball Reese had thrown her brother.

* * * *

Galena cast her senses out across the garden, wild rainbow blooms dancing on the late spring breeze in what was left of a beautiful sunset. Lavender, mango, and midnight blue blended on the horizon and stretched across the hillside protecting the castle. No visible signs of her mate registered, but he was there somewhere, likely tucked inside the arbor at the garden's center.

The stone balustrade scraped her palm as she moved along the terrace. She'd expected Eryx to grill her on the details of her visit when she returned. Instead she'd learned her fireann had been holding out on some pretty worrisome information for their race, an emotional slap she'd failed to cover. Even now her pride stung.

She sifted through the reasons Reese might have withheld his trust and wandered down the castle steps, through the winding white sand paths. The simple cotton sheath she'd worn to council left her arms bared to the cooling evening air. Exotic perfume and the fresh bite of greenery surrounded her, soft like her footsteps. Only the fine hairs that escaped her intricate braids tickled her neck and face, an odd but interesting sensation after years of feeling her hair's weight on her back and shoulders.

This wouldn't be the last of what she and Reese would face together. If she trusted him enough to take him as a mate, she had to believe in him long enough to give his reasons. To set the expectations for their future and grow as a unit.

Her steps quickened, the need to see him, to connect with and touch him, driving her heart to an urgent rhythm.

The arbor came into view, natural walls thick with ivy and dotted with ivory, bell-shaped blooms, and a wrought iron dome with more riotous vines. Their link promised he was inside, but it wasn't enough. Not until she laid eyes on him. She rounded the edge and her breath slipped out on a slow sigh.

Reese lay stretched out on the center bench, hands tucked behind his head as he peered through what he could of the ivy. One foot rested on the bench, knee bent, a casual pose to anyone else, but it was a ruse. She felt the knowledge to her bones. Maybe not as succinctly as Lexi or Eryx might manage, but this was her mate. His unease jangled against her nerves, a scratching tension along her arms and legs.

"Reese?"

He started and stood up, another clue how deep his worry ran. Sworn warrior or not, his skills were on par with an elite and no one caught such a man unaware unless his emotions distracted him. "You finished with Eryx quicker than I thought."

She should have known when he'd said he'd wait for her at the castle something was wrong. "Eryx doesn't beat around the bush when he's anxious for time alone with his mate." She closed the distance between them and wrapped her arms around his waist, resting her head against his chest. The soft cotton of his ivory shirt tickled her cheek. "I'm beginning to understand why."

He hesitated a second as though she'd shocked him, then hugged her back. His kissed the top of her head. "He told you everything?"

She inhaled deep, the smell of forest and spice unlocking her tension. His heart pounded beneath her ear. "Everything."

He stroked her spine, long calming sweeps that left a delicious heat in their wake. "Does he think I'm nuts?"

Damn. She should have seen that coming. A person with a pristine history and a rock solid reputation would have had a hard time dropping information like that with Eryx, but with Reese's background, it had to be nervewracking. "Eryx is more open-minded than most. You forget it was dreams that led him to Lexi. He's got a healthy respect for things he doesn't understand."

He cupped the back of her neck. "And what do you think?"

So, this was why he hadn't told her. "I think I've heard a tiny voice in my head too many times to dismiss the concept." She pulled back to see his face. Gold lashes lined his hooded eyelids, his forest eyes broken only by sage slivers. "If I'm honest, something spoke to me the night I saw you in front of Maxis' house." She cupped one side of his face and his evening stubble scratched her palm. "I wish you'd told me."

Reese pressed his forehead to hers. "I wasn't sure I was supposed to, let alone if anyone would believe me."

"I believe you."

He tightened his grip at her waist.

She tilted back, needing eye contact. "So what are we going to do about it?"

Reese's laugh rumbled against her and his lips curled in a sardonic slant. "See if we can find a way to get my brother to surrender, cure the realms of hunger, and negotiate peace for all of them while we're at it?" He sat on the center bench, pulled her between his knees, and tugged her onto his lap.

"You joke, but it sounds like the spiritu think you're the key in all this," she said. "That you have the angle necessary to bring Maxis around."

Reese cradled her close and she let her head lull against his shoulder. "Clio said I was the hook in Maxis' life. The one bright spark. Though how they intend for me to leverage that, I don't have a clue."

The V of his shirt hung open and Galena splayed her hand along the exposed skin. Faint hairs teased her palm, his warmth spreading up her arm. "Your mother is what you have in common, maybe that's where you should start."

"Start how?"

Galena shrugged. "Tell me about her. Did she talk much about Maxis?"

Voices sounded from far away, laughter moving away from the castle as the bulk of workers made their way home.

"She hated leaving him," he said. "It was the one regret she had, leaving him behind."

"She talked about it a lot?"

She felt more than saw him shake his head. "Maybe once or twice when I saw her looking sad, especially when I was younger. Most of it I read."

Galena pushed away. "Read it where?"

"Her journals." His gaze grew distant and his lips tilted in a sad smile. "I found them after she died. I don't think I really understood how bad leaving him bothered her until I read them." His eyes sharpened.

"What?" she said.

He focus on the hollow of her throat, his brow furrowed as though puzzling out a complex riddle.

"Reese, what?"

"The pain in those books, you can't help but feel it. The first time I read them, I couldn't put them down. She had a gift for words. A way that made me feel like her experiences were my own."

"You think the journals might be the key?"

Reese eyed her. "It can't be that. It's too—"

"Easy? Why? Because it's not about strategy and warfare? Swords, electricity, and fire?" She couldn't help but laugh at the irony of it all. "Isn't the basis of the spiritu's message that more is gained through peace than violence?"

He squeezed her leg, his thumb working in a distracted circle.

"I'd imagine getting Maxis to read journals would be the tough part," she said. "Getting them in front of him when we don't know where he's at makes it even more of a challenge."

"You really think what's in the journals might sway him?"

Galena let the idea simmer. "From everything you've told me, Maxis has lived his life on nothing but revenge and believing everyone he loved abandoned him. If I were him and I found out I hadn't been abandoned by choice, that my mother not only loved me, but wanted me with her? Yeah, I think it would rearrange my life."

Reese sat forward, urging her to her feet.

"What? What are we doing?"

He wrapped his fingers around her wrist and tugged her behind him. "Come on. I need your help."

Chapter 27

Maxis pushed the thick slab guarding the private tunnel to his estate open. Two days out of his healing and he was good as new, ready to put his plans for Eryx in play.

"We shouldn't be here." Serena grumbled and burrowed into her fur coat.

"We shouldn't be anywhere else." He ushered her through and resealed the entrance. "I left my men behind to fight once before and all it got me was an insubordinate strategos and a slew of dead men. Besides, Eryx would be hard pressed to find our camp beneath the mountains and snow. No tracker is that good. And even if they did find us, I've got enough escape hatches to ensure we're long gone before they find us."

Serena squeezed the coat's lapels together. He'd be willing to bet her mouth was drawn into a superior pucker behind all that sable. Mated barely a week and already he was learning her patterns. Weren't they a cozy pair?

Her low voice vibrated through the shaft. "I've put myself out there for you. Done the things you asked and sacrificed the only mother I ever really knew to your benefit, and you repay me with keeping me in the dark?"

So that's what her foul mood was about.

She glanced over one shoulder.

He grinned, and her steps picked up, sandals slapping on the cavern floor as she stormed away in an incensed fit. It was cute, even understandable given her background, but not something he'd tolerate.

He struck, coiling the Earth's energy around her waist and hips and slamming her against the uneven stone walls. Her head snapped back on impact, eyes wide with fear and a little shock. Surely she hadn't expected he'd accept such out outburst. Or was she simply surprised he'd cushioned her crash against the rock?

"Such temper." He prowled forward.

She twitched beneath his invisible hold, struggling for release.

He might've stolen a good number of the gifts he now wielded, but those of the Earth ran strong and natural, a power she'd never escape. "If I didn't know better, I'd say you were trying to bait me."

"I'm not doing anything. I'm pissed."

He pressed close.

She snapped her head away and glared down the corridor.

Praise the Great One, her fire unsettled him, crackling against his skin at the damnedest times. "I thought you trusted me, Serena." He skimmed her jawline with his lips. "I know what you've given. I value it." He tickled the shell of her ear with his nose. "You'll have your answers, but you'll have them my way, in my time." He stepped back, his cock a heavy rod behind his wool pants.

Serena barely deigned to look at him, but she shook with the same lust he felt, no matter how she longed to hide it.

"Now." He straightened his long coat with a firm tug on the lapels. "I've got an ellan tucked away and awaiting our arrival. I'd hoped to have your perspective on the conversation, but if you're not fit to—"

"I'm fit for whatever you can dish out and then some." She might not have a crown, but she was regal to her very marrow.

He ducked his head to hide his grin and ambled down the corridor. With a flick of his fingers, he released the binds surrounding her. "Perhaps later, mate. For now, we've got some negotiating to do."

His steps rang through the tunnel and a chilled, steady draft bit his cheeks. Silence trailed him at first, then the determined clip of Serena's sandals. She kept one pace behind and to the left of him, more of a silent protest than submissive acceptance.

Ahead, the corridor fanned out to a wide opening. Morning sunlight filtered in from tubes at the top of the vast cavern to cast a pale yellow haze over the bustling troops below.

"Come." He held out his hand. Dissension in private was one thing, but public remonstration was something else. "We're late and Uther's temper has grown short. Angus doesn't seem to care for his manner of treatment."

As far as olive branches went, the tidbit seemed to sooth his baineann. She slid her hand in his, chin lifted, and kept pace beside him. "Angus? I thought he'd outlived his usefulness after his poor timing with the council."

"His temper got to him." Maxis guided her around a corner and lowered his voice as they neared a scared wood door, the paint faded to a drab olive. "Doesn't mean we can't revise and repurpose."

The door opened, Uther beside it, the scowl on his strategos' face enough to elicit an empathetic chuckle. *"Have a care, friend. He's not without his purpose,"* he said to Uther, keeping the thought between the two of them.

Uther's frown deepened, but he crossed his arms in quiet acceptance.

Angus sat blindfolded and bound in a gold, brocade chair near a modest hearth. The crackling firelight danced along one side of his face. He straightened as Maxis and Serena entered the room. "Who's there?"

"Not to worry, Angus." Maxis closed the door with a thought. "I assured you you'd be in good hands and you will continue to be." He motioned to Uther to remove the blindfold.

Uther complied with obvious reluctance, but kept the binds at Angus' wrists in place.

"The secrecy is necessary," Maxis said. "No matter how valuable you might be to me, I think it's best for both our interests if you remain innocent to my whereabouts."

Maxis eased Serena's coat from her shoulders, displaying his mark on her forearm. He guided her to the free wingback situated opposite their guest. "Angus Rallion, meet my baineann, Serena Steysis."

"You look familiar." Angus leaned forward and squinted. "You're Reginald Doroz's girl."

"Not anymore." Maxis stood beside her. "And you'd be wise to keep my mate's existence and family relations to yourself until we're prepared to release the information. I want my plans behind us before I share my good fortune. Understood?"

Angus sneered. "Hard to agree when I've yet to learn your plans."

Gods, but the man was a stubborn old goat. "Despite the fact you bungled the last opportunity I handed you, I've opted to give you another chance to put Eryx in a corner, one he'll have a hard time getting out of and that won't come back on you." He leaned against Serena's wingback. "Assuming, of course, you're interested."

Angus shifted in his chair and nodded, obviously uncomfortable with his hands bound behind his back. "Any action that takes Shantos from the throne interests me, so long as it has merit."

"Then I'll pose a scenario for you." Maxis paused, more for effect than to gather his thoughts. "How would the ellan perceive it if a person charged with treason were to come forward in surrender only to be executed by one of the malran's men in cold blood?"

"I assume the treasonous party in question is you?" Angus shook his head. "He's already said you'd face death for your actions."

"Without a trial? That's hardly the fair ruler he presents himself to be."

Angus scoffed and did his best to recline in a nonchalant manner. "You'll have a hard time getting a fair trial, not after those humans he brought forward. Their memories made a mighty impact on the council." He studied Serena a moment, then refocused on Maxis. "Still, if it were clear up front you meant to surrender, no fight and a stated desire to atone, he'd look like a bloodthirsty barbarian out for vengeance. The problem is you'd have a hard time proving it."

"Unless there were ellan to observe it." Maxis let the idea sink in for a beat. "If someone were to convey to a few unbiased council members that my surrender was about to occur, but that I was concerned as to whether or not the malran was capable of following due process, that could ensure a witness would be present to keep things above board. Correct?"

"Most likely," Angus said.

"Then all you need do is find the right individuals and get them there at the appointed time." Maxis grinned, his best, non-verbal taunt. "Assuming you still have any sway with the council."

Angus struggled to free his bonds. "It's a foolish plan. You intend to stage some type of bogus attack? How would you ever convince them and manage to live through it. They're too leery of you and tricks at this stage."

Maxis waved off Angus' concern and aimed a curt nod at Uther. "Suffice it to say, those details are handled. So long as you keep the malran away from my corpse, we'll be fine."

Uther stepped forward and replaced the blindfold around the old man's head.

Angus sputtered and wriggled to keep Uther from his task.

"You'll need to work quickly." Maxis cut in before he lost Angus' focus entirely. "Uther will have you safe and sound at home in no time and will give you all the details. Tell them I've requested a location in Evad, a place I can be sure the malran will keep his impressive powers in check for fear of exposure to humans. In truth, it'll be to provide us more cover. Time for me to get away, and a whole lot of clean up for the malran to contend with. The key is to keep the information close until the last moment possible. We don't need Shantos showing up before we're ready."

Uther urged Angus to his feet. "Any questions?"

"This is preposterous." Blindfolded, Angus' unsteady balance belied his confident words. "It won't work."

"It'll work," Maxis said as Uther guided him from the room. "And you'll aid me in our plan or you'll go down with the rest of us."

That shut him up, leaving only the hiss of his shuffling sandals against the stone floors.

The door clicked shut behind them.

Serena considered him and a smile curved her ballet pink lips. "So, the human swipe you wanted me to share with Reese isn't real."

"Not this time." Maxis took Angus' chair and crossed one leg over the other. "It's a setup to prod the malran into swooping in to save the day and surrounding me in the process. If Eryx mans up the way I think he will, Uther ought to be able to blend in among his men without problem.

"Naturally, I'll realize we're outmanned and will offer my surrender. When I raise up my hands, Uther will throw his bolt, I'll feign death, and you and the humans go into hysterics. My men spirit you and my corpse away while Angus and his cronies act as witness. With the unexpected fireworks, Eryx will be too busy with crowd control to do much in the way of stopping us."

He paused, rotating his crossed foot in measured circles. "Satisfied?"

Serena's smile grew, slow, but infinitely devious. "Immensely."

* * * *

Eryx eyeballed every person in the room—Reese, Galena, Ludan and Ramsay. The warrior compound's round strategy map sat all but forgotten. "You wanna do what?"

Reese flinched. "I want you to give me a chance to get Maxis to surrender."

"And you want to do it with a book." It had to be a joke. Maxis surrendering under any circumstance was nearly improbably, but luring him with a book? No.

"It's not just a book, Eryx." Galena leaned into the ancient stone map and gripped its edge. The topography of Eden's many regions was carved into the tableau, the fine detail spotlighted by the noonday sun piped from above. "They're journals. Real life, raw emotions that could make a difference, even for someone like Maxis."

Eryx turned away and fisted his hands. He glanced at Ramsay who for the first time in forever didn't look angry, but seemed as off kilter with Reese's idea as Eryx. "We can't do it." Eryx faced the couple and braced his fisted knuckles on the stone surface. "This is a chance to nab Maxis and I want it."

"It's a trap." Reese's hesitancy evaporated and an air of certainty swept in behind it. "If you show up you're playing exactly like he wants. This is an entirely different tactic."

Eryx hung his head and his braids fell forward on either side of his face. Pressure built across his brow and behind his eyes, and the need to punch and shout ratcheted by the second.

"I let it get this far." Eryx let out a tired breath and pushed upright. Ludan had prodded him time and again not to ignore Maxis and the rebellion. "If I'd taken action none of this would have happened. Not those human women, not Ian, not Lexi." He lifted his chin toward Reese. "Hell, he probably wouldn't have even made it to you if I'd done more."

He paced along the map's rough edge, focused on Evanora's estate. "I'm not about to make the same mistake twice. If I've got a shot at him, I'm going to make sure I take it."

Reese stepped in to catch his attention. "At what price? Even if you manage to out-think whatever Maxis has planned and you take him out, what if the spiritu was right and it's not enough to counter balance the bigger picture? Are you willing to risk all our races for such a simple idea with zero impact on you and your men?"

"Reese." Galena edged forward.

Reese stayed her with a terse shake of his head. "No. There's no need to risk anyone but me. If it works, we all win. If it doesn't, no harm, no foul. Eryx can move ahead with this attack."

Eryx rubbed the back of his neck, the weight of decisions and consequence pressing on his shoulders.

"What makes you think you can even find him?" Ramsay asked. "We've had men out scouting for days and no one's seen him. Evanora's estate has been empty of all but a few guards, nothing substantial enough to warrant a raid."

Reese motioned for the emerald leather-bound book gripped between Galena's hands.

Galena glared at her mate. "You never said anything about going solo."

"Galena." His voice dropped and he brushed his hand along hers, comforting. An intimate stroke Eryx appreciated from the perspective of a caring mate, but could've done without witnessing with his baby sister. "Trust me. This is the right thing."

A blush spread up her throat and across her cheeks, and her lips pressed so tightly together they lost all their color. The visual lock between the two of them seemed charged enough to power half an Evad suburb.

She ducked her head and handed over the book.

Reese took it and kissed the top of her hand. "Galena's the one who found a clue on where we might find him." He released her with obvious reluctance and thumbed to a dog-eared page. A faint hiss sounded as he ran his finger down the parchment. "This is her first journal, penned right after she'd left Evanora's estate. She makes references here to slave farms. A big stretch of land north of the castle where the region's weather gets nasty."

"They had actual farms?" Ludan pushed off the wall and twisted for a better look at the journal.

"Nothing too large, but sophisticated." Reese pointed at a section on the stone tableau, a mountain range beyond Evanora's land. "If I'm reading her notes right, they'd be right about here."

"And you think that's where he's hiding?" The derision that had been prevalent in Ramsay's voice for days was gone, replaced with genuine curiosity.

Reese leaned in, a bit of the camaraderie Eryx had once seen between the two men sputtering. "If you were about to make a slave run, what would you be doing?"

"Getting the cells ready," Ramsay answered.

"Exactly." Reese focused on Eryx. "I found him at Evanora's place just before Maxis met up with Serena. The place was spotless, like he was about to move in. The two fit."

"No leads with the trackers though," Ludan said taking his place back at the wall.

"Unless you didn't go far enough north." Reese met each man's stare in turn. "All I want is a chance to scout and get one or two of the journals in where he can find them. In and out."

Galena lifted her chin and tapped her thumbnail on the tableau's edge. The idea of her mate on this crazy errand obviously didn't sit any better with her than it did with Eryx.

"That's an awful lot of risk based on a huge amount of old knowledge and assumption," Eryx said.

"Not if I mask."

Eryx chuckled and paced toward the plush, yet well-used gold leather couch along the rear wall. "I haven't met anyone that masks better than a Shantos and even I'd be hesitant to try that stunt."

"He's better," Ramsay said.

A startled silence filled the room.

Eryx sat the foot he'd been half way to putting on the table back on the floor. "Come again?"

"Reese is better than either one of us." Ramsay grinned at the floor and scratched the back of his head before he finally looked up. "Used to drive me nuts when we'd practice against each other. He's a pretty respectable tracker too."

Son of a bitch. Eryx stretched his arms out on the sofa back. Ramsay might not yet be ready to let bygones be bygones with Reese, but he'd manned up enough to admit Reese's strengths, which meant they had to be damned impressive. "You think this plan has merit?"

Ramsay shrugged and studied the map. "If the spiritu story is true and you can nab Maxis without a fight and risk no men, it's worth it."

"He shouldn't go alone." Galena leveled every man in the room with one of those feminine glares most men dreaded. "Any one of you would take at least one or two men with you."

Eryx shook his head. "You're missing the point, Galena. We can't risk anyone from our crew being there. If Serena wasn't playing us and a bunch of us get caught, we screw our chance to catch Maxis. If Reese goes it alone…" He glanced at Reese. "Well, he's just a pissed-off brother out to get even."

"So you're agreed?" Reese said.

Praise the Great One, if Eryx had any compassion at all, he'd give his sister her way and forbid the whole thing. The idea reeked of a suicide mission. On the other hand, if the spiritu thing was true, he'd be an idiot not to let Reese try.

He pulled in a deep breath and braced for impact. "Yeah. I agree."

Chapter 28

Snow sparkled beneath Reese's airborne form, the rich purple, blue, and red of the mountain rock pulsing up through the blanket of white. Bitter wind whipped around him, the mask hiding him from the dilapidated structures below no protection from the fierce gusts.

No way was the mess below him Maxis' hub. Rock walls were all that remained, wood beams broken and strewn in haphazard patterns.

He breathed into the high neck of his full-length coat. His warm breath ricocheted off the lambskin lining to heat his checks. He'd known the region was treacherous, but damned if he'd expected this. Not one footprint marred the snow's surface, no scent or sign of smoke and no activity. No noise beyond the wind's steady whir.

There had to be something. Evanora's place had been in perfect condition when he'd been there less than a week ago, only a trace of stagnant air beneath some kind of citrusy cleanser.

He squinted against the glaring overcast skies. Every gust vibrated through his thick coat and to his bones.

Wait a minute.

He closed his eyes and focused on the steady thrum, a constant tremor beneath him that went against the wind's surge and fall.

The tunnels from Maxis' hideout came to mind, crude but efficient and nearly undetectable if one didn't know where to look. Reese cast his energy out in a wide arc. One ping, one pattern out of context was all he needed.

Wind whistled around him, the quiet of the barren region almost suffocating.

A steady rumble sounded on his right.

Reese drifted toward it, feeling along the tall ridges with mental sweeps. His brow burned from the chill and his shoulders ached from the constant clench of his muscles, one hour too long in this forsaken ice cube. Probably closer to two by now.

A scrape of stone on stone sounded.

He spun and froze, gritting his teeth at the knee-jerk reaction. The weather and the need to prove himself were making him sloppy. His blood had all but turned to liquid steel when Eryx had agreed to his plan, but he'd never prove himself worthy if he ended up dead. If he didn't get a grip and act smart, he wouldn't make it another thirty minutes.

He flew toward the sound. His fingertips pulsed and prickled despite his deep pockets, and his nose grew numb.

A rock jutted out by an opening on the top of the ridge, almost identical to the ones at Maxis' Asshur hideout.

Adrenaline rushed his sluggish bloodstream. No men were visible, and the place was void of detectable energy. Odd, he'd keep the place unguarded. Then again, Eryx had decimated a good chunk of rebellion men in their last battle.

He pushed the cover aside, and slipped inside.

Bingo. Just like Maxis' cave, complete with slow burning torches at regular intervals.

Less than twenty feet in, a buzz registered against his senses, the same thrum he'd felt from above, only more so. It took at least a few hundred bodies to stir that kind of energy, or maybe double that. Pinpointing the origin was next to impossible, though, with so much rock between him and the source.

If you'd forged links with your men the way Ramsay does, you'd have found the new camp in a blink. Then again, they could have tracked him as well. And didn't that put a whole new light on how much trust Ramsay put in his men? The exposure his old friend faced everyday, knowing any one of his warriors could find and double-cross him, showed how much faith Ramsay put in those who served.

No wonder he hadn't been able to ignore Reese's secrets.

He wound down the shadowed tunnel and pumped his fists to urge more blood to his tingling fingertips. Every step clicked in his head. Fifty feet he'd traveled, north to northeast, assuming the thick mountain hadn't muddled his connection to the sun. It had sure thrown his tracking skills.

Ten more feet he traveled, the rock's bland surface blending with the darkness to create the sensation of blindness. At this point he couldn't even see the warm puffs of air from his mouth.

A draft rushed his right side and lightness registered on his left. He paused and strained to see through the darkness. An intersecting tunnel, this one wider than the one behind him. The scent of fire and roasting game wafted from the light.

He glanced from right to left, and gauged the long-winding path behind him to the outside. Closing his eyes, he visualized the energy around him, his tracker sense more heightened with the flush of adrenaline. A path of energy sparked from the light on his left to the exit tube behind him. Only recent and frequent use would leave such a bright, vibrant residue.

He crept toward the darker corridor on his right. It was stagnant in comparison to the others, though not void of energy. Another step in and his senses tripped, feminine energy, light and colorful catching his attention.

Serena.

Checking his position against the sun, he mentally mapped his location. Evanora's estate lay just over two miles away. Maxis loved his escape plans. To mine an elaborate labyrinth between his troops and Evanora's castle made sense.

Three paths to choose from, two toward danger, and one toward safety. He'd taken the safe road before with Ramsay and look where it got him.

A new intersection.

Funny how the spiritu's words had proven to be so literal, or maybe she'd known all along. He stepped toward the light and halted. Maxis hadn't once marched or trained with his men in the time Reese led them. Why would he start now?

He turned toward the darkness instead and crept forward. His heartbeat thickened and with every step, its tempo built. Sweat lined his chest and back, his fur coat stifling.

Time eked by and his doubts raged. Fatigue and the constant mask he held along the two-mile stretch drained his energy until he could barely stand. Every second, the sun slipped closer to the Earth's horizon. Half a mile more to Evanora's estate if his internal map calculated right. And then what?

He shook his head and tried to release the thought. He'd get the answers when he needed them. And if he didn't, well, at least he'd die with a free heart, a clear conscience, and Galena.

His heart stuttered. Galena would be safe, her and the rest of their race if his plans actually worked.

Up and on the left, a darker pocket of color covered the tunnel wall. No, not color, but a door, inset and well scarred.

Reese scanned for energy behind the gray planks and came back with nothing. Relying on touch over telekinesis, he eased the door's iron latch free and prayed for well-oiled hinges. A high-pitched, grated squeak sounded for a second, then silence.

He pulled the door wide. Smoke and the scent of sweet cloves assailed him as he stepped into an aristocratic studio apartment, a king size bed to one side with ornate carved posters on each corner, and an elaborate desk on the other. A cozy hearth nestled in the middle with barely glowing coals in the grate and wingbacks on either side. Every inch was decorated like something from the 1800s complete with dark colors and gold embellishments.

Just like Evanora's castle.

He hustled to the desk and touched the map spread across the top. Energy echoes rushed up his forearm. Fresh, four hours ago at most, but probably closer to two. He pulled the journal from the inside of his coat and thumbed to the page he'd bookmarked, the one his mother had penned the first night she'd spent without Maxis. Wedged in the crease was the note he'd written for Maxis before he'd left.

Trust me enough to read it. It's never too late to do the right thing. Never.

Not the most prolific guidance, but all he'd been able to come up with. His hand shook as he situated the note, fatigue making his movements short and clumsy. He had thirty minutes, forty-five at best, to get outside and drop his mask before he blacked out.

He set the book in place and re-checked his location. Definitely at Evanora's castle. If he could find another way out he had a much better shot at making it, but he could just as easily burn what little time he had looking. He'd give himself five minutes to find an out, and then he'd have to take his chances in the tunnel.

He felt along the open wall near the bed, fingers pressed to the gold filigree accents.

Serena's harpy voice chirped from the rock corridor.

Reese froze.

The door opened and Serena swooshed inside, all drama and tittering laughter. She grinned over one shoulder as Maxis entered behind her, and tossed her coat over the back of one wingback. "We should celebrate. Have a little pre-event, one on one. You're back to full strength after all."

Reese edged toward the still open door and prayed his steps fell soundless. He didn't dare levitate with his energy stores this low. Better to risk his shaking legs than clipping Maxis' interest with a shift of air or energy.

Maxis shrugged out of his own coat. "Getting ahead of yourself aren't you, my devious mate?" Staring at the desk, Maxis tossed his coat over Serena's.

The journal.

Fuck, he'd wanted Maxis to find it, but after he'd hightailed it home would've been nice, or at least with a fighting bit of energy left in him. He managed another few steps toward the opening.

Maxis sidled closer to the desk.

A draft from the tunnel tickled the back of Reese's neck. Almost there.

Leather hissed against wood as Maxis dragged the book across the desktop.

Serena crept up behind him and laid a tentative hand on his shoulder. "What's that?"

Reese backed through the doorway.

Maxis snapped the book closed and flicked his hand toward the entrance. "Nothing."

The door skimmed no more than three inches from Reese's nose and slammed shut just as Reese's vision wavered.

* * * *

Galena paced the castle parlor. The center window arched high and wide before her, but her mind was somewhere else. Four hours since Reese had left, three and half since his voice had floated through her thoughts with a sweet, *"I love you."* Then he'd crippled her heart and extracted a vow she wouldn't check in or leave the castle. Too much risk, he'd said. He'd need all of his focus to keep his presence masked and wouldn't want to stir unnecessary energy.

She stopped at the window and glared at the crescent moon. A bold purple lined its edges and a cheerful silver streak sparkled beneath it. She'd rip them both from the sky if she could, the image far too happy for her anger to abide.

Watching Eryx and Lexi had been worse. She'd holed up here just to avoid them. The way they ogled each other and the way their hands stayed intertwined all the way home from the warrior's compound.

She grumbled and fisted the window ledge. Her whole life she'd stood behind her brothers, her whole damned life and they sent her mate in unprotected. For what? So they'd have a better chance at killing Maxis? It was a perfect deal for them really. The troublesome sister potentially loses her tainted/traitorous mate and they get the madman in the end. A total win-win.

A low click sounded behind her.

She watched the parlor door open in the window's reflection, the night's black backdrop making the image nearly mirror perfect.

Ah, the happy couple. Galena sucked in a slow, fortifying breath. "I picked this room because no one uses it."

"And I'm here because we need to talk." The bantering, placating tone from dinner was gone, replaced with a sharp edge.

Galena faced them, smoldering beneath the angry tirade she barely held in check.

Lexi's mouth was screwed up as tight as Galena felt and red colored her cheeks. She didn't know her new shalla all that well, but she certainly knew a pissed-off woman when she saw one.

At least Lexi had her fireann here to fight with. Hers was off The Great One knew where. Alone. Galena gave them both her back and scowled at the moon. "Now's not a good time."

Eryx's heavy footfalls stopped behind her and Lexi slid up on his right. "You don't have a choice in this one. Turn around."

Galena knew that tone. This was her malran behind her, resigned and formal.

Prickles spread along her neck and spine. Goose bumps rose on her forearms and a chill shot through her heart. "Reese." The whisper slipped out as she reached for Reese through their link. To histus with her promises, she needed contact. She needed—

"He won't answer." Eryx gripped her shoulder and urged her to turn.

"No." Galena jerked from his touch and staggered toward the parlor door, part run, part stumble.

Eryx shot between her and the door. "He's fine." He gave her a subtle shake. "Look at me."

"He's fine, Galena." Lexi came up beside her. If her brusque delivery didn't spell out how pissed she was, the set of daggers she aimed at her mate did the trick. "Eryx is a secretive dick, but he's got news you need to hear."

Galena sucked in a deep breath and focused on her link to Reese. Somehow Lexi's anger strengthened Galena's spine and helped fortify her focus. She nodded, but kept her gaze rooted on Eryx's sternum. "Talk."

"He made it in and out, then flashed out five minutes from some tunnels that lead to the rebellion warrior camp."

Galena tried to duck out of his grip. If Reese was out in that kind of weather, especially in Brasia, he'd be dead in no time.

Eryx gripped her chin between his thumb and forefinger and forced her gaze to his. "Ramsay and Ludan were close by."

Her brain sputtered. "What?"

A sound that crossed between a vile curse and a scoff tripped passed Lexi's lips. "Yeah, that's what I said."

Lexi pushed Eryx's hands off Galena's shoulders and guided her over to the wide, crimson couch. "Turns out our boys might not have gone with him, but they lined out some contingency plans." She glowered back at Eryx. "Without telling the little womenfolk."

Relief blasted through Galena. She should focus on her breath and keep an even head so she'd be ready to help him. Reese's link pulsed in her mind, there but too fragile to gauge the distance. "How far out are they?"

"Ramsay said another twenty minutes," Eryx said. "He's unconscious, but alive. Took them fifteen minutes before they could get to him without detection, but Ramsay doesn't think he sustained any injuries. Nothing visible anyway."

Twenty minutes and no visible damage was good. Something to hang onto.

Wait a minute. She looked to Lexi then Eryx. "Ramsay?"

Eryx sat in an overlarge gold chair on her left and a sardonic grin twisted his lips. "Ramsay offered Reese his link just before he left. He told Reese it was to make sure Reese was on the up and up, but about five minutes later, he cornered Ludan and the two of them followed."

Galena braced her elbows on her knees and white-knuckled her hands together. "Twenty minutes." If she could make it that long she'd take care of him herself. "And then what?"

Eryx covered her clasped hands and squeezed. "We get your man healed and hope his efforts pay off. If not, we go out and kick some rebellion ass."

Chapter 29

Maxis adjusted the ugly maroon baseball cap low over his brow and shifted on the ass-numbing metal bleachers. The jeans Uther had talked him into wearing didn't do much to help his blood flow either.

The baseball stadium was nearly filled to capacity.

"I'll give you credit," he said to Uther beside him. *"You picked a popular team."*

Elbows rested on his knees and eyes trained on the field, his strategos looked like he'd been to a million high school championships. *"You did say you wanted a crowd."* He glared over one shoulder. *"I delivered."*

Delivered indeed, and picked a decent climate as well. It wasn't Havilah by any stretch, but Texas in late April was tolerable.

Maxis fidgeted with his hat again. He hated the damned things, the bulk of his hair tucked underneath making the discomfort worse.

Uther's voice trawled through Maxis head. *"You're awful jumpy."*

Maxis blanked his expression and shifted to check the scoreboard. *"I'm trusting a man I've known ten days not to overestimate his skills and fry me to a crisp. Call me cautious."*

Uther stood and lifted his chin in the direction of the parking lot. *"Time to get in position. You throw your hands up and I'll try not to hit any sensitive spots."*

Maxis held his tongue and let him pass. Ever since the healing Uther had been different. More familiar, like family. A low grumble rattled free and the couple in front of him glanced back with uncertain looks.

Uther was right. He was jumpy, out of sorts and disoriented to the point he couldn't contain his thoughts or actions. It was that damned book. His mother's journal. He'd done more than read the passage Reese had marked, he'd read the whole thing, a few parts multiple times. All this time he'd thought his mother had abandoned him. Left him in favor of a child sired by a human. But she'd wanted him. Missed him.

It's never too late to do the right thing. Never.

"And that's the game folks." The announcer's tinny, distorted voice blared through the sound system. "Let's hear it for this year's 5A high school champions."

Maxis stood with the crowd and ambled with the rest of the human herd toward the parking lot. His men would be waiting, seven chosen for their noticeable stature and sure to draw the malran's notice as soon as they came together.

All this time he'd thought himself alone. If he'd known how his mother felt, he'd have killed his father sooner and found her on his own. He tucked his hands in the front pockets of his jeans and clenched is fists. Seventy years without family. His life could've been different.

The visiting team's bus sat parked along a building adjacent to the field, a parking lot and a steady stream of humans all that stood between him and his fate. He aimed toward the bronze wildcat statue centered at the main entrance and tugged off his ball cap, tossing it in a trash bin near the corner.

A big man in jeans, a white T-shirt, and black leather cuffs on each wrist stepped forward and took position on his right. Another fell in on his left with a different color shirt and the same cuffs. More filtered in behind them, their Myren energy more dense than the human crowd. If their size didn't tip the malran off, then the pure mass and energy striding against the flow of bodies toward the bus would.

He could forgo his plans. Vanish and start over. Maybe reach out to Reese after time had passed.

No, he had a mate now. Plans and opportunity to finally gain his revenge. He'd chosen his ship and one way or another he'd steer it.

He slowed and checked the building rooftop. No visible sign of Serena, but her presence wavered through their link exactly where she should be. That meant the ellan were there too, waiting and watching.

Eighty feet to go. Seventy. Sixty.

Eryx ambled from behind the bus, Ramsay and Ludan on either side of him. Another cluster of men strode from the other end, each warrior marked as the malran's men with a mix of gold and silver cuffs.

The wall of energy at his back lessened, his men falling away as they'd been directed.

Reese stepped from the shadows.

Maxis stopped. He'd expected the twins and Eryx's somo, but Reese was a surprise. His hair was bound and a mating mark spanned his forearm. Not just any mark, but the winged Shantos horse. Son of a bitch,

Serena hadn't mentioned that little tidbit. He guessed his brother ended up getting his heart's desire after all. Maybe Reese was right. Maybe things could change.

"Throw your hands up," Falon crooned in his head. *"Give the signal and stick to the plan."*

He should move, step forward and lift his hands in surrender as planned.

"You're a fool if you think your fate will be as fortuitous as your brother's." Had Falon's voice always been so grating? A brush against the grain?

Reese paced closer, fingers loose at his sides. Dark circles marked the space below his eyes and his cheeks were drawn and hollow. Why?

Movement registered on his left, a splash of turquoise out of place in the crowd and long blond hair. His mate. He should acknowledge her, but he couldn't look away from Reese. Something held him. Not a physical hold, but something born from emotion.

"You think I'd let you screw us both?" Falon taunted. *"Ruin my plans?"*

Reese drew closer. Two more steps and Maxis could talk to him, ask him all the questions he wanted and learn more about their mother. He could always throw his hands up after and stay to his plans.

"Look out." Serena darted forward and shoved Reese away.

An electric bolt shot from beside Eryx, Uther standing behind him as a wicked blue arc emanated from his palm.

This wasn't the plan.

Maxis dodged left, distrust unlatching his feet from the asphalt.

Serena spun. In her right hand a dagger flashed against the stadium lights, and her face burned in a wild rage. "I won't let you."

Pain flared sharp at his chest. Steel grated against bone and vibrated through his torso. He couldn't breathe. Sound dropped to nothing and people shoved and pulled all around him.

Serena yanked the knife free. It was Serena wasn't it? Or was it Falon? No, it was his mate, though her eyes were black like Falon's.

He fell to his knees and his head jerked forward. White edged his vision. His muscles gave way and gravity took over, his body surrendering to a thick, unyielding weight. His head smacked the ground, no pain issuing beyond a dull rattle in his skull. The white crept closer, the black sky above him barely bleeding through.

Reese hovered above him. His mouth moved, but no sound registered. How fitting to have him here. A comfort.

He shook on a rough exhale, and the white took over.

* * * *

"Maxis." Reese rolled his brother to his back, the frenzied crowd knocking into him on every side. He pressed his palms against Maxis' wound. "Galena!"

Humans screamed and pushed around him. Behind him Ramsay and Ludan barked orders. Beside him Eryx wrangled Serena.

"I had to do something. It was a set up." Serena flailed her arms before Eryx clamped them in a brutal bear hug. "He'd have killed Reese if I hadn't stepped in."

Warriors circled to create a protective wall.

"Ramsay, get Reese and Maxis out of here." Eryx slung Serena over one shoulder and zigzagged through the crowd toward the isolated spot they'd picked for their portal.

Reese pressed harder on the wound, his gut cramping from the pain ripping inside him. Maxis had been close to surrender, Reese knew it to the root of his soul. The hope and raw vulnerability in those last seconds had made Maxis look as innocent as a five-year-old child.

"Reese." Galena's voice reached through the dark shroud choking him. "Reese, look at me."

Blood coated his hands, thick and warm. "He was almost there."

"We gotta go, man." Ramsay kneeled beside them. "Eryx fried all the closest electronics, but that's not gonna buy us much time. We've got smart phones everywhere."

Galena covered Reese's hands with hers and squeezed. "Reese, we have to go. We'll take him with us, but there's nothing you can do. He's already gone. You can't save him."

Reese coughed to cover the sob that pushed up his throat and levered himself off his knees to a crouch. He lifted his brother's dead weight off the asphalt. His shoulders and biceps shook, still weak from his flash out the night before, but he cradled Maxis close. "I think we already did."

Chapter 30

Padding from Galena's bathroom, Reese swiped a thick cotton towel down his chest. Steam billowed out behind him and his skin still stung from the scorching shower. The castle was the last place he wanted to be, but with all the madness going on he'd capitulated to Eryx's "request" he and Galena stay close. As if anyone would go against the malran's wishes.

He paused at the open window. Galena's suite sat on the corner of the third story in the royal wing and gave a perfect noonday view of the ocean beyond. Twelve hours since he'd watched his brother die and no real sleep to speak of, but at least he was alive.

The image of Maxis' body stretched across an ebony marble slab at the warrior compound flashed cold and eerie in his head. They'd left him in the jeans, white T-shirt and boots he'd worn to Evad, a rusty crimson stain covering most of his torso. Reese laughed to himself. Maxis would have thrown a fit if he'd known he'd die in human attire. Maybe Eryx would look the other way and let Reese give his brother a funeral pyre, one at the homestead where he'd said good-bye to his mother.

The door latch clunked behind him and the wind drafted through the open window as the door opened.

"A naked fireann fresh from the shower." Galena nudged the door closed with her hip, hands full with a tray of pastries and coffee. "No complaints from me." She picked up a steaming coffee mug and sauntered to him. "I come bearing food."

"And news?" He wrapped the towel around his waist, took the mug, and pulled Galena close.

"Lots and lots of news. I ran into Lexi and Orla in the kitchen." She tilted her head back for eye contact. "Eryx has all kinds of problems on his hands. For starters, humans are spouting stories to the press, some of them accurate, some of them closer to a sci-fi flick. Second, the ellan are in a panic over the exposure to humans. And finally, Serena's under arrest and telling anyone who'll listen her actions were to protect you and the Myren race from the rebellion."

She stepped away and headed for her own coffee. "She swears everything was an act, a desperate endeavor to shield the malran she's always loved, despite him choosing another woman over her." She blew across the surface and took a cautious sip. "Lexi's so pissed, Eryx had to order Ramsay to keep Serena under guard at the compound for her own safety."

No question who'd win that contest. He'd lay everything he owned on his new malress.

Galena stared at him across the mug's rim and took another drink. "She says Eryx wants you in the throne room in thirty minutes."

A jolt shot up his spine. "She say why?"

She sat her coffee down and strolled back to him, head tilted at a playful angle. The attempt at casualness didn't quite reach her eyes. "You haven't done anything wrong. He probably just has questions for you. Whatever it is, we'll face together." She rubbed his sternum. "Then we'll go home, spend some time alone and get you healed up."

Every part of him zeroed in on her touch. "Then let's get it over with. I've got a fresh deed and a new mate who needs attention."

Reese dressed and focused on the promise of time alone with Galena. He could deal with Maxis and the fallout of the events in Evad later.

They neared the closed throne room doors and his worries crashed through all his peaceful thoughts. "Kind of a formal place for questioning."

Galena squeezed his hand. "Probably busy with ellan. The old ones love anything with pomp and circumstance."

He opened the doors. No ellan waited inside, but a host of others stood waiting. Ramsay and Ludan were up front along with some folks he'd seen around the castle. A young girl Galena had called Jillian hung next to Brenna, and Lexi's friend from Evad, Ian Smith, kept a space beside her. He knew Ludan's father, Graylin, from his training days, and Orla he remembered from running with Ramsay.

At the center were Eryx and Lexi, seated on their thrones and decked out in full regalia. Reese stepped forward and focused on Galena's hand in his. How quickly she'd become his anchor. *"They're wearing crowns. Doesn't look like anything straightforward or simple to me."*

"Not everything has to be negative," she answered. *"Just go with it."*

At the foot of the dais, he drew to a halt. He started to kneel, but Galena tightened her grip and shook her head in a barely perceptible move.

"This isn't how I wanted to do this, but things are about to get hectic." Eryx shot a quick grin at Lexi. "I thought we'd better take care of an important detail before we all move into damage control."

"You mean Serena?" Reese nearly kicked himself at the thoughtless question as soon as he saw Lexi's glower.

Eryx hung his head, more to hide what Reese suspected was an even bigger grin from Lexi. When he lifted it, the only levity was in his eyes. "Serena's one. Human relations are another."

"That woman's a snake." Lexi gripped her armrests. "I wouldn't trust her as far as I could throw her."

"A wise statement from your malress, Eryx."

Every head spun toward the unexpected voice at the back of the room.

Clio stood, dressed the same as she'd appeared the first time Reese had seen her. "Serena's path is yet unclear, but her actions weren't her own. Not entirely."

Eryx spoke from behind Reese. "And you are?"

"My name is Clio." She smiled at Reese, a tiny one that hinted of secrets still untold, then focused on Eryx. "I believe Reese has shared with you the existence of my race and our purpose."

"I thought you couldn't show yourself to anyone else." The statement slipped out before Reese could censor it, his second snafu in under five minutes. At this rate he'd end up banned from family functions.

"I said I was only allowed to show myself to you, not that I wasn't capable. Given the weight of the action I'm about to take, The Great One has granted an exception." She floated to Reese's left, no footsteps, or swinging arms, just the subtle fan of her hair where air brushed it. "Before I take my final step, I wanted to support my warrior's claims and implore you to carry on with the wisdom he shared in your battles."

"Wait a minute." Ramsay stepped forward. "How could Serena's actions not have been her own? I saw her drive the dagger home."

"Reese told you of the dark rogues?" Clio said. "Those who strive to let the dark passions rule?"

Hesitant nods issued all around.

"One of them crossed an unforgivable line. Falon was Maxis' guide through much of his life. It was he who guided Serena's thoughts. In the final moments, he overpowered her will and forced the blade into Maxis chest. Crossing that line makes his existence forfeit. It also negates the weight of the deeds he's managed to incite to date, thereby greatly restoring the balance between light and good, not to mention putting a nice dent in the dark rouges' plans."

Clio surveyed those gathered. "The balance of dark to light is now well in hand, the larger crisis averted." She zeroed in on Eryx and the air cracked with tension. "Have a care though. Your exposure to humans promises many new and challenging obstacles, and it is only a matter of time before the prophecy begins to unfold. Falon may no longer be able to guide Serena's mind, but we don't yet know her guide going forward and how they might use the Rebellion in their schemes."

"Final step." An uneasy sensation slithered down his the back of Reese' neck. "You said, 'before I take my final step.' What does that mean?"

Clio tilted her head, pensive. "All aspects of light and dark must be kept in balance. If a dark spiritu is lost, so must a light spiritu go with him. I volunteered, so I've come to say good-bye and to witness the acknowledgement of your faith and good deeds, the detail the malran has called you for today."

Eryx smirked from his perch. "So the spiritu can see into the future?"

"We see it as it is at any given moment, but free will can and does shift. We also talk amongst ourselves. Remember, you and your mate are not without your own spiritu." She lifted one eyebrow, an imperial gesture that put Eryx's to shame. "How else do you think we managed to guide you to your mate?"

Eryx's smirk stretched ear-to-ear. "Fair enough." He stood and picked up an onyx box from the small table situated at this right.

Lexi rose and followed Eryx down the dais steps.

Ramsay and Ludan strode to either side of them and stood at attention.

"Reese Theron, come forward." Eryx's formal intonation rumbled through the long hall and the bystanders near the windows straightened.

Prying his hand from Galena's grip, he stepped forward.

"Kneel."

Reese went to one knee and his stomach clenched. His heart pounded and a slow cramp built behind his sternum.

"Do you pledge yourself to uphold the tenets of our race?" Eryx said. "To protect our citizens and stand as guard between those with and without power, maintaining the balance as The Great One commands it?"

The warrior's oath. A swearing in. He peeked from his bowed head at Ramsay for some kind of confirmation.

Ramsay stared dead ahead, but his mouth twitched. *"Eryx's patience is pretty shot. Might want to step it up with the answer."*

Shit, it was the oath. And Ramsay sounded, well, like Ramsay again.

Reese swallowed as best he could and forced his lips to move. "I give my vow."

"Will you follow and fight as your malran and strategos direct without hesitation? Placing none but your family before them?"

Family. He had that now, and so much more. "I give my vow."

Eryx handed the black box to Lexi and raised the lid, lifting a warrior's torc from within.

An odd tingling spread across his collarbone and down his arms, and his shoulders snapped back. Not just a new recruit torc, but the white gold of an elite. The Shantos winged horse sat etched in onyx at its center, and platinum bars lined either side.

He caught Eryx's smug expression and quickly bowed his head. Stupid. He knew better than to break protocol.

"You're family now," Eryx said in a way that implied he didn't mind the break in decorum. "The platinum seemed fitting." He shifted behind Reese and lowered the torc over his head. The metal settled around his neck. "Just so you know, this is a formality. Ramsay said he'd made his decision before you left. He didn't want his acceptance to look like a trade in exchange for your efforts, so he chose to wait."

Eryx stepped out from behind him.

Reese chanced another glance at Ramsay. The only change was a subtle lift of his chin, an extra inch to the already proud slant.

"Stand." Eryx offered his hand, palm up. A warrior's greeting.

Reese took it and when Eryx clenched his forearm, a part of Reese's soul locked in place.

Eryx nodded. "Welcome to the fold, briyo. You've earned it."

Galena came up on his right and clasped his upper arm, a smug expression aimed at her brother. "I'm glad you finally came around to my way of thinking."

Ramsay stepped in, palm outstretched. No witty remarks, no formal congratulations, just an unspoken olive branch and awkward quiet. Ludan followed next, formal yet disconnected, as though he'd suffered through one too many of these formalities.

"You've done well, Reese." Clio drifted toward him in her ghostly way. The midday sun sparkled off the crystals adorning her brow and the bottom of her soft-white dress fluttered on a nonexistent breeze. "While not without its challenges, serving as your guide has been a pleasure. One I would volunteer for again should time be replayed."

But she was leaving, not just him, but this life through no fault of her own. "You shouldn't have to give up your existence because of something someone else did."

Clio smiled and the whole room lightened, the same as when the sun came out from behind a thick cloud on a summer day. She cupped the side of his face and traced his cheekbone with her thumb. "Who says I don't relish this step into the afterlife?"

Deep, abiding love spread through him, an all-encompassing warmth like what he'd felt from his mother as a child only more so. An emotional equivalent of a down blanket and a fresh summer rain.

"I've walked this planet for three of your generations, long enough I no longer count the years. To join my maker is to find peace and rest." She lowered her hand and faced Ramsay. "Though, there are those of you who still have journeys ahead."

A heavy silence sparked through the room.

Ramsay's posture might have been relaxed, but Reese knew his strategos. Inside he was poised and alert. It was how Ramsay operated, how he soaked in every detail of his environment without the slightest tell as to the sharp analysis spinning in his head.

"Remember, Ramsay," Clio said. "Not all battles are fought with weapons. The heart is a valiant weapon for those brave enough to wield it."

"What's that supposed to mean?" Eryx said.

Clio kept her gaze on Ramsay. "When the time is right, he'll understand."

With a last glance at Galena and Reese, Clio's form began to fade. "Enjoy your life rewards, Reese. Smile, embrace your mate, and listen for the voice of inspiration."

Her words hung in the air as she disappeared, and Galena's hands tightened on his arm.

Ramsay, Eryx, and Lexi all stared at the empty space where Clio had been. Even Ludan seemed pushed from his usual bored demeanor, his brow furrowed.

"I think now might be a good time for the two of you to leave." Eryx's chagrined voice echoed in Reese's mind, an indicator he'd shared the directive with more than Reese.

The blush spreading across Galena's cheeks confirmed it.

"If you're lucky," Eryx said, *"you'll get a few days of undisturbed quiet before I call you in for duty."*

A low, ironic chuckle sounded from those gathered at the side of the hall.

Reese and those around him turned as one.

Ian Smith, the man he'd had a part in saving, shook his head, shaking with silent laughter. "Newlywed or not, I wouldn't get your hopes up. The way things are happening around here, something's bound to interrupt it."

Lexi sucked in a surprised gasp.

Galena's nails clawed Reese's forearm.

"Did he just—"

"He heard you?"

"Shit."

Lexi, Ramsay and Ludan all spoke at once, the last, most in-your-face bit unsurprisingly from Ludan.

Eryx rubbed the back of his neck. "Go, Reese. Now. Before I change my mind and put you on duty today."

Reese faltered only for a second, the prospect of his future so profoundly perfect he couldn't help but pause long enough to savor it. He gripped Galena's hand, his anchor and his mate. The healer for his soul.

"Come on." He tugged her close, not giving their audience a chance for good-byes. "I know a secluded place with a great waterfall."

Galena's laughter settled deep as they cleared the formal room and headed for the foyer. For the first time in his life, he felt whole and free of shadows, healed by the love of his mate.

Glossary

Aron - Mainstay livestock in Eden used for food and clothing. The hide is tanned to provide a soft, supple leather and is the predominant source of protective outerwear in the colder regions. The animal's fur is a cross between that found on a buffalo and a beaver in the human realm. The thickness and warmth of a buffalo, but shiny and soft as a beaver.

Asshur - A region in Eden. Sun isn't unheard of, but tends to be more cloudy and rainy than the other regions. The population has dropped off in the last few centuries with inhabitants moving to more hospitable areas.

Awakening - A Myren ceremony where people between the ages of eighteen and twenty-one are brought into their powers. The father (or paternal representative) is typically the trigger for the process, where the mother (or maternal influence) acts as an anchor for the awakened individual.

Baineann - The female within a bonded union.

Briash - The Myren equivalent of oatmeal, although its color is a deep brown and the flavor has a hint of chocolate and cinnamon.

Brasia - A region in Eden. The terrain is covered in mountains, with heavy snow and difficult conditions prevalent in the higher elevations.

Briyo - Brother-in-law.

Cootya - A type of cafe that sells common Myren beverages and snacks. Myren fruits and vegetables are the most common menu items, but some pastries can be found. Most feature an open-air area where customers can relax, while kitchen and serving areas remain indoor.

Cush - The capital region of Eden. Densely populated with elaborate buildings.

Diabhal - Devil.

Drast - Field issue protective garment worn by warriors to protect the most vital organs in battle. Made of fine, metal threads, the garments fit their bodies closely. Day-to-day drasts are sleeveless, but the most formal version covers 3/4 of their arms. The necks are boat-shaped to allow for greater comfort when fighting with the metal threads blocking most fire and electrical attacks.

Drishen - A fruit found in Eden. Looks like a grape, tastes like lemonade.

Eden - Another dimension, unknown to humans, within the fabric that surrounds Earth.

Ellan - Elected officials that govern the Myren race alongside the malran or malress. Like most governing bodies, there are a mix of honest servants who seek prosperity and growth for the Myrens and corrupt, "lifers" who stand on antiquated ideas and ceremonies.

Evad - The realm in which humans reside.

Fireann - The male within a bonded union.

Havilah - A more affluent and less populated region in Eden. Rain occurs, but mostly in the evenings with pleasant days full of sun and comfortable temperatures.

Histus - The Myren equivalent of hell.

Kilo - A fish the swims in many lakes in Eden, but is most prevalent in Brasia. A popular mainstay of protein in the Myren race, most often prepared by smoking in apple wood and basting with an apple and cinnamon glaze.

Larken - A long-winged bird known for its singsong chirp. Colored primarily in cobalt blue, but the tips of their wings are lavender.

Lastas - A favorite Myren breakfast pastry.

Lomos Rebellion - A faction of Myrens that have long pursued the enslavement of humans and sought to overthrow the tenets of the Great One.

Lyrita Tree - An exotic tree exclusive to the Havilah region. Trunks are dark brown. Leaves are long and slender, sage green in color. The blooms are exceptionally large and run from pearl to pale pink in color. Average height for a mature lyrita is thirty to forty feet.

Malran - The male leader of the Myren people and the equivalent of a king in the human realm. Leadership has descended down through the Shantos family line since the birth of the Myren race, with the mantle of malran (or malress) falling to the first-born.

Malress - The female leader of the Myren people and the equivalent of a queen in the human realm.

Myrens - A gifted race in existence for over six thousand years that lives in another dimension called Eden. They are deeply in tune with the Earth and the elements that surround her. Their powerful minds and connection to the elements allow them to communicate silently with those they are linked to, levitate, and command certain elements. Their women typically have more healing or nurturing gifts, where men trend more toward protective and aggressive abilities.

Natxu - A regular and expected practice of physical discipline for all Myren warriors. The moves and postures are grueling yet meditative in nature, resulting in peak physical performance and enhancing their tie to the elements.

Nirana - The Myren equivalent of heaven.

Oanan - Daughter-in-law.

Quaran - The Myren equivalent of a General within the warrior ranks.

Runa - Region in Eden, predominantly used for farming.
The black soil is rich and sparkles with minerals. It's
surrounded by "the blue ridge", a crescent-shaped formation
of mountains that appear blue from ground level.

Shalla - Sister-in-law.

Somo - Sworn personal guard to the malran or malress.

Strasse - A highly intoxicating Myren beverage
made from berries found only in Eden.

Strategos - Leader of the Myren warriors.

Torna - An annoying Myren rodent. Larger than an
armadillo, but similar in color with the skin surface of an eel.
While not typically aggressive, their teeth function similar
to a shark and aren't afraid to come out fighting.

Underlands - Not considered a region by most,
but more of an uninhabited wasteland. The lack of
rain makes agriculture nearly impossible.

Vicus - A vegetable known for its extremely tart
flavor, popular among the older generation.

Zurun - A thick flaky pastry with a thin layer of icing
in the middle, twisted in the shape of a bow.

Rhenna Morgan is a happily-ever-after addict—hot men, smart women, and scorching chemistry required. A triple-A personality with a thing for lists and an almost frightening iPhone cover collection, Rhenna's a mom to two beautiful little girls, and married to an extremely patient husband who's mastered the art of hiding the exasperated eye roll. When she's not neck deep in the realm of Eden, or living large in one of her contemporary stories, she's probably driving with the top down and the music up loud, plotting her next hero and heroine's adventure. Check out her website at www.rhennamorgan.com for all her social media links, and signup for her newsletter for snippets, upcoming releases, and general author news.

Be sure not to miss Rhenna Morgan's first Eden book

UNEXPECTED EDEN

Paradise, love and power...and a prophecy with a price.

When Eryx's nemesis tags Lexi as his next target, Eryx insists on taking her home where he can keep her safe. Lexi had no idea "home" would mean the one-and-only land of creation...or that she'd trigger a prophecy that could doom her newfound race.

A Lyrical Originals Novel

Learn More about Rhenna at
http://www.kensingtonbooks.com/author.aspx/31625

Chapter 1

Slow breaths in, slow breaths out. All Lexi had to do was focus on the thump of Rihanna's latest hit, keep the drinks flowing, and stick to her half of the bar. The mother lode of testosterone on Jerry's side couldn't sit there all night. Could he?

"Don't suppose you've noticed, but there's a scrumptious not-from-around-here type giving you the eyeball." Mindy grinned and handed over the latest round of drink orders.

White t-shirt, killer muscles, and dark chocolate hair halfway down his back? Yeah, she'd noticed. Repeatedly. And every time she went for a visual refill, his silver gaze shocked nerve endings she'd long thought dead.

"Drop it, Mindy. Guys like that are an occupational hazard and you know it."

"Honey, that man is way past hazard. More like Chernobyl." She leaned into the trendy concrete countertop. The modern pendant lights spotlighted her platinum hair and ample cleavage. One thing about Mindy—she knew how to work her assets. "I'll bet the fallout's worth it."

"It's packed tonight. You gonna get those drinks out and stash a few tips, or waste 'em on eye candy?"

Mindy's dreamy smile melted and she pulled the loaded cocktail tray close. "All work and no play, huh?" She shook her head and turned for the crowd. "Have fun with that."

Well, hell. Another social interaction down the toilet. At twenty-five-years-old, you'd think she could handle a little female bonding in the form of man-ogling. Especially when four of those years had been spent tending bar. But damn it, some things weren't meant for discussion. Her overactive man-jitters being one of them.

Crouching to snag a fresh bottle of vodka beneath the counter, she peeked behind her.

Lips guaranteed to make a girl forget her name curled into a sly smile. Busted.

She spun away too fast and scraped her forehead against the rough edge of the bar. "Son of a fucking, no good piece of shit." Head down, she counted to three and fought the need to check for witnesses, thankful the music was loud enough to cover her curse. The graceless gawker routine wasn't normally her deal, but for the last thirty minutes she'd come up woefully short in the finesse department—and it was all the dark-haired man's fault.

New bottle ready for action, she faced two middle-aged men dressed like frat boys and settled into her pour-and-bill groove. The routine was a comfort, a stabilizing rhythm to counterbalance the ever-present gaze heavy on her back.

"Hey, Lex." Jerry smacked her shoulder and motioned behind him, never breaking stride as he headed for the register. "Tall, dark and handsome wants to see you."

She wouldn't look. Not again. The giggling trio of barely legal blondes fighting their way into ordering range wasn't nearly as nice on the eyes, but at least they kept her anchored. "Since when did you take up matchmaking?"

"Since the guy offered me a Benjamin to make sure it was you who took care of him."

What? She spun.

The stranger met her surprised stare head on, his smirk a potent mix of humble and confident. "Sold me down the river, did you?"

"Damn right." Jerry winked, shoved a stack of wrinkled bills into the register, and swaggered toward the waiting blondes without so much as a wish for good luck.

Lexi huffed and took an order from the none-too-shabby twenty-something guy right in front of her on principle. Mystery man could cool his jets for a minute or two. Besides, if his banter matched his looks, she'd need every second she could get to batten down the hatches.

She filled orders with slow deliberation and an extra bit of bravado, grabbing snippets of recon where she could.

A vicious looking man sat next to her dark-haired hunk. Lazy raven waves fell to a hard jawline, a tightly trimmed goatee making his harsh face a downright menace. Entirely the wrong selection for wingman material.

Out of customers and bar space, she faced both men and wiped down of the counter. "What can I get you?" The catchall phrase came out shakier than she wanted, and tried to cover it with an intensive, yet completely unnecessary study of the bottles stocked below the counter.

"You disliked my tactic." God help her, the man had a voice to match his face. An easy glide that left a slow burn in its wake. Kind of like fifty-year-old Scotch. "I admit it's not my style, but I was desperate."

Not exactly the approach she'd expected from a hottie, but it did help ease her tension. "There's not a thing desperate about you and we both know it."

He answered with a megawatt smile that damn near knocked her off her feet. Utterly relaxed, he rested muscled forearms on the bar and raised an eyebrow. "Have dinner with me."

She shouldn't be able to hear him in such a crush, let alone register a physical impact, but damned if she wasn't processing both loud and clear. "I don't even know you."

He offered his hand. Long, strong fingers stretched out, showing calluses along his palm. "Eryx Shantos."

Wingman stared straight ahead, his aqua eyes cold enough to freeze a soul.

"Lexi Merrill." As their palms met, a rush fired up her arm and down her spine, and she shook as though she'd cozied up to a blow dryer in a bathtub. She ripped her hand away and rubbed the tingling center up and down her jean-clad hip.

Eryx didn't so much as blink, his sword-colored gaze glinting with dare and determination.

Maybe fatigue was taking a toll on her imagination. Or the flu. Or a desperate need to get laid. Gripping the bar for support, she took an order from a cute little brunette trying to avoid a middle-aged, bald guy's come-on.

Except for a slow pull off his beer, Wingman stayed stock-still. His angry expression screamed, *"Stay the fuck back."*

"Now you know me," Eryx said. "Have dinner with me."

"I have to work."

"Then lunch."

"I work then too." A lame excuse, but true. Two jobs and part-time college didn't leave a lot of room for being social. Not that socializing ever managed to work in her favor.

"Breakfast, then."

A half-hearted laugh slipped out before she could stop it. "You're persistent, I'll give you that."

"You have nooo idea." Wingman tipped his longneck for another drink, fingers loose around the dark glass despite his tight voice.

Eryx shot him a nasty glare.

"Your friend doesn't talk much." Lexi grabbed a few empties and dunked them in a tub of soapy water.

"His name's Ludan. And he may not be able to talk at all by the time the night's over. Depends on if he manages to keep his tongue intact."

"Yo! Need a few Bud Lights." Two college-age men in need of a manners class shoved their way to Ludan's free side.

Ludan straightened and pushed the men back a handful of steps with nothing more than a glare.

No way was she dealing with the fallout from a brawl, even if the young punks could use the lesson. "Stand down and kill the scary badass routine."

Ludan faced her, his eyes a shade closer to white than blue. It took a tense breath or two, but the muscles beneath his black t-shirt relaxed and he smirked. He eased down on his barstool and snagged his beer. "Your woman's got bite, Eryx."

She snatched a pair of Buds from the cooler and popped the tops off. "I'm not his woman."

"Not yet." Eryx's calm retort landed between them—part taunt, part promise. The sheer resoluteness in his expression sent a rush she didn't dare analyze clear to her toes.

Better to get down to business and add some distance before she did something she'd regret. "Tell me what you want to drink. I gotta get back to work."

"I've already told you want I want."

Lexi planted a hand on her hip and thanked God he couldn't see her pounding heart. "A tall order that's not on the menu."

Eryx nodded, a slow, sultry move that intimated a whole lot more than simple agreement. "Some things are worth waiting for."

A blast of déjà vu hit and left her stunned. A hot gush of frustration shoved in behind it and spun her back toward her half of the bar. With a thump on Jerry's arm, she motioned toward Eryx. "He's all yours. I want the sane side back."

She worked her portion of the crowd with single-minded enthusiasm. *Worth waiting for.* It was just a line. Guys like Eryx were landmines waiting for a trigger.

A couple nuzzled nose to nose, an out-of-place intimacy amid the harsh lights from the dance floor. Her heart stuttered. Was she bypassing something good? Maybe she should circle back. See if he needed another—

He was gone, his wingman with him. A gaggle of women, one with a naughty tiara and last-night-of-freedom sash wrapped around her, crowded between the leather and chrome barstools.

The tiny thread of hope she'd refused to acknowledge snapped in half. She snatched a bag of ice from the back cooler and shook it over the longnecks along the front bin of the bar. She knew better than to wish for things like love. Hell, she hadn't even done a double take on a guy in more years than she could count. She could get a massage from a team of Chippendales and she probably wouldn't get excited. What made her think she'd ever find anyone worth laying her heart on the line?

She turned for the rear register and shoved her disappointment deep. Better to study that topic later—say in about five years. She'd finish out the night, prep for tomorrow like she always did, and be glad she'd avoided the drama.

Pinpricks raced down her spine and warmth surrounded her. Not the slick and humid dance floor variety, but comforting, infused with leather and sandalwood. Out of place. Delicious.

Ordinary patrons reflected in the wide mirror before her, faces bright with the glaze of alcohol. Nothing stood out. No danger.

But she could have sworn warm, rough fingertips grazed her cheek.

* * * *

Perched on the high retaining wall at the end of the parking lot, Eryx glared at the streetlight overhead. One flick of his wrist and he could fry the whole damned contraption with an electric pulse. Better on his patience for sure, but not so great for his plans. Smart women like Lexi weren't usually keen on dark parking lots at two-thirty in the morning.

Tapping his boot heels against the wall, Ludan cracked his knuckles and scanned their surroundings for the fiftieth time. As Eryx's somo, Ludan looked out for his wellbeing, but the nasty bastard sometimes took the job too deep into mother hen territory. "We need to go back to Eden. Recharge for a few days and then come make a play for your woman. If the Rebellion catches us here with our energy this low—"

"The rumors are just that. Rumors." Eryx shifted on the cold concrete, anything to get the blood flow back into his too-stationary ass. "The Rebellion hasn't launched an attack worth merit in over seventy years. I bet I couldn't find five people who've seen Maxis in more than that. I'm not cranking my men into a tizzy over hypotheticals."

"And the ellan?" Ludan's cool gaze slid to Eryx. "You gonna keep ignoring them too? The old coots are chomping at the bit to know what's got you so tied up in the human realm."

"Only half of them are old coots. The rest are as young and eager to modernize our race as we are." If you could call one hundred and fifty-two years old young. From the human perspective, it probably seemed closer to eternity.

Ludan looked away and gripped the ledge. Better than throwing a punch——which would probably be his preference.

Hard to blame the guy. Ten years helping Eryx look for the woman who visited his dreams every night would send most people running. Ludan? Loyal to the core and still right here with him. But that didn't mean he'd give up on his argument. Ten more seconds tops before he chimed in again. Ten. Nine. Eight. Se——

"You're the malran. You call the shots." Ludan crossed his arms. "But even without the Rebellion threat, you're risking your throne and a death sentence."

And there it was. The lecture he'd had coming since he finally tracked a clue from his dreams to Lexi's workplace. Humans were a no-no. Do business with them? Walk freely in their realm? Tangle in a bout of good, hot, sweaty sex? All fair game. Fill them in on the Myren race or interfere in human destiny? That shit earned you the axe, a mandate passed down by The Great One himself when he'd created Eryx's people.

"We've been here too long," Ludan said. "Both our powers are damned near gone. Any attack outside of one-to-one and we're screwed."

The service door *kachunked* open.

Eryx shoved off the ledge.

"Sorry, man." The bartender he'd bribed ambled toward the mid-size pickup on Eryx's left with a sympathetic shake of his head. "You've got it bad."

Eryx leaned against the brick wall, crossed his arms, and notched one boot over his ankle. "You telling me she's not worth the trouble?"

The man's keys jangled against the quiet night and a perky chirp mixed with a flash of headlights. He shrugged and tugged open the driver's door. "Hard to say. Never met a man who made it through the gauntlet." He tossed his black duffel bag across to the passenger's side, shot a man-to-man nod at Ludan then smirked at Eryx. "Good luck."

"Fan-fucking-tastic. Your dream woman's the hard-to-get type." As the truck pulled away, Ludan leapt to the asphalt and planted his hands on his hips. "We're never getting home."

Crickets and the drone of cars on the interstate filled the silence.

"Would you go back if you were me?" It was an underhanded question. Ludan knew the toll Lexi's dream visits took on his ability to reason. How he woke strung out with need, zeroed in on the single purpose of finding his mate. "If you were this close, would you risk losing her?"

Ludan didn't exactly hang his head in defeat, but he sure studied the asphalt hard. "No." He turned and stuffed his hands in his pockets. "Better not to fuck with The Fates."

The door rattled and eased open.

His skin buzzing, Eryx pushed to full height.

Ludan sidled further away and switched to telepathy. *"You sure you wanna do this? You can't be sure she's Myren."*

"I'll figure it out. The pictures in her mind were definitely of Eden."

Under the unforgiving street lamps, Lexi's tan skin glowed. Soft-black hair brushed her shoulders and her hips swayed, slow with an unpretentious sexuality. A distracted frown tugged at her lips, her face downcast. She looked up and froze, bits of gravel crunching beneath her fancy shoes. "You gotta be kidding me."

"I told you I was willing to wait." He tried for a lighthearted tone, no easy task. A decade of tracking one irresistible woman did crazy things to a man's insides.

She zigzagged a look between Eryx near her red Jeep Wrangler and Ludan a stone's throw away then glanced at the closed door behind her. She adjusted the purse strap at her shoulder and narrowed her blue-gray eyes. "You're one step past stalker."

He held up his hands. "I swear it's not like that. I really do want to take you to breakfast." So he'd gone a little further with his scan of her memories when they'd shaken hands than he should have. She always caught an after-work breakfast with a man who looked to be in his mid to late fifties, and she drove the Wrangler parked behind him.

"It's nearly three AM."

"And we're all hungry. Perfect timing." He lowered his hands and hoped Ludan wasn't sporting his perma-scowl. Non-threatening wasn't his strong suit.

"Smart girls don't go to breakfast with strangers." She nodded toward her Jeep. "Let alone get near a vehicle with unknown men nearby."

"Your bartender pal clued me in." Hopefully, she'd buy the lie, not that it felt good on his tongue. "And you could always call a friend to join us. Public place, your own car." He paused to let the idea sink in. "What's there to lose?"

A breeze ruffled her loose hair. Her face slackened and a flutter of energy drifted across the parking lot, barely perceptible.

Ludan perked up.

It was Lexi. It had to be. Humans couldn't generate such a ripple—at least not any he'd ever met.

She tugged her purse to her chest and rooted around inside. "Waffle House. A few miles down the road." A wad of keys settled in her palm, she dropped the purse back to her hip. "I meet a friend there after work. A cop, just to be clear. So don't get any ideas."

Satisfaction fired hot in his veins, the fact some strange older man would be along for the ride a paltry detail. He closed the distance, slow and steady, and traced the angle of her cheekbone.

Her eyes widened.

The Fates were never wrong. They might be coy with their reasons and damned vague in their instructions, but there was one thing he was sure of. They'd led him to his mate.

CPSIA information can be obtained
at www.ICGtesting.com
Printed in the USA
FSOW02n0133041115
12947FS